"IF YOU WOULD HALT ME, HALT ME NOW."

Beset by a passion she couldn't fathom, Flora desperately tried to think. Sorley was right. She was a child no longer. She was a woman, free of the ties of father or husband, free to make decisions for the first time in her life. And this strange man she hardly knew commanded her heart even as he gave her this choice.

In a lucid instant, she made her decision.

"Will you take care with me?" she asked, stroking the hollow at the base of his throat.

Sorley nodded, then kissed her on the lips, lightly at first, then deeply, until she was sure he would drink her straight down like a dram of whiskey. "If you're not certain you'll have me, you may yet decline," he said softly.

"I'm more certain of this than of anything else that has gone before," she said. Too often she had let the needs of others determine her lot, but not now. Now she would listen to her heart, and her heart was with the mysterious Gael. Did he love her? For the moment, it didn't matter.

BOOK YOUR PLACE ON OUR WEBSITE AND MAKE THE READING CONNECTION!

We've created a customized website just for our very special readers, where you can get the inside scoop on everything that's going on with Zebra, Pinnacle and Kensington books.

When you come online, you'll have the exciting opportunity to:

- View covers of upcoming books

- Read sample chapters

- Learn about our future publishing schedule (listed by publication month *and author*)

- Find out when your favorite authors will be visiting a city near you

- Search for and order backlist books from our online catalog

- Check out author bios and background information

- Send e-mail to your favorite authors

- Meet the Kensington staff online

- Join us in weekly chats with authors, readers and other guests

- Get writing guidelines

- AND MUCH MORE!

Visit our website at
http://www.zebrabooks.com

ONCE A ROGUE

Megan Gray

Zebra Books
Kensington Publishing Corp.

http://www.zebrabooks.com

ZEBRA BOOKS are published by

Kensington Publishing Corp.
850 Third Avenue
New York, NY 10022

Zebra and the Z logo Reg. U.S. Pat. & TM Off.

First Printing: November, 1999
10 9 8 7 6 5 4 3 2 1

Printed in the United States of America

Chapter One

Edinburgh
September, 1745

It was truly a miserable bit of stitchery.

Flora stabbed at a few stray strands of charcoal-colored floss that elevated themselves defiantly from the torn seam of the much-mended gown. Two years ago it had fit her quite well. Now all the sewing in the world—especially if she was the seamstress—could hardly save it. Why was it, she wondered, that so many ladies could work true wonders with needle and thread, while she had neither the skill nor the patience to repair a side seam? She tugged at the piece of linen, then gasped as her needle jabbed her finger. "Oh, Mrs. Leckie! I fear I've no head for this work whatever!"

Flora looked up into the round face of the housekeeper, which looked pale in the glow of the rare autumn sunlight that burst through the open window and flooded the tiny upstairs sewing room. "Let's have a look, lass." The older woman, who was mending a frock coat belonging to Flora's father, laid down her work and craned her neck to peer at Flora's dubious efforts. Her face collapsed by degrees into the frown of a professional critic. "No' the best, no' the worst. But see—you've gone and dinged yoursel'." Mrs. Leckie pointed a sausage-shaped finger at a drop of blood on the heel of Flora's thumb. "Puir lambie! I'll attend to it."

She would have risen from her comfortable station on the window seat, but Flora laughed and made her stay seated. " 'Tis nothing. Don't rise on my account." She sucked at the pinprick, which, for all its diminutive size, burned like a bee sting. "In truth, it's no less than I merit, judging from the muddle I've made of my work." In a sudden fit of frustration, Flora tossed the gown, needle and all, on the window seat beside her. "I'm better with a book, I'm thinking."

Mrs. Leckie nodded, a small smile cracking the weathered surface of her face. "Aye, but you could do both, ye ken. Your mother was a great one for stitchery, as well as the reading. Many's the time I've seen her at her embroidery, the hoop in her hands and a book in her lap. How could a body read and tie a French knot at the same time, I'd like to know, but do it she did."

Flora sighed and leaned back on a chintz cushion. Her mother. She had been only seven when her mother died, taking an unborn child with her. For a reason she couldn't comprehend, Flora could recall only shadows and fragile fragments of the woman she had loved so much. She could still feel the gentle touch of her hand, could still smell her fragrance. She remembered strange words, too, words that she herself had once spoken, words that sounded like the wind keening through the treetops. Her mother had been a Gael, and spoke the old tongue.

"Tell me again about my mother, Mrs. Leckie," Flora said softly, overcome with a powerful longing for the distant innocence of her past. How many times had she heard the same stories? It mattered not. She never heard them often enough.

The housekeeper tucked a silver curl under her mobcap. "She was beautiful, like you, lass, with hair as golden as sunshine on barley and eyes like amber. It's uncommon rare to be gifted wi' such coloring, y'ken."

Flora gave a careless wave of her hand, trying to brush aside the woman's compliment. "Go on with you! I'm scarce a beauty." Her tousled curls, untamable regardless of how many pins she used on them, were much too unruly to be praised in good company, and she herself had always favored blue eyes over brown.

Mrs. Leckie's smile only grew wider. "So ye say. But ye have been locked up in this auld house and the convent at Auchincairn for these eighteen years past, so what know ye anything of the beauty of women?" She picked up the frock coat, then immediately set it down as if it had growled at her. "Nay, I trow it won't be long before the lads will be swarming about here like bees in the harebells, begging your father for your hand, and then ye'll ken the worth o' a comely face and dainty figure."

At the mention of her father, Flora glanced nervously about the room. She had been in the house only a month after living six years at Auchincairn with the saintly sisters, and the mere thought of her father was enough to distress her. He had once been so kind, so loving, but strong drink had destroyed all that. She had vague memories of her mother sitting in a corner, weeping, while her father raged in front of her, an empty bottle in his hand.

"Here I was thinking it was my mother we were discussing," she said, trying to dispel the ugly image. "Won't you tell me about the simple boy?"

"Ach, the puir thing!" cried the housekeeper as she resumed her mending. "It's well he met your mother when he did. She always did have a kind word for the most wretched o' the earth. Well, there we were one morning, your mother and me, taking the air on our way to market— fresh currants she wanted, and cream and peaches. It was before the bad times came on your father, ye ken, and we had nae need to count pence. Yer mother, rest her soul, heard people shouting tae wake the dead, and there before us was the dairyman's lad on his hands and knees in the stour, using a tin cup tae collect the milk he had spilled into the street. His master was skelping the puir creature wi' a wooden spoon, and giving tongue tae sich language I hope I ne'er have tae repeat. The lad was simple, it was plain tae see, for he poured the filthy milk back in his pitcher, as though he thought he still might sell it. Folk stood about laughing so hearty you could see the backs of their teeth, and this but made the dairyman a' the more distraught, and he beat the boy worse than before. Then yer mother up tae the man . . ."

Flora closed her eyes and smiled. Though the memory wasn't really her own, she had often played out in her imagination just how the incident had happened, could clearly see the look of trust on the round face of the simple lad and the flash of righteous anger in her mother's eyes. ". . . and strikes him—*hup*—directly in the face wi' her basket," Flora continued, speaking for the housekeeper. "The people watching are struck dumb. My mother turns to the boy and tells him to come with her, that she has better work for him to do; then she *pays the dairyman* for his ruined goods. Heaven protect her soul! She took the simple boy back home with her and put him to work in the stable. He had a way with horses, and a few years later he was riding champions at Newmarket and winning race after race, all because of my mother's generous nature, which would not allow her to ignore the less fortunate.''

Flora opened her eyes, surprised to find herself in the parlor, not at the teeming marketplace in the city's high street. "Wasn't it just so, Mrs. Leckie?"

The stout woman snorted, her indignation at being clipped off so abruptly by her forward young charge writ in uppercase upon her blunt features. "Aye, but who's telling the tale, me or thee?"

"Forgive me," Flora said, patting Mrs. Leckie on the knee. She hoped she had not offended the woman, her only friend in this somber, brooding city that had seemed so cheerful to her as a child. Mrs. Leckie was the last to remain of a houseful of servants, and even so Flora was aware that the good widow had not been paid for her services for at least a fortnight. Only her devotion to Flora and the memory of the loving family had kept her from leaving. "The devil was in me, wasn't he? I meant no offense."

"For certain ye did not," Mrs. Leckie said, smiling again. "Oh, but how ye put me in mind of your mother, too high-spirited for a woman, if the truth be told."

"Too spirited?" An overspirited lock of wheat-colored hair flung itself into Flora's eyes, and she hurriedly brushed it aside. "High spirits are to be admired in one sex but not the other?"

Mrs. Leckie stared at her needlework, pretending a sudden and intense interest in a slightly uneven row of stitches. "You know very well what I speak of," she said softly.

Flora did indeed know. Even as a child she had always been aware that her father had once stood accused of her mother's death. Nothing was ever proven, and eventually her mother's shattered neck had been attributed to a tragic but purely accidental fall down a steep staircase. "Whatever happened to my mother," she answered thoughtfully, "it wasn't her high mettle that killed her. That was what drew my father to her in the first place. Indeed, 'tis my observation that gentlemen are bored to death with these fainting creatures that decorate a house like a vase of flowers, with a personality to match. Men desire women of wit and vigor, who speak their minds frankly and act with honesty and compassion."

"Indeed?" Mrs. Leckie murmured. "And where saw ye such women at Auchincairn among the sisters? Honest they are, aye, but surely not much given to bold language, especially in the presence of gentlemen."

Flora hesitated. She had encountered few such women in the flesh, but many in the novels she had smuggled into the convent and read in rare private moments, when she should have been at her devotions. The creak of the floorboards caught her attention, sparing her the awkwardness of an answer. She turned toward the doorway just in time to see the door lurch open and slam against the wall.

Her father stood in the entrance, listing slightly to the left, his shoulder-length wig of coal black curls off-center to the same degree. A puzzled frown marred his once-handsome face, pinched and wasted now after years of wanton indulgence in aqua vitae. Flora held her breath, hoping that he was not as incapacitated as he seemed. As if to belie her hope, he stumbled into the room and fastened a glare on Flora's face. "Damnable Jacobites!"

Flora turned away. Mrs. Leckie gazed at the floor. "Mr. Buchanan, the young lady . . ." she implored him.

But Flora knew her father was far beyond the reach of fine scruples. The sharp tang of brandy wafted from him like the odor of sweat from soiled linens. Somehow he collected his wits long enough to walk to the window seat, intrude himself between his daughter and housekeeper, and peer warily out the window. "What will become of us when those Highland savages storm the town?" he muttered, more to himself, Flora thought, than to anyone else.

"Storm the town!" cried Mrs. Leckie, her hand leaping to her mouth in astonishment.

"The Jacobites are no' taking Edinburgh by force," Flora said quietly, although she was far from willing to stake her life on her information. "They are within a day's march and hope to raise many supporters here. Their entrance will be peaceful and triumphant, I ween, with no violence of any sort. They say the prince is exceeding handsome and noble, and brooks no misrule among his Highlanders." As she finished speaking, Flora saw her father turn toward her and stare at her in disbelief. For an instant she thought he might strike her, but she gulped back her fear and ended her say. "I should like to see him and his army when they enter the city."

"See him!" her father shouted. "That Papist fop!" Flora winced, but her father ranted on, apparently forgetting for the moment that his own daughter, like her mother, was a member of the Roman Church. As far as she could tell, her father was neither fish nor flesh when it came to matters of the eternal soul, and the only spirit that held his interest was sold in casks. "Indeed you shall not! And where in the name of the devil himself did you hear the shite you just spoke, hussy?"

"If you please, Mr. Buchanan!" Mrs. Leckie again struggled to steer her employer into polite discourse, but he simply waved his hand impatiently in her direction and said nothing.

"It's all right, Mrs. Leckie," Flora said, in an attempt

to soothe her friend. Then she took a deep breath and addressed her father. "This very morning at the baker's the question of the Jacobites' intentions arose between two ladies, and a well-dressed gentleman also present offered his opinion. He spoke with such conviction and candor I could no' but believe him. If I have done wrong, Papa, then I beg you forgive me, but I've heard others venture much the same news."

Her father was quiet a moment, his face perfectly blank. Then, like dry sack draining from a breached hogshead, the life seemed to flow from him and he collapsed into the sole chair, opposite the window seat. Flora, close to terror only a moment earlier, felt her heart fill with pity. She feared her father, and at times she detested him. For all that, however, he was her only support. Though she shuddered to admit it, she needed him.

Flora knelt down beside her father and took his limp hand in hers. "Papa, you're ill. You'd best take to bed. I'll bring you some broth and a compress for—"

"Silence." Her father was not shouting now. Indeed, he was almost pleading. He pulled his hand away from hers and pressed it to his pale forehead. "Forgive me, lass. It's the terrible times we live in that bring me to this state." From the corner of her eyes Flora saw Mrs. Leckie shake her head in silent disagreement. "Whatever happens to the city now, there's naught you nor I can do to change the course o' events. But ..." He raised his hand and gazed at her thoughtfully. The intensity of his look made her tremble inside. "But we can attend to our own affairs and fetch the best prices for our own labors."

Now it was Flora's turn to shake her head, utterly baffled. Her father often failed to make sense, but this time he appeared to have some knowledge that she did not. "I beg you, speak plainly. What affairs? What labors?"

The man pushed himself a little straighter in his chair as he gathered the remnants of his scattered mind. "My dear, I'll admit I have not always been the most careful of fathers." Flora could not contain herself, but sighed at this greatest of understatements. "Nevertheless," he continued, "I'm endeavoring to make up for past errors, y'see, and to do right by you as best I may." He paused, searched her face a moment, then went on in a softer voice. "You will remember the most excellent Capt. Henry Stelton?"

Flora nodded. The captain—a proud, closemouthed English career officer with eyes as gray and hard as steel—had visited the house twice since she had arrived from Auchincairn. He lost no chance to comment on the poor condition of the rooms, the lack of servants, and the humble furnishings. Once she had been suffered to play whist with him in the dingy parlor. Another time she had undergone a long tête-à-tête during which she had felt obliged to hunt for suitable topics of conversation while he sat quite still, his eyes locked on her in attentive silence. She did not care for the captain, who made her feel like a hare pursued by a hound. "I recall him very well, Papa." She noticed Mrs. Leckie's gaze drop into her lap at the mention of the name. The woman had taken an instant dislike to the haughty officer.

A sly look played over her father's face, a look she had seen on many occasions, whenever he was hiding the truth or angling for some advantage. "And you found him an honest, decent gentleman, I wager," he said.

Flora rose from her knees, which were beginning to ache, and seated herself beside Mrs. Leckie, at the last moment brushing her needlework out of the way to make a place for her wide skirts. "I found him tolerable as a guest, Papa, but in truth I must say I'd be grateful to learn that we are to be quit of his company. It's no fault in his

manners, mind you, but in the way he makes me feel."
She hesitated a moment, unsure how to voice her other
objection. "Then there is the matter of his reputation."

Her father blinked. For a moment, his eyes flared; then
he brought himself under control. His voice dropped to
an even softer level, and Flora knew her answer had not
pleased him. "The captain is well known as a gallant soldier
and a tireless defender o' His Majesty and the govern-
ment," said her father carefully. He hiccoughed once during this statement, but sought to hide it by clearing his
throat.

Flora wondered absently how much liquor he had consumed and of what quality. She breathed in the trenchant
fumes of his intoxication, fighting to suppress a cough.
"Yet there is more to his fame—or infamy—than that,"
she said quietly.

"I daresay you refer to his reputation among the
women," her father said, the volume of his voice increasing
with each word. "Well, he's been imprudent now and then
in the company he keeps, but what man has not? The
captain is seeking to make amends in his private circumstances by taking a wife above reproach."

A terrified gasp escaped Mrs. Leckie's lips. Flora took
note of it but didn't readily comprehend the reason for
it. Surely it was fortunate that the captain was taking a wife,
for then he'd no longer have either time or inclination to
disrupt the daily rhythms of her household or belittle the
delicate poverty of her life. "Above reproach?" she echoed.
"I must say I have nothing but sympathy for the poor lady
who ends up as his bride. With such a husband, she'll be
scorned by all society and treated no better than a drab
in a bawdyhouse. Worse yet, she'll not be able to trust the
captain one step beyond the door, and her life will be
nothing but loathing, shame, fear, and constant worry."

Her father took her completely off guard by bursting into a fit of laughter, during which he rolled in his chair in paroxysms of glee. Suddenly he became still, and his voice was serious. "Ye impudent hoyden! I'll warrant you'll change your tune once you become Mrs. Henry Stelton, mistress of Highgate."

Flora felt her mouth sag open as the meaning of his words struck home. Mrs. Stelton—he was speaking of her! It couldn't be possible! "I beg you not to taunt me so, Papa. It's cruel to use your own daughter for amusement, considering all that has gone afore." She cast a glance at Mrs. Leckie, who patted her shoulder, whether in encouragement or consolation Flora could not tell.

"Amusement?" Her father's eyes glittered with anger and his face took on a look of fierce determination as he heaved himself out of the chair and onto his unsteady feet. "I assure you, mistress, this business is most grave. A matter o' life and death." He turned his head aside, collected himself yet again, and faced Flora once more with some semblance of composure. She tried to protest, but he cut her off with a clap of his hands. "Hear me out. Were you aware that rental monies on this poor hovel are past due? No? I thought not. Mrs. Leckie will be glad to tell you the sorry state o' the family's finances. The good soul hasn't been paid in two months." Flora stared at the woman in horror, but her father hurried on. "My import business has not been thriving. To be blunt about it, for some years now I've been on the verge of ruin, and the sums I'd set aside for hard times have been exhausted. In short, we are penniless, my love, penniless."

Flora's anger overpowered her better judgment. "And was it brandy or port that drowned what silver you had left?" she snapped.

"Enough! I'll not have you speak to me thus, ungrateful tyke!"

But Flora felt her face burn with indignation, and she could not curb her smoldering emotions. It was no fault of hers that her father had drunk away their livelihood. The thought that he would force her to wed a notorious rake simply to be rid of the expense of keeping her was more than she could bear. "I must speak my mind, for it's I who stand to lose the most," she said, her voice soft but trembling. "I take it the good captain has forgone all hope of a dowry?"

Her father sighed. "It's far more pertinent than that, my bonny Flora." He paced about the room one, two circuits, his gait more certain than before. When he returned to the chair, he did not sit down, but gripped the back of the seat firmly with one hand, as if to anchor himself to the floor. "Captain Stelton has agreed to provide me with an annuity of two hundred pounds as long as I shall live if I but give my blessing on this union and arrange it."

"Two hundred pounds a year!" Mrs. Leckie echoed in shocked reverence.

"Papa!" Flora felt the air leave her lungs as the force of his words hit her. Her knees shook, and she lowered herself to the window seat, where Mrs. Leckie gathered her in her arms. "Am I nothing to you that you'd sell me into bondage?"

"Why, pet, you mean the world to me. In truth, I'm not abandoning you but rather preparing you for a life o' luxury. As an ancillary benefit, I'll also have what comfort I may in my declining years." He sighed deeply and let go of the chair. "It vexes me sore to see you take the news so badly, but it can't be helped. The bridal date is set for a fortnight from today. Make ready to see your future husband early on the morrow."

"Nay! It cannot be so!" Flora felt hot tears of rage burn a path down her cheeks. She clenched her hands in impotent fury, and for a moment her proper English gave way to the broad Scots dialect she encountered daily in the streets. "It canna be saé! De'il tak' ye! I'll no' be ravished yet again!"

"We are speaking of the sacred union of marriage," her father said, "not the past crimes of a diseased mind. Bear up, now, mistress, and mind how you express yourself. You're a lady, after all, or soon to become one. Understand that far worse could befall you." He turned to leave, his balance fully recovered, but Flora leaped forward and seized him by the arm before he reached the door.

"You forget, sir, one important detail," she said, controlling her sobs and her language. "I am not above reproach. I shall bear the shame of that day forever, on my body as well as in my heart. I know you've not forgotten it. Surely you have some remorse as well. The captain or any other suitor will no' be duped, if Mrs. Leckie has advised me correctly." The housekeeper blushed deep scarlet.

Her father nodded. "D'ye think I could ever put such a thing from my mind? Nay, be assured that Captain Stelton already kens the whole of it, save for that bit about the scar. When he discovers it, you'll be wed, and then it will be too late for second thoughts."

"You'd dupe the man!" cried Flora. "He'll shout my shame from the roofs of the city."

"He'll tell no one," her father insisted. "Neither will our good Mrs. Leckie. In truth, not another soul is privy to your sad past or the conditions surrounding it."

"Not so," Flora whispered. "Sister Brigid and others at Auchincairn know of it. I confessed it to them."

A look of fear blazed over her father's face, then was snuffed out so quickly she wondered if she had truly observed it at all. The man shrugged. The gesture revealed just how thin and ravaged he had become of late. She hadn't noticed the extent of his decay until that very moment, the poor fit of his clothing, the gaunt hollows of his face. In many ways, he was more of a stranger to her than the people she passed by chance in the market square of a morning.

"They've taken a vow to remain silent on the subject, so what harm lies in their knowing it?" he said. "Now away with you, and make yourself as ready in mind and spirit as you may in dress and disposition. And, mistress . . . if you won't have the captain, there's others that would pay good silver for your services. Don't think for an instant that I'd turn them away."

Tugging his wig into place, he straightened himself to his full height. For one breathless moment he reminded Flora of the father she had known as a tiny child, a father whose every word commanded respect and obedience. "And daughter—for God's sake, take care to speak the King's English, like a person of worth, and not the low prattle spoken by tinkers and beggars." Then he was gone.

"Oh, my puir wee thing!" cried Mrs. Leckie, clutching Flora's shoulder as she dabbed at her own eyes with a pocket kerchief. "Promised to that brute of a Sassenach!"

Flora stood looking out the open door, still dazed by the abrupt revelation of her demonic wedding plans. "That, or sold to the stews," she whispered.

"Oh, wha's to become of ye?" wailed the housekeeper, giving full vent to a stream of tears.

Flora sighed, a single tear plunging down her nose and onto her breast. "I know not," she whispered. Marriage to Stelton boded a disastrous future, but to be cast aside by her father like an empty sherry bottle—that was scorn indeed. "But I assure ye, if I can find an honorable path out of this catastrophe, I shall take it."

It could not be happening, but it was.

Flora had lived it before. Now she was living it again.

Shadows played around her in her bedroom at her father's house. In the shimmer of a single candle, the porcelain faces of her three dolls quivered with fear. Their china lips parted, their glass eyes stared at the door, transfixed. Terror gripped her like the talons of a hawk. What was real and what was not merged into an unstable dimension balanced between past and present, light and darkness.

She was in bed. Her twelfth birthday had just passed. Wilting yellow roses and a half-eaten box of raspberry sweets scented the air by her bed with sugar and perfume. She ran her hands over her body, her swelling breasts, her womanly hips. She was not a child!

The door opened, revealing the figure of a tall man, his wig in disarray, his face flushed as pink as her dolls' painted cheeks. "Mr. . . . Mr. Macinally," she murmured, sitting upright. "But you're . . . you're . . . dead."

Suddenly her father's business partner was standing beside her. A brilliant merchant with an infallible instinct for the import of liquors, Macinally had unfortunately too often fallen victim to his own product. A cloud of alcoholic vapors surrounded the man, and as she breathed in, Flora began to feel giddy. "Please leave me," she said, longing to scream but completely unable to speak above a whisper.

"I hae a gift for . . . for yer birthday," Macinally croaked, and proceeded to pluck a white silk handkerchief from his pocket. Flora touched it, admiring its softness, but an instant later the innocent-looking cloth had somehow snaked around her wrists, binding them tight. She whimpered in pain, but still she could not cry out. "Mr. Macinally! Mr. Macinally! Begone!" she begged, but still he stayed, stretching out beside her on the bed. She felt a hand on the shirred bodice of her nightdress and writhed under its inquiring touch. In the semidarkness, Macinally's face, once so pleasant and kind, transformed into a sneering mask. One by one she could hear her dolls falling to the floor, shattering, crying out in a voice as high and pathetic as that of a startled infant. A bolt of pain rent her in half, tearing a silent scream from her throat. Then the pain was gone, and she was hovering over a terrified, defiled child and the besotted creature who feasted upon her. Such a hideous sight, but she was powerless to intervene. Powerless.

Flora awoke in sweat-damp sheets. That night would never leave her, no matter how many years passed, no matter what room she slept in. It did not even matter how assiduously her father tried to stitch up the remnants of her life, first in Auchincairn, now with an arranged marriage to a man obsessed with the appearance of purity. Oh, if only her mother were still alive! Together they might have been able to postpone the wedding, if not prevent it.

Unable even to contemplate sleeping, Flora pushed back her goose-down coverlet and eased herself out of bed. She hated the darkness, the shadows and the chill of the night. It was fitting that winter was coming soon, she thought, now that an early frost threatened to strike down any hope of happiness in her life.

Quickly she set about repelling the darkness. She stoked the dying fire, though her hand shook each time she wielded the firebrand. As flames burst into life, they painted streaks of salmon-colored light on the stained wallpaper. Cheered by the light, she kindled two tallow candles in sconces on the wall. A stern face glared at her.

Flora caught her breath, then let it out, laughing to herself in relief. It was her own face that had disturbed her so, scowling back at her from the polished depths of the small mirror above her washstand. The ugly red scar that Macinally had slashed across her chest was just visible through her nightclothes. It traversed the upper part of her breasts, as if the devil himself had run his nails across them. Hastily she turned away. Captain Stelton knew nothing of the scar. He might not take lightly the fact that his young bride was so disfigured.

Still shivering from the nightmare, Flora could hear Macinally's words to her that night as he stood gripping his dagger, almost as if he were still in the room with her. "I'll claim ye as mine, mistress. No other man will have ye once I've finished with ye. The auld man will let me take ye away, for he'll never be rid of ye otherwise."

The memory of the steel against her flesh had seared itself into her consciousness: it would forever lie right beneath the very surface of her thoughts. But she did rid herself of Macinally. Her shriek of pain and outrage had been so loud that even her besotted father had heard it. Waking from a stupor induced by Macinally's best Jamaican rum, he had lunged into the room and shaken his associate with the vigor of a terrier worrying a rat. The dagger fell from the man's hand as he tore himself from Buchanan's grasp and raced from the room like a man on fire. Her father knew at once what had happened. The blood that fouled her bed and nightdress laid the truth of the matter bare.

Flora sat down heavily in the one chair in the cramped bedroom, exhausted but oddly alert. She recalled little of the rest of that wretched night, save that her father had

summoned a physician, who bathed and dressed her
wounds. She had fallen on a carving knife, her father had
explained. The good doctor had snorted in skepticism
when he heard this news. " 'Twas no carving knife that
claimed her maidenhood," he observed wryly. Whatever
his private thoughts on the matter, however, he said nothing further but fed her a dose of laudanum, which soon
rendered her senseless.

Days later, when the pain from the wound and the haze
of the drug had subsided a little, Mrs. Leckie had told her
that a man of Macinally's height and weight had been
found dead in the gutter, his face bludgeoned to a pulp.
The victim of a thief, guessed the bailiff.

Was it Macinally? Flora could only hope so. Whatever
had happened to him, she suspected her father had a hand
in it. Once she found him in possession of Macinally's
pocket watch. On another occasion, she had seen him
speaking in the drawing room with a ragged brute of a
man who, under ordinary circumstances, would not have
been allowed in the house. Her father was handing money
to the man. When Flora approached the room, the door
slammed shut in her face. She thought no more of the
strange visitor.

The merchant's name was never mentioned in the house
again, nor did her father ever speak with her at length
about the occurrences of that fateful night. When she had
recovered as well as she might, in body if not in mind, she
had been sent to Auchincairn. Her father had never asked
her leave nor even sought her opinion on the matter.
"Fate has decided the course for us," he had told her.
"Not I." She might not have seen him again if it hadn't
been for Henry Stelton. The captain had chanced to see
her portrait in the parlor during a visit and demanded her
return, claiming he could not exist unless he beheld the

painting's subject in the flesh. If not for him, she realized, she would have completed her novitiate. Now she was to suffer an existence just as isolated as convent life—without the benefits of spiritual inspiration, good works, and the companionship of saintly women.

Flora awoke some time later, still in the hard embrace of the wooden chair, her back aching. She didn't even recall falling asleep. Sunlight flooded the room, and the fire was a heap of ashes. The shadows that had disturbed her so the night before were gone, and the morning was rich with the songs of thrushes in the beech tree outside her window. She sighed, relieved, then remembered she had no cause for relaxation. The morrow had come, and with it the visit from the man who sought to seal her miserable fate. This day, which dawned so commonplace, was poised to free her spirit or damn her eternally.

Chapter Two

"A splendid likeness, though not one-tenth so fair as the original."

Seated by the parlor window, half listening to the shouts of passersby and the clatter of horses' hooves, Flora looked up into the captain's uncompromising gray eyes. Hanging within reach of his outthrust arm was the portrait he had just praised—a study in oil of a pretty, half-grown girl with a beribboned straw bonnet framing distrustful brown eyes. Flora barely recognized herself, just as she barely recollected the actual execution of the painting. Presented as payment on a debt owed her father by a foundering young artist, the canvas had been completed only weeks before her journey to Auchincairn. The panic of the night that had changed her life still hovered about the face of the young subject, creating the odd impression that at any moment she might cry out, turn, and flee her painted prison.

"Thank you, Captain Stelton. You are too kind," Flora rejoined, without enthusiasm or sincerity. She played with the fringe of the thin blue shawl that covered her breast and shoulders. Her father, seated by the fire, twirled a stemmed brandy glass between his fingers and coughed to show her his discomfiture. She was not about to give herself over timidly, however. If she were to be sold into marriage, she was determined to go down struggling. Flora turned back to the window, wondering when and if the Stuart prince would come and, if he did, whether she might appeal to him to put a stop to her father's desperate plot. An idea occurred to her, and she spun around to face Captain Stelton. " 'Tis a pity others are not as gracious in their descriptions of your private life, sir, as you are in praise of my likeness."

Stelton's eyebrows raised a fraction of an inch. Her father glowered at her with thoughts of murder clearly showing in his eyes. "Alas, Miss Buchanan," Stelton said, "one will never be satisfied if one depends on the graciousness of others."

"Be that as it may," Flora persisted, "if we are truly to commit ourselves to this unfortunate business, let us be about it without undue delay. If I understand my father aright, we are soon to be wed, though in truth I hardly ken your name, and have seen you but thrice in my entire life, if one might be so generous as to call it that."

Flora saw her father's face turn several shades of red before fixing on purple, but, surprisingly, the captain seemed amused rather than mortified. He aimed his bright, white smile at her and reared back his head, affecting delight. "A lady of spirit and wit—how enthralling!" he said. Flora knew at once that it would not be easy to deflect Captain Stelton. He was a fighting man, and evidently enjoyed fencing with words as much as he must have enjoyed fencing with blades. "My dear, I must say the more I am exposed to your company, the more I relish it."

Flora drew a deep breath. If she had any hope at all of dissuading the captain from this union, she would have to be more than enthralling. Still, if she insulted him outright, she might succeed only in incurring his undying enmity, hardly a desired outcome. "Since you have opened the discussion to the topic of company, pray let us continue it," she said evenly. "I have heard certain particulars about your company, sir, that are no' complimentary. Your name is linked in common discourse with married women, courtesans, lowlifes. . . . I need not mention names, I ween."

"Be silent, you impudent creature," said her father, his jowls shaking. "Enough of your accusations! Would you hang the poor gentleman on evidence no stronger than the word of fishwives and stable lads?"

The handsome captain, however, merely laughed, as if to show Flora that all rumors of his debauchery meant nothing to him. "Please, Mr. Buchanan, save your wrath for a more deserving victim. Your delightful daughter is merely baiting me in the style of the salons, to test my worthiness." Again he skewered Flora with his razorlike glare. "I daresay you are quite right, mistress, for I have appeared in public with such as you name and provided for their well-being. It is one of my hobbyhorses, you see, to affect reform in the downtrodden and raise the wretched of the earth to respectable levels. As for the wives of my friends and fellow officers, I find married ladies far more witty in their conversation than other females . . . present company notwithstanding, of course."

Flora returned his gaze but his bold lies made her shake her head in dismay. The captain's exploits were well known, and no trifling sums of money spent on the poor, with the intent of saving himself, could repair the damage he had done to his reputation. She had far more faith in the words of the local fishmonger, whom she knew to be an honest soul, than in the polished answers of the officer. "I beg you, let me make my position plain, for I mean you no discredit," she said, choosing her language as carefully as she could. "I don't wish to be your wife. I am quite unworthy, having been taken by force in my youth, and thereby sullied."

Stelton knelt and took her hand in his. He had not yet removed his black leather gloves, and she hid a wince as the hard seams dug into her skin. "Of that I am most aware, Miss Buchanan, and trust me, it matters not one whit. Your father assures me the incident was not of your doing, and that none are aware of it, save we three and your loyal servant. You are as pure as you are fetching, and you may rest assured that no one will ever know of the unfortunate event."

"Aye, indeed they shall!" she cried, no longer able to keep her rage or her brogue at bay. "I shall tell all to any who wish tae hear." A sudden rush of noise outside the window distracted her for a moment. Several boys raced through the street, shouting with great urgency, but she could not understand them. She turned herself back to the matter at hand, though the captain was clearly disturbed by the boys' commotion. "If I am forced tae go through with this . . . this masquerade o' a wedding, then ye may be certain that half o' Edinburgh will know every detail o' my shameful condition within the week. Wha' little may be left o' yer good name will be down in the dirt with my own."

With that she tugged the blue shawl off her shoulders to reveal a low-cut bodice. The mark of her dishonor screamed its presence on her chest.

Her father rose and began rumbling curses at her, but the captain, though shaken and white-faced, seemed more interested in the disturbance beneath the window than in either her threat or her scar. Now Flora could hear a loud wailing sound that pierced the hubbub of the city like a dirk. The pipes, she thought, and instantly the shrieking music became louder and more insistent. She watched in awe as men and women alike spilled through the streets like rainwater in teeming gutters. Their cries were unmistakable: "The prince is coming! The bonny prince!"

"The Jacobites!"

"The Highland host is taking the town!"

"God have mercy on us!"

Her father rushed toward her, and for a moment Flora was certain he would kill her. Instead he merely brushed past her and stood at the window next to Stelton, transfixed by the hordes below. People of all ages and conditions were streaming toward the High Street in a rush of noise and color. A few cautious souls crept indoors and cowered behind closed shutters.

Flora's mind raced with wild thoughts. What if she left the house now, while the men were distracted? It would surely take them some time to find her in the crowd, time she could use either to effect an escape or reconcile herself to a life of misery. Before she was quite aware of what she was doing, Flora crept from the room, certain she had eluded the notice of her father and the captain. She hurried on, through the dining room, past the little reception room her father called "the gentleman's parlor" and into the central hallway, stopping just long enough to drape the shawl over her bodice. Mrs. Leckie emerged from the parlor, her eyes round with fear. "The Jacobites," she said in a quaking voice. "Lord protect us! The savages are in the streets. They're likely tae slay us all!"

Flora tried to comfort the woman with a few words, but her mind was elsewhere. "Mrs. Leckie, could you not fetch me my cape and straw bonnet? And my pocketbook as well. Make haste, if you please."

Mrs. Leckie stood as if carved from the same mahogany as the double doors behind her. "Mistress? You'd not gae out among the heathens, would ye?"

"Hurry, hurry!" Flora urged her. "I must leave at once, and they are not heathens, but good Catholics."

Finally the housekeeper set off, only to return a few moments later with the items Flora had requested. "My dear lass." Tears brimmed in the older woman's eyes. "Must ye leave? Ye'll be killed!"

Flora smiled. "I shall be well, but only if I go," she said. "At once." The murmur of men's voices made her catch her breath. "Say you did not see me. Forgive me for asking you to dissemble so, but desperation drives me to it."

The housekeeper's face was a mask of worry. Still, she asked but one question, "Would ye hae me accompany ye, dear?"

The poor thing is fair falling apart with fright, Flora thought. It had taken great courage to make such a suggestion. "Please, stay here. Mind—you did no' see me." The voices drew closer. Flora slipped out the door and heard it shut quietly behind her. Despite the unexpected warmth of the afternoon, she draped her green wool cape about her shoulders, eager to conceal her identity as long as possible. She all but ran through the garden gate and into the lane, plowing headlong into a torrent of nervous, fearful, and exuberant humanity that carried her toward the High Street.

The scream of the pipes grew steadily louder as the people surged forward. Faces, buildings, wagons, and the occasional bewildered horse blurred past Flora as she floated on the human tide like a leaf on a millstream. Fearful at first of being trampled underfoot, she relaxed by and by when she realized she was in no real harm. Her capture, she knew, was imminent, only a matter of hours at the very most. Still, it was wonderful to be free for just a short time more, to drink in the danger and excitement of such a riot.

Like a river plunging against a dam, the crowd came to an abrupt halt. Flora worked her way past a motley assortment of fellow citizens, most of them badly in need of a good wash, until she found herself at the very front of the crowd. She stood on the edge of the huge cobbled road that cut a straight swath through the heart of the city. Before her lay a small square ringed with apartments, some of which boasted narrow iron balconies that overlooked the road.

The air rang with shouts and cheers. Flora knew well enough that most of the people of Edinburgh were Royalists, strongly opposed to Prince Charles Edward Stuart and his claim to Britain's throne. Perhaps, she thought, they would rather give the appearance of a hearty welcome than risk the outcome of a cold one.

As she stood staring into the square, glancing overhead now and then to watch children waving makeshift banners from windows and balconies, several people in the crowd began to cheer. The wailing of the pipes became unbearably loud. A band of men swept around a corner of the High Street and began marching toward her. And what men they were! Her mother had often spoken of Highland clothing and customs, but Flora had never before seen men dressed in belted plaids. As they drew closer, she could make out three pipers in front of a large column of Highlanders, their bare legs gleaming under elaborate folds of tartan cloth. Their hair fell to their shoulders, held in place by flat blue woolen bonnets. A wealth of weapons clanked about their persons—muskets, steel pistols, basket-hilted broadswords, long dirks, and round leather shields studded with brass.

Though the Highlanders kept in good order, they moved unlike any other soldiers Flora had ever seen. Instead of marching with frozen, expressionless faces, these men strode along, lithe and easy, nodding to the throngs they passed, even smiling and laughing from time to time. She thought them most splendid, in an exotic, barbaric fashion, and compared them to the leopard, zebra, and other beasts she had once seen in a traveling menagerie.

The first column was followed by another, larger one, whose members wore a different assortment of tartans, and it dawned on Flora that these must be two different clans, as her mother had told her about so long ago. In short order she became caught up in the frenzy of the crowd, shouting, "Hail to the Stuarts!" and "Long live the rightful king!" For the time being, her father's fierce political loyalties were entirely overshadowed by the drama of the parade before her.

"Brazen hussy!"

At first, Flora did not recognize the voice or realize that the epithet was directed at her. Then a strong hand shot out of the mass of bodies behind her and seized her by the shoulder. She yelped in surprise as the hand drew her back a short distance from the street, cutting off most of her view of the triumphant Jacobites. "Unhand me!" she shouted, though she could scarcely hear herself over the tumult of the spectators.

"Indeed I most certainly shall not!" Her father's head and shoulders thrust through the crowd, his face distorted with anger. "Come wi' me, ye sorry wench." He tugged her arm, but she managed to break away from him and

slip again to the edge of the street. A small company of
Highland soldiers were stepping past, and for some reason
she could not discern, the people about her were shoving
each other with abandon, baying like hounds on the scent.
Someone pushed her down onto the cobbles, and in an
instant her father was on her, manhandling her to her
feet. She recognized him more by the reek of the distinctive
German brandy he preferred than by the features of his
face.

She called out for help. The crowd ignored her, intent
on something behind her in the street. Suddenly she felt
a huge hand on her arm. A firm and strangely familiar
voice said, "Sir, desist. Leave the lady be."

Startled, Flora leaped backward and struck a warm,
unyielding mass. She turned quickly and beheld the most
arresting figure she had ever seen. He was a tall Highland
soldier about thirty years of age, dressed like his fellows,
except that his clothing fit him better and hung about
him more gracefully. He was clean-shaven, and his long,
midnight-colored hair fell in glossy waves around his neck
like the mane of a horse. His lips were full and sensuous,
his chin square and permanently outthrust. Flora fancied
she could trace the ridges of his mountain homeland in
his uncommonly high brow and cheekbones. But most
striking of all were his eyes: one was as green as a spring
meadow, the other sky blue.

She would have stared at him longer, so intriguing was
the contrast between his fierce appearance and calm
demeanor. But her father gripped her hand and began
pulling her toward him, cursing her and her would-be
rescuer all the while. As the Highlander stepped forward
to assist her, Flora caught a glimpse of a handsome young
man on a gray Barbary horse, some fifty feet up the High

Street. The crowd shouted anew and, with a single soul and purpose, lunged toward the elegant rider.

"The prince! The prince! Long live His Majesty, Prince Charles Edward Stuart!"

All at once a wriggling mass of limbs and sweating bodies encircled Flora. She screamed as her father cried out and fell beneath the onslaught, his face ashen. Flora tried to run forward to aid him, but she could not move. Her arms were pinned to her side in a grip of iron. She saw in a moment that it was the odd-eyed Highlander who held her. As she struggled to free herself, the horde pressed against her with such force she could barely breathe, let alone move. Just when she was certain she would be smothered, her Highland protector swept her up in his arms, cape and all, and leaped into the street. Flora heard the whinny of a horse. She felt a breeze in her face as the beast reared up in fright, its iron-shod hooves inches from her nose.

"Mon Dieu!" cried the young rider, even as he maintained his balance and brought his steed under control. Townspeople and Highlanders flocked around him and the trembling animal, but he was such a superb horseman that he kept his seat with ease. "Sorley Fior, what are you about? What are you doing with the young mademoiselle? Or perhaps I shouldn't ask." A mischievous smile spread across the rider's face as he glanced first at his officer, then at Flora.

"Your majesty!" the Highlander exclaimed.

Overcome by the possibility that Prince Charles Edward Stuart had directed his attention to her, Flora found herself unable to speak a word. Instead she averted her eyes and nodded her head respectfully in lieu of a curtsy, which, under the circumstances, was impossible. The man who still clasped her protectively, though she no longer needed protecting, was at no such loss of words. "I beg your leave," he said, inclining his head. "This lady was in danger of being trampled, and I but prevented her fall. Forgive me for frightening your horse."

Grateful that he had not brought shame to her by mentioning what had actually occurred, Flora scanned the crowd, looking in vain for her father. She began to worry for him, recalling the plunge he had taken into the crushing throng.

The prince, however, seemed satisfied. *"Très bien,"* he said. "You can be sure it will take more than a misstep to unseat me." He patted his horse's steaming neck and murmured something to the animal in Italian. Then, brushing aside well-wishers and his own concerned retinue, he suddenly urged the stallion forward under the nearest balcony. Before the stunned crowd, the prince kicked his feet free from his stirrups and stood up on his saddle. Then, as quick as a cat and no less graceful, he sprang upward, grasping the wrought-iron bars that formed a sort of fence around the balcony. After he pulled himself up into a standing position in front of the astounded apartment-dwellers, he turned and faced the throng.

With fear and admiration Flora noted that he stood upright on a space between the bars, no more than two inches wide. She held her breath, but the crowd cheered even more loudly. Then, as hundreds gazed upon him, the young prince swung onto the railing of the balcony, grasping a flagstaff for support. He stood like a god in tartan trews, his face aglow with exertion and exhilaration. The crowd was oddly silent, awed by the young man's performance. Flora felt the Highlander who held her grow tense. Should the prince stumble, she thought, this man would leap forward to save him. It seemed to be in the fellow's nature to watch over others.

"Citizens of Edinburgh! Fellow Scots! My friends! My subjects!" shouted the prince, boldly waving his blue bonnet. His accent was neither French nor Italian, but a pleasant marriage of the two. The people, as if jolted by a bolt of lightning, roared in approval. The prince continued, shouting to be heard over the general discord. "Too long have you endured the indignity of being ruled by a foul, sausage-eating sluggard who claims to be your sovereign. Today, I announce to you that you are free from tyranny. All of you who can, come swell our ranks and throw the usurper from the throne. Join us in a Stuart victory and reclaim the kingdom for your own people!"

Again the crowd cheered, but Flora knew that few of them, in their hearts, approved of Charles Edward Stuart. They saw him as a usurper, and King George as the rightful monarch. No matter how gallant he sounded or how noble he looked, the prince was just as foreign to them as the plump monarch from the House of Hanover, and a Papist as well. Even those who despised the king were loath to replace him with a Catholic.

But the prince was pleased. He held his arms aloft and smiled like a triumphant athlete before descending from the balcony and dropping onto the cobbles, apparently none the worse for his acrobatic display. Flora felt the arms that grip her relax as her protector realized the prince no longer risked breaking his neck. Spurning all offers of aid, Charles Edward vaulted onto the back of his charger and rode onward. As he passed Sorley and Flora, the prince bent forward slightly in the saddle. "See to the lady's safety, Sorley Fior," he said. "Rejoin us as soon as possible at Holyrood House, where we now repair." With that he trotted on, at once regal and boyish, his back perfectly straight, his bonnet slightly askew.

Again the Highland host began to march, and again the

crowd fell back to let them pass. But Flora's Highlander stood to one side, as if he had no idea what to do with his burden. "Set me down, if you please!" she cried over the roar of the masses, then repeated this request until the man seemed to come to himself and did her bidding. Moments before she had had no thought but to escape her father. Now, even though she felt no kinder toward him, she could think of nothing but locating him. She had to know, for her sake as much as his, what had become of him.

Flora darted from her self-appointed guardian without another word and was deep into the still-cheering sea of bodies before she began to regret her hasty action. Some of the crowd were beginning to disperse, and Flora was soon caught in an eddy of people, male and female, young and old, some standing still and others wandering in all directions. What was she doing? If she located her father, she would surely return to the house to face Captain Stelton and a marriage that was doomed before it had begun. Should she run off and try to find the high road out of the city?

She was standing by the gate of a strange house, her hands pressed to her temples in an attempt to clear her mind, when she sensed that someone was staring at her. She raised her head and saw the man called Sorley not four feet from her in the lane, his fairy eyes fastened on her own. His presence unnerved her. "Why do you follow me?" she blurted out.

The tall Gael smiled and gave a short bow. "Mistress, I was charged with seeing you to safety, and faith! I cannot think you look very safe, standing in the road with your head in your hands. Shall I see you to your house?"

Suddenly Flora realized that this man had most likely saved her life, and she had scorned him. "Forgive me," she said, dropping him a curtsy, at which his smile burst into a grin. She was surprised to see what white, straight teeth he had, though one of his front teeth was slightly shorter than the other. His unbalanced smile only added to his otherworldly appearance. "I owe you my life, I'm thinking, and for that I'm grateful."

"You're most welcome," he said. "You overstate the matter, I fear."

"Tell me, are you as close to the prince as you appear to be?"

"Not so very close," the man replied. "I am one of his cadets, as he calls us. *Breaman,* we would say in the Gaelic. His train. I carry his sword when he chooses to be rid of it." Flora was about to wish him well and send him on his way when he continued in a very different strain. "Tell me, mistress, who was that creature that laid hands on you? Say but the word and I'll track him down, tear open his windpipe for him, and make him whistle through it."

The violent image took her aback a moment. She supposed the Highlander had led a hard life and was used to brutality, on both ends of the sword. Still, she had seen her own share of suffering, had she not? "It was my father," she answered. "It's him I'm seeking now."

"Mo dhia! That was your sire?" he said with a gasp, his voice subdued by honest shock.

"Aye." The crowds had now fled for the most part, and Flora was becoming more concerned than ever. Her father was nowhere to be seen, and already the sun was descending. Soon gloaming would come, shrouding the city in half-light, hampering her search.

Sorley shook his head, clearly baffled. "Forgive me, mistress, but you'd seek out the man who meant you ill? Father or no, I'd think you'd be fleeing the brute, not running to him."

Flora couldn't deny the truth of his words. "What else am I to do?" It was less a question than a statement of her desperation. "I have nowhere to go but into his care, which, I'll grant you, is not of the best."

The Highlander made a noise that sounded like pure exasperation, then grumbled something incomprehensible in his own tongue, under his breath. "Let me fetch the man for you," he said at length, "if you're certain that it's him you want."

Flora did not wish to see her father now, or perhaps ever again, but her alternatives were limited. Perhaps she would be able to think more clearly if only the persistent Highlander would leave her be. "I can fend for myself, thank you."

He cocked his head by way of agreement, as her mother had done when conceding a point. It was a charming gesture. "Aye, likely so. The way you gave me the slip back there, I can tell you're a woman to be reckoned with. But if I don't do as the prince requests, then I'll be disciplined. So you see, I'm merely thinking of myself and my own fortune."

Here was sheer madness, Flora thought, making bargains with someone she didn't know, half gentleman and half savage, whom she'd first cast eyes on but minutes earlier. Yet he had assisted her when the rest of the world had harried her like a deer. Moreover, she did not wish to see him punished, especially for her sake. Then there was always the possibility that her father would behave more prudently if forced to deal with a muscular Gael instead of a short, slender daughter with an impudent tongue.

"Very well," she conceded. "His name is Alexander Buchanan, and he is most likely found at the Saracen's Head or the Dappled Cob, both on Kinnis Row. Do you mark me?" The man nodded, and she went on. "I trust you'll know him if you see him. I myself shall be at the bookseller's on Speedwell Wynd. Anyone can show you the place. With luck, the shop will be open and I shall wait for you within."

He gave another quick nod, and before she could wish him well he had turned and run off into the deepening shadows. She wondered if she would see him again or not, and which of the two possibilities was the better.

When Flora reached the tiny bookshop on Speedwell Wynd, the old proprietor, a Mr. Anderson, was in the process of locking his door. When she asked him if it were not too early to close, he had an intriguing answer. "Well, Miss Buchanan, what with the shouting and marching and general mayhem that has taken place today, the good folk o' the town are ill inclined tae bury their noses in a book just now. Not a soul has crossed the threshold since early morning." He looked up from his lock and key, a distinctly mercantile expression brightening his wizened face. "Was it something particular you were searching for? The latest French romance, perhaps? Or Mr. Defoe's chronicles on Highland rogues, in keeping wi' today's events?"

"Nay, neither, thank you," Flora said. She glanced about the lane, expecting her father to come stumbling toward her at any moment. "I was hoping you'd be open, so as to allow me inside to await a . . . friend." After all, she thought, it was the least old Anderson could do, considering all the money she had spent in his establishment in her younger days.

The old man smiled and unlocked the door. "As you like, mistress, but only if you can play two-handed whist.

I much doubt anything will get done the day save card playing.''

Flora heaped thanks on the merchant, and together they entered the dusty shop and began playing cards. They had not finished the second round, however when the bell attached to the door gave a furious jangle, and in burst a Highland soldier, his plaid swirling about his hips as he jolted to a stop amid the bookshelves. "Heaven preserve us! We are besieged!" cried Mr. Anderson, scrambling to his feet with far greater alacrity than Flora thought him capable of.

Not sure whether to be concerned or not, Flora peered through the gloom at the intruder. Even half-hidden in the shadows cast by unsteady stacks of books, the man's graceful bearing was unmistakable. "I think we're no' in mortal danger," she assured the quaking bookseller. "Sorley, is it you?"

The Highlander stepped forward, coughing on the dust raised by his entrance. "It is, mistress. You must come with me at once. The news is not of the best."

Flora knew not what to make of this dire announcement, but hurriedly thanked Mr. Anderson and joined Sorley outside in the lane. He set off up the wynd so briskly that Flora was forced to kilt up her skirts and trot to keep up with him. "Wherefore in such haste," she asked, panting "and why?"

"Mistress," he said over his shoulder, "forgive me for asking, but your ties with your father . . . how close are you to him?"

Flora, unused to thinking while pounding down the cobbles at a rapid pace, took some time to frame an answer. "He is my natural father . . . my only living kin," she said, puffing mightily, "but put to it, I'd say that . . . Mr. Anderson has been more fatherly to me than . . . Mr. Buchanan."

Then the import of his question hit her, and uneasiness began to gnaw at her innards. "Has my father been injured?"

But Sorley said nothing more, only increased his speed as he led her past shuttered shops, overflowing taverns, and quiet houses. Blue twilight smothered the city. Darkness was still an hour away, but torches already cast their wavering light down the larger streets. Though Sorley had stated just the opposite some time ago, Flora began to worry that he might be flogged if he spent further time attending to her "safety." Surely, however, that was his decision, not hers.

Finally the Highlander stopped at one house which bore a weathered hanging sign—ADAM BARCLAY, PHYSICIAN—on an iron mount beside the door. The panic of that afternoon and the fearful look on her father's face as he disappeared beneath the frantic mob came back to Flora as she mounted the steps and was admitted into the house, with Sorley at her heels. A very young maid showed them into the doctor's examination parlor, where the air stank of camphor and other aromatics, which made breathing difficult.

A man's corpse, naked to the waist, was laid out on a table. The body was black with bruises and spotted with blood. Its wigless head was covered with gashes, and the right temple caved in. Despite the mutilating wounds, Flora knew her father at once. "Christ have mercy on us!" she whispered, crossing herself. She should have felt grief, she thought, or sorrow or pity, anything of a compassionate nature, but all she felt was relief.

For a moment she recalled the doting father of her earliest youth, who used to carry her on his shoulders and surprise her with sweets. Her heart yearned for that father. Her vision blurred, and she brushed the back of her hand against her eyes to uncloud them. The aching was gone almost the moment it had begun, and in its place a perverse but comforting numbness crept over her. It gave her the courage to stare with bald curiosity at the crushed man, the father who had beaten his wife and almost sold his daughter into a loveless union.

"Most unfortunate affair," said a voice behind her. It sounded too English to be Sorley. She turned and saw a round little man with an ill-fitting peruke staring at her with intense brown eyes. "He was breathing when he was brought to the surgery, but there was no power on earth that could save him. Miss Buchanan?"

Flora extended her hand for him to kiss, but it was some time before she was able to speak. "Aye, I am his daughter, Flora," she said cautiously, feeling somewhat uncertain of just who or what she was at that moment. "And you, sir? Are you Dr. Barclay?"

"Your servant," the little man said, with a slight bow. Though she could not put her finger on the reason, Flora distrusted him at once. She glanced sideways at Sorley to ascertain his feelings about the man, but the Highlander's handsome features were passive. "Let me be among the first to offer my condolences," said the doctor.

Flora, still benumbed, did not know how to respond. She was now most certainly cut adrift from all society and any means of supporting herself. Cobbling together enough money to return to the convent at Auchincairn seemed out of the question, and surrendering herself to Captain Stelton would be utter folly. "Thank you," she murmured. "Forgive me if I seem stupid. I'm in a hundred pieces over this and have no idea how to proceed."

"For now, perhaps 'tis best I return you to your father's house," Sorley offered.

Dr. Barclay shook his head vigorously, and the rest of

his considerable self shook in sympathy. "Sir, whoever you are, I'm afraid that cannot be. Miss Buchanan, the men who brought your father here and identified him implicated you in his death. They swore they saw you push him to the ground, where, as you can see, he was severely trampled. I myself don't believe them, but I'm afraid the bailiff must be notified, and it is my civic duty to do so."

Flora gasped. "The bailiff? I implore you, sir, don't summon him." She was far less worried about being accused of her father's death than she was of being dragged before the captain, who doubtless had already dispatched lackeys all over the city to hunt her down.

Sorley stepped up and tapped the doctor's forearm with one long finger. "For certain you can see that the lady's no' constructed for tossing grown men into the street," he said, his voice gentle but his purpose firm. "Perhaps you needn't summon the bailiff at once. You could wait until morning, for that matter."

"He might be difficult to reach at this time of day," Barclay conceded.

Flora looked back and forth from Sorley to the doctor. They were engaged in some sort of negotiation, she thought, but she had no idea what it might be. Suddenly Sorley reached out his hand toward her. "You and I have private matters to discuss," he said, half leading, half dragging her to the door.

"What . . . what can ye be speaking of?" she stammered. "Private matters?"

The Highlander ushered her into the hallway. "Have you any coin?"

The forceful way he spoke, coupled with the fierce light in his mismatched eyes, led her to believe he had asked the question often before. Was he robbing her? If not, what was he doing? "Coin?" she echoed.

Sorley rolled his eyes. He snorted and tossed his head, looking more like a horse than before, if such a thing were possible. "To cross the good doctor's hand with, woman. Why d'ye think I'd be asking for it?"

"You'd bribe the doctor?" she asked, more delighted at his ingenuity than dismayed at his morals.

"Aye, for certain, to ensure he keeps his neb shut." He glanced back into the room, but Barclay had busied himself with his medicines and seemed lost in a world of his own. " 'Tis an easy matter to buy a physician. Bailiffs are harder, but it can be done. Any higher and it takes more silver than I've had at one time."

Flora stared at him with a mixture of admiration and outright terror. "You speak as though you had experience in these matters, Mr. . . . Mr. . . ." With some embarrassment she realized that she had blithely followed the man over half the city but didn't even know his surname.

"Sorley Fior MacAilean of Clan Cameron," he said. "Upright Sorley, as they call me, Alan's son. But no 'mister' for me. That's for the Sassenach and you Lowlanders. Sorley is fine. As to experience, I spent my youth in the cattle trade, before and behind the law, but now I've pledged myself to the prince. So . . . have you any silver?"

Flora considered asking him how a former cattle thief might be called "upright," but she decided to let the matter lie. "I have five pounds in my pocketbook, which I was thinking to use for my father's burial." She fished the money from her purse. It seemed only fitting that she should use it to bury her father, since she had lifted it from his purse just that morning, intending to shop for some necessities at the market. "Why do you need to buy the doctor's silence?"

Sorley held out his palm. "You need to, woman, unless

you want the bum bailiff after you, clepping at your skirts. Quick, now, lest the fat wee paddock change his mind.''

Flora laughed, imagining the doctor as a toad, as Sorley had suggested. She laid one of the five coins in his hand, then paused. What proof did she have that he was telling the truth? Might he just take the money and be on his way? She sighed, then gave him the other coins. ''Now my father will lie in a pauper's grave,'' she said.

Sorley snatched up the silver and grinned. ''And his soul will lie somewhere a little warmer, Miss Flora, but have no fear. I'll see to your da.''

Flora followed her guardian into the doctor's room, where the two men spent considerable time discussing matters of money, law and the rite of Christian burial. Flora could not hear all that they said, but when the doctor at last showed them out of his house, he seemed pleasant enough. Back in the lane, Sorley handed her a single coin—the pound he had not needed. ''Physicians are easily bought, as I said. The doctor will hold his whisht until the morn. And you may rest at ease about your da. Whatever belongings he owned will be sold to pay for the long sleep. Barclay pledged me his word it was so, though I can't help but think some of your father's gear will end up in the good doctor's pockets.''

''Thank you,'' Flora said. ''You've been kind to me.''

'' 'Twas your silver, no' mine.'' He brushed her damp cheek with one finger, and she shuddered at the gentle intimacy of his touch. ''You weep. Even in your sorrow you are uncommon fair, mistress, if I may be so bold. *Arrah!* I trust you're no grieving for the man who misused you.''

''No, indeed.'' It was thoughts of Mrs. Leckie that brought tears to Flora's eyes, tears she could not produce for her father. She wished she could see the dear woman one more time, but she knew it was not to be. A housekeeper with her skills would have a new position in no time, Flora told herself. The stolid Ayrshire woman was better off in a new house, with a family who would cherish her. It was a sad thought, but comforting. "Now in truth you must be on your way, or you will suffer for your own decency."

"Nothing of the sort," Sorley replied. "You are in just as much danger as you were before, only now I am better able to see you to safety, as I was charged."

"I'm afraid I don't understand at all," Flora said. As she stood close to him in the darkened street, a breathless, dangerous feeling invaded her, and she wondered if she would ever meet any man half so captivating as this devoted Gael. What drove him to shadow her every step? She had never asked him for a moment of his time, let alone his generous assistance. It was all most curious. If only Captain Stelton were half so steadfast and honest as Sorley. Flora felt a pressure on her fingers. Looking down, she saw that the soldier clutched her hand tightly in his. She was distressed to realize how much she liked the pressure of his grip, the warmth of his flesh. For the first time since she was a child, she felt a bond of undeniable trust with another person, and the feeling both frightened and comforted her. It was as if she were connected to the universe at last after floating in ether for many years. She was about to ask him to free her when he suddenly released her hand, crushed her into his arms, and kissed her deeply on the lips.

Flora wriggled in his embrace like a trout still flapping and gasping in the fishwife's basket. How dare he! Was this the cause of his fidelity, then? Did his nobility extend no further than his lust? The face of Macinally appeared before her but quickly vanished. She knew, in some deep reaches of her body if not her mind, that the Gael had no intention of ravishing her. Indeed, she was fairly certain he had formed no intentions at all. He was simply doing first, thinking second.

She pressed against his chest, then pushed against it, then struck it with both fists, but still he would not break his insistent embrace. Her face grew burning hot, and her skin prickled with a thousand minute bursts of an intense sensation she could neither name nor explain. Some unassailable force was pulling her toward this man at the same time that eighteen years of careful upbringing were pleading with her to stop. Against her best judgment, against her parents' stern counsel and all she had ever learned in polite society and in the company of the good sisters of Auchincairn—at the risk of her very soul itself, she was sure—she surrendered to his kiss.

Flora was past caring what she thought, or what others thought of her, if only she could extend the sweet pressure of that kiss to last forever. Even when his tongue teased her lips apart and entered her mouth, searching and thrusting, she started only once. Unlike the brute Macinally or the self-important Stelton, Sorley belonged this close to her, if not closer. The moist intimacy of this kiss seemed right, perhaps even holy. It was most certainly not innocent.

Without warning Sorley drew back and released his hold on her. The spell was broken, and the wonderful closeness Flora had felt in his arms was suddenly, inexplicably gone. Once again she felt the chilling desperation of her loneliness descend on her. "You'd ask why I dogged you so," Sorley said, his strange eyes glittering in the twilight. "Well, the hope of a kiss such as this was the answer. Now you may strike me if you like, and faith! I deserve a good skelp."

Flora stood speechless, unable to tell whether he was toying with her feelings or not. He had taken supreme liberties with her, yet she had allowed him to. While slapping him might restore her dignity somewhat, it was not an honest way to treat the man. "Consider yourself paid for your services, then," she said slowly, "though I fear I'm in as much danger as before, if not more, as you yourself have said."

The Scot looked up and down the street, then led her to a deserted spot inside a garden behind a large house. A torch bathed the overgrown patch of grass and rambling roses in flickering light. His touch on her arm was most businesslike, and, had she not known better, Flora might have believed that their kiss had never taken place at all. When he drew his dirk without a moment's explanation, she jumped back and flattened herself against an iron gate. Two passing strangers glanced in her direction, then hurried on before she could summon her wits to scream. This incomprehensible man—was he lover, guide, or murderer?

Sorley studied her fear with interest, then laughed outright. "Your hair," he said, nodding at her wild curls, which had come unpinned during their embrace. "It all must go, woman. I'll have you looking like a boy yet."

"A boy! Pray, why might you do that?"

The Highlander laughed yet again. "Those who seek you seek a woman, aye? They'll no' seek a lad. Some breeks, a blouse and waistkit, stockings and brogues—ach, you'll be fine, provided the blouse is cut loose enough. All you'll need is a place of refuge. If not your father's house, then where? Have you no family, no friends?"

Slowly Flora began to discern his plan, though she was far from ready to agree to it. "The convent at Auchincairn, not far from Perth," she said, dragging each word from her throat. Much had happened to her in a short time, and she was beginning to feel as weary as a corpse, reanimated and forced to walk the earth. "The sisters would take me back if I asked them."

Sorley shrugged, as if prepared to accept the best of a bad situation. "Now there is an uncommon waste of a beautiful woman," he said. Flora thought him bold, but she appreciated his compliment nonetheless. She could still taste his mouth in her own, and wondered if and when he would attempt another such liberty. "Listen well," he continued. "I pledged to see you to safety, and I shall. I can arrange for your safe conduct to Perth. A livery owner here in the city is heavily obliged to me, and he will provide you with a horse and guide. I'll tell him you're my cousin, going to live with kinfolk up north for a bit. If fortune is with us, he'll ask no questions."

"Did you mean what you said before, that I must dress like a lad?" Flora sputtered, her head reeling with the speed at which her life was changing. She had begun the day as a daughter on the brink of becoming a wife, and was about to end it as an orphan, and a boy to boot.

Sorley nodded. "And I meant what I said about your hair, too. Come, let it down."

Under the command of his blue-green gaze, Flora could do naught but obey. She pulled the remaining pins from her hair as if he willed her hands to do so. Her hair was unruly, but it was hers, and the thought of having it lopped off made her feel diminished, reduced. Unwomanly. Suddenly she stopped, a hairpin in her hand. "I shall tie it back in a queue, as is the mode with so many young men," she said. "No one will be able to identify me."

Sorley tapped the point of his dirk on his jaw, deep in thought. "Aye, then, as you like. Only let me trim the length at the back. Few lads wear their hair quite so long."

Flora, amazed that he had accepted her proposal, happily consented, but, when minutes passed and he was still hacking away at her yellow curls, she knew she had been duped. Long tresses filled his hands and slipped to the cobbles, like straw spread on the square on market day. "My hair!" she lamented, running her hands over the cowed remnants of her once-rebellious locks. They now dawdled down to her chin, a little longer in back. "I'm as bald as a scone! Ye've shorn me as Delilah sheared Samson, which is fitting, deceitful rogue."

Sorley sheathed his blade and stepped back to admire his work. "It's not likely I'll be changing professions from soldier to barber," he confessed, "but at least now you can pass for a man, given the proper attire. And I was no' deceiving you," he added, brushing a flurry of golden hair from her shoulder. "I said I would attend to the length, and I did, though perhaps beyond what you fancied."

She might have been bone-weary, destitute, and confused, Flora told herself, but she would be hanged if she'd stand by idle like an empty-headed belle, waiting for the beaux to pay her court, and let this stranger mock her. "Attend to me no more," she said. "Leave me be! I can carry on well enough by myself."

The Highlander loomed over her like a thunderstorm. She could see in the torchlight that his face was set and square, full of the conviction lacking in her own voice. "Forgive me for my rashness," he said, and Flora could not tell if he were apologizing for the kiss or the brutal barbering. "I will vex you no more if you but come with me to the hostler's and get started on your journey. *Mille murthair!* This has been the hardest day of the campaign, and not a red soldier in sight."

The desperation in his voice moved her deeply. "Lead on, then." She pulled her hood over her decimated curls and hurried after the man as he snaked his way once again through the narrow streets. It was evening now, and the shadows that leaped out of alleyways and corners to startle her were black and cool. Did the Highlander never eat nor rest? She was about to give voice to her exhaustion when Sorley stopped. Flora breathed in the warm scents of hay and manure. She became aware of the whickering of curious horses and could see their great white faces shining in the semidarkness. "What place is this?"

"A hostelry just south of the city," Sorley explained. She was fascinated by the fact that he, an occasional visitor to Dunedin, was better acquainted with it than she was. "I'll rouse MacPhee."

"MacPhee," she repeated, no longer surprised by his sudden revelations. "The hostler, I ween."

"Aye. You take your ease until I return." He pointed to several bales of hay.

Wrapping herself in her bedraggled cape, Flora threw herself onto the sweet-smelling straw and listened to Sorley's footfalls growing fainter and fainter as he once again set off in pursuit of her elusive safety. As she closed her eyes for a moment, Flora doubted that either of them might ever find it.

Chapter Three

The light of morning streamed into Flora's eyes. Assorted whinnies, neighs, nickers, and squeals clamored in her ears. She sat up amid the bales of straw, painfully aware of an aching stiffness in every joint of her body, and looked straight into a pair of rheumy blue eyes set in a broad, red face bordered with rust-colored whiskers. She had the disturbing feeling that she knew this man.

"Wake up, lad," he said, giving her arm a good shake. "Auld Wull is up and mounted, and yer mare is being saddled. Did ye forget ye had tae be on yer way in the morn?" He clapped her on the knee and rose, a goodly amount of straw rising with him.

Dumbfounded, Flora looked down at her arms and legs, which appeared quite foreign to her. Her gown of rose linen—as well as her cream-colored underskirt, her pinafore, and other clothing—had been replaced with brown brogues, white hose, gray wool knee britches, a blue waistkit, and a linen blouse. A tricorn hat with a silver buckle nestled beside her, as innocent and unassuming as a small black cat. Flora stared at her transformation, struggling to remember when and where she had changed her clothes. Had Sorley dressed her? If so, had he seen the hideous mark of her dishonor? She couldn't bear the humiliation of this prospect, and so refused to contemplate it. Since the big man was still staring at her, she took a calculated guess as to his identity. "Mr. MacPhee?" she said, trying to force her thin voice into deeper tones.

"Aye?" As he seemed to await a question, she offered him one.

"Where is Sorley?"

MacPhee snorted. "That redshank reiver! Why, he was off and awa' last night, lad, after the three of us settled on the details o' yer journey north. D'ye not recollect him leaving?"

In truth she didn't recall anything of the night before, save a vague image of Sorley and MacPhee drinking whiskey together, and the sensation of falling asleep in the sun-scented straw. "Of course," she said, "now that you've reminded me." She scrambled to her feet, brushing handfuls of hay from her clothing. The garments were clean and durable, but worn soft in several places and obviously the veterans of much use. It occurred to her that she must have dressed—or been dressed—before MacPhee had seen her; otherwise he would surely be aware of her ruse.

As she took a step forward, hoping to find a private place to relieve herself, her sense of balance flew from her and she stumbled heavily in the straw. Then she remembered that she had eaten nothing for an entire day. "Is it ill you're feeling?" MacPhee asked, true concern showing on his coarse face.

"Have you any bread?" she murmured. The weakness in her voice displeased her.

The hostler nodded, then shambled into the darkness at the front of the stable. When he returned, he carried a small pewter pitcher full of milk and a wooden bowl containing what looked like the leavings of several other meals. "Eat up now and be on yer way," MacPhee instructed, thrusting the pitcher and bowl into Flora's hands. "The redshank said ye must be off by dawn, and dawn's long past. It's three days' ride to Perth, so the sooner begun the better."

Flora sank back down among the bales, hesitating only an instant before reaching into the bowl and gobbling up the bits of crust, oatcake, and greasy cheese. She tried not to think about who had bitten into the food before her. Downing the milk was more difficult, as she had never drunk from a pitcher before, but her thirst was greater than her awkwardness, and she soon swallowed every drop. When MacPhee left to check her mount, she slipped into a horse's stall and made water. The big gray gelding glared at her all the time in a most indignant manner.

The unfamiliar breeches were a bother, but she finally did up the buttons and emerged from the stall just as MacPhee returned, shouting a man's name at her. Then she remembered: Davey. It was what Sorley had chosen to name her. Davey Crookshank.

Flora followed the hostler into a small courtyard dulled by a leaden sky and chilling mist. She clamped the tricorn on her head in what she hoped was a manly manner and tried to walk as she had seen Sorley walk, his head high, his stride double that of a woman's, but she kept tripping on the toes of the clumsy brogues. As MacPhee held forth on distances between towns, road conditions, and the care of hired horses, Flora sought to pay attention, but the rough feel of fabric between her legs vexed her sorely. "This is Wull Taggart," the hostler said, nodding at an ancient man on the back of an equally ancient white stallion, which stood with its muzzle nearly touching the ground. The rider slumped so far back in the saddle that Flora feared he would topple over his horse's croup. "Wull will see ye intae Perth, as Sorley arranged," MacPhee went on, "then return wi' the beasts. Are ye agreed?"

Flora, still troubled by her trousers, nodded before realizing that she must needs find the convent of Auchincairn by herself. But she had been through so much already, she consoled herself, surely locating the sisters would not be insurmountable.

Without another word, MacPhee led a stocky bay mare into the courtyard and ordered Flora to mount up. She froze. She had ridden a horse only twice in her life, and both times on a sidesaddle. Each time a groom had assisted her onto her mount. Now what was she to do?

She walked up to MacPhee and stood by the beast, hoping that, through some miracle, she might ascend to its back without embarrassing herself, exposing her charade, or breaking her neck. In desperation, she turned to face the hostler. "I've no' ridden oft," she mumbled.

"No?" said the big man, who seemed not in the least perturbed. Seizing Flora by one knee and one elbow, he hoisted her into the saddle before she could think of protesting. Somehow reins appeared in her hands. "Bess'll follow the auld stone-horse," MacPhee said. "Pull her up when she'd run off on ye, and take care not tae wind her."

He pushed something cold and hard into her hand: a compass in a brass case, like a pocket watch. It was quite old, with a smiling sun etched on the front of the case and a thoughtful moon on the back. In a moment he had shown her how to use it. Flora, distraught at having been handled so roughly, had just enough presence of mind to tuck the compass into her pocket and mutter her thanks.

" 'Tis from Sorley," MacPhee explained. "Wull's dependable when he's sober, but not when he's had a dram too many. Remember, the road runs northwest tae Sterling, then northeast over the River Forth tae Perth. If ye keep tae the high road and the towns along it, ye'll most likely avoid any thieves, or worse yet, the damnable Jacobites."

"Jacobites?" Flora said, trying not to show her incredulity. "But the army is here in Edinburgh. I saw it myself."

"Aye, the army," MacPhee replied. He raised his head high as he looked at her, as if to indicate his superior knowledge. "But it's no' just the chiefs and their armies that support the prince. There's worse than that out there. Stay off the heath, and ye'll do fine."

Flora hadn't bargained on outlaws, and the thought of facing such brutes gave her pause. She put her hand to her heart, where the compass lay. Just knowing it was from Sorley made her feel braver. Though she was unlikely to see him again in this life, at least she had some token by which she could remember him.

Northwest, northeast, she chanted to herself as she and Wull rode from the courtyard and into the empty street. Merchants were just beginning to set up their stalls in a small market square, and the morning air was ripe with the autumn scents of kale, mutton, and cheese. A short ride on the high road brought them to the edge of the city, where houses did not stand cheek by jowl, but were separated by a small copse or pasture. By noon they were well into the countryside. The fine road had deteriorated into a rutted path the width of three horses. Houses were few and widely scattered. Often nothing more significant than a plume of smoke indicated a human habitation in a brown wilderness of forest and field.

To divert herself from her loneliness, Flora sometimes reached her hand up to her tricorn as she jounced along and stroked what was left of her reckless hair. She certainly didn't feel like a lad. Did she look like one? Though she reckoned she had seen thousands of boys and men in her lifetime, she had no clear image of how a man moved, spoke, or acted. Her one consolation was that she had fooled MacPhee, or appeared to. More important, she wondered, had she fooled Wull?

Wull himself was a poor model of virility, a shrunken creature as bony as his decrepit horse. He proved a dour companion as well, incapable of saying much beyond "aye" and "nay" whenever Flora tried to incite him to conversation. Since even these pitiful attempts at communication left him in a glum mood, Flora held her tongue, vowed to ignore the growing discomfort in her bladder, and thought of Sorley.

In truth, she tried hard indeed not to think of him, but he was always with her, marching beside her in her thoughts. No one save her mother had shown her such kindness and devotion, and not even her mother had saved her life. She knew nothing of love, though she had read much of it, and at last decided that what she felt for the Highlander was nothing more than affection. Deep affection, perhaps. She was not worthy of the love of such a man. But what did it matter? She'd never see him more. A shame, that, since she hadn't even had an opportunity to thank him properly.

Sometime in the afternoon they stopped at a wretched inn to eat. Flora was almost ill from holding back her water, and was overjoyed to find a privy behind the ramshackle tavern. The food was so greasy and unappetizing she ate but little and was glad to ride on, despite her aching bottom.

Wull was no more amiable than he had been earlier,

and Flora found herself longing for company of any sort. She pulled the compass from her pocket and absently rubbed it with her fingers as she rode. When she at last, quite by chance, happened to glance at its face, she could not believe what she observed. She and Wull were traveling nearly due west. But MacPhee had clearly said northwest, then northeast.

She showed her evidence to her implacable guide. "Do you see, Wull?" she said, holding up the glittering bit of brass, "we're far off the trace. We must amend our path, aye?"

The old man eyed her suspiciously, then spat into the heather. "We need nae amending," he announced. "D'ye dare question my route? That loadstone o' yours is nae worth a pint o' pish." With that he rode on, and Flora was obliged to follow him, full of misgivings. She promised herself that, when they came to an inn for the night, she would get proper directions and force Wull to see the error of his stubborn ways.

But it was nearly dark when they stopped at an inn, and it was all Flora could do to eat a little soup and bread, find a private place to relieve herself, and drop into a dead sleep on a straw mattress. The morning dawned cold and dreary. After a breakfast of oatcakes and cheese, Wull mounted the mare, forcing Flora to ride Siller, the doddering stallion. They rode from the inn in such haste that the sun was high in the sky before Flora remembered her resolve to find the road to Perth. She suspected with growing anger that Wull had a secret resolve of his own.

"Why must I ride this bag o' bones? Bess is for me," she shouted to Wull.

He had no reply save, "Hauld yer whisht," and she could neither coax nor coerce anything more enlightening from him. The landscape grew hilly, and after several miles of stumbling across rises and valleys in a light rain, Flora lit on the reason for the shift in mounts: astride Siller, she could come no speed, should she ever wish to. There was no hope of escape on the cow-hocked nag.

After about an hour had passed, Flora again checked the compass, and again it pointed due west. Sorley knew the straits she was in, she thought. He would never have given her a faulty instrument. The notion gave her courage. When the rain finally abated, she halted her horse and shouted out to Wull, who twisted about in the saddle to face her. The dark scowl that distorted his face made her almost regret her decision, but she felt obligated to confront him once more, for Sorley's sake as much as her own. The Highlander had risked so much for her; she could not cower like a child and let someone else undo his kindness. Perhaps Wull was leading her astray on purpose, she thought . . . or perhaps he was simply too stubborn and proud to admit a mistake. If on purpose, what purpose might he have?

"I'll ride no farther with you," she said firmly, "until you tell me where we are headed and why. I know full well we're off our course. Deny it not."

To her utter amazement, Wull's face blossomed into a beautiful smile, and she could see that, in his youth, he had been remarkably handsome. "Weel, Davey, lad, ye're uncommon clever, are ye no'? 'Tis true enough, I've led ye west, but only for yer own good. This road is safer. Fewer thieves and broken men and such-like dangers. Ye'd no' have me lead ye into a nest o' reivers, aye?"

Flora took in the hills around them, a dark wilderness of moorland without so much as the likelihood of a house or village nearby. This road was no safer than the road they'd left. Indeed, it no doubt led through the very heath that MacPhee had warned her to shun. Though she had no idea what his motive might be, she knew Wull was telling her false.

She tried to speak, but she'd lost her tongue completely. What could she say to him? That she did not believe a word he'd told her? Surely that would do her no good. She fingered her reins, longing to break the silence of the moorland.

Wull smiled at her again, the conversation at an end, as far as he was concerned, and urged Bess forward. But something was not right. The mare pranced and whinnied, tossing her head like a wild beast. Wull cursed as he fought to control the frightened animal. Even Siller raised his skeletal head and gave such a cry of fear that Flora's entire body stiffened at the sound. Although she could see nothing out of the ordinary, she felt the chill of someone's gaze upon her.

Siller began to paw the heather. Flora tightened the reins, recalling what MacPhee had said about checking a horse to keep it from galloping off with her. Wull was still wrestling Bess into submission when Flora saw a man walking toward her, a disreputable fellow in torn breeches and jerkin. "Who are you? What do you want?" she cried, thinking all the while how stupid she must sound. The man stopped short, then gave a piercing whistle. Another man rose from the heath, not far from the first, then charged toward Wull and Flora, shouting obscenities and brandishing what looked like swords.

Stunned at first by the sight of the outlaws, Flora at last came to herself and kicked Siller furiously in the ribs. Since she still held the reins quite taut, the old horse had nowhere to go but straight up. Suddenly the earth shifted under Flora as Siller reared into the air. She gasped as she tumbled forward over his shoulder, certain that his flailing legs would strike her senseless. At the last instant, the animal flung himself aside, and for the second time in three days Flora avoided death under a horse's hooves.

The ground reached up and struck Flora on the side. The air shot out of her lungs. She struggled for breath. Her vision dimmed and the world became a blurred confusion of shapes and colors. Men were shouting all about her. The stench of whiskey and tobacco lay thick on their breath. Hands ripped at her midriff, groping for her breasts. She gasped in agony as someone grabbed her hair and hauled her to her feet.

A fist gripped the front of her waistkit and rent it from her body. Flora cringed, hoping Macinally's horrible brand would not show through the opening at the top of her blouse. Then again, she thought, her blouse likely would not be long on her back. She clenched her teeth, anticipating the same horrors she had undergone so long ago.

"Now we'll have a proper look at ye, *Davey.*"

Flora recognized Wull's voice at once. When her eyesight returned to her moments later, she saw Wull's watery blue eyes and gaunt face. The three were in league together! "How . . . how can you have known?"

"Yer scent," said the old man, drawing a small knife from his belt. "They're no' the same, ye ken, the smell of a woman and the stink o' a man." Flora writhed in the grip of her captors, but they held her fast. Wull pressed the blade to the base of her throat. She clamped her eyes shut, waiting for the bite of the knife. It didn't come. Instead Wull sliced open the front of her shirt and tore it from her. Tears ran down her face as she sobbed in outrage. She snapped her head back and tried to bite the fingers of the men who held her, but the rogues were too swift for her. Too late she saw that they held cudgels, not swords. A clout on the side of her head made her ears chime like cathedral bells.

Wull needed only a moment to appraise his trophy. "Ach! Ye're damaged, hussy! Wi' tha' great ugly thing on yer paps, wha' man would pay to lie wi' ye, even should ye prove tae be unbroken? Wha' stew would have ye, at any price, even in Glasgow?"

The men who held her shook their heads, muttering their disappointment.

Through a mist of humiliation and anger, Flora grasped Wull's meaning. He and his tattered friends meant to sell her into a life of degradation in a distant city. Despite her pain, the finely wrought irony was not lost on her: in seeking to escape a plot to sell her as fine china, she had walked squarely into a plot to sell her as earthenware. And Sorley? He could not have been involved, she told herself. And yet . . .

"Wha's tae be done wi' her?" asked one ruffian, absently running his filthy hand over her exposed breast. Again Flora struggled to break free, and again one of her captors struck her in the head, this time with the back of his hand. She shrieked her pain into the hills. Blood filled her mouth.

"Why, doubtless two hot-blooded gentlemen such as yourselves hae an answer for that," Wull replied, his beautiful smile lighting up his weathered face. "Myself, I'll keep an eye on ye and offer suggestions. If there's anything left o' her afterward, we may yet scrape it up and get a few pounds for it."

As if he had only been waiting for this suggestion, one of Wull's companions flung himself on Flora with such fury that she crumpled to the ground. She vowed to fight back. She must not let what happened before happen again. The man caught her by the wrists and held her fast. Desperately he sought to remove her breeches, but she was equally desperate. When she freed her hand to use his own, she clawed at him with her nails and pinched his big red ears.

''Well, ye're a clever lad indeed.'' She heard Wull laugh. ''Just what is it ye're attempting tae do tae the puir doxy?''

The other scoundrel, who had up until that moment stood immobile, apparently content to be a spectator, ambled into action. He seized her arms from behind, freeing his friend to remove the remnants of her clothing. Rendered completely helpless, Flora did not even have the will to cry out any longer. Tears streamed down her cheeks as she remembered Macinally.

''Hold, in the name of His Majesty, *Prinnsona Tearlach Eidird Sturaich!*''

The two men, in the act of ripping apart her breeks, paused. Flora tried to locate the source of the command, thinking it might have been Wull, but the old brigand was busy looking about the heath, also in search of the mysterious speaker.

''Hold, or all three of you are dead!''

Flora wondered if the beating she had taken had affected her hearing. The voice was almost that of a child, high and airy, but with a masculine edge that made it unlike any bairn's voice she had ever heard. Where was this strange rescuer? she asked herself.

As if he had intercepted her thoughts, the intruder shouted, ''Can you not see me?'' and burst out of the heather not six feet from where Flora lay half-naked on the ground. She could see only the top of his head and the white cockade pinned to his blue bonnet, identifying him as a supporter of the Stuart cause. She was glad to have this stranger's assistance, rebel or not, but she wished mightily that she did not have to expose herself to yet another male.

Suddenly Wull began to laugh wildly. The others joined

suit. Flora wriggled into a sitting position and saw at once the reason for their derision: the man who dared to threaten them with death was no taller than a six-year-old child. His huge head was surmounted with a thatch of brown hair, and his body was likewise big and burly. His arms and legs, however, were so shrunken that they seemed inadequate for their purposes. The Highland plaid belted tightly about his waist emphasized his tiny limbs and added to an appearance that, under any other circumstances, Flora would have thought comical. She remembered having seen dwarves in pageants and carnivals when she was much younger, but never had she encountered one so fierce, so commanding.

"Leave her be and go on your way, or suffer," the little man continued. He drew a dirk from his belt to emphasize his words. Another, taller man, she thought, might have drawn a broadsword, but this brazen homunculus could never wield such a heavy weapon. "I'll be taking the mare in the name of Prince Charles," he said. "You may keep the nag."

This announcement drew a loud snort of disbelief from Wull, who strolled forward until he was within arm's length of the diminutive Gael. "Take my mare? Likely not. Do ye hae a name, wee mon?" Wull said, as if speaking to a child. He crouched low until his face was level with the intruder's and smiled.

Flora marveled that the dwarf was not in the least put out by this indignity. "I am Ewan Fada MacEwan of Glen Strone," he said, without a quaver in his voice, though Wull was nearly twice his height, and the other men as tall as Titans compared to him. "If you don't heed my words, then 'tis the last name you'll ever be hearing."

Good Lord, the creature was cocky! Flora looked out over the heath but saw nothing, only brown bracken and gray granite. She pitied this brave but obviously mad little man who had rushed, however foolishly, to her service. "Please, sir, save yourself!" she cried.

"Whisht, woman!" he piped in his reedy voice, rousing Flora's captors into another fit of laughter. "You're bold wights, sure enough," he taunted them, "three of you to one female. I trow you've no stomach for scrapping with a man."

"Hah!" Wull shouted. "And what man might tha' be, ye wee cripple?" Wull gestured to the larger of his two companions. "Come then, Archie, and show this banty cock wha' a man is."

Flora watched as Archie reluctantly released his grip on her left breast and lumbered toward the dwarf who called himself Ewan Fada. The outlaw had raised his cudgel and was within striking distance when the crack of a musket shot tore apart the silence of the afternoon. Archie squealed. Streamers of blood sailed from his head. He sank like a rock into the dying heather.

Too shocked to cry out, Flora stared at the dead man, then at Ewan, then back at Archie's body. At last she saw someone rise from the heath, a man of normal height, carrying a musket. A cloud of black powder was rapidly dissipating over his head. For a long time all four men waited in silence, looking at each other and the corpse. Flora could sense their anxious excitement as they sized up the odds against one another. The young man who had backhanded her stood up, fingering the pistol at his side. Finally Wull asked the intruders, "Are there more o' ye?"

The dwarf lay his stunted arms across his chest in a poor imitation of a normal man crossing his arms. He shrugged. "How badly do you wish to find out? Now listen well. Leave the woman and the mare, take the nag, and be gone."

"Your pistol, Jamie!" Wull bellowed.

His startled henchman pulled the gun from his belt, but Flora could not tell if he intended to fire it or not. Rallying what was left of her strength, she aimed a kick at his knee and struck his shin. He hopped backward, and the pistol slipped from his hand.

There was a whistling sound, then a gasp. Jamie's eyes bulged as he looked down at his chest. An ashen shaft half a yard long protruded from his flesh. He slumped to his knees, then onto his side. Underneath him the ground turned scarlet.

A scream died in Flora's throat. She turned away, burying her face in her hands, half expecting to feel an arrow slam into her own chest. When she raised her head, she saw not one but two men behind the dwarf—the musket bearer and a bowman. Wull, still alive and whole as far as she could tell, was on his knees, his hands clasped prayerfully before him. "Spare me, gentlemen, please!" he begged. "We meant ye no harm!"

Ewan laughed. He turned to his comrades, said something to them in his native tongue, then glared at Wull. "Nay, you'd brain us and shoot us, deceitful cur, and throw your lackeys' lives into the bargain. I'm a compassionate man, but my patience wears thin. Ride off, as I said afore, but leave the mare . . . unless you'd still care to be knowing how many more men are with me."

Wull needed no further invitation. He ran to the pine snag where he had tethered both horses, mounted Siller, and, through some enchantment known only to himself, coaxed the ancient beast into a gallop. Flora marveled at man and horse, amazed that either could be so fleet of foot. When she could see Wull no longer, a huge sigh shuddered through her. In the past three days, she had watched three men die brutal deaths; she prayed she would never see such a thing again.

As she tried to put her tattered clothing to rights, she all but forgot about the rebels who had saved her honor, or what was left of it. When Ewan called out to her, she jumped like a child caught making mischief.

"Ach, sir," she said, "forgive me. You . . . you've been most kind. Those men . . . I fear they meant to slay me." She glanced at each corpse, then away. Her gorge rose at the reek coming from the dead men, and she had to fight down a sudden wave of sickness.

The little man jogged forward a few steps. "Aye, slay you or worse. How fortunate you were that we were close by, on the trail of the prince. In any affair, you gave a good account of yourself, screaming like the *ban sith* and kicking like the water horse."

Flora almost smiled at the mention of these two Highland legends that her mother had often invoked. She assumed the dwarf was paying her a compliment and thought to thank him, but her mind was spinning so fast from her ordeal that speech became a daunting task. "My horse . . . if ye'd be sae kind as tae fetch her . . . I'll be on my way."

Ewan walked up to Flora and looked her up and down with the air of a man used to assessing the results of carnage. "On your way, eh? *Mo dhia!* On your way to your grave, I trow. Look at the face on you, woman! Your nose looks like a handful of raw venison, and your eye! *An diobhail!* I've seen dead dogs less swollen. 'Tis a wonder you can think straight, what with your brains rattled about like oats in a cup."

Through a fog of pain and dizziness, Flora realized he was right. In the unlikely event that she was able to wheedle the Jacobites into giving her Bess, she knew she'd not be able to ride three steps without falling off the mare's back. "Mayhap . . . mayhap I'll need to rest a bit before I start . . . start back to Perth."

"Perth!" Ewan stared at her. "Woman, you're at least five days' ride from that fair city, if indeed you were able to ride. Now rise and we'll have a better look at you. What in the name of the fiend himself has brought you out on the Heath of the Hundred Sorrows?"

"I . . . I've been duped," Flora murmured. Five days! If she ever saw that terrible creature Wull again, she'd bite off his nose.

Flora could not stand by herself, and so allowed the dwarf's two companions to take her by the arms and help her rise. However, the moment she stood up the earth began to pitch beneath her feet and she toppled back to the ground. She tried a second time, but her legs turned to pudding and failed to support her. "I'll just have a moment's rest," she said, stretching out in the sweet-scented heather. Vaguely she worried whether her scar were visible, but she hadn't the strength to see for herself.

A wonderful feeling of peace ebbed over her, and she began to forget Wull, the two dead men, even her father and the deadly accident that had driven her north in the first place. The world began to look dark around the edges as her vision receded until she could see nothing but the dwarf's round, kind face. The last words she heard before slipping into a welcome blackness were Ewan's, but as he spoke in Gaelic to his friends, even those brief instructions were encased in mystery.

Chapter Four

Flora awoke to a flurry of barking. Where was she? On the open heath, far from Auchincairn, she reminded herself, on the Heath of the Hundred Sorrows, some of them hers. What dog was this, then, that shattered the quiet?

She sat up and looked about her, not certain whether she was truly awake or waking only in a dream. Plaids and deerskins hung all about her, stretched on a rude framework of boughs, and she reckoned she was in a tent of sorts, pitched in a hurry to shelter her from the rain. Taking stock of her shirt, she found it ripped in half, completely ruined. By good fortune or, more likely, Ewan's kindness, another blouse of gray homespun lay rolled up under her head. She slipped it on. Though the garment was so long and wide she felt lost within it, she was grateful for the concealment it offered her.

The barking was still in full force when Flora crawled from the makeshift shelter and stopped abruptly at the

entrance. What she saw persuaded her she must have been
dreaming. A dog indeed stood close by, a grotesque black
beast with the head of a mastiff, the body of a deerhound,
and other parts that appeared to have been donated by a
wide variety of breeds. But it was not the dog that caused
the commotion. It was a man.

The marksman who had shot Archie knelt some twenty
feet from Flora, staring at her even as he snarled, snapped,
growled, bayed, and barked in a manner more befitting
the panting creature at his side. Flora gazed back at the
man. She felt like a deer caught in the hunter's sight. Not
knowing whether to run away or dive back into the refuge
of the tent, she remained motionless, bracing herself for
an attack.

She did not have long to ponder her indecision. To her
utter fascination, Ewan careened across the heath on his
stubby legs and launched himself at the barking man. As
both Highlanders collapsed in the heather, the dog finally
emitted a halfhearted woof. The man's mad barking was
overwhelmed by a torrent of angry Gaelic as Ewan scrambled upright and began berating his comrade, punctuating
his statements from time to time with a slap to the man's
thigh or shoulder. Although she recognized precious few
of Ewan's words, Flora knew his intent well enough: You're
frightening the woman. The word *cu,* meaning dog, was
familiar to her, and as she listened, she came to believe
that Cu was not a reference to the patchwork hound, but
the name of the doglike man.

When he had at last expended the greater part of his
distress, Ewan Fada walked up to Flora and gave a deep
bow, which made him look even more childlike. She had
not so much as blinked during the incident, and it took
great effort of will to acknowledge the dwarf with a nod.
"Have no fear of Cu here, mistress," Ewan apologized,

"though I'll warrant he seems fearsome enough. He's as good a man as any born, but when the anger's on him, or fear or weariness, he cries like a hound. Sometimes his body shakes, and sometimes he hammers at the ground, but pay him no mind. He's a bonny shot and a good-hearted soul, and of no harm whatever."

Flora looked doubtfully at Cu, who now sat brushing bits of heather from his plaid like any ordinary man. He was decidedly of harm to Archie, she thought, but said nothing. After all, Cu had only been protecting Ewan. "I shall take your word for it," she said. She took his outstretched hand, smaller than her own, and stood up, thankful that her head was clear, her balance restored. "And what was it brought about his display just now?" she wondered aloud.

"Cu, the lady inquires as to the cause of your fit," said Ewan to his man. With his bearded chin held high and his stubby fingers resting on his waist, the dwarf cut an almost preposterous image of misplaced pride, yet Flora confessed to herself that there was something about him that would never allow her to laugh at him. What magic did the poor creature have that inspired her unquestioning trust? In that respect, he was something like Sorley, she thought.

Cu rose, a sheepish expression on his sanguine face, and made a little bow of his own. "Mistress, forgive me for frightening ye," he said. Flora was relieved to hear him speak in an ordinary voice, and in tolerably good English to boot. She had suspected he might growl an answer at her. "I was worried that ye didn't waken for so long," he went on, "but Ewan Fada forbade me from disturbing your rest. We had words on the matter, and ye can see where they led me. Is all well with ye?"

Flora smiled at his look of concern. With his large brown

eyes and shaggy black hair, he could almost pass for a distant relation of the mongrel hound. "Well enough, I warrant, thank you. I trust you'll not get into any further disputes over my welfare." For the first time since she had risen, Flora took in the land around her. The sky was full of threatening gray clouds, but the place seemed less barren, less hilly. Pines and red rowan trees fringed the distance, and the musty perfume of a peat bog scented the air. "Is this the heath where Wull deserted me?"

"O, nay, mistress," Cu reponded. "This is Mialach Moor, the Moor of the Lice, and in truth, I've ne'er been bit so much in my life as last night."

"How much closer to Perth are we, then?" Flora asked. When Ewan and Cu shot sidelong glances at each other, she immediately became apprehensive. "Surely we are closer to Perth now," she ventured, assessing the distance to the hills on the horizon.

"Seven days' ride," Ewan murmured, "had we a horse to ride. The thief's mare went lame, mistress, and we had to leave her with a crofter. But," he said, smiling, "we are only a day or two from the prince's army, and only half a fortnight or so from the border. Then we triumph!" He paused, then added, "That is, Prince Charles will triumph, of course."

"Seven days from Perth!" Flora gasped. The little knave and his overwrought partner had abducted her as surely as Wull, if not as cruelly. At this pace, she would never find rest nor the safety that Sorely had fought so hard to win for her. "Ye left Bess in a farmer's care, but ye carried me off? What am I tae do?"

"Why, come with us, for certain," Ewan suggested. "Join the rising against the despot, King George, and his smarmy minions. What else might you do? I swear on my father's grave that you'll suffer no indignities from my men, nor any violence. You'll not fight, of course, but you may help us cook and mend, and nurse the wounded. Once the prince takes his rightful place as king of these islands, I myself will see you to wherever you wish to go, Perth or Paris, or the moon, if you wish." Ewan's voice thundered with bravado. He thrust out his chest, nearly obscuring the rest of his ill-made body.

Flora was unconvinced as to the wisdom of this plan, or even whether Ewan offered it in jest or in earnest. She paused, considering her choices. Returning to Edinburgh and facing the captain was just as absurd as the thought of walking to Perth alone, without money or provisions. But Ewan's proposition was scarcely less foolhardy. Her father, never much impressed with the military life, had once explained to her the customary relationship between women and soldiers, and she wanted none of that. Again she asked herself, what was she to do? Getting to Auchincairn was her only solution, even though she had little desire to live such a spare existence, without children, without color, without joy. Her head swam with weariness and hunger.

Were Sorley here, he'd establish his bearings before doing anything else, she told herself. The thought brought her peace. Fishing Sorley's compass from the pocket of her worn breeches, she tried to gauge true north. When she looked behind her, she leaped backward, dropping the compass. "Heaven preserve us!"

Several men gaped back at her with interest. Their appearance made even the dwarf and the barking man seem ordinary by comparison. One fellow was huge, almost three of Ewan in height and weight, with an expression as blank as that of an ox. The fellow beside him bore a hideous red mark over half his face and neck, creating the impression that he had been lying in a pool of claret for some time. His right arm was normal, but his left so wasted that it was no bigger than Ewan's. The third and most monstrous creature of all was a truncated boulder of a man whose face was distorted by folds of flesh. His body, though large and powerful, slumped to the right as if frozen in the act of melting. Next to these unfortunates stood a fair-haired boy of thirteen or so, who seemed free of deformity, and three much younger lads, the eldest of whom could not have been more than eight years old. She recognized a normal-looking man about Sorley's age, with bright red hair and a slender, wiry build, as the archer who had brought down the outlaw, Jamie. All eight gazed on her with a mixture of admiration and—to her overwhelming disbelief—fear.

"What . . . wh-who . . . ?" Flora stammered, backing up still farther, until she was standing between Ewan and Cu, who seemed not in the least disturbed by the menacing apparitions. On the contrary, when the dwarf answered her, she heard a definite ring of paternal pride in his forever-adolescent voice.

"This is my regiment, and I its captain," he said. "Good men all, some more capable than others. I ween they take some getting used to, mistress, and it's sorry I am if they surprised you. Almost all of them have some English, except for Dughal, who is too simple to learn one language, let alone two. Shall I make introductions?"

The desperation that had been mounting inside Flora since she had woken up that morning finally overpowered her. She caught Ewan by the front of his shirt and screamed at him in a way that she knew would not be sanctioned by the sisters of the convent at Auchincairn. "Ye despicable wee man! Ye'd carry me into the wilderness to help ye support a cause that's uncertain at best and no' of my own choosing. Then ye force me into the company o' cripples, monsters, waifs, and wheybrains, and wish tae *introduce* me tae the brutes. Why would ye think I'd care tae be in their presence? Regiment? These sports o' nature? Are ye daft?''

Ewan drew himself up as tall as he might go, which brought his eyes level with the top of the dog's head, and clenched his knobby hands. "Faith, woman, I've never seen anyone reel from genteel language to broad Scots with such speed as yourself. But it's no' only your language that changes. One moment you're civil to Cu, and the next you're laying the lash on his comrades.''

Ewan gently pried her hands from his shirt. "Mistress, think on this. Say a company of honest men should come to the aid of a woman dressed in man's garb and beset by wretched knaves. Say also that this woman should be so badly injured that she falls into a swoon for two days, compelling these decent men to care for her and take her with them instead of abandoning her on the heath. Now if this same female should then complain because the men fail to look as she'd wish them to look, then I'd put it to you that she is the one lacking in humanity.''

The fierce expression that crept over the dwarf's face as he finished speaking gave Flora pause. She knew the men could do nothing about their defects, nor were they to blame for them. Hadn't her own mother shown compassion to one of their kind? The thought of being so close to succor, then being rudely ripped away from it, broke through her rage and loneliness. She was as good as helpless, at the mercy of a clutch of the strangest strangers she had ever encountered. Thoughts of her childhood raced through her mind, and she burst into tears, struck by the depth of her aloneness.

At the sound of her sobs, the youngest of the three little boys began to weep with such force that the big, ox-faced man grasped him by the back of the collar and hauled the child into his arms. Flora's tears came to a sudden halt. "Save the boy!" she shouted. She clawed at Ewan's shoulder as she envisioned the child with a broken neck.

The dwarf laughed so hard that he seemed fit to choke. "From what? Too much affection? Look for yourself."

Flora saw at once that Ewan was right. The child quieted immediately in the giant's arms and lay back, sucking his fingers like an infant in a cradle. Flora stared at the pair in wonderment. She patted her eyes dry with a sleeve of the voluminous shirt. Somehow the gentleness of the huge Gael was almost as unsettling as his capacity for violence.

"What may we call you, mistress?" said the man who looked like molten rock.

Suddenly it was important to Flora that these people know who she was. If she were to die on the open moor among the desperate and the dispossessed, then at least they would know her as a person, with kin and history. "My name is Flora Buchanan," she said, aware as she spoke that even Ewan did not know her name until that very moment. "I've lived in Edinburgh most of my life, with my father, God rest his soul. I've been ill-used by my family and my guide, and I'm much obliged for what you've done for me."

Ewan cleared his throat and touched her hand. "You're more than welcome. Now sit and eat with us, and I'll learn you the names of my brothers-in-arms."

"Very well," she said, still surveying the ragged group that eyed her back. Indeed, her two-day fast had made her light-headed, but she was not about to show her weakness to these oddities, who for all their concern were still unknown to her and required her caution. She stooped to pick up Sorley's compass, but the tallest of the little boys was quicker than she. He dived down into the heather, plucked up the shiny instrument, and held it out to her with a shy smile. She thanked him, but he merely ducked his head in reply and scurried back among the others.

"Take a dram of this, mistress. It'll do you good," Ewan said, handing her a leather flask. She sipped from it, expecting whiskey, and was relieved to discover water sweetened with red wine. Then the dwarf clapped his hands once and his bedraggled regiment broke ranks. They scuttled about, building a fire from bits of wood and peat, and in a short time began cooking oatcakes on a griddle. "You've an appetite on you, I'll wager," Ewan said with a grin, bestowing on her the first cake browned by the fire. Though it was so hot it burned her hands, she managed to chew off the edges and work her way toward the steaming center.

After he had given her two oatcakes, Ewan made good on his offer to introduce his followers. Pointing in turn to each man seated around the fire, he proceeded to cast out an imposing string of Gaelic names, each as peculiar as its owner.

"I . . . I don't have the Gaelic," Flora told him, angry at herself for not knowing her mother's tongue. "The odd word or phrase, aye, but nothing more. What are their English names?"

Ewan sighed thoughtfully, resting his bewhiskered chin on the back of his wrist. "I was coming 'round to that," he said. "It strikes me, though, that you should first know who we are when we're together. The *sona* call us *An Damainte,* the Damned, and I suppose we are, to their way of thinking."

"The *sona?*" Flora savaged another oatcake, astonished by her own ferocity.

The little man took a long pull from a whiskey skin resting in his lap. "Aye, mistress, the fortunate ones—the ones taller than myself, with more wits than Dughal, less accursed than Cu or the others. But we are the prince's men, nonetheless. We watch his back and do whatever else we can for him.''

Flora felt completely befuddled by the dwarf's proud claim. "But the army is nowhere in sight. If you fight for the prince, why are the lot of you not with your chief and clansmen?"

"We were separated from the prince's army some time ago," Ewan answered. "When they choose to travel quickly, we can't match their pace. But no matter what the circumstance, we'd never risk our lives among the ranks."

Flora nearly choked on a mouthful of food. "Risk your lives? Your own people would slay you for taking their cause?"

Ewan gave a high, sad laugh. Cu, stretched out beside him, made a sound that was half chuckle, half growl of contempt. "It's clear you speak as one who has never been despised by many, Miss Flora," Ewan continued. "Nay, the clans will take the maimed and the halt, the deaf and the slow, but they'll not have us. We're a curse on the entire undertaking, y'see. That's why we stay at the rear. *Far* at the rear. Now myself, I might pass muster with the *sona*. I'm good with my dirk, and a distant kinsman of my chief, Lochiel. But these creatures ..." Ewan indicated the Damainte with a sweep of his hand, and each man looked up as he gestured. "Without someone to shepherd them and plead their case, they'd only get themselves killed, by Jacobites or Royalists; it hardly makes a difference. Think on it, now: if you'd held a pistol when Cu was raging at you, would you have spared him?"

"Faith, I don't know." Flora set her half-eaten oatcake aside. She was no longer hungry. So often she had bemoaned her fate, which had appeared to her as black as doom, as cruel as eternal damnation. And here were men who lived damnation every day, even at the hands of their own kin. Suddenly she felt how incredibly circumscribed her world had been, no bigger than a trinket box compared to the lives and woes of others. But she had no time to ponder her situation further, as Ewan gave her still more miseries to consider.

"Cu you know already—the dog, and y'ken the reason why. He's of Clan Donald, as is Dughal, the big man with the little brain. He speaks little, but he mostly does as I tell him. Strong as an ox is our Dughal, and just as likely to father children. His parents had him unmanned at an early age."

"Unmanned!" Flora cried. "How could they do such a thing?"

"Why, to prevent any mischief later on, mistress," Ewan explained, looking at her intently, as if she were the half-wit. "A man unable to control his passions is likely to get himself killed. Beside him is Creag, the rock, and a fine fellow he is, though a little slow of foot." Ewan nodded toward the misshapen man whom Flora had likened to a living boulder. "Donald is his given name, of Clan Gregor. As you can see, we are of many clans here, a sort of tartan of clans, with many colors and stripes."

"But ill-stretched and ill-woven," replied Creag, in a hoarse voice that sounded as if it had been lying unused for years. "Warm enough, but not to the taste of most folk."

Flora smiled at the man's homey comparison, although his appearance still frightened her. His gray eyes shone like bright pinpoints through the heavy creases of his flesh, and she wondered how it felt to be so disfigured.

"Next to Creag is Seumas Half-face," Ewan continued. The man with the port wine stain and withered arm gave a broad grin, which made his disfigurement seem even more ghastly. Flora barely managed to smile back. "Seumas is of Clan Stuart, and almost as brave as our noble prince," Ewan said proudly. "He's a good shot with a pistol, and the only married man among us. The rest of us, save Dughal of course, have sworn never to marry, for fear of fathering more monsters such as ourselves. But Seumas, where is your lovely wife, *mo bhalaich*?"

Suddenly Seumas was all eyes as he looked about the heath. "Where indeed? Losgann! You had charge of her." He grabbed the blond lad with his good hand and gave him a shake, then spoke to him in such rapid Gaelic that Flora could not decipher a word. The boy's speech was just as incomprehensible.

"Is the woman lost?" Flora asked Ewan.

"Perhaps, but Seumas will find her. Her memory is none of the best."

Flora was curious to see this lone woman who traveled with so many men, but before she could question Ewan further on the situation, he had continued his introductions. "And the weans here . . . we call them the Three Smalls." He gave Flora a quick bob of a bow. "No offense to you, Miss Flora, but sometimes our language is coarser than what you're used to, I'm thinking. Leastwise, there are three of them, and of no size at all, so the name seemed good enough."

Flora smiled at the two older boys, who gazed at her with deep emptiness and longing in their faces. The youngest lay asleep in Dughal's arms. *Where are their mothers?* she wondered. "I cannot call them what you call them. Have they no proper names?"

Ewan shook his head, then took another gulp of whiskey. *How much liquor can such a little man hold?* she asked herself, then realized she might not wish to know the answer. "They're city weans from Perth and Dunedin. Lowlanders, like you. They've lived in the streets for so long they've forgotten their given names, or indeed whether or no' they ever had any. What use they are to us I can't say, but we found them wandering on the moors and couldn't very well leave them go. Who else but wretches such as ourselves would take in the spawn of tinkers and strumpets? The two older ones call themselves Whoreson and Bugger, and claim they've never been called otherwise. Rattie is the wee one.''

Flora shook her head in dismay. ''I'll not curse them whenever I speak to them!'' she cried.

Ewan shrugged. ''It matters not to me what you call them.''

Already she began thinking of new names for the grimy children. ''And the older boy?''

''Losgann,'' Ewan said, ''the Frog.''

Flora frowned. Why would anyone call such a handsome lad such an ugly name? When Ewan called out to Losgann in Gaelic, however, she soon discovered why. The youth held up his hands, and Flora used all her presence of mind not to cry out at the sight of them. His fingers were about half the length of Ewan's and webbed like a frog's feet. She could see at a glance that Losgann could never easily pick up an object with those deformed hands, not a pistol nor a trencher nor any other useful implement. Surely his worth as a soldier was next to nothing.

She found Losgann especially pathetic, and quickly turned the conversation back to the rest of the *Damainte*. ''What of the red-haired man?'' she asked. When Ewan looked back at her with confusion on his face, she assumed he hadn't heard her. ''The bowman,'' she tried again.

''Ach, that's Gair,'' Ewan answered. He glanced overhead at a dark bank of clouds, then back at Flora, then at the blaze-haired archer. ''The Harebrained Man, I suppose you'd say, for he's as mad as a hare in the spring. No sense to him at all.''

Flora couldn't believe what Ewan had told her. "He had sense enough to shoot a bow and defend your life," she countered. "He can't be as damaged as you say."

Ewan cocked his big head, so out of place compared to his tiny hands. "Gair, the lady believes you must have something in that sieve you call a skull," he called out to the redhead.

"In my head there's only enough space for so little as will fit in the sea," Gair answered, nodding wisely, as if he had given an appropriate response.

Flora gaped at him, then decided to ask her own questions. Perhaps she had unnerved him somehow. "You may speak plainly with me," she said. "I mean you no harm. What brings you to travel with Ewan and these unfortunates?"

Gair looked at Ewan, but the little man said nothing. When Gair turned toward Flora, his face took on the sadness of a man who sensed his own defeat but could not prevent it. "How unjust it is that we can only see the stars when we wake," he murmured, "and cannot trace their course through the heavens."

Flora shook her head. "Either this man is a poet," she said to Ewan, "or he's daft."

"And some would say there's little difference between the two," Ewan answered with a laugh. "Nay, truth to tell, he's neither, Miss Flora. Watch now." As Flora and the *Damainte* watched, Ewan commanded Gair to unbuckle his sword belt and toss it onto the heather, which the stricken man did at once. Another word from Ewan, and Gair retrieved the belt and fastened it over his shoulder without hesitation. "He'll do exactly whatever I ask of him," Ewan said. "I've heard him speak like a man on more than one occasion, but most often he caws like a corbie, with just as much sense."

The dwarf was in the act of saying more on the subject of Gair's disability when Flora felt a drop of water strike her nose. More drops soon followed.

"Tha t-uisge ann!" cried Losgann and Cu.

"It's raining!" said one of the Three Smalls with a squeal. All the *Damainte* looked at Ewan, and when he nodded they raced to the tiny shieling Flora had left a short time earlier. She could scarcely believe they could all fit inside, but soon only she and Ewan were standing in the cold rain. Even the dog had disappeared. Though Flora had no desire to join the crush of so many bodies, all of them male, unwashed, and imperfect, Ewan clutched her by the hand and dragged her inside, deaf to her objections.

Once she was inside the makeshift shieling, Flora's protests began to fade. The little sanctuary was dry and warm, thanks to its many occupants, and though the air was pungent with their mannish scent, it was no worse than Flora had experienced in many a crowded marketplace. She squeezed between Whoreson and Bugger, who immediately fell asleep against her, and listened to the rain attack the deerhide roof with savage intent. Despite the dim light, she quickly noticed that one of the *Damainte* was missing. "Where is the man with the birthmark?"

"Seumas Half-face?" said the dwarf. At that moment, as if in answer to their questions, the plaid that covered the entrance to the shieling parted and yet two more bodies wormed their way inside. The space was so cramped that both Cu and Ewan were forced to clamber onto Dughal's broad lap, while Gair took Rattie, awake at last, into his arms. The two latecomers were wringing wet but had no choice but to shiver in their soaking clothes. Flora instantly recognized Seumas by his disfiguring mark and crippled arm; at his side was a bronze-haired lass with an uncommonly pert, sweet face and luminous blue eyes.

"Your wife?" Flora asked, inwardly congratulating Seumas on his good fortune in finding such a bonny bride.

"Aye," the poor man said, squirming against Creag in a vain attempt to achieve a comfortable position. "My Rosmairi. A rose among the thorns, she is." He worked his arm around the young woman, drew her even closer into his dripping plaid, and kissed her tenderly on the forehead. Flora's heart warmed at the sight, and she was glad to think that love could flourish even with such bleak prospects.

"What place is this, Seumas?" Rosmairi asked, in the soft accent of a Perthshire native. She looked about herself as if seeing the *Damainte* for the first time. Perhaps she was a very new bride, thought Flora. "Do I ken this woman? There's Ewan Fada, I ween, but who are the bairns?"

"I'm quite sure I don't know you, mistress," Flora answered, and quickly introduced herself. She was working up the courage to introduce the three boys as well when, to her surprise, Seumas named everyone in the shieling for Rosmairi, save himself and Ewan. He even reintroduced Flora. "Has your wife not met all these folk before?" she asked.

"Oh, indeed." Seumas nodded so violently that his entire face appeared red. "Every other day or so. I must acquaint her with them often, as she forgets." As if to illustrate her disability, the young woman stared at Flora and again asked her name. "We've been wed two winters," Seumas explained, "and it's been ever thus. Even after a fortnight of traveling with the *Damainte*, she can no more hold our names in her head than a net can hold water." He stroked his wife's red-gold hair with great affection. "Even mine." Once again he named everyone in the shiel-

ing, including himself and the dog, Crann, then turned
to Flora. "Pray don't be offended if she fails to hold you
in mind."

"What little there is of it," Ewan grumbled.

It was an uncharacteristically cruel remark, Flora
thought, for a dwarf who defended lunatics and barking
men, and she couldn't keep herself from speaking up for
the distracted woman. "Poor Rosmairi cannot help her
condition any more than you can help yours," she said
boldly. "You might just as well blame any of your men for
their defects." As soon as she'd spoken, she realized how
forward she'd been. She depended solely on Ewan's good
graces, and insulting her host was hardly the sort of action
that would endear her to him.

"Aye, well, mayhap," Ewan answered, looking about in
vain for a place to sit on the ground. "But I don't make
a habit of wandering in the heather like a sheep. The red
soldiers patrol hereabouts now and then, and they'd have
no second thoughts whatever about practicing their mus-
ketry on a poor woman who has forgotten where she
belongs. 'Tis easy to speak of being kind, but keeping
everyone alive is another matter entirely."

Flora was spared a reply by Seumas, who pulled a whiskey
skin from his plaid and passed the burning liquor around
to the entire company. Even the Three Smalls each took
a swig. Flora sipped the whiskey, pleasantly astounded by
the way it warmed her right down to her fingertips.

"Don't be too harsh on Ewan, Miss Flora," Seumas said.
"He has a hard time of it, being chieftain to such as us.
We all know only too well that every man, woman, and
child, even among the *sona*, has some wart, if not on the
outside, then on the inside. We reckon none of us are as
bad off as we could be."

Flora fell silent, thinking of her own secret. She thought

of Macinally, a devil of a man, and her father, who had
much to account for in the next life. When at last she
recalled her surroundings, she saw that half the *Damainte*
were asleep. This was a great advantage, given the wretch-
edness of their lodgings.

Flora longed for sleep, but her back was stiff and her
legs numb from crouching in the cramped quarters, and
the sighing of the wind through the deerhides only voiced
her own despair. Perhaps we are all monsters in some way,
she mused, thinking of what Seumas had said. At once she
thought of Sorley. No one, not even Mrs. Leckie, had been
so kind to her. But perhaps his kindness was no more than
part of some plot hatched with MacPhee and Wull, to sell
an unwary lass into depravity for a handful of silver. After
all, he had admitted to stealing cattle. Why not women as
well?

Surely that wasn't true. She remembered his kiss, so full
of tenderness. That wasn't the kiss of a monster. She knew
firsthand how monsters treated women. So what was her
Sorley then?

She thought she might try to avoid him. She could not,
however, avoid thinking of him. As she tried to imagine
where he was, what he was doing, and how he was surviving,
she fought back an image of him lying wounded in the
heather, suffering in silence and waiting to die. Nonsense,
she scolded herself. There was no point in terrifying herself
on account of a man who had perhaps used her ill and,
in any case, was as good as dead to her already. Still, it
was some time before she could put the discomforting
thoughts past her and surrender to sleep.

By morning the rain had passed. Everyone was relieved
to be free of the shieling, though wintry winds raked the

heath and made Flora's teeth chatter. Her arms and legs ached, and she balked at the thought of facing many such days and nights on the moors. Sorley's welfare was still on her mind. If only she could determine his guilt or innocence, she might be able to coax him into seeing her safely to Auchincairn, where she might actually escape the mad fervor of the Jacobites, if indeed she wished to. She would be safe at last, but the price would be high: thirty or forty years of pious tedium and isolation, waiting out her life instead of living it. Perhaps it was better than her present situation. Perhaps it was worse. Perhaps it was no better than she deserved.

As she helped Seumas and Rosmairi prepare a simple breakfast of oatcakes and drammock over a peat fire, she asked them whether they knew a man named Sorley. Rosmairi, of course, knew no such man, though Seumas reminded her that her own brother bore the name.

"I know several Sorleys," Seumas continued, as he poured oatcake batter on the hot griddle with his good hand. "This man you seek, what clan is he from?" But Flora could not recall. He was always only Sorley to her. "Ask Ewan Fada, then," Seumas suggested. "He claims to know every soul north of the Highland line. If your man's among them, Ewan will have heard of him."

Because Ewan was in a great hurry to join the Highland army, or at least come as close to it as he might be allowed, breakfast was a hasty affair. Nevertheless, the *Damainte* were cheerful at the prospect of aiding the prince, and jested with each other as they ate. Even the Three Smalls laughed, though Flora suspected they had no idea what was happening. The sight of so many damaged people in such high spirits disturbed her, and she wondered if any of them truly knew what lay ahead of them. After all, taking on the king's army was no light matter. Even worse, their

travels would take her still farther from Perth. If she found
Sorley, or chanced upon some other means of parting
from her unusual companions, she would have a long
journey back to Auchincairn.

Flora's mind was full of these dark thoughts and others
as the *Damainte* set out. She thought of herself as a
thundercloud in the midst of a blue summer sky. Ewan
seemed to mark her glum mood, for he offered her a dram
from Seumas's whiskey skin. Flora declined. She wanted
all her wits about her, lest she miss an opportunity to
escape.

Ewan led his people south at as brisk a pace as they
could muster, which was none too swift, due to Creag and
the Smalls. Flora found that walking eased her stiff muscles,
and she was glad she still wore breeks and hose instead of
a flowing skirt, or even an arasaid, the loose Highland
gown that Rosmairi wore. Flora had grown accustomed to
her heavy brogues, and could walk, even run, without fear
of tripping in the heather.

At noon the *Damainte* paused to rest in the shelter of a
grove of ancient pines, which roared in the wind and made
the air smell like the spice shop on the Cowgate back
in Edinburgh. Flora strode up to Ewan and tapped his
shoulder. The little man spun around like a wolf, but he
smiled when he saw her. "Ah, you're looking well, Miss
Flora. And to think that but a few days ago I thought we
might lose you. You have a question for me, I'm thinking."

Flora began to believe there was nothing she could keep
hidden from the shrewd dwarf. "Seumas tells me you are
well acquainted with many people in the north," she said.
"I wish to locate a man named Sorley, a member of the
prince's bodyguard, but I know not his clan. Have you
heard of such a man?"

"I know a hundred Sorleys," Ewan said, raising his chin

in the air like a cock robin. "Lochiel has a brother-in-law of that name, and our shadow-man bears it, too. Can you not be more descriptive?"

"Shadow-man?" Flora repeated, fascinated by the image of a slate-colored man without features. Such a fellow would be at home among the *Damainte*. "In heaven's name, what manner of man is that?"

Ewan laughed so loudly that Crann the hound began to bark at him. "Our connection with the prince's army," Ewan explained. "Charlie's worried about being out-flanked, and we do what we can to prevent that. Lochiel himself chooses a man from his ranks to direct us. We had us a fine shadow-man some time back, but he sundered his leg and had to be carried home to Lochaber. His second cousin has taken over for him, and a more miserable son of the devil I've never seen."

Flora hesitated. If this Sorley were her Sorley, then perhaps he would not make such a trustworthy guide after all. "You would know this man the instant you saw him," she said. "He's odd-eyed, blue and green."

"The man I speak of has gray eyes," Ewan muttered, "and a mood to match. There's almost no talking to the brute at all, he's so taken with his own opinions. But you can see for yourself, as Lochiel should be sending the creature to seek us out any day now. Come, we've rested long enough. I'll think on your question as we go."

The *Damainte* continued their trek, and Flora was quite pleased to find herself always at the head of the group with Ewan, who was forced to trot to keep up with her walk. The others dawdled behind, except for Cu, who was always at Ewan's side, and Losgann, who ranged far ahead of the group, scouting the terrain. Gair, most whole in body if not in mind, traveled at the rear, like a stallion patrolling the back of his herd, alert to dangers from behind.

The moorland gradually gave way to rolling hills of brown grass and leafless alder trees. Flora checked her compass often: they were heading due south. Ewan had just ordered another halt when Losgann came toward them at a dead run and slid to a stop an arm's length from Flora. His face was bright pink and he panted like a hunted deer. Crann frisked about the boy's legs, barking and whining. "What's amiss?" Ewan demanded.

Losgann gasped something in Gaelic, and Ewan replied with muttered curses.

"Are we off the mark?" Flora asked.

"Worse than that. Red soldiers," Ewan said. "Half a mile from here. They have a captive with them, and unless I'm much mistaken, you'll meet our shadow-man sooner than I expected, living or dead I can't say."

"Let me go with you," Flora entreated him, bending over to look him full in the face. "I may be of use to you, ye ken." As she spoke, she wondered what mad notion had bitten her. Here was an opportunity, not to escape, but to get herself killed. Nevertheless, some force she didn't understand was throwing her into the fray. It was exciting, and not a little terrifying.

Ewan scanned her up and down, then nodded. "Keep behind. If it comes to blows, fall down and lie like the dead. Hold this." He placed a Highland dirk in a leather sheath in her hand. She shivered at the thought of the murderous blade, so harmless now within its scabbard. Her chest ached at the memory of Macinally's dirk against her flesh. "I have another. Thrust upward, not down," he whispered, then gave Losgann a nod. *"A' ghille! A'shuas!"*

The boy darted off and Ewan leaped after him, his crab-bed legs working furiously to keep up. Moments later Cu followed with his musket, and Seumas sprinted by, his lone pistol drawn. Pulling Sorley's compass from her pocket, Flora gripped it as hard as she could, summoning the foolhardiness she needed to live up to her bold request. She cared not whether a Stuart or a Hanover bottom sat upon the throne, some saner part of her told herself as she scrambled after the rebel misfits. This was not her war. Why was she fighting it? And why was she so elated at the prospect?

Chapter Five

"D'ye see, mistress?"

Flora inched her head out of the prickly bracken, peeked over the granite boulders before her, and gazed in the direction Ewan Fada was pointing. The patrol of English soldiers was unmistakable: their scarlet coats burned like a bonfire on the distant hillside. The six of them were taking turns kicking a fallen figure barely visible in the heather, occasionally prodding their victim with their bayonets. "Is it the man you spoke of?" she whispered.

Ewan wagged his head. "It may well be, from what I can see of him, a long-leggit brute, dark as Glencoe in a storm. But shadow-man or no, we'd best go back and get the *Damainte* into hiding. I'll no' risk my people for a worthless reiver."

Flora frowned as she watched a soldier slam his Brown Bess against the figure on the rocky slope. "You'd let the man die?"

"And what else might you propose?" Ewan snorted and began to back away from the shelter of the massive rocks. "To march Cu and Seumas into the mouth of death to save a misbegotten wretch, clansman or no?"

Flora winced. She could hear the man moaning. Beside her, Cu growled deep in his throat. "Your clansman?" she wondered out loud. "What clan might that be?"

"Clan Cameron, as I've said afore," he replied. "You'd do well to remember—" Ewan's jaw snapped shut. Flora sat transfixed while a flash of tartan sped past her, out into the open. She blinked in disbelief. It was Cu, snarling as he ran like a mad thing from rock to rock, straight toward the astonished redcoats.

"Cu! Come back, ye whoreson knave!" Ewan shouted, stamping his dainty feet. "He can't abide the sound of a body in pain," he explained. Then, screaming in Gaelic, he drew his dirk and plunged from the rocks, in pursuit of his addled warrior.

Flora at first drew back, but a shriek from the soldiers' victim was so compelling that she crawled from the boulders and picked her way after Ewan, using the rocks to shield her approach. The redcoats had recovered from the first throes of shock and had begun to fire on Ewan and Cu, who were still beating an erratic path toward their captured countryman. A spent musket ball fell to the ground, only inches from Flora's feet. Another struck the rock beside her and sent a chip of granite slicing past her chin.

Suddenly the air filled with smoke as shots erupted all around her. Flora knew Cu and Seumas must have fired on the English, but they were not alone. She caught a glimpse of Gair on her left and Creag on her right, each lumbering uphill with a musket in one hand and a claymore in the other. But Dughal was running with them as well, and even little Whoreson and Crann the hound. Someone—Losgann, perhaps—had summoned the rest of the *Damainte,* at least those with any hope of offering a fight.

Through the cloud of black sulfur smoke burst a grenadier, his eyes closed against the sting of the gunpowder. Flora froze in horror as the man blundered past her and collided with poor Gair, only five paces away. The Gael rolled onto his back like a beetle, his legs and arms jutting into the air. The soldier regained his balance, turned, and faced the Highlander.

Rage tore through Flora like a flame and jolted her to life. She remembered Ewan's dirk, which she had not laid aside once from the moment she'd received it. She tried to draw it from the sheath, but the thought of Macinally made her hesitate.

The grenadier trained his gun on Gair, who had not moved a finger since his fall. Flora knew she must do something or bear the guilt of Gair's death for a lifetime. In a fit of desperation, she tossed the dirk, still in its sheath, as hard as she could against the soldier's red back. The man grunted as the dirk thudded against him and fell to the ground. He scowled over his shoulder at Flora for a moment only, then resumed his deadly stance.

It was just the moment that was needed. Flora cried out as Crann whirled past her and sprang at the grenadier's shoulder. The musket discharged into the bracken, so close to Gair's head that the impact sprayed his face with earth.

As the grenadier desperately hopped back and forth, trying to dislodge the dog's fangs from his scarlet coat, Flora searched for the dirk. She spied a glint of silver in the heather just as the Englishman succeeded in throwing Crann to the ground. She dived for the dirk, but when she tried to lift it, it would not budge: the grenadier had planted his heavy boot squarely on the blade.

Another shot thundered about her. The soldier screamed and collapsed. Flora clambered to her feet and saw at once that a musket ball had shattered the man's leg. Shards of bone protruded from his torn hose.

Flora turned away in horror.

Crann, once again on all fours, ran up to the man and began savaging him. As Flora took a step toward the dog, thinking to pull him off the terrified soldier, she felt a hand at the base of her neck. She spun around to behold Gair gazing down at her, a smoking flintlock in his hand. Flora sighed in relief. Gair clapped his hands, and Crann released his prize.

"A thousand thanks to you for stacking the peat," Gair said, his green eyes aglow with some meaning that only he could fathom. Flora knew it was likely as close as the man could come to expressing his gratitude, though she thought it was the dog that deserved it, not her. She felt ashamed to think that, because of her fear, Gair had almost lost his life. As she walked away, she tried not to listen to the cries of the grenadier as Gair dispatched him with his claymore.

Flora saw at once that the battle was over, if indeed such wild confusion could lay claim to the title. The *Damainte* had triumphed. Every trooper lay dead. Ewan and Seumas busily searched the bodies, removing gold, silver, weapons, shoes, and anything else of value. She rushed forward, eager to tend the injured. As much as she hated the thought of killing, Flora consoled herself that at least all her newfound clan had survived the conflict with nothing worse than flesh wounds and, in Cu's case, a cracked tooth that pained him mightily.

"No less than you deserve, half-wit," Ewan berated him.

"Had Losgann not been so clever, we might all be breathing in sod now." The boy beamed. Perhaps he was more useful than she had first thought, Flora mused. A distant groan made her remember the cause of the combat.

"What about your shadow-man?" she asked. "Is it he?"

Ewan nodded grimly. "Aye, and he'll be living long enough to cause us further misery, I'm thinking." He walked toward a patch of bracken. From its depths, a rumpled plaid emitted an assortment of angry noises. Flora followed, expecting to see a stranger. One glance at the man told her otherwise. Still, she had to look again to prove to herself that the bloody, squirming hulk before her was the man who was either her gallant protector or almost the cause of her undoing.

Sorley Fior raised himself on his elbows, cursing mightily. Flora had become acquainted with many Gaelic epithets over the past few days but scarcely heard them now, so intent was she on watching Sorley, lest he disappear from her again. And he most certainly was her Sorley. Even the blood and dirt on his face could not hide his flowing, flint-black mane or the beautiful asymmetry of his eyes. She did not know whether to be overjoyed at finding him, terrified at finding him, or shocked at how badly he had been used.

It wasn't long before his oaths slid into English. "God's curse on ye, Ewan Fada! Half a man! Whoreson! Son of hell! The lad says you would have left me for dead were it not for he. I'll give your back a salmon's roasting once I—" He stopped, and Flora saw that she had caught his gaze. His eyes opened wide. He smiled. At once he looked like a small boy noticing a sweet set in front of him. "Miss Flora!" he cried. *Mo dhia!* How came you here?"

"My guide proved to be a thief," she said, studying his face for his reaction. He seemed completely thunderstruck.

His lips moved, forming unspoken words. "The *Damainte* rescued me. We'll speak of it later. You're injured and must take your rest." She knelt beside him and began cleaning his face with the hem of his plaid.

"Injured? Ha! He's shamming, I'll wager. Trying to win my sympathy, Sorley Fior? Faith, you'll have a long battle ahead of you."

Flora looked up into Ewan's blue eyes. He stood a handsbreadth away from her, one doll-sized arm draped over Crann's shaggy neck, the other cradling a small bag filled with flintlock pistols and leather purses. In the excitement of finding her knight, Flora had all but forgotten about the fierce little toadstool of a man who had commandeered her life of late. "Ye knew I sought him!" she said shrilly. "Why did ye not tell me?"

Ewan lifted his head, his lush brown beard bristling like a thornbush. "As I said, I know a hundred Sorleys. This is but one, and one of the least, I'd say, though he is our shadow-man, and we are beholden to him. As you can see, his eyes are neither blue nor green, but as gray as bad weather."

Flora felt her jaw sag open. Then she remembered that Ewan had failed to recognize Gair as a redhead. "Ye're blind tae colors," she said simply. Her father's chief groom had had the same affliction.

The dwarf's face deepened into a dark scowl. "I'm blind to nothing."

"For the love of God," Sorley said, his voice as clenched as a fist. "Will ye not see to me? I've been stuck like roast mutton, and you two rooks can do naught but jabber!"

"Forgive me," Flora murmured. She began to seek the site of the Gael's wounds, prodding all around his arms, legs, and chest, but could discover nothing more serious than bruises on his ribs. At last Sorley gave a huge sigh, rolled onto his stomach, and drew aside the lower half of the belted plaid that covered his muscular haunches: they were pocked with a dozen bloody jabs from the grenadiers' bayonets.

Flora hesitated. She had bandaged many a cut and scrape among the servants when she was younger, and tended to the good sisters through a host of illnesses. She had patched up her father whenever he had fallen during one of his more spectacular fits of drunkenness, and played nursemaid to a hundred cats, dogs, rabbits, and birds. But she had never before dressed such private wounds on any male, much less one she had kissed with unfettered passion less than a fortnight ago. To her complete embarrassment, she found herself almost as curious as she was scandalized.

"If you'll not aid me, then shoot me," Sorley muttered.

"I'll warrant the lass has never afore been this close to a man's bare hurdies," Ewan observed, his face thoughtful. "Your flesh has dumbfounded her, shadow-man, but not me." With amazing speed he pulled a leather whiskey flask from his sporran, uncorked it, and poured the entire contents over Sorley's punctured bottom.

Flora leaped back as the Gael let loose a roar that made Crann whine in fear. The man's cries brought Seumas running, with Rosmairi right behind him, a bundle of linen rags in her arms. Man and wife sat down by the howling man and set about at once to dress his wounds.

"What have ye done tae him?" Flora cried. She pointed at Ewan in indignation. "See the pain he's in because of you. Would ye slay a man who means only to help ye?"

"I'm saving his life," Ewan said, his voice soft and even. "I trow it's unpleasant, but so is death."

Despite his agony, Sorley managed to spit out yet another flurry of invectives, half English, half Gaelic, all aimed at the dwarf. "Ye damnable half of nothing! *Uruisg! Bogiel!* Hobgoblin!"

Despite her anger, Flora realized that Ewan was right. She herself had used her father's brandy to cleanse the wounds of man and beast alike.

"It stings, God knows," Ewan said, "but otherwise the flesh will putrefy. A man may live without a hand or leg or foot, but he'll no' get on without his arse."

Flora gulped. Plain language still had the power to rattle her. "Fine, then. Only tell me how I may help you."

"I beg you, keep away," Sorley said through gritted teeth. "I'll not humiliate myself in front of you any more than I have already."

Flora was about to protest, but when Seumas shook his head, she turned her back on Sorley Fior. Tears came to her eyes, but they were tears of anger, not grief. She had meant but to help, and he had rebuffed her. What did it matter what part of him needed caring, as long as she was willing to tend him? She knew she should not take Sorley's words as an affront, but standing about useless while he was hurting maddened her.

At last Sorley was bandaged and prepared to travel. Flora helped Ewan and Cu fell two rowan saplings, then arranged the men's plaids on the stripped tree trunks to make a crude litter. Ewan cursed all the while as he helped Cu lift the wounded man and lay him on the plaids. "Little I imagined I'd have to go cold for your sake, creature," he scolded Sorley. Flora thought to ask him why he was so harsh to his own clansman, but held her tongue and vowed to ask Sorley about the matter himself, once he had recovered.

The *Damainte* and their groaning guest set off due south again, Losgann and Flora leading the way with Sorley's compass. It was lonely at the front of the group, since

Losgann knew but little English, and curiosity about Sorley's condition ate at her constantly. Was he feverish? Did he ask about her? Shouldn't she put him from her thoughts altogether?

Once, while Losgann ran ahead to scout a hillside, she paused to get her bearings in a drifting sea of mist. When she heard footsteps behind her, the memory of the grenadier leaped into her mind. She spun around only to encounter Ewan. Without his plaid, the stunted man looked even smaller and less imposing than he had when she had first seen him. Save for his beard, he might have been an ungainly tot, stumbling about the heath in its nightshirt. He peered up at her with a twisted smile. "Easy with your blade, mistress," he instructed her, "lest you do a friend a mischief. 'Draw in haste, laid to waste,' as they say, though I am glad to see that you didn't intend to batter me with it."

Flora glanced at her right hand. She had instinctively drawn her dirk. Her fingers quivered as she slipped the dagger back into the sheath at her belt. "Forgive me," she said. "Have you any word of Sorley Fior? Is he better? Worse?"

Ewan spat onto the stones at his feet. *"Arrah!* Mistress, you're much taken with the creature, or I'm as tall as he is."

"I'm in his debt for many a kindness." She thought of their first meeting, when Sorley had come between her and her father. "Please tell me, how does he fare?"

"The way he's healing, Seumas says he must be in thick with the Almighty. In league with Black Donald, the scourge of mankind, is more likely. You should hear him cursing and complaining, just like a drover at Crieff Market when he finds he's lost a dozen cows." He paused and reconsidered. "Well, perhaps it's best you don't hear."

Flora smiled in relief. "He's no' in any danger." Suddenly it was essential to her that this man live, though she wasn't quite sure why. Now that her father was dead and Mrs. Leckie far away, Sorley was perhaps the only soul who cared whether she lived or died. Except for Captain Stelton, she admitted, but that was different: She cared not what became of him. Overcome with a feeling she couldn't name, Flora sank into the heather and began to weep without restraint.

Ewan Fada hunkered down beside her. "Och, but you're exhausted, Miss Flora," he murmured. With considerable difficulty he pulled the neckcloth from his throat with his stubby fingers and placed it in her lap. "Dry your tears. I'll take the lead for now. If you're curious to see how that reiver Sorley is faring, you may go back and ask him yourself."

At the thought of speaking with the odd-eyed man, Flora stopped weeping and stood up. She relinquished her treasured compass to Ewan's care, since he had need of it. Although every mile brought them closer to the border, the country they traveled was still rough and barren. "Did Sorley tell you the location of the prince's army?" she asked. "We're on course, I trow."

"Aye. The prince is nearing Selkirk, if our shadow-man can be trusted to deliver the truth," the dwarf answered. "If we continue at this pace, morning will see us within sight of the clans. Charlie had wished to stay in Dunedin a while longer to recruit fresh troops, but volunteers were in short supply, I'm told. Lord George Murray, who has a good head on him and knows the army within and without, was for pulling back to the mountains until winter is past, but the bonny young man is set on conquest."

Flora paid little mind to Ewan's report, so eager was she to meet with the prince's messenger himself. She excused herself as soon as she might and made her way past Cu and Gair, who were almost unrecognizable in the mist. The appearance of a horse and rider caught her off guard for a moment, until she recognized Seumas Half-face on the back of the tall bay courser. One of the soldiers' horses, she told herself, no doubt destined to become a present for the prince.

Behind them shuffled Rosmairi and the Three Smalls. Flora noticed that Seumas's wife had taken over Gair's position as rear guard. She carried a pistol in her hand, and now and then looked behind her into the mist as she marched along, either in fear or longing. It was a wonder that the woman did not walk off by herself, Flora thought, and an even greater wonder that Seumas trusted her not to do so. Then she realized what was happening. The three children had a tight grip on Rosmairi's skirts, and in all likelihood were leading her forward. Damned or no, all members of the little troop had to play some role in its survival.

Immediately behind Rosmairi and the boys stumbled Creag and Dughal, laboring under the weight of Sorley's litter. The wounded man lay on one side, berating the two *Damainte* with a constant flow of oaths. He recognized Flora immediately, in spite of the billowing mist. "Hello, Miss Buchanan!" he bellowed. "Come up to me, now, and let me set eyes on you. Ach! Still doubling as a lad, are you? Your gown is back in Dunedin. I walked off with it when we parted company in the stable. Please forgive me."

I may have much to forgive you for, Flora thought. She fell into step beside Creag as the misshapen man trudged through the heather. "Nay fear," she said. "I could scarce run were I clad in more feminine garments, and I have run more in the past day than I have in the rest of my life." She was pleased to find the Gael greatly improved in health and aspect. His transformation made her wonder how much whiskey had gone down his throat as well as over his hind end. Since she knew not whether to trust the man or run from him, she decided to be wary. "You are in good spirits, sir, considering how badly you have fared."

"Aye. Much good spirit has gone into my spirits, and they are much elevated at the sight of you. I assure you, though, if I see MacPhee again, that piece of walking manure won't be walking far."

Flora studied his face intently. Though hardened by pain, his fairy eyes burned with such intensity that Flora was for one instant convinced of his innocence. Then doubt fell back onto her like a heavy blow. She had trusted men before.

Despite Flora's jumbled feelings, Sorley's compliment had not escaped her. She could not comprehend why she had missed him above all others, when he might have been no better than Macinally. Days ago she had fretted over the jaded monotony of her existence. Now, beset on all sides by betrayal, destitution, and death, she felt she could not take one step and feel certain of its outcome. "MacPhee may be innocent," she said. "I know not whom to blame." On an impulse she reached up and took his hand. He squeezed it, then let it go. An instant later, he slumped back in the litter, dead asleep.

Such long, strong fingers he had, she thought, yet so gentle they didn't leave a mark on her skin. That moment of warm contact had been enough encouragement for her. Even if Sorley had duped her, he was surely in no condition to harm her now.

After another hour of rugged marching, Ewan at last bade his weary followers make camp for the night in a clearing surrounded by pine and alder. Flora found Sorley

wide-awake, lying on his belly not far from a small fire. A
plaid lay underneath him, and his back and legs were
covered with another plaid. In between he was as bare as
an egg, save for the linen bandages that swathed his
wounds. "You must excuse my attire, Miss Flora," Sorley
apologized as she knelt beside him. "That is to say, the
lack of it."

"It's no matter," Flora murmured. "I assure you, worse
has befallen me." She tried to fix her gaze on his face,
but now and then found herself glancing at his waist and
beyond. What a wanton I am, she thought, hastily turning
away. She wondered if she were to blame in some way for
her own misfortunes.

"Aye, likely so. Such as what befell you after I left Mac-
Phee's livery. Won't you tell me what took place?"

With as little adornment as possible she unfolded her
adventure to him, thinking all the while that it was just
possible this charming creature had planned the entire
abduction, or at least had been aware of its existence. But
as she spoke, a look of genuine horror darkened his face,
though Flora could not say for certain whether he was
reacting to her travails or expressing the pain of his own.
When she had finished, he gave her a quick nod and again
gripped her hand. "I give you my word," he said with
great solemnity, "that I will see you to Perth once I'm free
to do so. If, indeed, you still wish to go there."

Suddenly the doubt she had been nursing for the past
day burst to the fore and overpowered her better judgment.
"What? Would you betray me again?"

He dropped her hand as if it were a nettle. His mouth
fell open, exposing his tongue and lower teeth. His eyes,
both golden in the light of the fire, glistened with shock.
"Betray you? Have you taken leave of your senses?"

Flora stared back at him. She didn't know what to think,

what to feel. Either Sorley had the skills of a stage player, or he was telling her the truth. How desperately she wanted to believe in him. "You might have hatched some scheme with MacPhee yourself, or with Wull Taggart or with the two of them." Her mind raced and her voice sped after it, spilling out thoughts she did not even know she harbored. "After all, by your own admission, you've dealt with your left hand when it comes to the law. Mayhap you stood to earn a few pounds of the profits once I had been sold to the stews, or else MacPhee or Wull paid you to deliver me to them. Do you deny it?"

The man reared back his head with a look of proud disdain. For a few moments he said nothing. Indeed, her accusation seemed to have struck him dumb. When he finally found his voice, it was not his voice at all, but a savage whisper that raked its claws across her chest and pierced her heart with its honesty. *"Mo dhia!* It's beneath me to deny such a charge. Procuring! Me, a full cousin to the great Lochiel himself! Here I thought you were a clever lass, but anyone who hasn't the wits to see what sort of man I am isn't fit company for me, so go on with you."

Flora hesitated. She hadn't meant to insult Sorley, only winnow the truth from him. She was now fairly convinced she had done so, and the scales tipped in favor of Upright Sorley. "I'm sure you can understand why I must be careful in my choice of companions," she said carefully. "A woman alone is a vulnerable creature."

But the Highlander was not to be pacified. He lifted one arm and thrust it out before him, as if he meant to shove her away. "Did you not hear me, wench? Away with you! Do you think I'd risk the censure of my prince and my chief for a few pounds sterling? Faith, if I wished silver, wouldn't I have taken yours when I had the chance? Christ and all the saints! I'd rather have Ewan Fada, for all his growls and scowls, than a woman who cannot recognize a man's sincerity. Now begone!''

He spat out his last words with such ferocity that Flora leaped back, anticipating a blow. None came. Hot tears of anger rose in her eyes, anger directed at herself. For certain he was right; how could she have doubted him? Without even trying to reply, she scrambled to her feet and hurried back toward the *Damainte*. When Ewan came up to her, she turned away from him lest he see her tearstained face. She felt a pressure in her hand. When she looked up, Ewan was gone, but Sorley's compass lay in her palm, parts of it glistening through a layer of grime.

The little instrument only reminded her of what she had surely lost and made her feel more alone than ever before. What might she do now? She had stupidly tossed aside her one slender chance for escape as carelessly as she might toss a stone at a rat. True, she had no real desire to return to the sisters. On the other hand, returning to Edinburgh would be an act of madness. Should she stick with Ewan's ruined souls and pray for the success of a gallant young man who might win or lose all? She was a king in an absurd chess game, caught in a checkmate, unable to advance, retreat, or stay in one place.

Rosmairi called to her. Scarcely aware of what she did, Flora curled up in a plaid on the hard ground with Seumas's wife on one side and the Three Smalls on the other. She tried to distract herself with memories of happier days, but thoughts of feather beds and linen sheets only reminded her of what she had lost. Though she managed to prevent a torrent of tears, several slipped through her defenses and slid down her cheeks.

A gentle voice interrupted her misery. ''Do I know you, mistress?''

Flora shook her head at the darkness. "Ah, dear Rosmairi! It's Flora Buchanan. Do you not recollect me?"

Her answer was met with a sound halfway between a snort and a sigh. "I recollect little, Miss Flora. Names perch in my head for moments and fly away as they please. But tell me, why do you weep?"

Flora considered the question. Why indeed? Because she had offended Sorley? It was more than that. She placed her hand on her chest and shuddered. "Consider yourself fortunate, Rosmairi. You've no past to grieve over nor future to fret about." No cause to weep for being an orphan, for having virtue torn away like a child's plaything, for railing helplessly against events far too powerful to control.

"Aye," Rosmairi whispered. For a long moment, Flora heard nothing save the harsh breathing of the children, the sigh of the wind on the moor, and the occasional snap of embers in the dying fire. Then Rosmairi spoke again. "Do I know you, mistress? Why do you weep?"

As Flora spoke her name yet again, she concluded that knowing just who this woman named Flora Buchanan was and why she wept might be no easy task.

When Flora woke the next morning, she found herself completely paralyzed. It was as if she were a butterfly inside a chrysalis, unable to break free. She squirmed about in panic, but could not move more than an inch. "Rosmairi! Lads! Help me!" she called out. When no one came, she twisted about just enough to see that the woman and children were gone.

"Lord save us, woman, what's become of you?" cried a familiar voice.

"Ewan!" Flora shouted. "What's wrong wi' me? I canna move!"

Ewan's face edged into sight above her, one eyebrow arched high. The dwarf always gave her the impression he could set any misfortune to rights; here was something to try his skills. "Small wonder, since your plaid is frozen fast around you. Wait, now. I'll soon have you free."

Ewan disappeared but returned moments later, holding a stout stick. To her horror, he began flailing at her shoulders and legs with the staff, sending a cloud of ice crystals flying all about himself. "In God's name, stop! Ye'll slay me!" Flora cried, but her protests merely made Ewan attack the frozen plaid with even greater vigor. By the time Flora discovered that she had not been harmed after all, she had stood up. The plaid lay at her feet on the heather in a tangled heap glittering with frost.

"A cold night," observed Ewan, as he tossed the stick aside. "Tonight, lie as close to the fire as you dare. And mind you, no more of that screeching, Miss Flora. Were any Royalists nearby, they'd be on us like down on a duck, so have a care." And with that the little man stalked off, whistling under his breath. Flora stared after him, half grateful, half outraged. She imagined that, had he been immobilized under a frozen blanket, he would be something less than silent himself.

The smell of fresh oatcakes caught her by the nose and led her to the cooking fire, where Seumas and Rosmairi were preparing breakfast. Cu, Gair, Dughal, and the Three Smalls sat about the fire, intent on gobbling down as many oatcakes as they could cram in their mouth. As Flora sat down to eat, she wondered if anyone had bothered to feed Sorley, as he surely couldn't be expected to fetch his own food. Perhaps a few oatcakes would help her win back his good favor and make him forget her rash outburst.

Flora wrapped two cakes in Ewan's neckcloth, which she still carried with her. She was on her way to check on Sorley when she beheld the impossible: the man himself approaching her, dressed in a belted plaid that covered him from knee to shoulder. He gait was stiff and slow, but he held his head high and his back straight. He wore no bonnet, and his blue-black hair whipped in the breeze like a banner. Even in his pain and humiliation, he still surpassed any man Flora had ever seen in form, feature, and sheer masculinity of presence.

But Sorley's courage and virility were lost on Ewan Fada. "Ha! Here comes Geordie's pincushion!" shouted the dwarf, drawing snickers from Cu, Losgann, and the three little boys. "Must ye walk because ye canna sit, shadow-man? Or d'ye wish to bare your bum again to the young Lowland lady?"

Flora felt her entire body grow fiery hot. She could scarcely believe that Ewan would speak in such a crude manner, especially when he had been so kind to her in the past. She knew some sore point festered between these two men, though she couldn't guess what it might be. She looked down at the ground in embarrassment.

But Sorley was a match for Ewan. "If I did, I doubt I'd shame her more than you have already. I know you took a stick to her. I saw it all." This drew a spate of questions in Gaelic from the *Damainte* which Ewan was obliged to answer.

Flora looked up at Sorley and gave him a small, grateful smile. She thought it best to try to avoid any mention of the night's grim discussion. "I have some breakfast here for you, sir," she said, extending the oatcakes. "But I see you are well enough to get your own. You heal with amazing speed."

"Aye, it serves me well," he answered. To her surprise,

he strode over to her, took her by the elbow, and steered her away from the chattering *Damainte*. "But not well enough to let me sit down, as Ewan so rightly observed. Will you not walk with me as I eat?"

Flora was only too relieved to have the chance to stretch her legs after a stiff night in the frozen plaid, and set off at a slow pace to accommodate Sorley. The morning mist was rising, revealing a path that led to a ridge that Sorley identified as Fionn's Spine. They climbed the slope side by side. The chill air prickled with the scent of burning pine. "Ach, but it's cold!" said Sorley. He looked up at the heavens, shrouded in gray and black, and took a deep breath. "There may be rain in it soon."

"How can you know that?" she asked, amused by his self-assurance.

"It smells like rain," he replied, "like peaty water and salt from the sea and the black earth itself. And then there's the wind. It's rising."

Flora sighed. To her, the air smelled like smoke, nothing more. She could not even feel the wind that Sorley spoke of. She had much to learn about the land, she thought.

Sorley threaded his arm through hers and held her close. She luxuriated in the warmth of the man and his plaid and for some time said nothing at all. Faint laughter from the camp of the *Damainte* set her to thinking. "You and Ewan are brothers-at-arms, but you're not friends," she said at last.

"Sure enough," he answered, biting into an oatcake. "But truth to tell, I admire the wee scraper. He's as fierce as a pine marten though hardly any bigger. As you've seen, he hasn't one good word for me."

"And has he a reason for his rancor then, or does he merely envy you your height?"

The Highlander burst into laughter. "Well, perhaps that

is the reason, **after a fashion**," he replied, his mismatched eyes aglitter. "**We courted** the same woman once, and she chose me. It **was clear** from the start his courtship was doomed, but he could not be dissuaded. And when I won Aimil, it turned him against me."

Flora started and would have drawn away, but Sorley had a strong grip on her. "Then . . . then you're wed?"

"I was wed," he corrected her. "Aimil died two years syne. A terrible sickness took her from me, and you can be sure her death did nothing to endear Ewan to me."

Flora nodded, sorry for his loss but happy to discover that she had not kissed someone's husband. She sought to find out more about his lost love, but his answers were brief, and she soon understood he wished to talk no more on the matter. She began to lead their conversation down another road. "You talk most congenially with me now, sir, though last night you'd have none of my company. I'm sore confused."

"Aye, you've every right to be," the Gael admitted. "I've been awake the entire night thinking on it, and I've come to the conclusion that I'm more brute than man. You were right when you said you must take care whom you trust. Faith, looking back at what happened to you, I can see how you might believe I had betrayed you."

They walked on through the brown heather, over a bare shoulder of granite and up to a massive bank of mist, where they were forced to halt. Sorley rested his head upon hers, not so much a bold gesture of possession as an innocent one of affection. Flora remembered her mother touching her in exactly the same manner. She leaned her head against his shoulder, trying to recapture the distant sweetness of that memory. "But indeed you didn't betray me."

"Indeed I did."

Flora immediately relinquished Sorley's arm. The man had been deceiving her all this time! "What! Ye were in league wi' that devil, Wull Taggart?" With growing fear she realized that Sorley stood between her and Ewan's camp. "I'll call for help should ye come one step nearer!" she cried, laying her hand on the sheath of her dirk. Sorley shook his head and chuckled, infuriating her even further. How dare the creature mock her helplessness!

"Hold your whisht, woman," Sorley said. "Troth, you're the sort 'twould run off a cliff before knowing it's there, aren't you? In truth, I had no idea this man Taggart would abduct you. What I did was arrange for MacPhee to return you to your father's house. Taggart was meant to take you there and escort you inside."

"My father's house!" Flora gasped. Her legs wobbled. She sank down in the heather. "You lied to me! To what purpose? So that the magistrate might accuse me of murder?"

Again Sorley laughed. Flora glared at him, but she could not diminish his mirth. "Murder? Nay, not for all the world." Sorley slowly lowered himself onto his knees, taking care not to sit on his heels. "I found the house myself and was well received by a kind woman and an English gentleman. The man said he was your intended, and he gave me his word that, if you returned to him, no harm would come to you. The woman was most anxious for your safe return. Christ and Mairi! Given the alternatives, I thought I was doing right by you."

"An English gentleman? Captain Stelton?" The Highlander nodded. Flora had nearly succeeded in forgetting him, and now Sorley of all people had brought him to light again. "My intended, he called himself?"

"He did. Is he mistaken?" Sorley leaned forward so closely that she could see green flecks in his blue eye and blue pinpoints in his green eye, fascinating blemishes she had never noticed before. His breath warmed her face, and she fancied she could feel the charcoal coarseness of his cheek against her own.

"Aye, very much mistaken," Flora said grimly. "I warrant he appears to be genteel enough, but every doxy from Edinburgh to London has lain in his arms. I'd as lief never wed than marry that ill-bred Sassenach. I'd far happier wed you."

She hadn't meant to say such a thing. The words had left her lips of their own accord. It was staring at his eyes, his magic eyes, that had coaxed such bold words from her. There was no reason on earth or in heaven she should say such a thing to a man who admitted that he'd lied to her. Then why had she said it? All her life, save for her earliest years, men were creatures to be obeyed, feared, and cared for. Sorley asked none of that from her. He had none of Stelton's stiff elegance or Ewan's swagger. He was himself and himself only, from the ropy sinews of his hands to the shocking nakedness of his iron legs. It was admirable, this unaffected sense of self.

She felt the warm pressure of his hand as he played with her rebellious hair. "Are you proposing a conjugal union, Miss Flora? *Arrah!* Were it not for His Majesty and the campaign, I might consider accepting. Call me forward if you will, but I've missed you sore these past days and was worried sick about you. Even worse was the fear that I'd never see you again."

Understanding flooded Flora's mind like sunlight. "Was that why you gave me the compass, then . . . as a token to remember you by?" she said. He surely didn't intend her to navigate with it. How could he think she would ever forget him?

"Aye, indeed," the Gael answered. "I couldn't bear the thought that you might never think of me again. For certain I'll never forget you."

Flora gasped. He had put into words exactly what she had been thinking. Then she knew that he had never meant her any harm. If he had, she would not be feeling as she did just then, the shameful, immoral, and all-consuming desire to surrender herself to the captivity of his arms. "The air's quite chill," she whispered.

"I'll keep you warm," he said. Pulling the ends of his plaid from his belt, he wrapped two yards of thick tartan around her and himself. Flora felt as if she had become some strange being, two separate entities within one skin. Enmeshed in the plaid, she found it hard to tell where she left off and the muscular Gael began. When his lips found hers, she opened her mouth at once to accept the gentle caress of his tongue.

Macinally! A flicker of fear ran through her, then dissipated. Sorley was as different from that devil as wine from water. But even so, what would the sisters say? Those good women had never been in love, she answered herself. Was this love, then? Ripples of flame tore up and down her body. A voice in her head was shouting at her to stop, but something even stronger, not in her head but deep in her very bones, persuaded her to continue. She gripped Sorley's plaid until her hands ached.

Sorley spoke to her in a hushed voice, a soothing mixture of Gaelic, English, and what sounded to her like the nickering of a horse. She felt a pressure against her blouse and realized too late what was happening. The horn buttons came undone, the frayed cambric parted, and a hand stroked her naked breast.

"No!" Flora broke away from Sorley's embrace and gathered her blouse to her chest. She mustn't let him see the terrible mark of her shame. "Please . . . no more!"

Sorley stared at her in remorse. "As you like," he said. "Forgive me. I meant you no harm. Come. We'll return now." As he stretched out his hand to take hers, Flora was besieged by a sudden image from that night so long ago. An outstretched hand, a gleaming blade . . . Again she felt the sting of the knife as it sliced into her bosom. Panic sent her flying from the vision, into the mist.

From what are you running? she asked herself, but she could not stop. She plunged through white wisps of vapor toward a darker patch within the mist: a clearing! She was about to fling herself into the veiled opening when something caught her arm and forced her to a standstill. A shape emerged from the mist. It was Sorley, his face glistening with sweat. "Do you see?" he said, pointing straight ahead.

Flora turned and peered into the mist. It was parting rapidly, and through the trailing gossamer banners she saw sunlight, then the brown of distant mountains, then a watery blue swatch of sky. Glancing down at her feet, she felt her heart sink to her belly. Not five inches from where she stood, the world ended. She was standing at the brink of a precipice some hundred feet above a glen mottled with many shades of green, brown, red, and amber.

"What a great fool I am!" she cried. Sorley circled her waist with his arm, and she clasped it with both hands. "You were right. I am the sort to run off a cliff. But how could you know it was here?"

The Gael chuckled. "You forget, mistress, that I've been this way before. When I could move faster." He smiled and ran his free hand over his hip.

"Thanks be to God that—"

"Wait." Sorley laid one finger on her lips. "Take another look ahead of you. A hard look."

His voice had a reverential tone she had never heard before, something akin to the sound of the good sisters when they intoned their matins and *angeli*. Flora gazed out over the glen, into the dwindling mist. Then she blinked and looked again. The colors she had first associated with plants and rocks were moving. They were not attached to objects bound to the earth, but men. Hundreds, thousands of men, most dressed like Sorley in subtle-hued tartans that echoed the colors of their country. She heard the distant neigh of a horse and the warlike clatter of weaponry. "His Majesty Prince Charles's army," she said softly, unwilling to disturb the grand scene with the sound of her voice.

"Even so," said Sorley, "in all its splendor." He pointed out half a dozen rippling banners attached to pikestaffs, dotting the field like so many martial flowers. "The flags of the clans," he explained, his voice deep with pride. "Clan Stuart, Clan Donald, Clan MacBain—the Clan of Cats." He nodded to indicate the various groups as he spoke.

As Flora watched the milling clans below, it occurred to her that not many miles separated the Highland army from the northern reaches of their enemy. "The prince doesn't intend to cross into England, does he?" she asked. The Jacobites were many, but not nearly so many that they could ever hope to stand up to King George's massed troops. It was a deadly dangerous venture for the clans to try to reinstate the Stuart line where it was definitely not wanted.

"I believe he does, mistress," Sorley answered. "To kill the badger, you must go where he lives, and so must my prince. Our numbers aren't great now, but he says they will swell once we set foot over the border. He says the Stuarts have more supporters in England than one might think.''

''And you?'' she asked, twisting about until her eyes met his. ''Is this what you believe as well?''

Sorley shook his head. ''It's no' my place to think one thing or the other,'' he said. ''I must only serve my prince and my chief, the Lochiel.'' She sensed that he felt uneasy, for he quickly tried to distract her. ''Can you see the red flag with the yellow arrows, Flora? 'Tis my clan, Clan Cameron. Are we no' a fine sight? Ah, but the Sassenach will be wetting their breeks when they see us! They'll run from us like rabbits, as they did at Prestonpans.''

Again Flora felt Sorley's cheek nestle against her head in the gesture she loved so well. The man's arms tightened around her as he reveled in some moment of past triumph. Though her ribs ached, she felt supremely secure in his powerful embrace. In the face of such tenderness, the memory of Macinally retreated to the deeper caverns of her memory. ''Prestonpans?''

''Our noblest victory!'' Sorley seemed to become aware of her predicament, for his arms relaxed and his grip slackened. His voice, however, still brimmed with passion and held her entranced. ''You should have seen us! We took the red soldiers by surprise at daybreak at the edge of a marsh, rising up around them like wraiths. They bolted from us, wild with terror, and even their general lost all control over them.''

Flora listened, impressed but afraid. Her father had been to war and claimed it was the reason he sought to drown his memories in drink. She knew from him that war held a great deal more suffering than glory. ''But many men died, did they no'? The prince's men? Your clansmen?''

''Aye.'' Sorley sighed, clearly uncomfortable with the

notion of discussing the darker moments of his people's proudest hour. "In war, Flora, men die. There's naught to stop it. You've seen it yourself. But the fine thing of it is that we defeated the Sassenach, routed them, in fact. What we did before we can do again." He paused, and Flora could see by the lines that furrowed his lean cheeks that she had stirred some deeper sorrow within him. "Thirty, forty, perhaps. I myself lost my youngest brother, a lad but sixteen."

Flora reached up to pat his rough cheek in what she meant to be a gesture of consolation. Instead, the moment her hand made contact with his hard jaw she was shocked by the intimacy of the touch. He pressed his lips against the back of her hand in a kiss more intimate and full of emotion than the passionate embrace they had shared only moments earlier. "Oh, Sorley! I'm sae sorry to hear it. Your wife and your brother both! You must—"

A shout drowned out Flora's attempt at condolence.

"What are you doing to her, devil?"

Flora tensed at the sharp words and their cruel accusation. Quickly she withdrew her hand. "Who'd dare be so bold?" she whispered.

"The midge himself, unless I miss my guess," Sorley replied. He released Flora and spun around so abruptly his plaid brushed her face. Startled, she tottered sideways. The abyss loomed dark and empty underneath her for an eternity before she recovered her footing and caught her breath. So near to oblivion, she thought, and within sight of the prince himself!

"Harm her and die!" came the voice again.

Flora stumbled to Sorley's side and gripped his belt for support. Squinting into the remains of the mist, she could see a figure make its way toward them. A very small figure indeed. "Ewan Fada!" she cried out. So Sorley had been right after all, if not kind. "Come! Come look!"

Ewan trotted up, his plaid back to rights around his middle once again. "If this rake has compromised you, mistress, I'll make him wish he were back with the grenadiers." He dismissed Sorley with a waggle of his hand.

For the life of her, Flora could not fathom why Ewan was forever thinking the worst of his clansman. "Indeed not. What would ever give you such a notion?" she said. "Look yonder! Prince Charles's army, dead ahead of us." Flora pointed toward the glen in an effort to draw Ewan's mind toward a more pleasing subject. The groan of the pipes and the shouts of many men floated up to her from below, lending credence to her words.

"Dead, aye, all the better for some of us," Ewan said with a snarl. He glowered at Sorley, then strode up to the edge of the cliff, took one long look, and faced his rival again. "Come down with me, shadow-man. We can deliver the horse and report to the prince's aides-de-camp about the six dead redcoats half a league back. Such news will set them hopping about like magpies, I trow."

"I canna wait tae see them!" Flora could hardly believe it was she who spoke. There was no denying it: she was becoming as caught up in the prince's quest as Sorley and Ewan. The last few years of her life had been filled with nothing but obedience and dreary repetition, and against this great gray expanse of dull granite, the Jacobite cause glowed like an amethyst. It was like one of the fanciful stories her mother used to spin for her as a child: the banished prince, surrounded by his few but loyal retainers, triumphs over evil and corruption to reclaim his legitimate inheritance as ruler of the kingdom. She wanted so desperately for such a lovely ideal to become reality that she began to believe it might be possible. "Perhaps I'll glimpse His Majesty as well."

Ewan squared his broad shoulders, the very picture of a bulldog. "Indeed you won't! I trust the *Damainte* to honor all women, but I put no store in any other of my sex, including this two-legged stallion here." He scowled sideways at Sorley before returning his gaze to Flora. "Do you expect me to lead you into the midst of six thousand men who might just as soon ravish you as look at you?"

Flora crossed her arms firmly over her chest. If only Ewan could see her as an equal instead of some frail female in need of constant protection. Of course, she had been just that at one time, she reprimanded herself, but no longer. "His Majesty would brook no such behavior from his men," she said, "and in breeks and waistkit, I may yet pass for a lad."

Sorley, who had been standing to one side, draped his great arm around her narrow shoulders. She felt glad that she did not have to face such a powerful sword arm in battle. "Though it pains me to say it, Ewan Fada is right," he said. Flora looked up at him, aghast. She'd felt certain he would have supported her, but she had read him wrong. "You'll remember that you did not fool Wull Taggart," he reminded her. "And while it's true that most of the prince's men would no sooner harm you than they'd harm their own daughters, what of the others? With so many men present, some are bound to be unprincipled."

Flora protested, but she could not dissuade the two Highlanders. When she refused to follow them back to camp, they merely exchanged a few words in Gaelic, turned on their heels as one man, and marched off into the drifting mist. They were a ridiculous pair, one tall and straight, one gnarled and squat, but both enveloped by such an air of determination that, for an instant, they could have been

Megan Gray

brothers. Flora hesitated only a moment before setting out in their wake. As much as she bristled at the idea, she was at the mercy of these two admirable and infuriating men. While she could afford to be patient, she could not afford to be abandoned.

Chapter Six

By the time Flora returned to Ewan's camp, the mist had conjured itself into a light rain, which in short order swelled into a thunderstorm that hammered the clearing without mercy. The *Damainte* threw together their miserable shelter of hides, rowan boughs, and plaids on the edge of the forest. Flora crawled into it without a second thought about the strong funk of bodies or the muddy ground beneath her. It wasn't until Cu made a pathetic fire from a handful of twigs that she took a good look around her and saw that two bodies were missing. "Where are Ewan and Sorley?" she asked. She wanted to have the pleasure of watching them wait out the storm.

Cu made a rusty, whining noise, and Crann, crouched at his feet, replied in kind. Their cries were just audible over the rattle of rain against the deerhides. "Setting off to find His Majesty, I'm thinking," Cu said.

"Setting off! In this!" Flora waved wildly at the damp

plaid inches from her head. She had the compass. How would those two fighting dogs get their bearings in the storm, or even agree on a path?

"They'll manage." Creag's words rasped from his wrinkled throat like flint on granite. "A wheen of raindrops won't stop Long Ewan and Upright Sorley when they've set their minds on a matter. Don't worry on their account, mistress."

And she did not worry, at least for the next few minutes. But as the pounding overhead grew fiercer and the wind picked up and the little shelter began to shake like a drenched dog, worry crept into her mind. Experienced mountaineers like Sorley and Ewan weren't likely to topple over a cliff as she almost did, but they might become lost, or indeed they might fall on the slick stones or boggy ground. Had they the compass, they could be sure of taking the most direct route to the Jacobite camp. They could not have gone far in such a downpour, she reasoned, especially dragging a frightened horse behind them. She could easily catch them up by following the track of the animal's steel shoes in the wet earth. And then . . . and then she might also persuade the two Gaels to let her join their mission.

"I must go out," Flora announced. Using Dughal's broad shoulder to pull herself to her feet, she stood bent over in the tiny tent. "Privy needs."

A bolt of lightning sizzled outside, followed by the crash of thunder. Flora trembled. She caressed the compass in her pocket to bolster her resolve. Cu, Seumas, Creag, and Gair gazed up at her, their faces full of doubt. "Haste back," Seumas warned her. "Keep low."

"Dinna leave, Miss Flora!" cried Rattie.

Flora smiled and patted the lad's wild black hair. "I'll soon be back," she assured him. Had his mother said the same to him once, she wondered, only to desert him?

Gair said nothing, but reached behind his back, drew forth a black shadow, and laid it in Flora's arms. It was a sealskin cape, ripped along one side and worn paper-thin in several places, but still good protection from "damp weather." Flora smiled and draped the skin over her head. As she ducked outside, she could hear Rosmairi ask her husband, "Who is the comely young woman in breeks?"

It was a driving rain, as cold as snow and as heavy as hail. Walking was much harder than Flora had anticipated, but she had the good fortune to find the track of the grenadier's horse almost at once. It had churned the dead grass into a muddy soup that even she could follow. But after stumbling through the storm for several minutes, she noticed that the trail became disturbingly faint, eroded by the constant assault of the rain. Better to return, she thought, but when she tried to discover the track she had followed, she found nothing but flooded earth, a giant, shallow puddle that defied navigation.

A fear as cold as the rain washed over Flora. She considered staying where she was until the storm abated, but could not bear the thought of standing still when just over the next rise she might find Sorley and Ewan. She plodded on, her heavy brogues encrusted with mud, following what was left of the horse's hoofprints. When at last she could no longer make out the tracks, she fished the compass from her pocket and followed it due south. She had almost forgotten why she was seeking the two men in the first place; now finding them had become the single most important goal. Why she must do so was irrelevant.

Footsteps.

Flora raised her head from the dial of the compass. She listened but heard nothing save the roar of the rain. After a moment the sound returned, then increased in cadence. Running footsteps, muffled by the downpour. She squinted into the lashing rain but saw nothing. Were the steps from behind her, from the front, from left or right? She couldn't tell. She pocketed the compass and gripped the scabbard of her dirk. Beneath the sealskin cape, her own skin rippled in dread. Some ancient impulse goaded her to run, but she stood steadfast. Whatever it was, she would meet it head-on.

The blow came from behind. Flora cried out, not in pain but surprise. She tumbled to the ground onto a tangle of briars that clawed at her hands and face. As the rain beat down into her eyes, the earth jolted around her, then became still once more. Something heavy lay atop her, nearly crushing the breath from her. Though she knew she should be terrified, she felt oddly at peace.

She recognized his scent.

"My dear friend." It took all the breath she had left to muster the one phrase.

The weight on her chest and legs shifted and eased somewhat as the man sat up. "A hundred thousand murders!" Sorley angled his face into hers, so close she could have licked the rivulets of water streaming from his chin. "Flora! My God! In this weather I took you for a red soldier. What in Saint Bridgit's name brings you here?"

"You," she said. "I was following you."

He nodded, as if this were a reasonable answer. "We're making a practice of stumbling about together, that's certain." He ran his hand over her wet hair in a gesture that was at once intimate and casual. *"Dia!* I did murder your tresses, didn't I! Can you never forgive me?"

"You're more than forgiven. Now I beg you, let's quit this . . . this deluge!"

Before she could take another breath, he had grasped
her by the shoulders, raised her upright, and began leading
her by the hand through the squall. Once, when she stumbled, he braced his arm behind her back and all but carried
her through the rain. She ran blindly, aware of nothing
save the constant lash of raindrops on her body and an
overwhelming relief to be once again by Sorley's side.

Flora thought they must be racing for the shelter of the
forest, but suddenly she became aware of another torrent
beside her: a tumbling river, incited by the storm into a
seething white mass of foam. Sorley slowed to a trot, then
stopped and faced her. In the darkness of the tempest, his
eyes flashed with an unearthly brilliance. "Down here.
Follow me," he muttered. "Mind the rocks."

"Down where?" she said, wondering whether the Gael
intended to drown her in the wild river. "I canna . . ." But
Sorley had already slipped over the rocks beside the river
and stood dappled in shadows. When he reached out to
her, she gripped his hand until her knuckles ached. She
felt she had no contact with the world itself save for that
sure grip, invisible in the darkness but undeniably real.
And if he let go of her? she asked herself. Would she still
exist?

Flora shuddered, gathering her scattered wits, and picked her way after Sorley down the glistening boulders. Spray
from the river danced into her face. The roar of the water
thrummed in her ears. With a rising sense of horror mixed
with curiosity, she realized Sorley was ushering her directly
into the roiling cascade.

My charge is to lead you to safety. Had he not told her so
a dozen times? Now she had only to believe him. Yet she
could hardly even see him. She took a gulp of misty air
and plunged into the nothingness that surrounded the

man. The thought came to her as bright and momentary
as a flame: only love could elicit such trust.

"Gle mhath!" shouted Sorley. "Well done, my calf!"

Flora felt his hands around her waist, his long fingers
nearly reaching right around her. She sank against his
chest, half expecting to fall into a pool of cold water, but
her feet struck against bare stone. When her eyes became
accustomed to the darkness, she saw that she and the
Gael were standing on a damp, rocky shelf beside the
thundering river. "A cave!" she shouted.

"Barely a niche in the rocks," Sorley replied. "Still, we'll
be dryer in here than out there." He nodded toward the
silver curtain of rain. "I told you I knew this country, did
I no'?" His hands still circled her waist, and as he spoke,
they inched down across the slim flare of her hips. It was
too intimate a touch, she knew, yet she said nothing. The
feel of his strong fingers against her flesh seemed right to
her, if not proper. Bereft of a loving touch for so long,
she was determined not to lose it again. He stared into
her face, his eyes reduced to their normal luster. His long
locks were plastered to his neck like wet leaves clinging to
a tree trunk. "You're well aware, I trow," he continued,
"that I can find my way through the rain without assistance."

Something about him had changed. He held himself as
stiff as a loaded musket. "Indeed I am," she said. "I've
no explanation for why I had to find you, other than I felt
in my heart that I must. When Creag said that you and
Ewan . . ." Mentioning the name aloud made her abruptly
conscious of the dwarf's absence. "But where is the bold
wee fellow?"

Sorley laughed, breaking the rigidity of his stance. With

a completely unaffected sweep of his arm he crushed her close to his chest and wrapped his soaking plaid about her shoulders. Voices from her former life protested; she ignored them. She was no longer that Flora, although who she had become was still a mystery. She drank in the wet-wool smell of his plaid and the musky fragrance of his skin. An uneasy warmth enveloped her.

"Don't fear for that halfpenny," said the Highlander. "D'ye expect him to pop up again to shout, 'Hold, knave! Release the lady!'? I warrant he's at the prince's camp by now, seeing as he rode while I walked." Sorley sighed. Flora felt his body tense as his haunches twitched beneath his plaid. "And just as well, since I can scarcely sit on the ground, much less sit a horse."

It troubled her to think that he was still in pain. "Come, turn around. I'll have a look at you."

"You will?"

She reconsidered, suddenly aware that she had asked to see him naked. "Aye, if you're willing to let me. You may think me bold, but how else may I judge how your wounds are healing?"

In the dim light of the cave, she could see his face broaden into a grin that exposed his uneven teeth. Sorley was not handsome in the way that most men were hand-some, with strong, symmetrical features. No, the Highland-er's nose was too long for his face, his cheekbones too prominent, his lips too full. But, like the base metals in an alchemist's vessel, all these imperfections mingled with the stunning imbalance of his eyes to produce a look that was far beyond mere comeliness.

"Faith, I guess you'll not see anything unfamiliar to you," he said. "But I'm as good as healed already."

The disturbing warmth she'd felt just moments before

began to dissipate as Flora felt herself slip into the comfortable role of nursemaid. "Not so hasty," she scolded him. "There's always the chance of putrescence and corruption, and you'd no' want those."

Sorley released her from his plaid, then unbuckled the long, damp garment and spread it over the stones at the back of the little cave. "If I must humble myself," he said, "I should at least make myself comfortable first."

One limb at a time he stretched himself out on the plaid, his face to the ground, and lifted his gathered shirt up to his chest. Flora knelt beside him. Her impudent curls kept falling into her eyes, though she continually brushed them away. Sorley had been right. His wounds were healing without the slightest intimation of infection. She probed his taut flesh with her fingertips, glad to see that there were no signs of permanent damage. That was not the case with his back, however, which was a ridged tartan of pink, white, and purple scars from beatings long ago.

"These scars . . ." she began, but could say no more. Her gorge rose, and she had to look away from the maggot's nest of stripes on Sorley's broad back.

"My da," he said, and it was clear from his iron tone of voice that rage still burned in him. "I was a feckless lad, and Da was fond of disciplining his weans."

"Disciplining them within a breath of their lives, I ween." Flora snorted in anger. Sorley was silent, and she decided not to press him for an answer. No doubt his memories were as painful as her own. "Do they ail you?"

"No longer," he replied. "Lay your hands on them."

Somehow she found the courage to look at the scars again. After a few moments she laid a finger on one red river of knotted tissue and followed it down over waist and haunches to its delta on his right thigh. Sorley's flesh was warm and fairly throbbed with life. Flora ran her hands over the sinews of his legs, fascinated by the hardness of his muscles and the satin sheen of his skin. She had spent many years in the company of women, modest women at that. The sight, touch, and scent of the man entranced her. She felt as if she had entered some holy shrine that she had hitherto been forbidden to visit. She touched his skin as she might stroke the gleaming wood of a cathedral door.

The Highlander groaned, a soft, earthy sound barely audible above the roar of the water. Had she hurt him? Flora hastily drew one corner of the plaid over Sorley's legs and tucked her hands between her knees. The man propped himself up on one elbow and tilted his head back to look at her. "That was no healer's touch," he said, without a trace of laughter in his voice. "So a wife touches her husband." He paused, his eyes wide-open in thought. "Or a mother a child. Or a child its mother."

Flora tore her gaze away from his bewitched eyes. How could she tell Sorley that he was right, that she felt like wife, mother, and child toward him? She did not even know it herself until he had laid it out before her in plain speech. "Life hasn't been a simple matter for me, Sorley Fior," she whispered, still not daring to look at him. "My mother died when I was very young, and from that day onward I've seen naught but struggle. Forgive me if I've offended you, but many a year has passed since anything akin to love has been in my life."

The cave filled up with silence broken only by the rush of water. "Is it something akin to love that you're feeling now?" Sorley said at last. "Would you know if you felt it?"

She shook her head. "I can't say. My relations with men have ne'er been o' the best."

"Your father and that Englishman. Stilt, you called him?"

Flora smiled to herself in the darkness. "Stelton." She stopped. If she went on, she might lose Sorley's respect forever, but if she did not continue, she'd not be able to respect herself. Sorley was her champion, an unbidden champion, right enough, but a decent man of good intentions. Such a man deserved the truth. "Not the best men, but not the worst."

"And who was the worst?"

She took a deep gulp of the stale, humid air. Sorley slipped his hand over her cold fingers, squeezing them back to life with the naked power of his affection. That alone gave her the courage to go on. "His name was Macinally," she began, but her voice failed her as she recalled that distant night. She bowed her head and clamped her eyes shut, trying to fight off the terror that enfolded her. Once again she was a child. Once again a shadow faltered at her bedroom door and a voice stumbling with whiskey called out to her.

Flora clenched her teeth and thought of Ewan and the *Damainte*. Those damaged folk faced real horrors every day. What sort of woman was she if she could not master for five minutes the pain of a nightmare long since dead? Every muscle in her body shivered. She could taste the salt sweat trickling down her face.

Suddenly a voice spoke up, as though it were her own but deeper and surer. "And this man Macinally, he seemed a good sort, a gentleman," said the voice, "but indeed, 'twas but a mask to hide a dark soul gripped by the devil himself. He was given to drink, and, though he brought fine gifts and spoke fine words, he was more fiend than friend.''

Flora looked up and stared into Sorley's uneven eyes, which gazed back at her with hawkish intensity. He still held her hand, gently caressing it with both of his, as courage flowed from his body into hers. She could barely contain her amazement long enough to form words. "How did you know this?" she whispered. Perhaps Sorley was as enchanted as his appearance suggested. "Almost none know save I. Surely the captain didn't tell you?"

The Highlander shook his head. "Nay, you told me, but not with words. When I touched you as we stood on Fionn's Spine and you darted away as if you'd been seared with a brand, I knew some man had treated you ill. I haven't been sleeping through these past thirty years, Flora. There's much I've seen, both noble and evil. I'm well aware of the cruelty a man can visit on a woman.''

He sighed, and Flora tried not to imagine the kinds of cruelty he had seen. She should have known she could hide nothing from him, she thought. God save him! Here he was, telling her own story to her and not thinking the worse of her for it. She ran her free hand over both of his, the callused hands of a man who had seen hardship and despair, who understood fear because he had lived it himself.

Flora drew another deep breath, then began to speak. The words rushed from her like the tumbling river, so fast that she could not believe they made sense. But they did. She listened to her own story as if for the first time— the assault, the pain, the shock of comprehending what Macinally had done to her. She spoke of her father's arrival, Macinally's disappearance, her utter denigration before the surgeon and, ultimately, her banishment from her own household. Her voice held fast, but she could feel her tears streak down her face and fall from her chin onto her hands and the Gael's. She didn't look down. Neither did Sorley.

After she had finished, she waited for him to respond, but he was as silent as a midnight kirkyard. His face was pale marble, blank and immobile. Just when Flora was certain he would rise up and leave her alone with her disgrace, Sorley flung back his head and began to keen like a father mourning his child. His cry broke through the stone walls she had built around her feelings, and suddenly all her terror and self-hatred came flowing forth. She threw herself into Sorley's arms and joined him in his wild lament for her ravished childhood.

The release of passion so long kept in check was a new sensation for Flora. She reveled in the power she felt, giving voice to her misery after so many years of silence. Some time went by before she realized that her voice was now the only one that defied the clamor of the river. She stopped at once. Sorley's face hovered just above her in the half-light of the cave. He gazed down at her with a look that bespoke both compassion and a raging desire held under massive restraint. "Flora, I am not Macinally," he said.

She felt his hand travel slowly up her side and settle on her left breast. This time she did not flinch. "No, indeed you're not. You're a friend, not a fiend."

He leaned closer and kissed her burning cheek, gently, almost reluctantly, she thought. "And you are not a lass any longer, but a woman, as fair as you are strong."

"Do you think so?" Until a moment ago, she had never thought of herself as strong.

"Aye," he answered, his voice suddenly subdued. "Strong enough to bind me in chains."

He pressed himself against her, but she pulled away.

"There's more," she murmured. She would discover just how strong these chains were. "You must know it all." Flora carefully undid her waistkit and blouse, revealing the innermost secret of her ruined past. "Can ye see it?" she murmured. "More of Macinally's work. Tell me, do ye think I'm comely now?"

Sorley gasped when he saw the wound, but recovered himself at once. "Every bit as comely as I said. Maybe more." The kindness that always burned in his eyes took on an edge of malice. "The only pity of it is that I'll likely never have the pleasure of killing the brute myself. Slowly, I'm thinking."

Flora gaped at him, almost as angry as she was grateful. "Can ye no' see that I'm deformed?" she cried, grasping the front of his damp shirt. Water seeped into her hands.

"Nay," he said. "I see a splendid woman, a queen among women."

Flora longed to believe him, but Macinally, Wull Taggart, and even her own father had assured her otherwise. "You yourself cried out at the sight of it," she persisted. "I'm as much an outcast as any of the *Damainte*."

Sorley's eyes flared wide-open. His lips drew back in a snarl. For the first time since she had known him, Flora truly feared him. He seized her by the waist and pulled her to his chest before she could cover her naked breasts. At first she recoiled from the rough touch of his linen shirt against her bare skin; then she shuddered as an over-powering and boldly physical delight engulfed her.

"I cried out at the thought of the wrong done to you," he said, bristling, "not the mark on your skin. The *Damainte* are what they are, but you're not of their kind. Faith, woman, the lash marks on my back are uglier by far than that kiss of the knife on your beautiful body. It means naught to me, and I shall prove it."

Without another word Sorley bent his head and pressed his lips against the ragged scar. His hungry mouth inched downward, seeking her teat like a suckling babe. Ribbons of flame flickered over her, destroying all thoughts of right and wrong, proper and profane. Her back arched as she thrust herself toward the Highlander, pressing herself against him so hard she fancied she might push herself through him. If only she might! They would be one, then. They would possess each other.

Sorley lifted his head. The fire that had been devouring Flora from within wavered, then flared anew. The Gael eased himself down onto his plaid and drew her into his arms. Heat emanated from him like steam. There wasn't so much as a breath between their two bodies. Flora felt the hard ridges of his hip and rib cage dig into her side, but the pressure only gave spur to her desire. "If you would halt me, halt me now," Sorley said, panting. His big hands cupped her face. She stared directly into his eyes, as luminescent as pearls in the perpetual twilight of the cave.

Beset by a passion she couldn't fathom, Flora desperately tried to think. Sorley was right. She was a child no longer. She was a woman, free of the ties of a father or husband, free to make decisions for the first time in her life. And this strange man she hardly knew—but who commanded her heart and soul as readily as Ewan Fada commanded the *Damainte*—had given her a choice.

In a lucid instant she made her decision.

"Will you take care with me?" she asked, stroking the hollow at the base of his throat. He removed his shirt, and the dim light danced blue on his bare skin. "Ye ken the reason."

Sorley nodded. "You suffered, I'm sure. But the bastard that ravished you was an animal, not a man."

"And you?"

He kissed her on the lips, lightly at first, then deeply, until she was sure he would drink her straight down like a dram of whiskey. After a time he stopped and sat down with great care. "I'm no more or less than a man in love with a magnificent woman. If you're not certain you'll have me, you may yet decline."

"I'm more certain of this than of anything else that's gone before," she said. Too often she had let the needs of others determine her lot, but not now. Now she would listen to her heart, and her heart was with the mysterious Gael. Did he love her? For the moment it didn't matter, and the moment, the poets had assured her, was all that mattered. Life was a rose in bloom, they said, waiting to be seized and enjoyed.

Sorley smiled. "If your mind is set, then some introductions are in order."

Flora glanced about the cave, expecting to see Jacobite warriors. "What can you mean? We're as alone as two people may be."

"Aye, alone, but you haven't met Himself."

"Himself?"

Sorley shifted his weight. He flicked his hand toward his belly.

She followed the movement and saw at once what he meant. It rose between his legs, and she was amazed at how proudly it held itself erect. "Is there so much room inside me?" she mused aloud, tense as a bowstring but not frightened. Sorley might surprise her, but she knew he would not willingly harm her. Hadn't he thrice saved her life?

"There is if you wish it so," said Sorley. "There's some that say it's because of Himself that I'm called Upright Sorley," said the Gael, "but he's not always thus. He stands up only in the presence of enchanting Lowland ladies with

eyes like whiskey and golden hair that's been hacked off
by a madman.''

Flora smiled at his jest and the way he insisted on
addressing his own body as a separate presence. ''Forgive
me if I appear simpleminded,'' she said, ''but for a fallen
woman, I've no knowledge of men at all.''

''The fall belongs to Macinally, not to you,'' observed
Sorley. ''Woe to them who've told you otherwise. As for
knowledge, you may easily attain it.''

''Many men would despise me.''

''Mayhap you've noticed that I'm no' among them.''
Sorley lowered himself back down on the plaid. ''Speak ill
of yourself no longer. Take Himself to hand if you like.
You may have feared men for many years, but you needn't
be loath to touch any inch of me.''

Flora hesitated. Mrs. Leckie had told her a little about
men and women, but she had not prepared Flora for such
an audacious act. Not knowing what to expect, yet
expecting something, Flora reached out and gently took
Sorley's member in one hand. Again her body burst aflame
as she realized how deeply Sorley trusted her. Stroking
upward, she was pleased to find that he lay in her hand
as if he had been carved to fit her fingers.

Sorley groaned. He writhed on the plaid like a man with
a fever.

In an instant Flora released him and flung herself down
beside him. His arms encased her as he surged against
her, pulsing with desire. An overpowering longing enveloped her, a feeling far stronger than any of her doubts.
She wanted the Highlander. She wanted, not to become
him, but to possess him, to include him in her own being.

''My treasure! My heart's joy!'' he whispered. ''For the
love of God, I beg you not to decline just now!''

But she knew she had already gone well past the threshold of return. Somehow she summoned the wits to speak: "Never, love!" She felt caution and prudence drop away from her like broken shackles as her heart soared upward into a tangled garden of the senses.

The salt taste of his skin burned her lips. She felt his heart slamming against her chest and fancied she could hear it as well. The fragrance of his passion rose into her nostrils; she drank it in like a prisoner inhaling fresh air. She sank her fingers in his shadow-colored hair, luxuriating in its glossy texture.

His lips sought hers. His tongue filled her mouth. At the same moment, Flora felt his hand fumbling at her waist, undoing the buttons of her breeches and tugging the fabric down around her hips. When he lunged against her once again, she ground herself into him with a hunger she had never felt before. Something nudged her belly, then her thighs. There was a breathless moment of entering, traveling, and arriving, and Sorley was inside her. The longing she had felt earlier gave way to exhilaration as she realized she was one with the man she loved.

Time and space melted from Flora's mind. The world reduced itself to man and woman, here and now. Each rhythmic thrust against her body brought a dozen new delights to her senses; each caress of his lips sent threads of lightning all over her body. But even in the midst of such wonderful chaos, it was Sorley's beautiful passion that fascinated her more than her own. He was no hunter bagging a quarry or soldier conquering a foe, but a man in love, overpowered with his own happiness. He filled her body, yes, but he also filled up other empty places within her, the gaping caverns in her soul and heart so long void of affection.

Like a child she watched entranced as light and shadow played across the Gael's face. She was caressing his silken neck and coarse chin, trying to lock the beloved textures forever in her mind, when another face burst into her thoughts and twisted itself into a cruel parody of Sorley's passion. No, she told herself, I will not have you defile me yet again. She clenched her eyes shut, but Macinally's face still sneered at her. You will not drive Sorley from me, she screamed silently at the apparition.

"O, mo lurag! Tha gul agam ort!"

The words washed over her, stunning her with reassurance. She knew them well. They were words of love her mother had sung to her a thousand times: *Oh, my jewel! How I love you!*

She opened her eyes to behold Sorley's face, not Macinally's. His skin shimmered with sweat. A look of elation so intense that it might have been pain rippled over his features, and she sensed she was witnessing the moment of his ecstasy. A strange pride overpowered her. She had brought him to that height. When Sorley gave a final thrust, she was unprepared for it. The world fell apart around her in a fountain of red embers. Exquisite pleasure shot through her veins like living lightning and burned her to ashes.

Moments or eons later, she knew not which, she sank back on the plaid, exhausted but again in one piece. What had happened to her? Mrs. Leckie had told her nothing of these matters. Perhaps she had thought that with a husband such as Captain Stelton, Flora would never have need of such knowledge.

Smiling, she reached out toward Sorley, who lay beside her completely spent, less a man than a sack of barley. Something glistened on his belly. She ran the tip of one finger playfully through the silver jelly, then licked it from her hand. It was unexpectedly sweet. If this was what ruin tasted like, she decided she could withstand it. "It's you who's magnificent, y'ken," she said.

Sorley lifted his head from the plaid. Flora could see at once that all wasn't well within her beautiful new paradise. The man who had exploded in joy only a moment earlier now looked as though he had dire news to tell her.

Flora swallowed hard. She had given much to Sorley Fior, including her body and her soul. Faith, she hadn't much more to give him. Perhaps he had second thoughts about bedding her. Tears seeped into her eyes, and she dashed them away with her wrist. "I hope it's not Flora Buchanan who's distressed you so, love."

"*Mo dhia,* woman! How can you say such a thing after what just passed between us? Nay, it's myself I'm angry with, for not asking you beforehand."

What could the man mean? "Asking permission to bed me? You needn't have asked. I gave it freely. Do you think for a moment that you forced me?"

"Devil take you, woman!" Sorley grumbled something in Gaelic. "That's not what I mean." Suddenly he gathered her into his arms and planted fiery kisses all over her face and neck, rekindling the coals of her passion. Once again they made love on Sorley's plaid, slower this time, with no forethought and even greater rapture.

Once Flora could think again, she remembered the high price she'd surely pay for the pleasure Sorley had brought her. "I fear you're right," she said, draping herself over the Gael's chest. "The devil will take me. My only consolation is that he'll take us both, and I'll no' be bereft of your company."

Sorley took her head between his hands and gazed straight into her eyes. "Nay, my darling Flora. You'll not live in disgrace any longer. I mean to make you my wife, if you'll have me. A soldier's wife, aye, so there'll be danger in it, but I reckon you're acquainted with danger."

"Are you proposing marriage, Sorley Fior?"

"I am." His voice was calm, his forehead cool. He seemed rational enough. "I love you, as I said, in your tongue and mine. If you have any feeling for me, as I think you have, and if we live through the coming year—which will be no small matter, I assure you—then I think we'll make a tolerable pair."

Flora sat up, suddenly very much aware of her nakedness. She arranged her bedraggled blouse around herself and pulled her trousers over her hips. It hadn't occurred to her that the man might ask to wed her. The thought of becoming his bride was exciting, even frightening. She loved Sorley, that she knew well enough, but she didn't know him, nor did he truly know her. Ewan, the most honorable person she'd ever met, did not trust this shadow-man.

"You hesitate," he said softly, his voice burdened with disappointment.

"Oh, Sorley! You must know how dear you are to me! But so much is happening so rapidly. . . ." Flora reached for his hand, but instead of clasping warm flesh, her fingers closed on cold metal.

It was Sorley's compass, the very one she had been trying to return to him. "You dropped it when I found you in the storm," Sorley explained. "I trust you'll use it now to find your way back to me, love. Ever since my Aimil died, I've had a hole inside me that no amount of drinking or eating or whoring could fill. I thought I'd never wed again. Then I saw you in the streets of Dunedin, and it was as if the Lord had written me a promissory note for a new life." He took her hand, which still held the compass, and kissed her fingers. Then he rapped the instrument's brass case.

"You needn't speak. Put it in my hand if you'll no' have me."

As Flora sat locked in indecision, she saw Sorley cock his head. He might have been a hound, hearing the snap of a twig a quarter-mile away. Then Flora heard it, too: the unmistakable scatter of rocks that heralded the presence of an intruder. An icicle of fear slid down her back. The hand that had been reaching into the darkness gripped her fingers. Joined again to Sorley, she waited.

Chapter Seven

Extravagant curses preceded the intruder as he slid on the rocks, then staggered into the cave. Flora saw a foot, a shaggy beard, a blue bonnet, and finally the entire man, crouched at the entrance. She blinked, and looked again into the gloom. The man was not crouching; he stood fully erect.

"Sorley Fior?" Ewan's voice, normally so welcome, cut through Flora like a winter wind. She held herself as still as she could behind Sorley's body and prayed that Ewan did not notice her. "Is that you, shadow-man, sitting about as naked as a day-old pup?" squeaked the dwarf.

"Aye, to your sorrow," answered Sorley, squeezing Flora's hand even tighter. "Why are you here and not with Clan Cameron and the prince? Away with you now and let me be."

Blithely ignoring Sorley's demand, Ewan held up a long, limp garment. At once Flora recognized Gair's sealskin cape. The little man perched on a rock, the cape a wrinkled mass at his feet. "The damn nag threw me on my arse, and I was obliged to track down the creature. When I found this, I thought that Gair had lost what little sense he possessed and had taken to running wild on the moors. Apparently he has more wits than you, however."

Sorley twisted sideways in a hopeless attempt to shield Flora from the dwarf's gaze. In silent answer, she pressed herself against the horrible tapestry of his back. It was futile to hide, and part of her wished to stand up and reveal herself. Indecision paralyzed her mind. "Leave me be, Ewan Fada," Sorley said. "You've no need of me."

"To be sure," Ewan replied, "though I'm baffled to find that others do. Aha! You're curious to ken my meaning. Well, then, come now and dress yourself. Himself awaits you."

"Himself?"

The word echoed in the rocky niche. Flora gasped. Had she spoken? She must have. Sorley turned to look at her, anger glinting in his eyes. How could she have been so daft? Ewan was clearly speaking of some worthy man, an entity far different from the one she had just encountered.

"Miss Flora?" As the little man gazed full at her, his look of wonder deteriorated into a snarl of horror. "A thousand devils! He's ravished ye!" He charged toward his tall clansman, dirk in hand, but Sorley was on his feet in an instant, swerving to avoid the sharp blade. Both Highlanders roared at each other in Gaelic. Terror pulled Flora to her feet. She pleaded with the men to stop, but if they heard her, they paid her no heed. Sorley grappled with his diminutive rival and tried in vain to wrestle the dirk from his grip. Ewan was as brawny as a wildcat and twice as fierce.

"Ewan! List to me!" Flora shouted. "Sorley has done

me no dishonor!'' This was true enough, she told herself.
She still held Sorley's compass, the pledge of his faith, in
her hand. But even though she had given herself willingly
to the Highlander, she knew Ewan Fada would never
believe her. "Lay up, I beg ye!"

But she might just as well have been calling to the rocks
or the wild river. The men continued their desperate strug-
gles, Ewan to eviscerate Sorley, Sorley to avoid harming
the dwarf.

They'll not stop until they kill themselves. The frightening
thought stabbed at Flora's mind and drove her out into
the open, determined to find help. The storm was over.
The air smelled as sweet as her father's favorite sherry, but
she had no time to enjoy it. Clawing her way up the rain-
slick boulders, she finally reached the top of the riverbank,
only to come face to face with a large, shaggy head. Flora
jerked back so quickly she almost fell down the tortuous
path she had just climbed up. A sorrel horse stood gazing
down at her inquisitively, its muzzle so close she could see
the steamy breath rising from its nostrils.

"Arrah! A lass in breeks!''

For a moment, in her confusion, Flora thought the horse
had addressed her. Then she saw someone astride the
animal, a burly man whose expression mirrored his mount's
curiosity. "Might you be Miss Flora Buchanan, the young
woman Ewan Fada spoke of?'' he said.

Flora gaped at the rider, wondering what Ewan had told
this stranger. Perhaps he was another Cameron. In any
affair, he was surely the "himself" Ewan had mentioned.
Some forty years old, he was dressed in the tartan trews
and silver-studded jacket of a wealthy Highland gentleman.
His blue bonnet bore three white feathers and the white
cockade, and his hair, as black as Sorley's, was pulled back
in a queue. Something about his forthright gaze and the

solid set of his jaw gave Flora the impression that this man was used to being obeyed. Five sturdy clansmen clustered about him, staring at her in disdain.

"I am indeed that unfortunate being, sir," she said, as she gulped for breath. "Ye look like a man of quality. Help me, I beg you. Ewan and Sorley Fior Cameron are at each other's throats in a cave in the rocks below, and I fear for their lives."

"Surely you exaggerate," the stranger said. "I've never known them to come to blows."

The thread of patience that had been holding Flora together suddenly broke. "I exaggerate nothing!" she cried in a burst of fury, clenching her fists at her sides. "Likely they'll slay each other while ye and I discuss the matter. Then ye'll know them no more!"

The rider gave an almost imperceptible start, then began snapping orders to his men in his native tongue. Four of them plunged down the slope, so close to Flora that their plaids brushed against her body. She turned to follow them when the rider called out to her. "Stay!"

She saw him stretch out his hand in a gesture that was more regal than haughty. Who was this imposing fellow? One of the prince's officers, perhaps? She decided to obey him, at least for the nonce. After all, she thought, a distraught woman would be more of a hindrance than a boon to anyone trying to subdue two raging rivals.

"Fear not, mistress," said the man. "I trow you're concerned for your friends' safety, but all will be well, I promise you. Come, stand by my side and wait."

"Very well, sir," Flora murmured, though she felt far from optimistic. Still casting glances at the river, she trudged up to the gillie who stood at the horse's head, holding its bridle. The young man was only slightly older than Losgann but with beautifully normal hands. With a pang of sadness Flora realized that this boy took for granted the simple tasks that Losgann could only dream of. The lad smiled at her, and she smiled back, thinking of the *Damainte* and wondering how they were faring without Ewan's guidance.

A sudden clamor destroyed her thoughts. Two familiar voices called out as one, and to Flora's puzzlement and deep embarrassment, it was the Gaelic version of her name—*Floraidh!*—that rang out above the rumble of the river.

The gentleman looked at her with something akin to compassion. "Ah! See?" he said, pointing down the hillside. "Already your admirers regret their quarrel. Here they come now, as hangdog a pair of rogues as you'd see in a day."

It was true. The two combatants clambered up the rocks toward her, Ewan in the fore—no surprise to Flora—and Sorley behind him, wearing his plaid but carrying his shirt. The other men followed some distance in the rear. Flora was relieved to see that her two Gaels had not seriously harmed each other, although Sorley's arms were laced with cuts from Ewan's dirk, and the dwarf walked with his head bowed. When the two men reached the top of the bluff, they paused briefly, then sank to their knees in front of Flora, the gillie, and the mysterious horseman. They seem repentant, she thought. She didn't know whether to thank God for their safe return or give them a proper tongue-lashing.

The gentleman had no such ambiguous feelings. "Get to your feet, you sorry creatures," he thundered. "How can it be that you and I share the same blood? You call yourself Sons of the Hound of Clan Cameron, yet you'd chew at each other like mongrels. Tear apart King Geordie's soldiers, if you must tear something."

Flora expected Sorley and Ewan to say something in their defense, but they merely rose and stood in silence, their eyes downcast. They looked for all the world like two schoolboys caught in some prank, their faces aglow with shame, not a bit like two warriors who had come within inches of murdering each other. The thought made her shudder as she remembered the tender embraces she and Sorley had shared such a short time ago.

"You have this young woman to thank for your lives, you wretches," the horseman went on, indicating Flora with an elegant turn of his hand. "I trust you'll treat her with the honor and respect she deserves."

At this Sorley sighed, and Ewan became so tense with rage that Flora thought he might explode. She tried to intervene for their sake, but the imperious rider held up his hand and bade her be still. He continued in the Gaelic, though Flora could tell by his tone of voice that he was just as angry as before. She could scarcely believe that anyone could have so much dominion over two men as indomitable as Sorley and Ewan.

Just when Flora was certain the censure would go on forever, the gentleman ceased abruptly, wheeled his horse about, and jogged off in the direction of the Jacobite encampment, his five attendants scurrying after him. Sorley and Ewan followed too. They motioned for her to go with them, but she hadn't the heart for any more adventure. She sank onto the damp ground, heedless of the mud that caked her breeches. The storm, her rapture with Sorley, Ewan's assault, and the puzzling incident with the stranger had exhausted her. Not even the thought of seeing the prince's army seemed quite as thrilling as before. Now that the danger was over, she wanted nothing more than to return to the *Damainte* and curl up to sleep beside the Three Smalls, but she doubted that she had even the strength to do that.

When Sorley and Ewan returned to her, she begged them to go without her. "I'll make my own way back," she said, hoping she sounded more assured than she felt.

"I'm no' leaving you alone on the moors," Sorley insisted. He took her by the elbow and helped her to her feet, then gave her a sip of whiskey from Ewan's flask. The strong drink refreshed her a bit. "You must come with us. I'll keep you safe."

Flora squeezed his arm to let him know how deeply she felt for him, but not so hard that Ewan might notice.

But Ewan was too preoccupied cursing Sorley and jabbing the tall man in the ribs to discern Flora's loving gesture. "Go on alone, ye whoreson, and let me take Miss Flora back to the *Damainte*. The lady may trust you with her honor, but I know better."

Sorley scowled at the little man. "Start no more brawls with me, halfpenny," he warned Ewan, "unless you want to face your chief's wrath again. We both must go as he bade us and speak to the prince about the soldiers you slew."

Flora had been letting her mind drift, recalling cups full of hot tea shared with Mrs. Leckie and bowls of raspberries and cream. At Sorley's words, her mind stowed away the comfortable memories as fast as servants clearing dirty dishes. "Chief? Do you mean the man on the horse?"

Ewan tilted his head back with a pride that far outweighed his person. "Himself. Donald Cameron of Lochiel, the chief of Clan Cameron, the best man in the prince's army. Did you not see the three eagle feathers in his bonnet? Thus may you always mark a chief. It's proud I am to be kin to him, no matter how far removed."

Flora shook her head in an effort to quiet her pounding

brain. Due to a lack of knowledge about headgear, she had berated Sorley's chief, one of the most powerful men in the kingdom. "I fear I didn't show him the proper courtesy."

To her consternation, Sorley burst out laughing. He was most handsome when he laughed, for then all the kindness inside him shone from his face. Flora could not maintain her anger with him, though she tried. "I don't know what you told him," Sorley said, "but faith! I would like to have heard it! Did Cousin Donald some good, I ween, to not have the whip hand for once."

Ewan glared sideways at Sorley. "And what words do *you* use to enchant him and the prince, shadow-man? It's surely not your wits that win you their blessing."

Sorley scowled down at the little man. "Would you accuse me of currying favor with Lochiel and His Majesty?"

Ewan would have replied, but Flora had had enough. It was incomprehensible that Ewan would still bait Sorley in spite of his chief's stern reprimand. She thrust herself between the two clansmen and tried to shoulder them apart. "In Christ's name," she said, crossing herself, "will ye not desist?" The men immediately fell back but continued to glower at each other. Flora congratulated herself on her victory, no matter how temporary it might prove. "Go after your chief, but I assure ye, I'm too weary to follow."

Ewan peered up at her. "Mayhap you can't walk, but you can ride. The English officer's horse is tethered yonder." He pointed to a nearby grove of ragged rowan trees. Flora saw the glint of metal among the shadows of the boughs.

"The horse! That's fine, then," said Sorley. With no warning he bent down, picked up Flora in his arms, and hurried her off toward the grove.

"Set me down," she objected, although she secretly relished the rhythm of Sorley's stride and the pressure of his grip on her knees and back.

"I'll not," said the Highlander.

She threaded her arms around his neck and drank in the earthy smell of his plaid, which rose and fell with his steady breathing. "So be it." She sighed. " 'Tis not meet, but I haven't the will to contest you just now."

"Many fine things are not meet," he whispered into her hair. "I trust you know what I'm speaking of."

Flora said nothing, but she felt her face burn with passion and mortification. At that moment, Ewan ran past them, turned, and stood as still as a stump, blocking Sorley's way. "Set her down, you son of hell! I'll bring the horse to her."

Sorley snorted with impatience, increased his pace, and easily outdistanced his rival. Ewan trotted after them, muttering threats of mutilation, castration, murder, and damnation under his breath. Flora lamented his frenzy, but she understood it. Sorley, a tall, powerful *sona*, was in command of the moment. He was also his chief's cousin and a favorite of the prince. Strange that she did not realize earlier how much her short friend must have envied his shadow-man.

"Preposterous! I'll go where I please, when I wish."

The words clanged like iron bells. Flora awoke, wondering if she had encountered her father, come back from the dead. Muttering voices and the sharp scent of liquor surrounded her. As her vision adjusted to the flickering candlelight, she saw she was not at home in Edinburgh but slumped in the corner of a large canvas tent, such as might belong to a high-ranking military officer.

At least a dozen men were crowded into the tent. Flora
could hardly see through the thicket of legs—some bare,
some in breeches. She stood up and at once beheld the
prince, magnificent in blue silk and white linen, sitting
astride a folding campaign chair, as if he were still aboard
his charger. "First we shall take Selkirk, then proceed over
the border and on to London," he announced. "My supporters will swell our ranks along the way, and I am assured
that reinforcements from France are ready to embark." A
French-speaking officer beside him nodded, and the huge
jabot at his chin fluttered and danced. "Gentlemen, the
victory is ours for the taking." The prince punctuated his
statement with a brisk slap against a small table at his side,
and sent an empty brandy bottle tumbling to the floor.
He ignored it. Flora could not help but wonder whether
he had drained the bottle himself.

"Your Majesty!"

"Your Highness!"

"My prince!"

The crowd lurched forward, then settled itself again.
Several men spoke at once. Flora could make out Lochiel
even without his bonnet, a thickset Highlander named
Murray, the elegantly dressed French general, a stocky
Irishman, and an older Gael with flowing white hair.
Despite the flurry of voices, Flora understood the men's
meaning. The Scots all made much the same comment:
to march on England in bad weather was lunacy, if not
suicide. The men were weary and ill-fed, said Lochiel, and
urged that the Highlanders be sent home to rest. Disperse
now, Murray suggested, then renew efforts in the spring,
after fresh troops had arrived.

"His Highness must do as His Highness thinks best,"
offered the Frenchman.

"What happened to my brave Highlanders?" asked the

prince, shaking with exasperation. "Keppoch? Lochiel? Where are your hearts? Let us seize the day! Cumberland's army is scattered throughout the south of England, and Hawley's forces are split in twain, far to the north. They will never regroup in time to stop us if we but push the attack while the advantage is still ours."

More men voiced their opinions, most of which were contrary to the prince's wishes. Flora was intrigued, but she had no idea whom to believe. Standing on tiptoe, she could just distinguish a familiar profile among the russet shadows. It was Sorley, his face creased with a frown. Her heart ached for him. How torn he must have felt, caught squarely between his chief's wisdom and his prince's courage.

"Your Majesty," Lochiel said, stepping forward, his head slightly inclined. "Not two days ago my men surprised a Hanoverian patrol that had determined our position. They would have reported back to Cumberland or Hawley had my lads not cut them down."

Flora, wedged between a massive Highlander and the thickset Irishman, could not see the prince's reaction to this unnerving news. She thought he had dismissed it when Lochiel motioned with his hand and Sorley emerged from the shadows to present himself to his commanders. Flora eased herself between the two big men, straining to hear what Sorley said. As he was explaining his bottom-numbing exploits with the Sassenach, another speaker joined in. Although she couldn't see him, she recognized Ewan Fada's boyish voice, detailing the heroic actions of the *Damainte* and the cunning machinations of the English.

But the prince was not impressed. He tapped one forefinger against his chair in a graceful expression of his impatience. "Clan Cameron's bravery is undeniable, but what if the English had escaped? No harm done, I believe.

By the time they reported their news, we would have been
weeks ahead of any of their cumbersome armies. No, you
cannot deter me, Lochiel, nor you either, Lord George. We
continue south, or you will march without your prince." At
this Charles swung his leg over his chair, and stood up
abruptly. Those around him leaped back as if a flame had
seared them. Flora felt the two men in front of her draw
apart just as she began to push forward. Too late she saw
her error. Suddenly she plunged to the ground and lay
sprawled on the muddied Turkish carpet that served as a
floor.

Amid assorted gasps and epithets, someone stepped forward to help Flora stand up. Devastated by embarrassment,
she kept her eyes averted from her good Samaritan until
she saw the scratches on his forearms. "You've a rare talent
for making yourself known in a crowd," Sorley observed,
but his tone was kindly. She smiled as she looked up into
his unfathomable eyes, for that instant forgetting every
other person in the tent.

"Mademoiselle? *Mon Dieu!* It is the same young lady
whom I nearly rode over in Edinburgh."

Flora recognized the accent, the mellifluous voice, the
artful wording: Prince Charles Edward Stuart himself was
addressing her! The bones in her legs turned to pudding.
Her hands shook. She roused herself to drop a curtsy, no
mean accomplishment while dressed in breeches. "Your . . .
Your Majesty," she murmured, both pleased and amazed
that the prince had remembered their brief encounter.

Charles smiled and nodded. *"Enchanté."* An innocence
in his deep brown eyes captivated Flora and inspired her
to trust him. Sorley gripped her by the elbow, perhaps as
a gesture of courtesy, perhaps because he thought the
prince's charm might cause her to swoon.

"Your Highness, this is Miss Flora Buchanan," he said.

"She was accosted by thieves, and Ewan Fada here and his brave followers saved her from ruination." Sorley glanced down at the dwarf. Ewan glanced up at him. Flora felt the heat of their anger in what should have been a moment of camaraderie. Surely more than envy lay behind their hatred.

The prince sighed. He rested his chin in his hand, and for the first time Flora saw how remarkably young he was, barely in the earliest bloom of manhood. It must have been difficult, she thought, to carry so much responsibility on such youthful shoulders. "We are not graced by the presence of many ladies, Miss Buchanan, and none as ravishing as yourself, whatever your attire. I hope you will allow me to put a question to you."

Flora swallowed hard. She wondered why the spirited prince would solicit her opinion on anything. "For certain, Your Majesty," she whispered. "I am your humble servant."

"Mademoiselle, I trust you have heard at least some of the arguments voiced tonight, both for and against pushing our campaign over the border," said the prince.

"I have, Your Highness," she replied, "though I cannot pretend to have any knowledge of such matters." Flora stole a glimpse at Sorley and Ewan, hoping they might have some inkling of the prince's intentions. But she could tell from their wide-eyed expressions that they were just as mystified as she, or for that matter, the rest of the assembly.

"As modest as you are beautiful," returned the prince. "Nevertheless, I am interested to hear your opinion. This matter concerning the army's course is by no means concluded. Shall we go forward, or shall we allow my brave Highlanders a chance to visit their families? What do you think, hmm? I shall treasure your candid response."

From the corner of her eye, Flora saw several men inhale deeply. The tent was as hushed as a cathedral during Mass. Everyone waited for her to speak, but what should she say? She had the uncomfortable notion that the prince already knew how she would answer. "As I mentioned before, I've no head for such things," she said, then repeated herself when the prince gently urged her to speak up. "Your Highness alone must determine how best to proceed. However, my mother was a Highlander herself, and she told me that nearly all her people farmed the land. If this is true, then your troops might appreciate going home to tend to their harvests before the heavy snows come."

Flora saw Ewan roll his eyes. Sorley clenched his teeth. *I've said nothing that hasn't been suggested before,* she wanted to tell them.

"If I comprehend you correctly then," said Charles, leaning forward, his face radiant with expectation, "you suggest that we wait to invade England."

There seemed to be no air in the tent. Flora felt on the edge of suffocation. She had no intention of appearing contrary, but she felt obliged to speak her mind, as Charles had instructed. "Aye, if it's possible, Your Highness. But it is only one woman's impression on the subject, and a humble one it is."

The prince threw back his head and let out a laugh that sounded exactly like a cock's crow. "Spoken like a true courtier. Well, gentlemen, there is your choice: Will you march into George's lair and grip the cur by the throat? Or perhaps you'd rather tuck up your skirts and flee back to the north, as the lovely mademoiselle suggests?"

"Never!" cried the older chieftain, whom the prince had referred to as Keppoch. He laid his hand on the basket hilt of his broadsword and ducked his head in a brief show of fealty. "His Majesty does not command an army of women. Clan MacDonald has never cringed before any foe, and we'll not start now. Over the border, say I!''

"And I!''

"Over the border!''

Sorley and Ewan gazed at Flora in sympathy. Her stomach churned as she realized that the prince, whom she had so admired only moments ago, had played her for an ass. The tent erupted with wild screams of approval for the prince, even from those who had earlier opposed his plans. Only Lord George Murray continued to object, but the noise of the many soon swallowed up his desperate appeals for caution. Flora guessed that brandy and whiskey accounted for the tumult as much as the spectacle of her abashment. Still, the thought brought her little consolation.

While she stood petrified with anger, Sorley and Ewan each took her arm and began to shepherd her from the tent. But just as they were about to slip outside, Lochiel came forward and detained Sorley. Reluctantly he released Flora, murmuring words of encouragement even as he turned away from her. Before she could regret his absence, she was out in the cold night air with Ewan, staring up into a cloudy sky smeared with the red blush of sunset. A brisk breeze did nothing to control the fires of shame raging over her face. Never before had she felt so alone. Only twice before had she felt so betrayed.

A square of muslin worked its way into her hand, and she saw through her misery that it was Ewan who placed it there. "God bless you, my friend," she said, blowing her nose in the soft fabric. She knew she took the little man's good nature for granted sometimes, and this made her feel even more wretched.

"Take heart, Miss Flora," he said gently, patting her

hand. "The prince was unkind to you, there's no denying it, but you must try to see things from his view."

"His view!" Flora sobbed. "His view is absolute. He's a monarch and may do as he pleases, even if he wishes to use me ill." She paused to dab at her smarting eyes. "Indeed, I am nothing to him, but that's all the more reason to ask why he would mock me so."

Ewan cocked his head in the beguiling way he had about him. "Come with me. I'll explain the way I see it, but first you must have a bite and a dram." She followed him to a fire where several Highland soldiers were gathered, laughing and talking as they roasted strips of venison on the flames. Ewan spoke to them in Gaelic, and they plied Flora with bits of half-charred meat and a wooden cup brimming with whiskey. Then they graciously huddled together at one side of the fire, giving Flora and Ewan as much privacy as possible.

"His Highness didn't wish to mock you or belittle your courage," Ewan explained, pouring himself a cup of whiskey. "But when he saw that he would not have his way, that Lochiel and the others were pressing him to abandon the invasion, he felt he had to take strong measures."

Flora sighed. "So he shamed his officers into siding with him. Tell me, do you agree with his stance, or would it be better to wait, as I suggested?"

"Each course has its good points. Had it been me he was asking, however, I might not have been so quick to counter him. He is my prince, after all."

"And I, for his purposes . . . I'm naught but a helpless female." A hollow feeling began to replace Flora's fury.

"You mustn't take his action as a personal affront," said Ewan. "The prince was only protecting his campaign, which is more precious to him than his life." He drained his cup, then poured another. "No, I would not be concerned about His Majesty. It's someone else you should be fearing, a black-hearted wretch who's closer to you than he should be."

"Sorley Fior."

"Aye, to be sure."

Flora paused, a morsel of venison halfway to her mouth. For the second time since she had been aware of their rivalry, she had the disturbing sensation that Ewan resented Sorley for a reason that ran deeper than jealousy. Now, as she watched the dwarf, his face bathed in the lurid light of the fire, it seemed to her as if some poison had seeped out of his body and glowed on his skin like a badge of his loathing. "Why do you despise Sorley so? I'm aware that—"

"You're no' aware of the half of it," Ewan interrupted her, "but 'tis a long tale and night is coming. We must get back to the *Damainte.*"

"Tonight? In the cold and dark?"

"Aye. I've arranged to borrow ponies to make our journey easier."

He rose and began to shuffle off, but Flora caught him by the sleeve. "I've spent the last fortnight living in darkness like a frightened coney," she said, "and I'll have no more of it. It's true that I have warm feelings toward Sorley, as he has for me." She paused to consider her next words, fearing they might well turn Ewan away from her forever. "And unless you have good reason to object, then it is no concern of yours whether we keep company or no'."

Ewan looked at her with deep regret written in his beautiful blue eyes. "Sorley killed Aimil, his wife," he said in a fierce whisper, "and I don't wish to be laying stones on your cairn as well as hers. Wait now while I fetch the horses and I'll tell you more as we ride."

"Killed . . ." repeated Flora, but then her voice and wits failed her. She sat as still as a stone, and just as dead inside, watching Ewan walk off into the gathering shadows.

Killed his wife!

Chapter Eight

The moon crept out from among the clouds. Flora and Ewan rode in the moonlight on silvered horses, not a word breaking the stillness that lay between them like a fog. At last Flora shook off the daze that Ewan's revelation had wrapped around her. The image of her mother lying at the foot of the staircase, drained of life as well as color, flashed through her mind and vanished. "Killed his wife? Not Sorley Fior. You're mistaken."

"Make no mistake: he killed her." Ewan's voice was brittle with spite. "Aimil was always dear to me, even though I lost her to that son of the devil. When she fell ill I went to her and held her hand. Sometimes we spoke together. The day before she died she was in good spirits, and I thought she might yet conquer her sickness."

"But how can you be so certain that Sorley killed her?"

Ewan slumped in his saddle, as if the weight of bad memories rode on his shoulders. "I saw him. He sat at her bedside, pressing a piece of sheepskin over her face. Then she shuddered and lost her water. I saw it all. The creature smothered the poor woman."

"Oh, Ewan! I'm so sorry for ye! But ye must be in error."

Again they rode on in silence for several minutes. He couldn't be right, thought Flora. Her beloved Sorley would never stoop to such a heartless act. Although Flora burned to hear more, she knew how hard it must have been for Ewan to recount his bitter memories. She reined in her impatience as well as she might, and at last Ewan continued.

"An assize of Clan Cameron was held, and Sorley was charged with Aimil's murder. I told Lochiel and the others what I had seen, and not only that, but how I'd heard that Sorley had been consorting with another woman. Naught could be proven, nor could his sweetheart be found. Sorley denied all—that he was courting a new wife, that he'd killed Aimil. It was me saying aye and him saying nay, and the scales balanced exactly even."

Again Ewan stopped speaking. They continued on their way, the serenity of the evening broken only by the moaning of the wind and the tramp of the horses' feet. Finally Flora could bear the brutal silence no longer. "What was the outcome?" she asked. "You say nothing was proven."

"Sorley is not only Lochiel's cousin; he's his favorite," Ewan said, grumbling. "What might you expect? He was found innocent and set free. For the past two years, whenever I could, I've visited Aimil's cairn and wept over it and placed a stone on it, to show I've not forgotten her. My heart is sick with anger at this ill-named Upright Sorley."

Flora gazed at the ground as it lurched by under her pony's hooves. She felt as if she had been turned inside out and was slowly falling to bits. "I can't believe you."

"I can't make you believe me," Ewan answered, "but

I'm telling you my story for your own good and no other reason. List, now! I've taken an oath to remain silent about the matter, and I've broken that vow for your sake alone." Suddenly he leaned toward her and grasped her hand, a difficult task for a man with such short arms. "I'm fond of you, Miss Flora, and I want no harm to befall you. Stay clear of that murderer. He's handsome, true enough, but so is the devil. Faith, when I saw you in the cave with the brute, I feared the worst."

"The worst?" Flora wondered out loud. "You mean that he'd taken me by force."

Ewan shook his head. "Nay, for then you'd fear him. *Dia!* By worst I mean that you love the creature."

The statement took her aback. She had indeed thought she might love Sorley, until Ewan made his revelation. Now her thoughts were as scattered as leaves in a high wind. She needed time to collect them and make sense of her world again. She had to speak with Sorley. "He asked me would I wed him."

Ewan stared at her as if she had grown fangs. "Surely you did not consent," he sputtered.

The barking of a fox echoed in the stillness. The ponies pricked up their ears and whickered. A signal! thought Flora. "Robbers!" she cried. Dark memories of Wull and his bandits crashed through her mind like hounds through a thicket. *I'm glad I'm wearing breeks,* she thought. *I can ride like the wind if I must.*

She looked at Ewan, expecting him to take off at a gallop, but the diminutive Gael was unruffled. " 'Tis nothing to fear," he said and tightened his grip on her arm. "Did you consent?"

Flora shook her head. Ewan released her. "You were wise," he murmured. "Say nothing of this matter to anyone. Lochiel will have my head if he learns that I broke my vow." He then proceeded to astound her by imitating the very call that had disturbed the hush of the night. A man appeared suddenly before them, a silver shadow in the moonlight. It was Cu. Flora exhaled a quavering sigh of relief. Cu never strayed far from the *Damainte*.

As if sensing her thoughts, several of Ewan's band materialized from the heath. Losgann sprang up so quickly to take her horse's reins that she nearly leaped from the saddle. In a few moments she found herself crossing the moor at a swift trot, with Losgann and Gair running in front, Ewan riding at her side, and Cu panting along at the rear.

She was still pondering Ewan's grim revelation when she arrived at the camp of the *Damainte*. Little Rattie was so relieved to see her that he threw himself into her arms and refused to leave her. The others, excited by the prospect of invading the great nation to the south, huddled around a bonfire, chattering with an enthusiasm Flora had never witnessed before. She wished she could share their zeal, but she felt strangely apart from it. She knew all too well the dangers that Murray and Lochiel had tried to present to the prince. And now . . . what if Sorley were indeed the monster Ewan had made him out to be? She would have to face the coming months alone, without his love to sustain her. There was always the chance that Ewan was mistaken. If not, a doubtful future lay before her, one that even Rattie's sweet presence could not amend.

Thoughts of Sorley were still tumbling in her mind when at last Flora fell asleep by the fire with the waif in her arms.

A gust of warm breath struck the back of Flora's neck. She sat up, awake at once. An invisible sun was just rising, sending fingers of rose-colored light through layers of gray mist.

"Living on the moor has sharpened your senses, Miss Flora," whispered Ewan. He hobbled in front of her on his stubby legs as she tried to make sense of his sudden appearance. "There's snow coming. The air's as cold as steel."

"You didn't wake me to discuss the weather, I'm thinking," she whispered, for fear of disturbing Rattie. "Is all well?" Immediately her imagination produced a host of possible demons. "Has Rosmairi wandered away? Has anyone fallen ill? Are the red soldiers nearby?"

"A disaster worse than any of those," muttered the dwarf. He clawed at his beard in exasperation. "Our shadow-man is here and he insists that he see you. Seumas and Cu are keeping him at bay, but they won't hold him forever."

Flora surveyed the mist, but Sorley was nowhere in sight. Seeing that Dughal was awake, she gently laid the still-sleeping Rattie in the giant's arms. The boy stirred. The huge man clasped the boy to him like a kitten, his dull eyes reflecting for a moment the warm affection of one child for another. When she was certain that Rattie had fallen back asleep, Flora rose and faced Ewan. "I'm not afeared of Sorley Fior." *Confused, yes. Sick with worry and dread? Aye, indeed. But fearful of Sorley? Never!* He was no murderer. She knew it in her heart. "Let him come. What does he want of me?"

"How am I to know that?" Ewan answered, looking over his shoulder for phantoms attacking from the rear. "Speak to him freely, but mind you . . . not a word about Aimil."

So—not as free as she would like, she thought ruefully. If Ewan were right about his chief, then keeping silent was a matter of life and death, a burden Flora wished she didn't have to bear. But bear it she would, for Ewan's sake.

Suddenly, over the sighs of the sleeping *Damainte,* Flora heard a shout, then a whinny, followed by the sounds of a scuffle, scattered oaths, and finally the hoofbeats of a horse. Crann, dozing by the fire, leaped to his feet and began barking. Finally a horseman thundered through the mist, pulling up only an arm's length from the *Damainte* gathered around the smoldering fire. It was Sorley, mounted on the red gelding that Flora had first seen at the top of the riverbank. The animal was streaked with lather. Had Sorley charmed Lochiel into lending him the beast, or had he simply taken it?

Sorley dismounted just as the *Damainte* began to rouse themselves to stare at the warlike vision in their midst. Rattie awoke screaming. Flora knew the sound of terror all too well; it pained her soul to listen to him. Although part of her yearned to feel Sorley's arms around her, she stalked up to the man and began to berate him. "See what ye've done!" she cried, her anger releasing the brogue her father had so abhorred. "Ye've terrified the puir child! What can bring ye here so early?"

And in such a state, Flora added to herself. Sorley looked dazed or drunk, or both. His plaid hung in hasty folds around his body, and his hair, normally tied behind his neck in a neat queue, rose up around his head like a stormy halo. What force kept his shivering legs from buckling under him she could not imagine. She guessed offhand that he had not slept at all during the night. The more she chided him for his carelessness, the less he seemed to listen to her, but only gazed at her with a great, wordless longing that moved her deeply.

Ewan Fada joined in the abuse, slapping Sorley on the knees while spewing profanities at him in Gaelic. Sorley barely seemed to notice. At last he stretched his hand out toward Flora, just as he had during their idyll in the cave. "I've come to get an answer to my offer, mistress. The clans march south within the hour toward Selkirk, then on to Derby, then London, God willing. Five . . . six thousand men, hundreds of miles from home, without proper food or shelter, and no sign of support or reinforcements. Faith, even the Three Smalls couldn't have come up with a more reckless venture than this."

"Ye whoreson! You'd insult the prince and his bold plan!" cried Ewan.

For the first time since he had ridden into camp, Sorley took note of Ewan. "Nay, I don't insult him. If need be I'll die for him and his bold plan. Like you and your *Damainte,* I'd rather risk life itself than be ruled by a great slug of a German who cares not if my people thrive or starve." Again he turned to Flora. "Our time together is short and I must be knowing where I stand. I trust you still carry my compass. What say you, my bonny Flora?"

Murmurs rose up from the fireside where the *Damainte* were observing Sorley's frenzied announcement. Flora felt a strange uneasiness creep over her, as though she were an actress trying to remember crucial lines. "I . . . I must think further on the matter," she stammered. "It's twice in two days that ye have put the question to me, and I'm no' prepared to answer yet."

Flora hadn't expected Sorley to repeat his offer so soon, but what shocked her even more was that Sorley was still standing erect. She had expected Ewan to launch himself full force at the bigger man and lay him out on his back. Instead, the dwarf calmly cleared his throat and touched Sorley's wrist to gain his attention. "What question, shadow-man? And what's this about your compass?"

Sorley frowned, and it was clear that he was in no mood

for complex explanations. "As long as Flora keeps it, I know that she's considering my suit."

Sorley began to address Flora, but the dwarf interrupted him. "Oh, oh, so you're a suitor now, are you, you devil?" Ewan's eyes flared wide-open for a moment, but at least on the outside he maintained his ease. "Well, before you court this lady, Sorley Fior, perhaps you should be more forthcoming with her. Perhaps there are things she should know about you, things I should not speak of, but which you must. D'ye ken my meaning?"

Sorley had been paying little heed to Ewan Fada, but now he bent his head and fixed his sight on the fiery bantam. His fairy eyes glowed with ferocity, and even Flora took a step away from him. "Aye, I ken your meaning right enough," he said. "You burn with envy, I ween, just as you did over my Aimil. And now you're keen to steal Flora from me. Deny it and I'll call you a liar."

This was too much for Ewan. He drew his dirk and sprang at Sorley, but this time the shadow-man was prepared. As Flora looked on, ashamed of the dangerous spectacle her presence had created, Sorley twisted the dirk from Ewan's hand. He then grasped the bellowing dwarf by the elbows and held him up at shoulder height. Ewan squirmed mightily and hammered at Sorley's arms with both fists, but he could not break free. Cu, Seumas, and Gair gathered around the two men, but Flora sensed that the *Damainte* could not decide which side to take: that of their beleaguered leader, or that of Lochiel's favorite.

Flora knew that Sorley could break Ewan in half if he chose to. This was the second time she had seen him refrain from harming the aggressive little man, and she loved him for it. Still, it was hardly the time or place to plight a troth, if indeed she decided to take such a course. If only she could question Sorley without betraying Ewan's confi-

dance. "Enough o' this madness!" she shouted. "Sorley—
Ewan never will marry. He told me so himself."

"Aye, I'm aware of what he claims," Sorley replied as
he returned the struggling dwarf to earth and released
him. "But talk is cheap, mistress. It doesn't buy whiskey."

Ewan, not in the least chastened by his humiliation,
unleashed a torrent of angry Gaelic on his tall clansman.
Fearful lest the two set upon each other again, Flora thrust
herself between them, so close to each she could feel their
breath as they puffed and snorted at each other like stal-
lions. "Stop, if ye be Christian folk!" she begged them.
The men each drew back half a step from her, though
Flora could still feel the tension between them, as keen as
a blade. "Sorley, why do ye press me for an answer? Ye
must give me time to consider." *And to solve your secrets,*
she added to herself.

"Time? That would be a generous gift indeed, mistress,"
Sorley answered. "We've no time to dally." Standing with
a hand on either hip, he looked more like the fierce savages
Mrs. Leckie had warned her about and less like her Sorley
in the cave by the river. "Perhaps you need some persuad-
ing." While Flora stood divided between love and fear,
Sorley dived toward her. Driven either by whiskey or the
fire of his own passions, he caught her by the waist and
swept her against him. She resisted, bewildered, but her
daze vanished like snow in summer as she gave in to a kiss
so ravenous, so unbridled, so alive with hunger that she
forgot she was breathing.

She knew it was unwise to be indiscreet in front of Ewan,
but her desire overpowered her judgment. Too late she
heard the sounds of dirks rasping from scabbards and
flintlock pistols snapping clear of belts. She saw a blurred
movement, a flash of silver. Sorley whimpered. As she
watched, terrified, his magic-colored eyes rolled upward

into whiteness. His head tipped back, his hands slid away from her sides, and he toppled backward into the dry bracken.

"Sorley!" Flora was at his side at once, gently stroking a patch of red that glistened on his right temple. "You've killed him!" She laid her hand on his chest and knew at once that she was mistaken; his heart pounded against her palm like a mallet.

"By the saints, a tap on the crown won't harm that one." Ewan knelt opposite Flora and fingered Sorley's wound. As he did so, she saw that it wasn't he who had struck the blow but Gair, who stood with his head bowed, gripping a pistol by its barrel. The addled man examined the bloody weapon, babbling such a rapid stream of gibberish in both Gaelic and English that even the *Damainte* looked at him askance.

Seumas handed Flora a damp kerchief, and she quickly set to work cleaning Sorley's wound. "Gair would never strike anyone save on your command," she accused Ewan.

"Aye, true enough," admitted the dwarf, "but didn't that son of hell deserve it? Throwing himself on you like a stag on a hind . . . *Arrah!* What cheek! Never fear, Miss Flora; I'll send him back where he belongs and you'll see— he'll not be long in the mending."

"Send him back?" Flora gasped. "To the clans? But he's badly injured. Ye can see for yersel'. The kiss was an indiscretion, aye, but not a crime."

But Ewan had his mind set on ridding himself of his rival. Flora shouted in anger and Rattie began wailing again, but nothing could prevent Ewan, Cu, and Seumas from gathering up the unconscious Highlander and draping him over his horse's back. Flora tried to pull away the men's hands as they bound Sorley to the animal, but she might as well have been trying to uproot three oak trees.

In the end she could do nothing but watch as the gelding trotted off into the mist, more or less in the direction it had come from. Sorley bounced upon its back like one of the china dolls from her childhood.

When the horse was out of sight, Flora turned on Ewan. "Ye foolish wee man!" she upbraided him. "What if Sorley should die? What will Lochiel do then? He'll be black with fury! He's likely to slay all three of you before he even begins asking what happened—" She stopped, unwilling to contemplate Sorley's death any further.

"Hah!" Ewan spat. He waggled his head and rolled his eyes. "You underestimate the devil's endurance. Naught will happen save that Lochiel will understand the gravity of the situation and relieve Sorley of his duties as our shadow-man. His brainpan will ache for a few days, but no harm to him." The little man paused, then cocked his head, squinted, and eyed her like a falcon. "You don't have serious intentions about taking that murderer as your husband, do you?"

Flora mopped her face with a piece of linen. It was stained with blood. She knew at once it was the kerchief she had used on Sorley's wound. Choking back sobs, she shook her head. She wanted to hate Ewan just then but couldn't. The man was only trying to protect her, whether or not she needed protecting. Just like Sorley. "I don't know," she whispered. Suddenly she knew what she had to ask. Bending down, she gripped Ewan's shoulder. "You must let me question him. About Aimil, I mean. I must learn the truth."

Ewan's lips drew back in a snarl. He flung his stubby arms upward, breaking her grip. "Mary, Mother of God!" he cried. "I told you the truth myself!"

Flora felt her throat tighten in anger. "Aye, but I must have it from him as well."

"He'd only tell you lies, mistress," Ewan insisted. "You're fortunate to be rid of the creature."

Flora knew she mustn't give in to the little man. Above all, he admired persistence. "Ewan Fada, Sorley will do you no ill. You know it's true. Should he discover what you've told me, he won't betray you to your chief."

Ewan hesitated, and Flora could see that she'd touched something within him: hiding behind his hatred of Sorley was a sullen respect for the man. The dwarf leaned toward her, speaking in a confidential tone, though they were more than a stone's throw away from the others. "I'll give you leave to speak plainly to him," Ewan said at last, "but let me arrange your meeting. Does that suit you?"

Flora was about to tell him that it suited her fine, but he didn't wait for her answer. "That's settled, then," he said, as if she had spoken. Then his manner changed and he once again became the blustering fighting cock, forever in charge. "Sorley said the clans march within the hour, so we must be on their tail when they leave. Seumas will see to Rosmairi, but you must attend to the Three Smalls and take care they won't wander into the hills."

"Gladly," Flora said, and was about to thank Ewan for his compromise when he turned abruptly and walked off. His short legs rocked his massive body from side to side, like a stout boat in a rough sea. Before he reached the fire and the other *Damainte,* he shot her a broad smile and beckoned for her to join him with a toss of his head. As she ambled after him, a disturbing thought struck her: What if Sorley had chanced on the truth when he spoke of Ewan as her suitor? Misplaced affection might drive a man to lies, even a man of honor.

It wasn't the time to probe Ewan for answers to such intimate questions, however. He was a busy fellow, throwing instructions, curses, and exhortations around him like

a child tossing handfuls of wildflowers into the air. Flora
found that the Smalls had indeed disappeared, but with
Crann's help she tracked them down and herded them
back to the camp, which was now no more than a dead
fire and a square of crushed heather frosted with a breath
of snow. The *Damainte* were already on the march, with
Ewan and Losgann in the lead, Rosmairi, Seumas, and
Gair at the rear, and everyone else in between. It was
easy work following the army now: less than half a mile
separated Ewan's people from the clans. The Jacobite
forces left behind such a wide swath of trampled earth that
Flora thought they might as well have been tilling a field.

She had just shepherded the three urchins up behind
Rosmairi when Whoreson tugged at her cuff. "Miss Flora?"
he asked, without a pause in his stride.

"Aye?" Flora, gripping the younger boys firmly by the
hand, glanced at Whoreson but kept plodding onward.
"You've a question for me, Son?" She refused to call him
by his wretched name, no matter that it did suit him. He
was easily the sorriest-looking of the three, with pinched
cheeks, lusterless eyes, and pasty skin blotched pink with
the ravages of disease. Just looking at him made Flora vow
to find him and the other lost lads a home of some sort
after the campaign.

Without a word the child held up a familiar brass disk.

Flora released the boys and hunted wildly through her
pockets, though she knew the compass had to be Sorley's.
"A thousand thanks to ye!" she cried. How could she have
been so stupid as to drop it? Gratefully she scooped up
the bauble, heavy for its size. It made her think of its owner,
and thinking of him made her feel like weeping. She wasn't
even certain he was still alive. Could it be possible that the
man who had made her feel so much like a woman, so
alive, so complete, was lost to her forever? To distract

her aching mind, she tried to ruffle Whoreson's horribly matted hair. "God bless ye!"

"Devil roast him, ye mean," muttered a tiny voice by her elbow. It was little Rattie, youngest of all but the most outspoken. "The bastard thieved it."

Putting aside for the moment a lecture on the evils of coarse language, Flora leaped to Whoreson's defense, without quite knowing why. "He found it, I'm sure, Rattie." The older boy nodded with enthusiasm. "Why else would he seek to give it back?" Now that she thought on it, she recalled that he had picked it up and returned it to her before, when she'd first seen the *Damainte*. "It must have slipped from my pocket, but I'll be more careful of it now." She slid the compass into the inner pocket of her waistkit, but when she raised her head, the boys were far ahead of her. They had fallen behind the others, and now the three waifs ran like foals for the safety of Rosmairi's friendly confusion and Gair's elegant lunacy. Flora sighed. For the Three Smalls, nothing was more disastrous than to be left behind. Was Whoreson a thief, stealing, perhaps, for the sheer pleasure of the deed? Or had she truly been careless? Either way, she would have to keep close guard of her dearest possession. Though she no longer needed it for navigation, it still held the key to her life's journey.

Toward sunset the prince marched into Selkirk at the head of the clans. Flora did not witness the event herself, but she and the other *Damainte* were thrilled to listen to Ewan's description of it. He himself had heard about the triumphant entry from a talkative young MacIntyre lieutenant. Flora could well imagine the prince on his gray charger, the cheering people, the enraptured faces of the children. Her memory of the clans' entry into Edinburgh still fueled her dreams.

Two days later the army was again on the move. Half a mile or more behind, Flora could but catch distant glances of the Highland force through veils of mist and rain. While Ewan, Cu, Creag, and Seumas eagerly pointed out the clans to her, she could not discern one from the other and knew not how they could. She searched in vain for Sorley, though Ewan assured her he had seen his brash clansman from a safe distance, and that Sorley was walking and talking as well as he had before. The next time the shadow-man visited the *Damainte*, she promised herself, she would lay Ewan's accusation out in the open before him and let the shards fall where they might.

Less than five miles from England, the army was stopped by an early snowfall that spread a crisp white sheet over the rolling hills of the border country. The *Damainte* found shelter in a ruined byre, burned during an earlier uprising, according to Ewan. Compared to sleeping out in the open on ice-hard ground in a frozen plaid, the miserable shed was luxury itself. Flora had become used to a hard diet of oatcakes and gruel, so when Cu and Gair arrived that evening with half a side of salted mutton, a sack filled with loaves of bread, and even a small keg of ale, she was too delighted to question the source. As she choked down the splendid food, she remembered that the Irish quartermaster had not given the *Damainte* silver for the purchase of food. "Where did these victuals come from?" she asked Cu, half afraid to hear the answer.

Cu, as always, was blunt and honest. "From our enemies, Miss Flora, supporters of the king. The bread they gave us, hoping we'd be content with it. The meat and ale we took for ourselves, behind their backs. Soldiers have to eat, aye, and women and weans, too. We're far from friends and kinsmen here, ye ken, and there's little in the way of game.''

Flora knew he was right, but knowing that the meat was stolen ruined its taste for her, and she had to coax herself to finish her portion. She wondered how Sorley was faring and if he had enough to eat, no matter how it got into his hands. The *Damainte*'s favorite subject of conversation was Sullivan, the quartermaster who was more interested in filling his own belly with ale than feeding the clans. Such ill use didn't bode well for a long campaign. "Wee King Geordie should just have the decency to surrender," Ewan told her more than once. "His defeat is all but written in the stars anyway, and further resistance will do nothing but cause needless suffering."

Late in the afternoon the following day, the *Damainte* were dogging the army under a frowning, dark sky when Flora heard a great roar ahead. The sound made her think of the river by the cave where she had lain in magnificent sin with Sorley. But Ewan had told her of no river and, though a storm was certainly in the offing, the distant thunder did not come from the heavens.

"What is that noise?" she asked Creag, who lumbered along with her and the children, too weary to keep pace with the other men. The ungainly man-mountain laughed when he saw her face.

"Startled, are ye?" he asked. "And well ye might be, Miss Flora. 'Tis the men of Clan Donald and all the other gallant followers of the prince, raising their voices in triumph. That's the border into England they've just been crossing, or I miss my guess. Listen!"

Flora strained her ears and heard the whistling of the wind, just audible over the shouts of the clans. Then the sounds became notes, and she knew it was not the wind after all but the exuberant wail of the pipes, not the orderly martial airs that Flora had heard so often before, but a wild outburst of joy that had happened to take the form of music.

The other *Damainte* heard it, too.

"Over the border!" shouted Seumas.

"Aye, over the border!" thundered Creag. "And down the throat of the Sassenach!"

Before Flora had time to shout "Huzza!" her second family had engulfed her in its wild celebration. Creag, Seumas, and Gair raised their voices to the same pitch as their less disabled kinsmen. The little boys frolicked like pups, Crann began barking, and even Rosmairi threw her arms around Flora and gave her a hesitant kiss on the cheek. "Now mayhap we can gae home," she said.

"Oh, my poor Rosmairi!" Flora began, but she could say no more, for the rest of the *Damainte* had joined their brethren and the merriment grew even louder. The whiskey skin circulated rapidly amid a chaos of laughter and extravagant claims of victory. "We're still hundreds of miles from London!" cried Flora, grabbing Cu by the sleeve as he darted past her. "Where are the English Jacobites the prince spoke of?"

But Cu was so overcome with excitement that he could do nothing but yelp and howl in reply. In Edinburgh, such a man would have been locked up in a hideous cage, Flora thought, or hung as an agent of Satan. She was glad that she no longer lived in that overcivilized city. Though she had no idea what caused Cu to behave the way he did, she

liked him, and the others as well, with their secrets written
on their outsides, as Seumas had said.

Just when Flora decided that she was being entirely too
practical and should give in to her Celtic passions, a shot
shattered the air. Instant silence dropped over the
Damainte, except for the Smalls, who continued to leap
and shout like mad things, and Cu, whose howling had
turned to whining.

"To the devil with you! Brainless lot of cripples, women,
and weans!" Flora had not seen Ewan for hours, but now
he seemed to be everywhere—glaring at her, shoving Cu,
threatening the Three Smalls into a temporary standstill,
and thumping Creag and Seumas on the thigh with the
barrel of his smoking pistol. "What in the name of Jesu,
Bridgit, and the blessed Virgin are you all about? Shut
your nebs! Now!"

The *Damainte* cowered collectively before the wrath of
their master. Even Dughal, who was easily twice as tall as
his chieftain, crossed his arms in front of himself, as if to
blot out Ewan's fury. When she saw that none dared defend
themselves, Flora felt her own temper flare into life inside
her like an ember. How dare the wee creature abuse the
people in his care! "Ewan!" she shouted. "Enough of your
bullying. Your brave folk were rejoicing at the sound of
the pipes and the knowledge that the invasion is under
way."

"Aye, under way," Ewan admitted in his gruffest voice,
which was still sweetly childlike. He shoved Flora's knee,
not enough to hurt her, but merely to demonstrate his
iron authority. "Nearly three hundred miles from London,
two hundred from Loch Linnhe, almost as much to Edinburgh, and as much again to Glenfinnan, where the prince
raised his standard." Ewan stamped about the trail as he
spoke, waving his arms and doing all in his power to look

imposing. "I'd say we're square in the middle of the invasion, and no cause to celebrate anything yet. Once Charlie has his bottom planted on the throne we'll have time enough to shout and drink, but until then, we must show the *sona* that they're not the only ones with discipline. Drop your guard now and you're likely to end up with a ball in your back."

The *Damainte* glanced around the quiet landscape of gentle hills and rock-strewn meadows, searching for phantom riflemen. "But we've defeated Cope's army to the north," Flora continued, "and Cumberland's troops are far to the south. What harm in lifting a dram to the prince?"

"The harm lies in letting a city-bred lass speak for a regiment of fighting men," Ewan snapped. "Now fall in, all you sheepheads, and keep your wits about you." With that he spun around and hobbled off in the direction of the still-triumphant pipes. Flora watched, stunned, as the *Damainte* roused themselves from their stupor and, without a word, resumed their march in the same order as before.

Tears stung Flora's eyes. "Heartless wee cockerel," she muttered, falling in beside Seumas and Rosmairi.

"Nay, mistress," offered Seumas. "Ewan is right. We must no' drop our watch, and he must have order among us. The only reason he behaves so coarsely is because he thinks curses and pistol shots will make him seem bigger. Come, we'll teach you a fine song to take your mind off the long march."

Seumas began singing in Gaelic, in a clear, pure tenor, and Rosmairi soon joined him. She had no trouble remembering lyrics, Flora noted. But the song was as sad as it was incomprehensible to Flora, and it did nothing to lighten her mood. Only the thought that they must soon have word from Lochiel's shadow-man gave her the will to put

one foot ahead of the other. When the *Damainte* crossed
the border a short time later, she would not have taken
heed of it at all had it not been for a fluttering tartan
ribbon, tied to the bare branch of a rowan tree by some
less disciplined Highland soldier.

Chapter Nine

Even amid cold rains and scant provisions, there was no shortage of bravado among the least fortunate of the Jacobite army. As Flora tramped along, she loved to listen to the *Damainte* elaborate on their plans for the future, once the prince was king. They would be heroes, or at least noble veterans, and allowed at last to mingle with the whole and the hale. Seumas and Rosmairi wanted weans, and Ewan sought to petition Lochiel for more land. Cu longed to drove cattle, and a good idea, Creag said, for he would need no dog. The Three Smalls wanted only a safe place to stay, full bellies, and an end to their constant wandering.

They were very simple desires, Flora realized, but how much different from her own? A home, children, some say in how her life would unfold . . . and, of course, her beloved, cleared of the dreadful suspicion Ewan had mistakenly bestowed upon him. A family at last. Surely it was not too much to ask in compensation for a disastrous childhood and scars without and within.

Her first doubts about the fulfillment of her dreams arose one evening when the army was encamped just outside of York, well into England. Flora noticed several Highlanders slipping past the camp of the *Damainte* in a silent, orderly pack. "Where are they going?" she asked Ewan, pointing to the men, who were barely visible in the last glimmer from the setting sun.

Ewan sighed and patted her hand in a kindly way. "I fear, Miss Flora, that they are going home," he said.

"Deserters!" She gasped. Her father had told her of such men, traitors who were routinely hung if apprehended. It was unlikely, however, that the prince could spare any of his men to bring these few to justice. "But why?"

"They miss their families," suggested Ewan, "or else they are just tired, hungry, and cold. Ye ken that not a single soldier has received a penny for his service so far. A ship full of French gold for just that purpose was run aground by three English men-of-war only days ago."

Flora hung her head, ashamed that she knew so little about the hardships of the campaign. "Oh, Ewan! Surely the French king will send more gold and troops as well. The prince's cause depends on France. He's as much as said so himself."

"Aye, aye," said Ewan, tossing a handful of pine twigs into the campfire. "We'll have to see. In the meantime, I expect to spy more lads weary of waiting for their pay."

The army's reception in York was nothing like the false show of encouragement north of the border. Flora and the *Damainte* watched at a distance as citizens fled inside their houses at the first skirl of the pipes. Instead of cheering on the Highland host, the few folk who ventured out unarmed stared slack-jawed at the Highlanders in utter silence. Men stood in their doorways with muskets in their hands, as though they expected the Jacobites to leap upon them like wildcats.

Flora could not understand. "I thought these people supported the prince," she told Cu and Creag.

"Patience, Miss Flora," murmured Cu. "The people of York think of us as beasts, not men."

"You should be speaking," Creag said with a laugh, "you that are a beast, right enough."

"Aye, and you are neither man nor beast, but something the fairies stitched together," Cu replied. "Once we leave this miserable midden, there'll be conscripts galore. The English Jacobites will flock to our banner, for they have no more love for King Geordie than we do."

Flora hoped Cu was right. She knew that some Lowlanders and Englishmen had already joined the cause, lagabouts without steady work, young gentlemen seeking adventure, and others fleeing from the law. But while the Stuart campaign was sport to those men, it was deadly earnest work for the prince, the clan chiefs, and their clansmen.

Suddenly Flora heard the strains of the Cameron march, and knew that Lochiel and his people were passing through the unfriendly city. "Sorley!" she cried. She scanned the distant street for him but could not discern him among the hundreds of Camerons. "Do you see him?" Creag and Cu shook their heads. "Very well. Ewan says we shall see our shadow-man tonight, so I suppose that will be time enough. This time he won't receive a clout on the head, I trust."

She had meant the last words half in jest, but Cu's face betrayed no hint of humor. He peered at Creag from the corners of his eyes, then looked back at Flora. "Faith, that he won't," he said, his voice so void of expression that she could not tell whether he were teasing her or not.

Ewan had been overoptimistic: no emissary came that night. The next day, the *Damainte* plodded through mire as thick as treacle. Flora fell far behind the others. Even Rosmairi, Creag, and the children outdistanced her. When she limped into camp that evening, intent only on trying to find a comfortable spot to sleep, her weary heart gave a jump as she neared the fire. There stood Ewan, deep in conversation with a tall, dark-haired man who sat at ease with his back toward her.

"Sorley Fior!" Flora shouted. Ignoring her exhaustion, she jogged forward, but as she neared the man her spirits plummeted like lead. It wasn't Sorley after all, but an older warrior with dark eyes and brown hair. His long nose had been broken in some quarrel or accident, for it bulged at the bridge and rerouted itself slightly to the left.

The stranger rose and began speaking to Flora in Gaelic, but, at an interjection from Ewan, he swerved immediately into English. "Alas, young sir, I'm not the man you seek. Indeed, I've come to take his place. Alasdair Ard of Caillochie is my name, brother-in-law to our bold Ewan here."

"Take his place!" Flora knew how disappointed she must sound, but she could not disguise her anguish. "Forgive me, but . . . but . . ."

Ewan stepped forward, the firelight playing on his beard and buckskin jacket, and for a moment Flora thought he had in truth issued forth from the flames themselves. "Alasdair, the *shee* must be about tonight, making us mistake one body for another. This is no lad, but one Miss Flora Buchanan. She was forced to take a man's attire and, as we have no other, is forced to continue in it."

"Ah, is it so?" said Alasdair, and would have gone on, but Flora interrupted him. She was not about to let anyone divert her from her course.

"Forgive me, but you just now said that you've taken Sorley's place as our shadow-man," she said. "When will he return? Is he injured? Ill?"

"Mo dhia!" muttered Alasdair. "The last time a woman asked me so many questions, it was after I asked for her hand!"

"Alasdair is our new shadow-man," Ewan explained in a calm voice that was on the very brink of being smug. "Lochiel has decreed it, and *arrah!* 'Tis all for the better, I say. If you would know what's best for you, Miss Flora, you'd not bother your head over that *iargal.*"

Something in the little man's confident manner made Flora feel suspicious. While she understood why Lochiel might have appointed a new liaison after the incident at Selkirk, she did not understand Ewan. Only a few days earlier he had said he would prepare a meeting between her and Sorley; now she thought he might be retracting that promise. She decided to proceed with care. "No doubt you're right. Nevertheless, I must speak with him, if you'll give me leave."

"Aye, why not?" said Ewan, for once shockingly agreeable. "Alasdair, will you give Sorley a message from the lady?"

The tall man nodded. "What am I to tell him?"

Flora opened her mouth, but before she could answer, Ewan did so for her. "Say that it's of utmost importance that Flora speak to him tomorrow evening. Tell him also that he's welcome at the camp of the *Damainte,* provided he behaves himself." As if suddenly recalling that she stood before him, Ewan turned toward her. "I trust that's good enough."

Ewan's mysterious behavior and her own exhaustion left Flora speechless for a moment. Without waiting for her consent, Ewan launched into a long conversation in Gaelic with his new shadow-man, and Flora realized she was being dismissed. It was just as well, she consoled herself, as she was too weary to lecture Ewan on his rudeness. She was becoming used to his sudden shifts in mood, and she reckoned that years of hard living and cruel taunting had hardened the bold wee man.

She fell asleep the moment she curled up among the Three Smalls, but dark dreams plagued her throughout the night. Macinally prowled the shadows of her mind, sometimes turning a kindly face upon her, sometimes tearing her in half with fury. She awoke gasping at the first light of the morning, and some time passed before she managed to cleanse herself of the blood-washed memory.

When she could think straight, she saw that Alasdair had already left. The possibility of seeing Sorley again, of speaking intimately with him and, if she decided to accept his proposal, being intimate with him, filled her with restless yearning. While the *Damainte* still slept, she rose, coaxed the fire into life despite a heavy mist, and set water on to boil for drammock. Her efforts were for naught: the mist became a relentless rain, which woke the *Damainte* and sent them scrambling to construct their flimsy tent.

Once she was snug among Ewan's people, Flora tried to find the sweet sleep that had evaded her during the night, but it refused to come. Part of the cause was the Smalls, who fastened themselves to her like barnacles and, whenever she approached the welcome dark of unconsciousness, would utter just enough words to pull her painfully awake. Finally she became aware that Rattie was demanding something of her. "Show me the sun and the moon again, Miss Flora," he insisted, tugging at her arm.

"Sun and moon?" She had no idea what the child could mean.

"Your bonny timepiece with the arrow," whined the boy.

"He means that compass of Sorley's, I wager," Ewan ventured.

When Flora understood, she gave a weary laugh. "Of course. Do you want to see the arrow move by itself?" The boy nodded, and Flora searched her pockets. She searched them again, her stomach twisting as she realized the truth. "It's gone!"

Hearing her anguish, Rattie spun around and slammed his elbow into Whoreson's forehead. "Damned purse snatch!" he said, with the assurance of someone who knew something about the business. "Ye thieved it again!"

Whoreson battled back with one hand while rubbing his temple with the other. "I did naething!" he piped. His eyes were round and startled, and Flora thought he was telling the truth. But if so, where was Sorley's compass?

"Rattie! Leave him be!" she admonished the furious urchin.

"Doubtless you dropped it in the mire," Seumas said, and suddenly all the *Damainte* began to express their opinions on the whereabouts of Sorley's love token all at once. Even Gair added his incomprehensible advice, rattling off the names of a score of towns in Scotland and abroad. In the midst of this chaos, a black foreboding washed over Flora, and she fought to hold back tears.

Ewan glanced at her face, then roared and clapped his hands to restore peace. At last the tide of speculation abated. "Miss Flora, if Whoreson is the thief, we'll soon find him out," said the dwarf. The boy went dead white in the face at this, but when Flora questioned Ewan, he merely told her to wait for the storm to pass.

It was a long, heartsick wait for Flora. Some time past

noon the clouds broke and the wan sun made a brief appearance, raising Flora's hopes ever so slightly. Whoreson bolted for freedom the moment he wriggled out of the shelter, only to be chased down by fleet-footed Losgann and dragged back to the *Damainte,* bawling like a calf. Ewan called out a few words in Gaelic and motioned to Dughal. The giant hesitated, then stooped down, gripped Whoreson by the ankles, and whipped the lad upside down.

"Put him down!" screamed Flora, but she soon saw that the purpose of Whoreson's suspension was not to terrorize him, only to reveal his guilt or innocence. Dughal gave the boy a shake, and baubles began to cascade from the child's clothing. Flora recognized a tortoiseshell comb of Rosmairi's, two silver coins probably from Ewan's sporran, Gair's tobacco pouch, a roebuck's hoof that Cu carried for good luck, and various stones, sticks, and other worthless odds and ends. But no compass.

Seumas and Rattie helped Flora comb the camp up and down, but they discovered nothing. The compass was well and truly gone. Flora felt as if a piece of her heart had been hacked off and cast away. She tried to console herself with the thought that Alasdair would send Sorley to her, but even that knowledge could not dispel the inexplicable sense of doom that had visited her in the tent and now settled upon her like an evil odor. Long after the *Damainte* had broken camp, she continued to search her pockets. Though she knew she'd find nothing, she longed to believe that she could somehow lure back the compass, and its owner along with it.

The clans marched on through land burned black by Royalist farmers. Not a sheaf of oats or a handful of barley survived. But the prince encountered no other opposition.

Ewan explained the reason to Flora as they tramped along side by side: the Duke of Cumberland had clustered his army just outside of London in a protective embrace, unsure, perhaps, of the size of the Highland host.

Flora stiffened but kept walking. She had no idea how large Cumberland's force was, though she knew it must be superior to the prince's. Since she'd crossed the border, the invasion had ceased to be a noble adventure and had become little more than a numbing cycle of exhausting marches, bitterly cold nights, and aching hunger. It was a dream unraveled at its edges, exposing a nightmare underneath.

Macinally. The thought of him made her clasp her hand over her torn bosom. She would never be rid of him. Instead she carried the evil he had caused her around with her like a rotting carcass. Might he somehow be responsible for her situation now, perhaps even for the fragile state of the campaign? The thought was preposterous, she chided herself. If her life were in jeopardy, it was she who had made the decision, not some monster from her past. If only she could believe in Sorley's love, she might be able to put Macinally behind her forever.

Flora bore the hardships of the march in taut silence, but she could not bear the suffering of her second family. Their meager supply of grain was nearly depleted, and once she had seen the Three Smalls roasting mice that Crann had caught in his jaws. Nor was hunger the only menace. Rosmairi disappeared more often now, and Seumas had more difficulty finding her. Creag lagged farther and farther behind the others, his breathing labored and loud. Flora could not shift her sight from Whoreson, Bugger, and Rattie for a moment lest they strike off alone, perhaps toward the Jacobite lines, perhaps back toward the border, as their distracted spirits moved them. Once she found them lying together like a litter of puppies, asleep on a riverbank, inches from the freezing water.

"You'll be the death of the lads yet," she chastised Ewan one frosty morning as the icy wind whipped through her plaid and chilled her to the quick. "Perhaps the prince's soldiers can endure this treatment, but I assure you, all your people cannot. If you have half a heart in your breast, you'll send Rosmairi, Creag, and the Smalls back where they came from."

But Ewan was used to taking hard stands. "Why? So they may be despised and rejected by their people?" he said. "You'll notice it's not they who are complaining. Faith, they'll be going through worse than this before our wee jaunt is finished."

He paused, looking her up and down, and when he spoke again his voice was softer. "Mistress, you're not like the rest of us. You've got wits and beauty galore and, unless you take to wearing courtly clothing, no disfigurement to speak of. You can have a proper life, if you choose to. Say but the word and I'll have Cu see you safely back to Dunedin or Perth or wherever you wish."

His concern moved Flora. "Thank you, but I'm in it now. Besides, who would look after the little lads were I to leave?"

Ewan shook his head. Suddenly he seized her hand and caressed her fingers. "As strong as you are beautiful, I see. If only that creature Sorley hadn't enchanted you so." He turned such a luminous smile upon her that she was struck by just how handsome he might have been, had fate not stunted him. A charming, irritating fellow, to be sure, who sometimes seemed to tolerate her, and sometimes seemed to adulate her.

"I cannot wed you," she said. "Neither now nor later."

Devil take it! She hadn't meant to speak aloud, but now

her intentions meant nothing. She'd thrown her dart and it had hit home. Ewan's smile went out like a flame. He dropped her hand. "I'll never wed, as you well know. Now be of some use, mistress, and find those three weans. They're doubtless in London by now." He fairly ran from her, and Flora wondered: had she seen tears glinting in his eyes? Bold, self-sufficient Ewan, that defiant rooster of a man—he couldn't be in love with her. He couldn't. For if he were, he'd never be satisfied with mere friendship, while she would do anything to retain it.

The thought rankled in her as she collected Crann and set out over the desolate fields still spotted with ashes and char. "Seek, seek," she encouraged the dog. "Good lad! Seek Rattie!"

Crann shuffled ahead of her, sniffing at the barren earth. Ahead of him lay a small grove of gaunt birch trees, some still clinging to the remnants of their yellow autumn splendor, and it was to this grove that Crann trotted, as straight and true as the needle of a compass. The compass! Again she patted all her pockets, pulling them inside out while she ran after the hound. Of course she couldn't find the compass. And yet . . .

"Son! Bug! Rattie!" she called.

Crann darted toward the trees and in an instant disappeared among their pied trunks. As she neared the willow-scented grove, Flora froze. A patch of black and red tartan flashed among the birches, then vanished.

"Miss Flora!"

Rattie's hoarse voice floated in the chill air like a banner. The sound brought Flora back to life. Had she imagined the tartan? Perhaps it was only the sunlight playing on the birch bark. She rushed into the confusion of trees, brushing aside leafless branches and brambles. The trees gave way to a clearing, and in it Flora found the prodigal boys perched on a crumbling log. All three gnawed on chunks of bread but looked up when they saw her, their faces glistening with butter. Then they looked past her.

"Miss Flora."

She whirled around so fast that she frightened the dog. There stood her beloved Sorley, his hands on his hips, his head reared back.

"My dearest!" Flora cried, forgetting for the moment about the children behind her. Her chest tightened, and she felt her heart might burst from her rib cage. How she had missed him. Even she had not anticipated the joy that rose up within her at the sight of the powerful Gael and his unearthly eyes. His face, bronzed by the wind, was framed by wild black waves of hair far longer than she remembered. Although he was leaner than when they'd first met, he still held himself with the confidence of a stag stealing up behind a hunter. Only his expression worried her, part thoughtful, part troubled. It held her back, preventing her from running up to him and clasping his middle. "Oh, Sorley! It does me good to see ye again." She had thought he had deserted her, as so many had before, but she had been wrong. "Alasdair spoke with ye, I see."

"Alasdair?" Sorley crossed his arms in front of him and nodded at the boys, who stared back at him. "I must have a word with you, but not before spectators. You lads!" The Smalls raised their heads from their food but kept on chewing. "Can you find your way back to the *Damainte* without guidance?" Whoreson nodded, then Bugger, and finally Rattie.

"They can follow my footprints in the field," Flora suggested, gladdened by the thought of having Sorley to herself. "My tracks are clear to see."

"Did you hear Miss Flora?" Sorley shouted to the boys,

waving one arm in the direction of the camp. "Away with you! And tell no one you saw either of us, or I'll come after you and take back my bread."

Clutching their precious morsels against their chests, the three jumped up from the log and sprinted out of the clearing. As she watched them, Flora slowly realized that Sorley had used the bread to lure the boys into the grove. No doubt he'd used the boys to lure her to him as well.

Crann loped past her after the Smalls, but stopped at the edge of the clearing, sat down, and gazed at her with watchful adoration. He's guarding me, she thought. Even Crann did not trust the Highlander.

"You say you're glad to see me," Sorley said, still not making the slightest move toward her. "But by your other actions, I assume you mean the opposite. You're as confusing as you are bewitching, Miss Buchanan, and I dearly hope that you can scrape the muck from the water so I can see clearly how things stand between us."

Flora felt dread rise up within her like smoke. Her fingertips went numb. She thrust her trembling hands behind her back lest they expose her fear. "I . . . I know not what to make of this cold greeting, my love," she began. "I'm sorry to have caused you confusion, but I never intended to. Perhaps you misunderstood something Alasdair Ard said to you."

"I doubt that," he said, his scowl deepening, "for he said naught to me at all."

"What? Nothing?" The doubts that had been lingering inside Flora burst forth into full flame. She felt her face begin to burn. Her hands grew moist. "But I told him to arrange a meeting between us. Did you receive no word from me at all?"

Without shifting his eyes from her, Sorley rummaged in his sporran and drew out an object, which lay hidden in his hand. "Only this." He walked toward her until he was only a few steps away, then stopped and stretched out his arm before her. There in his broad palm lay his compass, snapped shut, the beseeching face of the moon staring up at her.

"God in heaven!" Flora ran her finger over the hard brass to assure herself of its existence. "How did you come by it?"

With a sharp jerk of his hand Sorley tore the compass from her. "Bad enough you spurn me, mistress, without also playing me for a fool. You know full well that you gave Alasdair the compass to return to me. That should have been the end of it, but the thought of not seeing you again fair ate the heart out of my body. I tempted the boys away, knowing you would follow, but now I'm not certain what to think."

"Sorley . . ." Flora felt a tear trickle down her cheek. "I lost the compass some time ago. I never sent it back to you, I swear it. Ye must believe me." Afraid to breathe, she held out her hand to him. Only when he gripped it did she sigh in relief.

"I believe you, Miss Flora," Sorley said. "But if that's so, then someone has deceived us." His voice simmered with an anger he could control but not conceal. "And I know only one man who's short enough to go that low."

"You cannot mean Ewan Fada," Flora said. "He's your rival, of course, but he's my good friend as well."

"Aye, good enough to protect you from a *bogiel* such as me, I ween," said Sorley. "Consider it well. Who else would wish to keep us apart?"

"Why, no one." The canny dwarf knew the power the compass held and had had a thousand opportunities to lift it from her. But what a monstrous deception! If he were the culprit, she didn't know if she would be able to trust him again. "He's terribly jealous of you, it's true," she conceded.

"He's never accepted Aimil's death, nor the fact that I was her husband." Gently he pulled her toward him and slipped the compass into her hand. "Enough of that half-penny, now that we've wriggled out of his snare. Say you'll have me, my beautiful Flora," he murmured into her ear. "I'm a patient man, but I can't restrain myself from wanting you." He fingered her golden curls, which had grown longer over the course of the campaign and even more riotous than before. "This time I'll allow you to keep your hair."

Flora chuckled, although Ewan's accusation began to flutter against the walls of her mind like a bothersome insect. She had just resolved to lay the damning question before Sorley when he gathered her against his massive chest and brushed his face against hers. His salty scent burned in her nostrils. All her intentions disappeared in a flood of passion so intense that it crushed every memory of her past and future. Flora Buchanan existed only in the one iridescent moment of time that had cast her into Sorley's arms.

Hungrily he pressed his lips to hers and devoured her. The last stirrings of propriety flamed briefly within her. Flora pulled away a moment, then returned his kisses with all the love that had been smoldering inside her throughout the long march south. Sorley was hers; she was his. At last she would have a husband of her own choosing, a man who sought neither to conquer her nor to keep her as a pet. If she had lost her virtue, then she would regain it through her love for Sorley. They would become man and wife, provide a home for the boys, have children of their own. . . .

Flora stroked Sorley's throat, delighting in the softness

of his skin, until nothing but her love for the man filled her mind and soul. Fiercely aware of what she was doing and without apologies for it, Flora tugged on Sorley's belt. But instead of stripping off his plaid, Sorley bent down, lifted Flora in his arms as easily as he might have picked up a lamb, and carried her to a nearby birch. Standing once more on the ground, Flora looked up at the Highlander. With her back pressed hard against the leathery tree trunk and her belly straining against Himself, they were as close as man and woman could be without coupling. The skin of his bare arms was hot and clammy, and she was certain it was love that stoked the fire within him. The same flames were racing up and down her own arms, her legs, her entire body, and she wondered that she was not reduced to ashes on the spot. "As God is in heaven, I will be your wife, Sorley Fior. How could I live without you?"

"Or I without you?" he murmured. "Will you take me, here and now?"

Aye, aye, oh, aye, my love, thought Flora. "I will. And our marriage?" she whispered.

"Afterward. You're as good as wed, I swear it." His huge hands encased her breasts, then with aching deliberation inched their way down her ribs to her waist. Flora felt his long, strong fingers undo the top buttons of her breeches. Her body convulsed with desire. Suddenly an exquisite wave of pleasure coursed through her as Sorley nudged against her, parted her, and thrust inside her.

Flora moaned as Sorley worked himself back and forth within her. He was a potter, and she clay. He could mold her pleasure any way he wished. Sometimes with hard, quick thrusts. Sometimes slowly, languorously, taking her up to the very point of paradise, then stopping, letting her subside, and easing her back down into another round of delicious, sensuous pleasures. At one point, when he rubbed his bewhiskered cheek against her neck, she found herself laughing deep in her throat.

"It's grand to see you're enjoying yourself," he murmured, his smile as broad as it was sincere.

"I have never . . . never been so happy."

Happiness. She rarely thought about it. Now, in Sorley's arms, with her body exulting in its freedom, she knew what it was like to love. To be loved.

Sorley raised Flora's blouse, exposing her small, taut breasts. He brought his mouth down over one, then the other. His tongue washed around her nipples, then over them, then over the red scar above them. Ecstasy exploded over her body. She felt herself go rigid, and for a moment, or perhaps much longer, she hung suspended in a pulsating web of rapture. Sorley flinched. She knew, in a distant but reassuring way, that he too had fallen prey to the power of their love.

He was the first to speak, in a gentle voice she'd never heard him use before, even in the cave by the river. "Oh, my Flora! *A'graidh!* How I love you! And not for this moment, I assure you. As long as there is a piece of Sorley Fior's heart somewhere, deep in the earth or under the sea, you'll be locked within it."

Flora laughed and gave his nose a gentle tweak. His words had touched her, but she couldn't resist teasing him. "I didn't know I was marrying a poet."

"Have no fear of that." He grinned. "Ask Ewan Fada about my talent with words, or any other good point I might have. He'll set you right. *Dia!* All the time we were parted I prayed to the Almighty that he hadn't succeeded in turning you against me."

With sudden urgency Ewan's bothersome midge of an accusation began to hum and thrum inside Flora's head again. She tried to smother it with the thought of Sorley's love, but it would not let her be. "He was wrong about you, dearest," she murmured. She cupped his face in her hands. If only she could look him squarely in the eyes, she would see the truth shining in them. "I didn't think him capable of so vile a lie. Desperation will drive a man to sin, I suppose."

Sorley's hands froze on her hips, then slowly trailed over her bottom, forcing their way between her and the birch. Without thinking she pressed herself against him. "What vile lie is this, my calf? Let me put it to rest and clear my honor, before you entice me astray again."

"Ewan says that . . . that . . . oh, 'tis too shameful to say aloud!" Flora dropped her voice to the barest shadow of a whisper, but even then it was difficult to form the damning words. "Oh, my love! Ewan accused you of . . . of killing your wife."

Sorley said nothing, only stared at her with burning eyes. She was about to repeat herself when he kissed her into silence. "He told you the truth," he said. "It's no less than you deserve. I did kill Aimil."

A moment earlier her body had been molten silver; now Flora felt her flesh turn as rigid as iron. Nausea gripped her stomach. Sorley looked as if he were standing behind a pane of glass that had been struck with a hammer. She pawed desperately at her world, trying to keep it from disintegrating. "Ye . . . ye didn't kill her," she stammered. "Ye couldn't have killed her."

"I did, my heart. I can explain it."

Slivers of her shattered happiness began to fall away, revealing a dark void underneath. Frantic now, she searched for a way to make sense of Sorley's confession. "A mishap?" she asked, digging her spine against the birch so hard that its bark crackled.

His gaze slashed across her face as he looked at her, then away, then back again. "Nay, *m'chreidh,*" he said, his voice cracking with grief. "It was no mishap."

The terror caused by these few words tore something loose from Flora's heart and mind. A flash of pure white light obliterated her vision, and in that flash she saw herself, just seven years old.

She was hiding behind a filigreed pillar near the head of the stairs in the stately house she used to share with her parents. It was a beautiful summer evening, and a fresh breeze from an open window blew through her hair.

Her father and mother stood arguing only a few feet from her, as they often did. But something was very, very wrong. Her mother wasn't weeping and her father wasn't bellowing. He was begging, pleading, sobbing, and he did not look like a man any longer but like a little boy whose dog had died. Suddenly her mother slapped her father. His sobs stopped. His arm swept out and connected with his wife's head. There was a small cry, then the sound of a stick snapping. Flora saw red spray fly from her mother's face and spatter in a thousand scarlet specks against the dark woodwork. Her mother pitched backward and disappeared down the stairs. Flora heard thumping sounds that seemed to last forever. Then silence. She waited for her mother to come up. Her father left. She waited. She waited until the larks began to sing and the morning light illuminated the scarlet spots on the wall. Her mother never came up.

Panic clutched at her. She couldn't move, could scarcely breathe. "Murderer!" she cried. "He killed her! You killed her!"

Sorley said something, but Flora could not hear him, only saw his mouth opening and closing, as if he were eating her alive. Her mother had died. Aimil had died. And she herself had been deceived. But she would fight to save herself, just as the *Damainte* fought every day to survive, just as the prince fought to reclaim his throne. Just as her mother had fought to leave her father.

Murderer! The thought gave Flora strength. She threw herself against Sorley's chest. The startled man leaped backward with the agility of a skilled swordsman, whipped his arm forward and snagged her elbow. "Murderer!" screamed Flora. "You'll not slay me!" Was it her father that stood before her or the Highlander? The two men looked alike to her now. She knew only that she had to free herself, or she too would suffer her mother's fate. She lunged forward. Her nails sank into the soft flesh of the man's neck.

"Dia!" Sorley yelped. Flora twisted herself free from his grasp and began to blunder forward. She had seen it she had seen it she had seen it. If only she hadn't seen it! If only she hadn't remembered it! If only it hadn't happened!

Sorley was on her at once. He pulled her to a stop and wrestled her to the earth. "A short life to you!" he said. "Hear me out, woman!"

"Murderer! Leave me be!" Flora struggled to rise, but the Highlander pinned her flat on her back, loomed over her, and stared down at her with his blazing, mismatched eyes. Angry tears blurred her vision. When Sorley reached out to brush them from her face, she shrieked like a child wakened by terrors in the night. The touch that had delighted her only moments earlier now repulsed her. Those very hands, so powerful and slender, had crushed the life out of an ailing woman.

She heard a bark, then a growl. A shaggy black bolt of lightning slammed into Sorley's shoulder. The man cried out. He toppled onto the ground beside her, his arms over his face to protect himself from the snapping hound.

She was free! Flora leaped upright.

"Stay!" cried Sorley. "You mustn't go! We're fated to be together, you and I!"

Flora hesitated. Her mind cleared, and she saw Crann in front of her, snarling like a rabid wolf. Before him stood Sorley. Whenever the Gael moved toward Flora, the dog bayed ferociously until the man stepped back.

Though some part of Flora wanted to return to him and lock her arms around him, a larger part of her despised him. "Once a rogue, always a rogue," she said. Just like her father. "I'll have none of you." Raising her fist to shake it at the Highlander, she stopped. Sorley's compass still burned like a golden flame ensconced in her sweating hand. She cried out at the sight of it and flung it from her as if it were a live coal. Certain that demons raced behind her breathing hellfire on her back, she ran from the grove.

Chapter Ten

Terror drove Flora heedlessly onward, and it wasn't until she returned to the safety of the *Damainte* that she stopped running. The resurrected memory of her mother's death still shocked her, but it no longer paralyzed her.

Several of Ewan's people trotted up to her, calling out to her in relief and concern. "By the holy rood," said Seumas, crossing himself with his good hand, as he approached her, "you're after coming back at last. I was a step away from hunting you down myself. The clans have already marched on."

"What happened to you, mistress?" asked Rosmairi, and through her heartache Flora sensed that the woman harbored some memory of her.

"You've been weeping," Creag observed. "And *arrah!* Your clothes!"

Flora looked down at her billowing shirt, sagging trews, and rumpled jacket. They had become soiled and threadbare over the course of the campaign, but she hadn't realized until that moment that her embrace with Sorley had left her nearly indecent. Dragging one tattered sleeve across her tear-streaked face, she drew a deep breath and, with great effort, pushed thoughts of Sorley and her mother's death to the edge of her consciousness, where they lay oddly intertwined. "I . . . I took a fall," she said, ashamed of the lie but just as ashamed of the truth.

"In more ways than one, I'll wager." It was Ewan. The dwarf swaggered up behind her, but the moment he saw her face his mood changed entirely, and if he'd had any notion of berating her, he dropped it at once. "Forgive me, Miss Flora," he said, subdued by her sorrow. "I know you've suffered much for the sake of that seducer. Only tell me, are you done with him at last?"

Flora nodded. "You were right in what you said."

"I'm always right," piped Ewan. "You'll see. You'll be much the better for your decision." He was so pleased he gave a laugh as clipped off as he was. How dared he be cheerful in the face of her pain, thought Flora, but she said nothing. "Now hurry, all of you half-wits, and prepare to leave," Ewan continued. "Derby lies only a hundred miles south, and London only two hundred miles beyond that."

London? So close? Flora wondered as she tried to straighten her disreputable clothing. The prince's soldiers were so starved and weary she wasn't certain they could reach Derby, let alone the teeming heart of the nation. And if they did, what then? Victory or disaster, of course, she answered herself. But in either case, the prince's quest was surely coming to a close. And when that happened, what would become of her? With Sorley gone, she was just as lost as before, not only without love but, what was worse, without means of support.

Except for Capt. Henry Stelton. She had all but forgotten him, and hoped one day to blot out his memory entirely. Marriage to him would be worse than a life in the stews, which, she reflected grimly, was also a possibility. Then there was Ewan, although he had in truth never asked for her hand and was honor-bound not to do so. Faced with such prospects, she decided never to marry. She'd return to the convent, if the sisters would consent to take her in. But then what would happen to Whoreson, Bugger, and Rattie? *That murderer!* He'd caused so much misery! She hoped she still didn't love him.

Crann did not return until evening, his coat bristling with mud and briers. He whimpered with hunger and exhaustion, and Flora guessed he had held Sorley at bay for some time. She patted and praised the animal for rescuing her, but all the while searched his muzzle and fangs for traces of blood. When she found none, she did not know whether to be elated or disappointed.

That night the *Damainte* were fortunate to find a farmhouse abandoned by its owners. One wall and part of the roof had been destroyed by fire. By all rights, the rest of the building should have fallen, but it still stood upright. To Flora, it appeared as though the structure simply lacked the energy to take its one last step into annihilation. Several ragged soldiers of Clan Donald had holed up in the ruin before the arrival of the *Damainte,* but with a great show of courtesy they allowed their accursed brothers-in-arms to curl up in one section of the house, provided they kept their distance.

The air was as cold as a bare blade, and even Flora's thick plaid could not keep it out entirely. While the charred rafters creaked and moaned above her, she tried to sleep, but horrible images plagued her mind. Macinally. Her father's sweeping arm. The sound of a breaking stick. The paneling spotted with blood. And Sorley's face, distorted with anger, glaring down at her.

Whenever she imagined him holding her, tears flooded her eyes and sobs threatened to tear her apart. How she missed him! But he was a cold-blooded murderer, as Ewan had said, and she was lucky to be free of him. Her mother had not been so lucky.

But Flora's luck had brought her nothing but pain. She wept into her plaid, so as not to disturb the others, but sometime during the night she sensed a warm presence creep up beside her. In the dim light from the remains of the MacDonalds' fire she saw Gair frowning at her, his bloodred locks straggling over his eyes like withered grass. For a moment she thought that she had awakened him; then she recollected that he was on watch. "The Irish say that King Connachar lost his beloved wife," he whispered. "It grieved him sore. Seven years he mourned for her."

Flora smiled, dabbing at her tears with her plaid. It was the closest she had ever heard Gair come to making sense. Despite her sorrow, his tenderness touched her. "My friend, thanks for your concern, but there's naught you can do. It's a hard thought, you and the others losing sleep over my sniffling, isn't it?"

"I don't give it a thought," Gair murmured, "but I can't speak for the rest."

"Gair?" Flora sat up, thoughts of Sorley suddenly less important than the miracle before her. "Do ye ken what ye just said?" She gasped.

The man drew back, his face masked by his usual look of puzzlement. He began to chatter wildly in Gaelic, then stuttered a bit as he changed into English. "What it is . . . is was what it was," he declared at last. "When the day sleeps, it breathes the darkness."

"Gair, Gair, list to me!" She grabbed his callused hand

in hers. "Just now ye said something and I understood you." He stared at her, dumbstruck, and she wondered how she might once more dispel the mists that shrouded his mind. "Tell me your name, your proper name."

Gair looked about the decrepit cottage, as if he thought the answer to her question might be hidden in its crumbling walls. At last he scrabbled backward, trembling in desperation. "Twelve crows over the house in flight nowhere *cluich na clarsaich,*" he cried out, once again a victim of his chaotic mind.

"Hold yer whisht!" shouted one of the MacDonalds wakened by their exchange.

Before Flora could stop Gair, he whirled away from her into the shadows and outside into the cold. Flora rose to her knees, considered following him, then sank back down on her bed of musty straw. Even if she found him, which alone would be an act of Providence, he would be in no condition to attempt rational speech again. Something she said had pierced the darkness of his mind—but what? A word, a phrase? Perhaps her tone of voice. She remembered only speaking words of assurance, as she might to a beloved child.

Gair's unexplained burst of coherence would not let Flora sleep. She devised half a dozen theories on how to unlock the man's secret, but in the end discarded them all. Life had failed her in so many ways. It had torn her virtue from her, driven her from her home, and destroyed the one love she had hoped to hold forever. It was hard to make sense of such a life or the mysterious Highlander who had captured her heart and smashed it to pieces just as easily.

But no matter how hard her life had been, she could not simply stop living. No, she must survive and do the best she could, for herself and those who depended on her. She would discover the key to Gair's sanity and try to provide for him, as she intended to provide for the boys. Her mother would have wanted it so.

The fire had died out completely by the time Flora fell asleep. Moments later, or so she thought, angry shouts woke her. She sat up to behold Ewan and Seumas standing in the open area created by the missing wall, waving their weapons and heaping curses on someone Flora could not see. "What's amiss?" she said, running up to Ewan. What she saw made her snap her mouth shut in surprise. Before her lay a world white with snow so deep that several spruce trees in the distance looked like white spear tips. Through the persistent snowfall, she could just make out the figures of five or six men stumbling toward the trees. "Who . . . ?" she began, but the word hung by itself in the frozen air.

"The damnable sons of Clan Donald, those who spent the night with us," said the dwarf. He drove his dirk into a burned board in impotent anger. "They're deserting the prince, going back to their homes."

Flora nodded at the sparkling wasteland before her. "Six men will make no difference one way or the other to His Majesty," she said. "But the snow . . . the clans will freeze."

"They'll manage," Ewan said, as though he did not quite believe himself. "They must." He sighed, gave a long look at the disappearing MacDonalds, then freed his dirk and sheathed it. "We cannot give up, not now that we've come this close, with King Geordie pishing in his breeks. There's not a man here whose heart wouldn't break like a week-old bannock if we were to turn back. The prince must go forward, and the *Damainte* with him."

The people in question, roused from their sleep by Ewan's protests, gave a feeble shout of approval. Flora couldn't help but admire them. There was no doubt they were among the prince's most devoted fighters. On the other hand, such devotion might well cost them their lives. This was bad enough for Ewan, Cu, Creag, and the others who understood the risk. But Dughal, Rosmairi, and the Smalls had no idea that at some point in the next few weeks they would in all likelihood be at the mercy of twenty thousand well-trained, well-fed troopers. She tried not to think of Sorley, who would stand at his chief's side, in the front ranks, when the two armies finally clashed.

Gair, shivering in a corner by himself, caught Flora's attention and made her remember the miracle of the night before. She told Ewan what had transpired, but his reaction disappointed her. "I told you that the man speaks sense on rare occasions," he said with an impatient wave of his hand. "Indeed, 'twould be better if he were always daft. Then we would know what to expect from him."

"I expect nothing of anyone," she said.

"Once you did," Ewan reminded her.

Flora grimaced. She remembered the feel of Sorley's lips on hers, the dear touch of his hands on her scar. She also recalled the sickness she had felt when he had revealed the truth about Aimil's death. "I was in error," she admitted.

When the snow abated, Ewan, Cu, and Seumas braved the cold to receive their orders from Alasdair Ard. As she waited, Flora helped Rosmairi search the house for food. They soon discovered that the MacDonalds had been obliged to leave behind an iron pot full of suet, a large sack stuffed with rock-hard, worm-eaten biscuits, and a salted ham. Pig meat, Creag explained, wasn't considered fit for eating in the Highlands, and neither he nor Losgann would set tooth on it, though both were listless with hunger. Flora soaked the bread in hot water to soften it, then fried it in fat and served it to the grateful Gaels. The meat she gave to Dughal Rosmairi and the boys, who didn't hesitate

to devour it. Gair ate nothing. Flora contented herself with
the scraps, which she shared with Crann. "It's just as well
Mrs. Leckie doesn't know her 'puir lambie' is eating this
muck," she told the dog. "She'd throw it on the midden
heap, and then what would we do, eh?"

When Ewan returned, he brought dire news with him.
They were to set out that very moment, as the prince hoped
to reach Derby by nightfall, at least with his advance troops.
Flora was loath to give up the meager comforts of their
temporary home for the forbidding fields of snow and ice,
but she knew she had no choice. She was less worried for
her own sake than for that of the boys, whom she feared
might sink into a drift or fall asleep in the snow, never to
waken. The best she could do was to swaddle the children's
worn shoes in rags to protect their feet from the cruel ice
and to persuade Ewan to let Rattie ride on Dughal's broad
shoulders.

Flora could remember nothing to match the march to
Derby for sheer exhaustion. At first she cursed the frosty
wind that stung her hands and the ice that slowed her
pace, but when the sun came out at last, the true ordeal
began. The blanket of snow melted, turning paths, fields,
and highways alike into a boggy soup of mud and water.
Sharp stones jabbed through her tattered brogues and
bruised her feet. Her wet breeches stuck to her thighs and
chafed her skin until she bled. Briefly she wondered how
Sorley was faring, then tried to forget she had had such a
thought. How could she have ever loved a man who had
murdered his wife?

Flora clamped her teeth together and plodded on
through the mire. If she survived this trial, she told herself,
she would acquire a dozen frocks of the best satin and

brocade, and never again wear men's garments, including the belted plaids of the Highlanders. While these were comfortable enough, they invited indecency at every turn. She was in awe of Rosmairi, who had difficulty recalling her husband's name but could readily identify his bare bottom.

To distract herself from her misery, Flora sought out Gair and tried to converse with him. She couldn't accept the notion that his moments of lucidity were mere coincidence. Even if she failed to repeat her triumph of the night before, she reasoned, her efforts had some reward. Gair was above all a polite speaker, and returned all her questions with charming, poetic madness.

That night the *Damainte* slept out in the open, soaked by rain and mist, but after a short march in the morning Flora finally saw the tidy whitewashed houses of Derby. She nearly leaped out of her skin with excitement. Creag and Gair, in back with the women and weans as usual, were just as enthusiastic. "Less than two hundred miles from London," Creag assured Flora, "yet there's not so much as a hair of General Cumberland or his fine army."

"With good reason," Flora said, shivering despite the plaid wrapped all around her like a tartan cocoon. "They'd have to be daft to set out in weather like this, wouldn't they?"

"Aye, daft or desperate," Gair answered.

"Gair!" cried Flora. She grabbed Creag's dripping sleeve. "Did you hear him?"

"I did indeed," Creag said, "but we're not likely to hear any more sense from him for some time, I'm thinking." He reached up and gently cradled Gair's face in his fissured hands. "What is your clan, man? Can ye speak its name? Use all your wits, man. Say it!"

"Say *saighe* sail slay *slainte!*" The words tumbled from

Gair's lips like pebbles rattling down a hillside. Tears shimmered in his eyes, and Flora suddenly became aware of the depths of his frustration. She remembered lying on her bed after her violation, terrified and mute. Perhaps, in Gair's case, it was better to leave well enough alone, as Ewan had suggested, than to tax a tired, half-starved man beyond his limit. Gair and Creag seemed to agree with her, for they said nothing more, only trudged on toward Derby in the tracks of the clans. This time, however, Flora did not forget the question that Gair had answered.

As the army poured into the town, Flora felt as though she were passing through a kirkyard. The thought unnerved her, especially since the incident in the birch grove still echoed in her mind like her frightening but unforgettable memories. Derby's inhabitants had either left the town or barricaded themselves in their houses, and the street was all but deserted.

The prince halted his forces at the edge of the village and commandeered a large house for his headquarters. Since the *Damainte* were no longer needed in the rear, Ewan sought to take refuge with a contingent of his own clansmen, led by none other than Alasdair Ard. Flora bridled when she heard the man's name, then resigned herself to Ewan's decision. Perhaps she should even be thankful to both men for saving her from her own headstrong passions. Weary beyond measure, Flora followed Ewan, Cu, and Losgann toward the cottage that the Camerons had commandeered, while the Smalls stumbled along at her heels.

"Halt there, you devils!" A guard brandishing a flintlock rifle stalked toward them. "Go back to hell where you came from! Would you bring a curse down on all of us?"

Flora's fatigue vanished. Although the fellow might have been Ewan's clansman, he was still a threat. She stopped dead, shooed the boys back into Rosmairi's arms, and stood like a shield in front of all four innocents, her arms outstretched. "Ewan!" she called out to the little man, but he didn't even slacken his pace. He strode up to the sentry shouting in Gaelic, and the two began a rather loud discussion in that dramatic tongue, punctuated with snorts and growls and the occasional shake of a fist. Flora understood only that the guard was far more frightened of the *Damainte* than they were of him.

A few Camerons ventured out of the house and joined the confrontation. A whiskey skin materialized from someone's plaid and circulated among the group. Flora waited, hardly daring to draw a deep breath, while Ewan and his clansmen exchanged muttered words that might have been threats as easily as pleasantries, for all Flora knew. When she looked behind her to see how the *Damainte* were faring in the face of such precarious negotiations, she was amazed to see that nearly every one of her second family, including the three urchins, bore an expression of benevolent boredom. Only Dughal paced about nervously, unable to comprehend what was happening. Ewan's people were used to such welcomes, Flora thought, but she was not.

At last the Camerons broke away and headed back toward their headquarters, the guard shaking his head and the others laughing and bantering with each other. Ewan drew himself up proudly and waved his arm in a careless fashion, as if he wanted his followers to understand that he feared nothing. "Come along, then," he called. "For what are you waiting? A piper to pipe you into camp? Step out, muttonheads!"

The *Damainte* dragged themselves forward. Flora, still somewhat rattled by the experience, was swept up among them. "Are we welcome here or no'?" she asked Ewan, when she at last caught up with him.

"As welcome as we accursed folk are welcome any-where," Ewan answered with a grim smile. "Come, mis-tress, and take your ease. These are decent gentlemen, and devil the man will harm any of us."

She recalled that once, long ago, Ewan had feared she'd be molested if she visited the prince's army. Apparently Clan Cameron could be trusted.

The soldiers neither welcomed the *Damainte* nor taunted them, but accepted them much the same as they might accept bad weather. She guessed that most of the warriors were too exhausted to fret about the ill luck that was said to surround her unfortunate friends, or else they had con-sumed so much malt whiskey that they had ceased to care about it.

The Camerons made a fine bonfire outside and crouched around it, laughing and spinning yarns. Flora, sitting among the *Damainte* just beyond the searing blaze, listened intently. By all rights, she thought, the Cameron soldiers should have been cursing their lives, and most probably that of the prince, but no, they seemed content enough. They even placed wagers among each other on how many days would pass before Charles became king. Flora wondered whether, by some miracle, these extraordi-nary men and their fellows might be just brave enough, foolhardy enough, and fierce enough to succeed.

Brave. Foolhardy. Fierce. She had loved such a man once. But where was he now? She did not see him among Alasdair's people, nor did she in truth expect him to be there. He was doubtless with his chief, Lochiel, or with the prince. But what did she care where he was or what he did? He no longer played any part in her life now, except in the ruins of her dreams.

Still, there would be no harm in asking about him, she thought. Indeed, it was important to determine if he were nearby, watching her in secret, perhaps even lying in wait for her. Flora didn't trust Alasdair Ard or his advice, and so turned to the Cameron nearest her, hoping he spoke English. "Know you aught of Sorley Fior, the tall man with the odd-matched eyes?" she asked.

The young man studied her face thoughtfully. "I do indeed," he said, then gave a soft, sad laugh. "Dead as Tam's mare by now, I'm thinking."

"What . . . what's that you say?" Flora couldn't believe the man's words or her reaction to them. "You're mistaken." Sorley couldn't be dead! But then, what did she care if he were, the murderer? Her mind whirled like a storm at sea.

An older man seated beside the first had been listening to her question with great interest, and now spoke up. "Coll here may be mistaken, mistress, or he may be right. We know nothing save that two days ago Sorley Fior gave away his pipe, tobacco, and snuffbox, and rode away on Lochiel's horse as though Black Donald himself were nipping at its tail."

This news overwhelmed Flora but also brought her some solace. Sorley might be alive after all. She tried to make some order of her scattered thoughts. Sorley had stolen his chief's horse and deserted the prince. That was unlikely, she admitted. Like as not Lochiel had sent Sorley away for some purpose, a purpose she couldn't guess. "Why?" she finally blurted.

Both men shrugged, and in the ruddy light of the fire Flora saw the strong resemblance they bore to each other—the same pale blue eyes and shaggy brows. Father and son, she guessed. Through her pain and panic, the terrible risk at the heart of the Jacobite campaign suddenly became clear to her: hundreds of fathers, sons, husbands, and cousins were wagering their lives and their families against the might of a great kingdom. They had so much to lose and little to gain save the satisfaction of their leaders' political desires. Given that, their loyalty was nothing short of incredible.

"You'd do well to ask Alasdair Ard, or even Ewan Fada," the older Cameron suggested, "but the Lochiel has a tight pair of lips on him and isn't much given to discussing his private matters."

Over the next few days, Flora found out that this was exactly true. No one in the Cameron camp knew any details about Sorley's disappearance, though they offered her a wealth of fanciful conjectures: Sorley was an English spy; Lochiel had driven Sorley away over some imagined insult; the prince had sent him to secure a shipment of gold from France. One young fellow, believing himself to be helpful, showed her the tobacco pouch Sorley had given him. Flora was hard put not to burst out weeping. Inside the leather bag among the dark red shreds of tobacco glittered a lock of her own golden hair, bound with a scrap of ribbon from the frock she had left behind in MacPhee's stable. She would never be able to reconcile these two Sorleys, the heartless slayer and the tender swain.

Flora finally summoned the humility to ask Alasdair Ard, but neither he nor Ewan could bring any light to the matter. Indeed, Ewan was delighted to hear about Sorley's disappearance and speculated that Lochiel had discovered the truth about his murdering kinsman. "Doubtless he got word from the woman that Sorley was courting," he thought out loud. "She must have told him all, and in a fit of rage he banished the brute. In revenge, Sorley made off with Lochiel's horse. Aye, it all makes sense." A hard smile distorted his boyish face.

"But it is only your fancy, not the truth," Flora reminded him, at the same time wondering why she was protecting Sorley from Ewan's vengeful imagination. Ewan had every right to be furious with his former shadow-man.

"It may be true enough," snapped Ewan, bristling like an angry badger. "Lochiel's a stern man, but he's warm wax when it comes to women. Go to him, since you have this itch to learn the fate of the murdering savage."

Flora hesitated to approach the chief with her worries. Lochiel had the fate of eight hundred men of Clan Cameron riding on his conscience and needed no distractions. Worse yet, if he had punished Sorley, he might not wish to speak about him. She decided to wait—for what, she wasn't quite sure.

That evening, she was trying to help the Smalls understand the concept of an alphabet when a young man barely old enough to grow whiskers strode into camp. The Camerons and the *Damainte* surrounded the youth at once. Some gaped at him in wonder; others glowered at him with suspicion. Flora was impressed by the ease with which he carried himself and his complete lack of fear in front of the Highland soldiers and the daunting-looking *Damainte.* He wore the white breeches and blue coat of a French officer and led a spirited gray horse that had a rather familiar appearance.

Alasdair Ard shouldered his way to the front. "What do you seek, lad?" he asked in a flat tone, neither friendly nor gruff.

The young Frenchman, clearly assuming he was in the company of inferiors, gave not so much as a nod. "I am here to collect a young mademoiselle," he said in heavily accented English. "By name, she is one Flora Buchanan."

"That is I," said Flora, stunned to hear her name spoken. "I'm the woman you seek." She began to step forward, but someone laid hold of her jacket and pulled her backward with substantial force.

"What do you want with her?" cried Ewan, pushing his way past a dozen men twice his height. "Who are you collecting her for, and why?"

Flora resented his speaking for her. "I have a voice of my own," she reminded him, then faced the Frenchman. "The questions are still good ones, sir," she said. "Who sent for me, and why in God's name would they do so?"

The youth gave her a slight bow and an even slighter smile. "The 'who' is His Highness, Prince Charles Edward Stuart," he replied. Every single man around her dropped back a step at this announcement, even Ewan. Flora alone held her ground. Now she remembered the horse, the fiery barb that had almost crushed her into the cobblestones of the High Street back in Edinburgh. She even recognized the prince's golden crest on the cobalt blue saddle blanket. "Mayhap he can explain the 'why,' " the Frenchman continued. *"Allons!* Make haste. His Majesty awaits."

The young man grabbed Flora around the waist. Unprepared for the quick movement, she cried out. Several of the *Damainte* laid their hands on their dirks. The emissary, ignoring them all, lifted Flora as her objections rained down on his head and all but threw her onto the pommel of the saddle.

"Harm one fingernail on her and I'll be holding your stones in my hand," Ewan said, waving his dirk in front of the youth's spotless trousers.

"Leave him be," Flora said, just beginning to catch her breath. She sensed the youthful messenger was a man to be trusted.

"Never fear for your lady," said the young man. "I shall personally attend to her." A moment later he vaulted behind her and wheeled the prancing stallion around in

a half circle. The horse leaped forward with such force
that she fell back against the Frenchman's chest. Then
they were flying along the road in the icy darkness of the
winter night. Flora gasped as the frozen air rushed into
her lungs and the stallion's billowing mane tickled her
face. The compromising nature of her situation dawned
upon her. A penniless woman with neither virtue nor family: What might the prince want with her?

As she resigned herself to find out, she knew she would
never give herself to any man ever again, no matter what
his station in life.

The atmosphere Flora encountered at the prince's headquarters was not what she had anticipated. The air smelled
stale, an uneasy combination of sweat and violet sachet.
The group of men clustered in the farmhouse parlor
looked more like a funeral party than a gathering of
debauched revelers. Flora recognized Lochiel, Keppoch,
and several other worthies, their faces all set in a uniform
expression of gloom. The prince appeared indifferent to
their worries. Slouched in a velveteen chair that had once
been elegant, His Majesty was well into the last half of a
bottle of claret. Three empty bottles standing at attention
at his feet attested to the depth of his capacity. When the
French cadet ushered her forward, she attempted a curtsy
using the tails of her plaid and disreputable coat. Although
he was splendidly dressed in green-and-red trews and a
black velvet jacket, Prince Charles was no longer the gallant
youth Flora had seen at the start of the campaign. He
was but twenty-four, she thought, yet looked as weary and
careworn as a man twice his age.

"*Merci,* Jean-Paul," the prince said to the youth. "How
pleasant to see you again, Miss Buchanan. As charming as

ever, I see, breeches and all. Rest assured I would have purchased proper attire for you in London."

The sad sound of resignation in his voice was unmistakable. *Would* have purchased? Where was the bravado that had guided the clans and the *Damainte* so far, so boldly? An air of defeat clung to him, as subtle as the scent of dead leaves.

"Doubtless you wonder why I tore you away from your companions in such haste." The prince quaffed his wine, and an attendant even younger than Jean-Paul refilled his glass. "It has become a personal habit of mine to seek your counsel . . . a matter of good luck, if you will, as I have always valued the company of ladies. No, I shall not dally, but come straight to the issue. My generals have ruined, abandoned, and betrayed me. They tell me I would be a fool to continue my attack and must prepare for the worst." He paused dramatically.

Flora was unprepared to hear this discouraging remark from the man who held so many lives in his soft, white hands. "The worst?" she repeated, in a desperate bid to fill up the embarrassing silence that stood between them.

The prince nodded. "Retreat," he said softly, and downed the contents of his glass.

"Consider it a temporary strategic withdrawal, Your Highness," Lochiel murmured.

The prince's word struck Flora like a hand across her face. "Oh, no, Your Majesty!" she cried. She knew better than to speak unless bidden, but words began to cascade from her mouth as she recalled what Ewan had said about the importance of going forward. "Your Highlanders are eager for the kill. A retreat would break their hearts. Why draw back now, with victory within your grasp?"

"Why, indeed?" mused the prince, examining his wine as he twirled the glass between his hands. "If only France would send us her support! Bring me Lochiel's eyes-and-ears again, so that he may instruct mademoiselle on our position."

Flora heard a rumble rise from the throng of chiefs and generals gathered in the small room that was more suited for intimate conversation than a council of war. Lochiel's strong voice pierced the clamor like a trumpet blast. "With all humbleness, Your Highness," he said, "I must protest this frivolity. The woman has nothing to say and my man is nigh dead with exhaustion. He's done the work of ten and deserves his ease. Besides, he has already told us all he knows."

The prince, having finished the fourth bottle, attacked a fifth. Flora had grown up around men who drank to excess. She studied Charles Edward for signs of inebriation—slurred speech, shaking hands, outbursts of laughter or harsh words. But, to her relief, except for a face flushed as red as the wine he drank, the prince looked none the worse for his indulgence. "I assure you, I fully appreciate the situation," he said with honest compassion in his voice. "Nevertheless, I will see him."

For a moment the room was silent as Lochiel seemed to balance the prince's whim against the welfare of his clansman. "As you wish, Your Highness," he said finally.

The prince nodded to Jean-Paul, who barked a short command in French to some unseen compatriot. A short time later the door to the parlor opened and in stumbled a dark man, stooped with weariness. He wore a grenadier's boots and scarlet coat, as well as a short plaid draped listlessly over his chest and shoulders. Because of his ungainly stance and outrageous clothing, it took Flora a moment to recognize him.

"Sorley . . . oh, my God!" she whispered. "Sorley! What have you done to yourself?"

He cut his eyes toward her for an instant, and she saw that the prince noticed this exchange. Sorley bowed as deeply as he could under the circumstances, both to the prince and to Lochiel. Flora concluded that only sheer stubbornness kept the man from falling forward onto the polished plank floor.

"I believe you know this gentleman, Miss Buchanan," Prince Charles said. "He's worthy of your acquaintance, I assure you. Not only did he beseech Lochiel for the opportunity to examine our opposition, he infiltrated their ranks and determined their numbers at great risk to life and limb. Indeed, he was nearly shot by his own people when returning to camp, were you not, my brave Sorley?"

"It was no great matter, Your Highness," Sorley replied.

"Ah, I admire a man of humility. And the numbers of the opposing forces? Once more, if you please."

Sorley took a deep breath and winced. Was he injured? Flora wondered. She saw not a mark on him. For a moment she set aside her doubts about him and beheld not a murderer, but a loyal and fearless soldier. Why did the prince demand this charade? He should have dismissed Sorley at once instead of insisting on these cruel theatrics.

"I can't be precise, but my best reckoning is twenty-five to thirty thousand infantry, five thousand horse, thirty heavy artillery pieces, forty light." Sorley paused and drew another shuddering breath. "Of the infantry, some fifteen to twenty thousand are fusiliers and ten thousand are grenadiers. Two thousand dragoons. The rest light cavalry."

Flora quickly calculated the odds against them. At most they could muster eight, perhaps nine thousand infantrymen, one regiment of hired Irish cavalry, a handful of other horsemen, and an antique fieldpiece scarcely worth dragging around. Almost five to one! She had never dreamed the Jacobites were so badly outnumbered.

"Then there is Hawley's army in the north, marching toward Edinburgh. They're said to number about ten thousand, including a thousand horse."

The prince sipped his claret. He offered Sorley a cup, but the Scot politely refused. "What is the distance of Cumberland's forces from our own?"

Sorley's considerable strength was fading. Flora could see the light in his strange, beautiful eyes flicker like a dying flame. Knowing that she risked the prince's anger, she begged for the Highlander's release. "Your Majesty, this man cannot continue. I implore you—"

The prince held up his hand, frowning. Flora stopped. If the Lochiel himself couldn't save Sorley, how could she?

"Their distance?" the prince persisted.

"Thr-three leagues, if that, Your Highness," Sorley said. "At a village called Kentleigh."

The prince shifted in his chair. He gave his glass to Jean-Paul. Now, thought Flora. The ridiculous charade was over at last, and Sorley could rest.

But Charles Edward wasn't satisfied. "Since you have seen our opponent and know his strengths and weaknesses, you must have some idea of our chances against him. What say you, gallant Scot? Can we best him? If you had the power to lead our force against Cumberland, would you do so?"

Sorley worked his jaw silently for a moment. Flora watched him, her inability to help him tearing her apart inside. Surely he had not answered such a question before. Whatever he said, he was bound to offend someone. Sorley stole a glance at his chief, then at Lord George Murray, the commanding general of the clans. The men's faces were blank, but their eyes blazed with a passion that bordered on fury. Flora guessed that they would not approve of what Sorley was about to say next.

"My prince, you've asked for the opinion of a man who has none to give, other than that of my chief." Flora saw Lochiel's face relax an infinitesimal amount.

"Come, come, man," said the prince, tapping the arm of his chair with his thumb. "I asked for your thoughts on the matter, not Lochiel's. He has already spoken his mind quite clearly, that back-stabber. And you?"

Flora was not prepared for what happened next. Perhaps, she thought, no one could have been. Sorley dropped to his knees before the prince, his back straight and his head erect. Now she saw what she had sought but failed to see earlier: a crimson splash on Sorley's scarlet coat, spreading like a deadly sunset behind his right shoulder.

She lunged toward him, but Jean-Paul caught her and held her back. "He's been injured!" she whispered fiercely. The cadet said nothing, only put his finger to his lips and tightened his grip on her elbow. Like a hare in the talons of a hawk, she watched and waited, sick at heart.

"Your Highness," Sorley began, "I know there is talk of retreat, but I beg you to press onward. The king's army is far greater in number, 'tis true, but size will never be our advantage."

Sorley stopped and swayed for just an instant, then steadied himself. Again Flora struggled to break free from Jean-Paul but failed. She resigned herself to captivity once more as Sorley continued. "Boldness alone will win the day, and I promise you, there's no lack of that among the clans. I for one am more than glad to lay down my worthless life for you, but to do that I must show Cumberland my sword, not my arse."

A tense, untenable silence fell over the room, and in it Flora suddenly understood Sorley's intentions. The terrible knowledge froze her blood. He had meant to place himself in harm's way. Like a man condemned to death, he had thrown himself from the gallows in front of the entire Hanoverian army and dared them to cut him to pieces. And why? Because she had spurned him?

This thought had no sooner entered her head when the prince pivoted in his chair and impaled her with his gaze. The pain of his officers' betrayal glowed in his soft brown eyes. "And you, mademoiselle? Do you agree? Do we press on or fall back?"

"Your Majesty, I beseech you, attend to Sorley Fior."

The prince nodded. "I shall. First, your answer."

Flora surveyed her choices. What should she say? Why should the prince care what she said? And yet he did. She remembered that he had played her for a fool before and could easily do so again. How should she answer? Winter weather had set in, provisions were all but nonexistent, and a vastly superior army of well-fed, well-armed professional soldiers was but miles away. All were good reasons to retreat. But to have come so far without a single setback or serious challenge, only to cast it all aside? Should she say what she felt, or exactly the opposite?

She decided to be forthright, like the *Damainte*, and hide nothing. "My answer is unschooled and therefore of little value, but I'm happy to give it to His Highness regardless. I agree with Sorley Fior. You may gain time if you retreat, but you will lose the moment, and the moment is in your favor. Press on, Your Majesty, press on."

Faced with such warlike speech from the mouth of a woman, the officers could restrain themselves no longer. The room resounded with their uproar. Hysterical shouts and bellowed pleas for restraint all but deafened Flora. And they say the fair sex is incapable of controlling its emotions, she fumed to herself.

"You'd listen to a female!"

"Sorley Fior is right!"

"*Mon Dieu!* Speed us not to our deaths!"

"*Dia!* We've already decided there's no choice but to fall back!"

"We will regroup come spring! All is not lost!"

"Hold your peace, the lot of you!"

The excited men surged around the bewildered prince, pushing Flora and Jean-Paul toward the doorway. Sorley and Charles Edward vanished before her eyes, engulfed by a tide of tartan and silk.

"I must tend to Sorley!" she cried, but Jean-Paul didn't seem to hear her. Instead of leading her through the fray, he lifted her in his arms and carried her from the room, then out of the house altogether. He came to a halt in a small courtyard where a dozen or so Highland gentlemen and French courtiers awaited their commanding officers. Flora shouted to these worthies for help, but they merely gawked at her as she kicked and twisted about in a useless effort to escape Jean-Paul's businesslike embrace. She clawed at his face, but succeeded only in breaking loose a spate of French blasphemy, musical despite its threats of damnation.

In this frantic state, Flora watched three shadows slide up in front of her and Jean-Paul. She struggled all the more, convinced that the legions of hell had indeed arrived to fetch her. Squinting into the dim light cast by a torch on the wall, she saw that she was right: the Damned had come for her.

"Ewan! For God's sake, help me!"

The smallest of the shadows nodded at her. "I'll take her now, lad," he said to Jean-Paul in the calm tone of a man soothing an enraged stallion. "Not a whit too soon either, I'm thinking."

"*Tabarnac!*" spat the young gallant. "This demoness! You are welcome to her, monsieur!"

Suddenly Flora found herself standing free and upright, surrounded by Ewan, Gair, and the hulking figure of Dughal. "Sorley's wounded. I must return to him," she tried to explain. But when she tried to re-enter the house, three fists shot out in unison and held her like steel pincers. "What are ye about?" she cried. "Unhand me!"

"Be still!" replied the dwarf, and began to pull her forward. "Come along in peace, I implore you, but if not, you'll come nonetheless."

Several gentlemen, attentive but idle up until that moment, stepped forward to her defense, and Flora's heart quivered with hope. But Dughal, his shaggy head lowered like a Highland bull, thrust himself into the torchlight, and Flora's would-be rescuers retreated with backward leaps that her childhood dancing master would have envied.

In rising despair Flora addressed her captor-friends. "Listen, I beg ye. Ye must help me!" She had just begun to tell them about Sorley's condition in extremis and the strange aching in her heart that compelled her to save him at all costs when Ewan muttered a word in Gaelic. At once Dughal picked her up and slung her over his immense shoulder, like a miller lifting a sack of flour. Her stream of passionate words ended in a pained *ooof* as her chest struck his flesh and the air rushed from her lungs. When she was able to breathe again, she hammered at Dughal's arms and head with what strength remained to her after her bout with Jean-Paul. The giant snorted once but otherwise disregarded her, and she soon abandoned her hopeless assault.

As Dughal bore her away, she saw a stout man dressed in a physician's drab attire and short-tailed peruke scurry into the farmhouse. The sight of the doctor stirred a grisly memory within her, and she recalled where she had seen

him before: in the chamber where her father lay, crushed
to death by a frenzied crowd. She shook her head to rid
herself of the grim recollection. Though she wondered
what Dr. Adam Barclay might be doing in the Jacobite
camp, she was glad of his presence. Apparently someone
else had wanted to preserve Sorley's life as much as she
did.

Dughal broke into a jolting run. The earth lurched past
beneath Flora's downward gaze and her face became
scorching hot. As she began to sweat, she fancied she was
melting. So much the better, she thought bitterly. Why
live only to be ignored, mistreated, and manhandled? Her
breath grew short, in part from outrage over her humiliation, in part because of her unnatural position. Tears
coursed freely down her face and spattered on Dughal's
bare legs. She writhed in fury at her utter helplessness.

Flora had no idea how long she lay across Dughal's back,
bouncing on his shoulder like a trussed lamb. It came as
something of a shock to her when Dughal stopped at last
and gently set her upright on the frost-covered ground
only a stone's throw from the Cameron camp, where she
could see some of the *Damainte* huddled around a cheerful
fire. She had traveled only a little over half a mile on her
unusual mount.

Flora's legs were numb and her hands so stiff she could
barely clench her fingers. She wobbled on her feet as badly
as Sorley had only minutes earlier, and her dignity was all
but shattered. Even so, her indignation still crackled inside
her like the *Damainte*'s bonfire. "Ewan, what have ye
done?" she said, towering over the fierce little man. "Sorley's life is in danger, and ye took me away from him. Why?
Why did you follow me? I had no need of ye just then."

Ewan straightened his back, which, she noted, he did
whenever his pride was threatened. "I am your chieftain,"

he intoned haughtily. "What cheek to counter my decisions! If you must know, I didn't like the looks of that French fop. And had you but seen yourself nearly trampled to death by the noblest feet in Scotland, you'd not have thought yourself so able."

"You saw it all!" Flora exclaimed. "Yet you did nothing!"

"I brought you out of harm's way," Ewan said, "and away from the devil that even now has you under his thrall." He paused a moment, a shadow of hesitation flickering on his face. "And I summoned the surgeon."

"The surgeon!" Flora remembered Barclay shambling into the prince's tent. "When did the prince acquire a surgeon?"

"Not long after the clans left Edinburgh," Ewan said. "Do ye ken the man?"

"I've met him once." Ewan gave a curt nod, then began to fidget with the scabbard of his dirk. Something was distressing him, Flora thought. She decided to try to provoke him into revealing it. "I would think you'd be the last person in Scotland to fetch aid for Sorley Fior," she said bitterly.

Ewan looked down at the ground as if it suddenly held great interest for him. "Aye, well, 'twas only fair, y'see . . . being as I was the one who shot him."

"What! Ye murdering brute!" Flora lunged toward the little man, but Gair grabbed her by one arm, and Dughal by the other, rendering her immobile. "How could ye"— she caught herself just before she said "stoop so low"— "do such a thing?"

"Hear me out," Ewan muttered. "The matter was pure mischance. I would not have shot him had I known it was he, but all at once a rider in a scarlet coat and knee boots and a dragoon's saddle comes thundering into camp, and what was I to think? I winged him as he rode past, and it was only after I got a look at him that I saw my mistake. But have no fear, Miss Flora. Barclay will patch him up.''

Flora felt her anger die down, like a fire that had consumed all its fuel. Dughal and Gair must have felt it, too, for they released her. Her arms trembled, and she crossed them over her chest to steady them. She believed Ewan, but she couldn't resist one final stab at him. ''Ah, but you'd be happy if he died, wouldn't you?''

''He would not, Miss Flora,'' Gair said, ''for he knows how much you fancy the man.''

For a shimmering instant Flora forgot Ewan and even Sorley as the answer to the riddle of Gair's tangled intellect leaped upon her with the force of a claymore slicing through brambles. ''Oh, Gair! Ye understand me when I end a sentence wi' a question in doubt.'' She felt more awe than triumph. Gair stared at her, confounded, and she quickly repeated herself, ending with the words ''don't ye?''

Gair smiled shyly. ''I know that I understood you just now, and a time or two earlier. 'Tis like the sun breaking through dark clouds inside my head when you speak sometimes.''

The joy of her victory cooled what was left of Flora's fury. She felt light-headed, almost giddy. Gair could speak! And she had unlocked his mind—more through luck than skill, of course, but who was she to quibble with fate? She clasped her hands together in front of her and laughed for the first time in many days. ''Ah, it's grand! A miracle!''

But Flora saw she was alone in that belief. Dughal's blank expression showed he hadn't understood her, and Gair's sweet smile of comprehension had almost faded. Ewan tossed his head from side to side in exasperation. ''Miracle?'' he said. ''Charlie's bum on the throne—that's the miracle we need, now more than ever if we are forced to . . .'' Unable to say the word *retreat*, Ewan spun around and would have walked back to camp had Flora not rushed up to him and blocked his path.

"This isn't folly," Flora tried to explain. "Gair can speak plainly."

"So I heard. Now come, the lot of you."

But Flora didn't move. She was not about to surrender her success so easily. "Gair can speak," she persisted. "Not normally, but well enough. He's a fine, clever man. Is that nothing to you? Do you prefer him mad?"

Ewan gave a deep sigh, as if he were about to explain a difficult matter to a rather backward child. "Here's the way of it then. Without his wits, Gair's the perfect soldier. He does all I ask of him without argument. With his wits, he's a contentious rogue who loves nothing more than to disobey me and pester the others."

The selfish wee crowl! thought Flora. She was on the point of telling him that Gair's mind lay in the balance, not Ewan's convenience, when something in the sly shift of the dwarf's eyes made her pause and rethink what he had just said. Then it struck her. "You're already aware of my discovery."

"Indeed I am," he said. "Only the two of us know, and I'd charge you to let this remain our secret, as least until the rising is over, one way or the other. After that, Gair may go to university for all I care, or to hell for that matter, but while I am the leader of the *Damainte*, I must have control over my men. Do I have your word on it?"

Flora nodded once and tucked her chin. She felt neither disappointed nor angry, only defeated. As Ewan passed her, she sadly took her place behind him, her spirits as low as her head. She couldn't believe sweet-tempered Gair was as contrary as Ewan made him out to be. On the other hand, she knew that discipline was important to any

regiment, even one as improbable as the *Damainte*. Even
more so now, when the fate of the campaign was in question.

She wished Sorley were with her so that she might ask
his opinion on the matter. Then she wondered if he were
still alive, let alone willing to discuss anything with her.
Although she yearned to see him once more, to hold him
and be held by him, she wished to her soul that she had
never met the magic-eyed Highlander. It was no easy matter, being in love with someone whom she should have
despised.

Gair trotted up behind her and grasped her hand. Perhaps he sensed her dejection, she thought. It was such a
warm, artless gesture that she almost burst into tears.
Quickly she caught herself. She would not abandon Gair,
no matter what Ewan said. "You'll still speak to me, won't
you?" she asked.

The former madman brushed a handful of shaggy red
hair from his eyes. Again she saw his gentle smile and felt
gratitude radiate from him like light from the sun. "May
my tongue cleave to my mouth if I don't, mistress."

Chapter Eleven

The prince's generals had their way, but the army that marched north out of Derby was not the same army that marched south into it five days earlier. Flora scarcely recognized the glum Camerons as the same confident men who had entertained her around the campfire with gruesome descriptions of how they would carve the red-coated Hanoverians in twain like so many turnips. Now they and the men of the other clans—great Clan Donald, Clan Ranald, Clan Chattan, the MacLachlans, the Stuarts, of course, and half a dozen more—plodded through the mud and sleet with their backs bent, their spirits quenched.

Ewan gathered a great deal of information, which he generously shared with Flora as they tramped over the same burned fields they had negotiated only a week before. Unfortunately, all the news was bad. After the retreat, Cumberland and the other Hanoverians had concluded that the prince had no firm strategy, which was all too close to the truth. According to Jean-Paul and other trustworthy sources, Prince Charles now consumed no less than three bottles of French brandy and four bottles of wine every day. Though he never showed any outward signs of drunkenness, he was taciturn and gloomy, another man altogether from the blithe adventurer who had enchanted Flora when he leaped onto a balcony in Edinburgh to declare his right to the throne.

The prince had no intention of giving Cumberland the impression that the Jacobites had been defeated or thrown back, Ewan explained. Therefore, the withdrawal moved slowly, perhaps more slowly than the prince's generals desired. An entire day was wasted at Manchester while the prince engaged in a clandestine tryst with his Lowland mistress, and he insisted on halting several days in Preston, for no purpose that Flora could see, other than to assuage his injured pride.

Although the slow pace of the retreat infuriated Flora, she conceded to herself that it was easier on the wee lads and poor Creag, who were always the last to arrive in camp. Because the Jacobites dawdled, Cumberland's army drew nearer every day. Flora wondered each morning when she awoke cold and hungry if a confrontation would take place before nightfall. Then, at the border, Cumberland hesitated and actually halted for four days. Even then Charles did not change his death-march pace, but he did put a comfortable distance between himself and the English general. Seumas, who knew almost as much about the situation as Ewan, told Flora that Cumberland's informants had been seduced into thinking that French allies were to arrive any day to aid the Jacobites. Like most rumors, it was entirely false, but Cumberland had believed it. From this, Flora deduced that Cumberland was either extremely cautious, or fearful of the fierce Highlanders he was pursuing. Or both.

All the time she was on the march north, two things stayed uppermost in Flora's mind and helped ease the misery in her heart as well as her body. One was her dream to provide for the Smalls, who were now sometimes so exhausted that they took turns riding Dughal's massive back two at a time. The other was Sorley.

From Alasdair Ard she learned that Sorley had been left behind in Preston to recover from his wounds. But ever since her meeting with Sorley in the birch grove, Flora trusted neither Alasdair nor his information. She persuaded Cu to inquire about Sorley among the Camerons, without Ewan's knowledge, but received the same intelligence: Sorley was last seen in Preston, his wounds serious but not mortal. The mysterious Dr. Barclay had disappeared, but another doctor sympathetic to the Jacobite cause had taken over his duties and shown at least as much competence.

The Highland army seized Carlisle, just over the border. There the *Damainte* appropriated a small cottage simply by walking into it and frightening away its rightful owners. Even deformity had its advantages, Flora thought. She had just bedded down the Smalls in comparative luxury on goose-down quilts and straw mattresses when Cu sidled up to her and touched her hand. "Miss Flora, I can't for the life of me fathom why you care for this Sorley creature," he whispered, casting a glance in Ewan's direction. "You told Ewan Fada that you were done with the man, but if that were so, it wouldn't matter to you whether he lived or died. You'd not have him for a husband, would you?"

"It's no business of yours," Flora snapped, then instantly regretted her harsh words. Cu had a point, after all. She wanted to forget Sorley but couldn't. His tenderness was seared upon her mind as surely as Macinally's brand was seared upon her chest. The slightest token summoned his memory—the sight of a dark-haired man, a birch tree, the flash of a brass buckle, or the smell of a rainstorm. She was hard-pressed to think of anything else.

"Forgive me," she told Cu. "You're quite right; it's not good to pursue him. I've determined not to wed him, but I can neither forget him nor abandon him." In truth, Sorley still commanded all the passions of her heart and played her any way he wished, just as a piper played the pipes. But the moment she actually imagined herself as his wife, an image of her father and her mother on the stairs broke into her beautiful vision and crushed it. "Please, ask me no more questions about the man."

Cu silently slunk away, but he had stirred such strong feelings inside Flora that she couldn't sleep. She was on the verge of rising and offering to relieve Ewan of his sentry duties when she felt a small hand on her shoulder.

"Miss Flora?"

Flora rolled to one side and encountered an enormous pair of dark blue eyes staring into her own. "Bug!" she whispered. "Can you not sleep?"

"Oh, aye," said the boy. Two years older than Rattie, Bugger was nevertheless half a head shorter and, despite Flora's assurances to the contrary, forever worried about becoming a dwarf. "But I dreamed about ye, and when I woke I remembered that I must give ye this." Flora smiled and tousled the boy's damp blond hair. It was the longest statement he had ever made in her presence.

"Give me what?" she asked. She leaned forward, pretending to be curious.

Encouraged, Bugger reached into his shirt. The odor of mildew filled Flora's nose, but she hid her disgust. After squirming about for a few moments, the boy withdrew something and slipped it into her hand. Flora did not have to see the object to know what it was. She could tell by the shape, the size, the weight, and the edges of the etched surfaces. Sorley's compass was a messenger dove that kept returning to her without fail, even when she drove it away. She sighed, rubbing the hard brass against her face and imagining Sorley's touch. "Are you taking up Son's trade?" she asked the child.

"He is or I'm Saint Peter."

The voice came from just below Flora's chin. It was Rattie, who had crawled beside her so stealthily she had not even noticed him.

Bugger gawked at Rattie blank-faced, then turned to Flora. "I didna pinch it, mistress; I swear it," he blurted. "The French popinjay that stole ye away on the horse gave it tae me and bade me take it tae ye."

"A likely tale," said the youngest member of the *Damainte*. "The tyke's lyin'. That's the shadow-man's clock."

"So it is," Flora said, "but I believe Bug." The urchin in question rewarded her with a glittering smile of relief. Sorley must have retrieved the compass, then, during his convalescence, asked the Frenchman to return it to her. She slipped the love-token into the front of her blouse, where it burned like ice. There was no use denying her passion for the man, whatever his failings. "Back to sleep now, the both of you. Tomorrow we march on Glasgow."

"Why are we running away from the Sassenach?" Bugger wanted to know.

"We aren't running away. We are withdrawing to familiar territory while we wait out the winter so we can press the attack come spring," she said, repeating the strategy she had heard back in Derby.

"Can I have new shoes in Glasgow?" Bugger held up

two flattened pieces of leather that could have once been footwear.

"And me!" added Rattie. "And a pasty filled with meat!"

"I promise it," she said, gathering the waifs in her arms. "Ewan says we shall all have new shoes, even the prince. And when the campaign is over, the two of you and Son and I can have a wee house of our own, if you like."

"I'd like that fine," Bugger murmured.

"Can Crann stay with us?" Rattie asked.

Flora laughed. "Aye, and mayhap Seumas and Rosmairi as well. We'll have new shoes every year and meat every day and—"

"And a da?" Rattie asked in the same tone another, more fortunate child might have used to beg for Christmas gifts. "Can we have a da, too?"

"If God is willing." Flora sighed as her carefree mood deflated. After a moment, she added under her breath, "And if I am."

Bugger and Rattie were not the only Jacobites in need of footgear. Flora herself had worn huge gaps in the soles of both her brogues, which she patched with scraps of cloth, leather, and whatever was at hand. To her disbelief, many of the Highland host went barefoot, even in the snow and ice, rather than chafe their feet with the rock-hard remnants of their shoes.

Ewan had pilfered several pairs of short boots from the dead grenadiers months ago and coerced Dughal into carrying them for him. The dwarf had no fear of going barefoot, even though the shoes were many sizes too large for him and gave his gait a distinctive waddle. "Now we are led by a duck and a dog, with a hare and a frog thrown in for good measure," Creag grumbled to Flora as the clans set out for Glasgow in a cold, roiling mist. "I suppose a lump of clay such as myself shouldn't complain, but I can't see what good we're doing, heading back where we came from."

"Aye," Flora agreed, "but it's the prince and his generals who make the plans, not Ewan and Cu."

She did share Creag's concern, though. Desertions continued among the Highlanders, and most of the English Jacobites who had joined earlier had stayed behind in their homeland. Rumors about aid from France scuttled like rats among the clans: the French had landed in the Isle of Skye, they were in Glasgow, they would arrive in Greenock in a month, a week, a day. While there was no shortage of news about reinforcements, the reinforcements themselves stubbornly refused to appear.

"You'll feel better when we reach Glasgow," she told her weary companion.

But when the Jacobites retook the city some days later, Flora realized she had been much too optimistic about the loyalty of the Glaswegians. She knew that the prince had taken Glasgow only four months earlier, with far greater fanfare and support than he had received in Edinburgh. Now, however, they might as well have been marching through Derby. Instead of cheering the clans, the citizens spat at the soldiers and taunted them with cries of "Traitors! Traitors to the Crown!"

As a rare honor, Lochiel allowed the *Damainte* to march through the city at the tail of Clan Cameron. Strangely enough, the townspeople said nothing at all, but gaped at Ewan, Dughal, Creag, and the others in fearful silence. Flora thought they must be struck dumb by the sight of such misery.

She saw the prince only once, astride his charger as the clans filed past him. Prince Charles sat slumped in the saddle, his head low. He had so much difficulty controlling his excited stallion that Jean-Paul had to hold its bridle. If he had been drinking, Flora mused, it was just as well. Then perhaps he would not suffer too much from the cruelty of the people he so desperately wanted to rule.

The Glaswegians' scorn did not extend to commerce, Flora was glad to see. Sullivan, the quartermaster, purchased shoes and warm clothes for at least part of the army. The *Damainte* received sturdy new brogues, and Flora even had a penny to buy a hot pasty oozing with beef and cheese for Rattie.

The army rested for a week in Glasgow, to the dismay of its unhappy citizens, who were forced to provide food and housing for six thousand men. Flora spent the time mending clothes, teaching the Smalls their numbers and letters, and trying to find them a permanent home among the city's orphanages and poorhouses. But conditions at these "humane" establishments were far worse than life on the open moor, where at least the boys were free from beatings and worse. In the end she decided that the Smalls would have a safer, happier life if they stayed with the campaign and risked the wrath of Cumberland's army. She only wished she could take all of Glasgow's rejected children with her.

Flora became adept at conversing with Gair, and tried to speak as often as she could with Rosmairi. She discovered that, by dint of much conversation and constant reminders, she could coax the woman to remember several names, including Flora's. But holding more than five names in her head at once was as much as poor Rosmairi could manage. When Flora tried to teach her Cu's identity, she forgot Ewan's. When it came to the boys, she called each of them "Small," a considerable improvement over their actual names.

Near the end of the week Flora sent Cu out again to learn if Sorley had recovered and received disturbing news. Sorley was no longer in Preston, but he was not in Glasgow either. "How may we know if he is even alive?" Flora worried aloud when Cu had finished his report.

"We canna know for certain," Cu responded, "but ye can look at his compass, if ye have it about ye."

Bewildered, Flora pulled the shiny instrument from a tartan bag that she had sewn to protect it. She opened the case. The needle was frozen at due north.

Cu leaned over her hand and inspected the compass with the diligence of a clocksmith. "It looks to be working proper."

"Aye, so it does," she said, still puzzling over the connection between Sorley's compass and his existence. "But why should it matter?"

Cu looked at her exactly as he might look at one of the Smalls, with tolerance shining from his eyes. "He gave it to ye, aye? To remember him? Then for certain it would break if he were dead." Flora began to protest, but Cu continued. "Laugh if ye like, Miss Flora, but things ken their masters. When my da died, I got his brace of pistols, but then they vanished like ghosts. For the next two years I felt compelled to visit the house of a man I couldn't abide, though I had no need to do so. Why? Well, that *bogiel* had thieved the pistols! They'd been crying out to me to fetch them all along."

Flora knew better than to counter the convictions of Highlanders. Her mother had believed in fairies, and who was to say just what forces might be playing touch-and-begone with people's destinies? "I'm not laughing, Cu," she said as she placed the compass into its bag and back in her blouse. "It's enough for me, just believing that

Sorley is alive." If she never saw him again, she would accept it. But he had to be alive.

Prince Charles fell ill in Glasgow and had to stay in the city under the care of a horde of doctors while his army set out to retake Sterling. The clans were fed and rested and, thought Flora, equally resigned to victory or defeat, provided they were allowed to fight. Though the weather was cold and wet, there was a faint promise of spring flowers in the scent of the rain.

Cumberland followed, days away but unshakable. Flora knew it was inevitable that someday, sometime, these two irreconcilable forces must meet, and one must destroy the other. They were ice and fire, ocean and shore, Saxons and Celts. She hoped for victory, but knew she would settle for survival.

One gray day, the *Damainte* came to a large, rolling moor just outside of Sterling. "This is the plain of Falkirk," Creag explained to Flora as they tramped over the field in the wake of the army. "Four hundred years ago the army of the great Wallace was torn to ribbons here by Edward Longshanks. A dark day for Scotland, that."

"I know about Sir William Wallace," Flora said proudly. "Robert the Bruce took up his cause and in time drove out the English. So may it be for us, I hope." She lengthened her stride, eager to get beyond the unlucky field.

Flora crested a gentle rise, the highest land around, and paused to observe a bank of large black clouds drifting her way. Crann came up to her and pressed his head against her thigh. "Wet weather's coming, lad," she said, stroking his neck. As she stood scanning the fields below for signs of shelter, she heard Crann whine. He pricked up his ears and gave her a searching look, as if to ask, "What's that?"

Just then a lovely music came to her on the wind. Not as shrill as the pipes but just as high-pitched, it reminded her of birdsong. A sort of rhythmic thunder accompanied it. She was about to ask Creag what on earth the sounds could be when the answer fell upon her.

She whirled on Creag and clutched his arm. "Listen! D'ye hear it?"

The man-mountain staggered back a step, then obediently raised his fissured head and listened. For several moments more he stood as passive as a rock; finally his eyes flew open and he stumbled back farther still. "Fife and drums! Damn them! The Sassenach!"

Flora fetched Gair, who was but several strides ahead. The three of them looked down into the vale they had just left. Far in the distance to the east a glittering line gilded the horizon. "It can't be Cumberland!" Flora gasped. "He can't have moved so far so quickly."

"Perhaps it's Hawley, traveling west from Edinburgh," Creag suggested. "Gair, lie down, man, and see if you can feel them."

Gair immediately dropped to his full length facedown in the earth. Flora looked from one man to the other. "Are ye daft, both of ye?"

But Creag and Gair ignored her. At length she understood Gair's tactic: by absorbing the vibrations made by the opposing army, he could judge its numbers. "Is it more than thirty thousand?" Creag asked. "Nod or shake your head, man." Gair raised his head just above the ground and wagged it back and forth in a highly exaggerated fashion. "Hawley, then," Creag mused. "We'll have to get Ewan and see if we can bring the clans back."

Flora stared at him aghast. "Bring them back? Ye are mad at that! They're already a mile ahead or more. Ye can't simply call them back like a dog."

"We must try," said Creag, who was winded most of the time now. "Otherwise, we'll all die like dogs. If we give up the high ground, we'll give up any advantage we might have had over the Sassenach."

Flora looked down at her feet. The high ground. The very ridge they stood on. If Hawley's army took the ridge, they could pick off the Jacobites with rifle fire or crush them like a boulder. "You're quite right," she apologized. "Forgive me." Without another word she sprinted ahead, found Ewan, darted around him, and slid to a stop in front of him. She said but the one word—"Sassenach"—and pointed toward the ridge. The dwarf snarled his rage, then raced back to the high ground with Cu, Losgann, and Flora hard behind him.

Ewan drank in the situation at once. He growled some orders to Losgann in Gaelic and the boy sped off as if he'd been shot from a musket. "What now?" Flora asked. Her wild dash had exhausted her, and she hoped whatever Ewan decided it did not involve further running. "Where's Losgann off to?"

"To summon Lochiel," Ewan answered, without even looking at her. He strode along the ridge like a general, his hands on his hips and his head in the air, miniature but martial. "Mind you, I'll take whatever he brings back. Clan Ranald, MacLachlans, MacGregors . . . they all travel at the rear. Now line up here across the crest, all of you, so the Saxons can see us. Spread out and cover as much ground as you can."

All the *Damainte* rushed to obey him, even Rosmairi and the Three Smalls.

All save Flora.

She had seen much in the past half year that set her head spinning, but none of it compared to this one mad request. Never mind that Ewan's plans were always larger than himself or his resources. In a world where folly was commonplace, this plan was lunacy.

Remembering that previous appeals to logic had never moved Ewan, she resorted to flattery. "You're a brave man, Long John," she began, knowing that the English version of his name amused him, "and a bold leader. But this is more than we're fit for. Women and weans and"—she hesitated, unsure what to call the others—"a handful of men can't guard this ground against *that.*"

Flora nodded toward the east. Instead of the glinting line she had expected, she now saw colors, even shapes, small lozenges of red, larger ones of black and red. Infantry and horse, she thought. Hawley's army filled the breadth of the valley.

Ewan glanced at the enemy, then reached into a saddle-bag slung around Dughal's shoulders and began passing out flintlock pistols and ammunition. "Is your musket loaded, Cu? Gair? That's grand. Here." He shoved a heavy pistol into Flora's quivering hands. "It's loaded. You have but to aim it and pull the trigger. Mind the kick when you fire it. Seumas . . . do you have your own pistol, man?"

Seumas Half-face studied the troopers in the distance. "Miss Flora is right," he told Ewan without looking at him. "Rosmairi and the Smalls shouldn't be here. If we have to run for our lives, they'll be left behind and slaughtered like calves."

Suddenly the two of them were arguing in Gaelic. Flora gritted her teeth. Ewan ignored her but not Seumas. A few minutes later she had to admit it was just as well, because Seumas persuaded Ewan to send Rosmairi and the boys to the protection of a distant grove. Flora doubted she would have had such success.

The fugitives left, taking Crann with them. "Mind you,"

Ewan said, "they'll be slaughtered anyway if the Sassenach ride over us."

Another glance into the plain assured Flora that her death was inevitable. Thousands of soldiers were assembling on the floor of the valley, still far off but spreading nearer, like a wine stain on yellow linen. "Explain to me once more why we must throw our lives away for no good reason."

"Hah!" The dwarf snorted and tossed his head. "I'll explain nothing. If you don't care for my command, you can go. Faith, you're but a woman. Perhaps you shouldn't be here, but cowering among the trees with your own kind."

Flora felt hot anger spread over her skin. "I'll not desert you," she said firmly. "I am a woman, but I can be of use to you. Truth to tell, Ewan Fada, you need me."

"I never said I didn't," Ewan retorted. "And I never thought for a heartbeat that you'd leave us."

A sudden shout caught Flora's attention. She looked over the top of Ewan's head and saw Rosmairi and the children, trudging across the wide meadow toward the grove. But beyond them the earth seemed to be heading toward her in bits of gray, green, and brown. Above this moving landscape sailed the black storm clouds, larger and lower than before. The strange scene completely entranced her, even when she realized what was happening. "Some clansmen are approaching," she said softly.

Ewan followed her gaze. When he saw the running Highlanders he gave a whoop, jumped straight up a foot off the ground, and began waving his bonnet like a flag. By and by his zeal began to wane. He crushed his bonnet back on his head amid a flurry of swear words. "Hell's curse on them!" he muttered. "It's that damned Sorley, back from the dead, which is where he belongs."

"Sorley?" The word shattered Flora's trance. She gazed again into the shallow dale. The man she loved and hated ran at the front of a band of clansmen who bore down upon her and the *Damainte* like so many stampeding Highland cattle. She tore her gaze from them and scanned the opposite valley. Hawley's troops advanced with an inevitability that was painful to observe. She could see the dragoons' horses clearly now, and just make out the muskets and white crossbelts of the infantry. We will all be ground to dust, she thought, more numb than frightened. Love, murder, kingdoms—none of it mattered in the face of such odds.

The *Damainte*, however, saw things differently. They were delighted that help had arrived, no matter how inadequate, and cheered Sorley and his fifty Camerons when they barreled up the ridge and shuddered to a halt at the top, puffing and wheezing. "You've saved us!" cried Seumas. Ewan scowled in silence.

Sorley had lost some weight and his face was unnaturally pale. Otherwise, he was the same captivating rogue Flora had run from in the birch forest. "How is it with you, Sorley?" she said, straining to remain calm. "You've recovered from your most recent wounds, I see."

"Floraidh! Mo dhia!" Sorley looked at her, then at the thousands of enemy troops on the Plain of Falkirk. The disbelief on his face was equal on both accounts. "My God! You must leave at once."

"I'll stay," she said, without raising her voice. "Ewan and I have already discussed the matter, and he's in agreement with me."

"Aye, unless I decide to have Dughal drag you away again." The dwarf frowned as he surveyed Sorley and his clansmen. "Are we to throw pebbles at lions then, Sorley Fior? Others are coming, I hope."

Sorley did not reply straightaway, but continued to gaze at the approaching Hanoverians and mutter quiet profanities. Finally he said, "The entire lot is coming, if you can hold your whisht long enough."

Flora noticed that others, in fact, were already there. A small group of feral, ragged-looking men that Ewan identified as MacGregors were plowing up the hillside at full attack. When they reached the crest of the hill, they would have charged right over it had Sorley not lined up his men opposite them and shouted for them to stop.

"Sassenach! I see them! At them!" yelled one big, bullish man, whom Flora took to be their leader. Ewan seized this fellow by one arm, while Sorley grabbed the other.

"Oh, aye, soon enough, Gregor," Sorley said, thumping the man's back in a brotherly way. "Meanwhile, you might pause to consider the wee matter that there are at least five thousand of them and but eighty of us."

"Fighting odds!" shouted the MacGregor. He shook himself free, and there was no telling what he might have done had Flora not remembered the Gaels' fondness for strong drink. Snatching Seumas's whiskey skin, she held it out toward the man.

"Will you have a dram, sir?" she said. She had a strange vision of sitting in the gentleman's parlor in her father's house in Edinburgh, offering tea and cakes to Capt. Henry Stelton.

"Ah, here's a right civil lad," Gregor exclaimed. He took a pull of liquor, then squinted hard at Flora. "I'm mistaken. Are we recruiting the ladies now?"

Sorley seized the skin and drank from it himself. "Enough foolishness! Line up your men along the ridge."

"Who gives orders to Gregor MacGregor of Strathbeg?"

A squeaky voice at Flora's waist proclaimed, "I'm chieftain here!"

Flora stood by with the whiskey as Sorley, Gregor, and Ewan quarreled among themselves as to which of them outranked the others. Meanwhile the sounds of fife and drum grew nearer. At last Sorley emerged as supreme commander, and Camerons, *Damainte,* and MacGregors alike fanned out along the rise. Flora watched anxiously as the English spread out over the field, drew up lines of battle, and waited. They've seen us, she thought. From a distance, Sorley's eighty men might have looked like the front lines of an entire army.

Flora was still standing, studying the indecisive Englishmen, when she felt a hand on her neck. She leaped sideways and drew her dirk. Sorley stood before her, sad and weary-looking. "I won't harm you, but you must go this instant. It's too dangerous for you here."

"Do you think I joined the *Damainte* to reduce the danger in my life?" Flora swaggered forward a step, trying to mimic Ewan. She waved the dirk in a threatening arc. "As I told ye before, I mean to stay. The prince needs every soul he can muster, male or female."

"Spoken like a woman of spirit," Sorley conceded, "but 'twill do you no good. Now go, damn you!"

A deafening *cra-aa-ck!* exploded over their heads. Flora looked up, wondering if Providence were indeed on Sorley's side. It was only lightning dancing among the rain clouds, which had almost obscured the meadow and were about to engulf the ridge. Thunder drummed in the distance. The sharp fragrance of rain perfumed the air.

"I'll go nowhere you tell me to!" she cried.

"Here they come, devil take them!" shouted a MacGregor. Flora knew he wasn't speaking of the ominous clouds. He meant the Hanoverians. The ground began to shake under her feet.

But something else held Flora's interest, something in

the distance on the other side of the ridge, something very large moving very fast through a curtain of rain. Here and there she spied a glimmer of steel. Wild music screamed above the tumult of the storm. "Here they come," she murmured, staring in awe at the thousands of Highland soldiers that poured onto the field, racing toward the ridge and the unseen enemy. "Oh, they are magnificent!"

"That they are, Miss Flora," Sorley assured her. "And they may yet win the day. But you won't see them do it."

His hand streaked out and slapped the dirk from her grip.

Flora gasped. She spun around and ran. He'd slay her for certain! Powerful arms circled her waist. She struck at them with her fists, but Sorley merely scooped her up as Dughal had and began to lope along the ridge. She howled and scratched and tried to kick free, but he was too strong for her. When he had run some distance, he picked his way down the slope a few feet and slid to a stop. I'll trip him up when he sets me down, Flora thought. The next moment she felt herself hurtling through the air. "Murder!" she tried to scream, but her breath rushed from her as she landed hard on her bottom. Shrieking in pain and defeat, she rolled over and over and over down the flank of the ridge, through brambles and across stones, until she finally tumbled into a shallow ditch near the bottom of the hill.

The ditch was full of water, which broke Flora's fall but chilled her to the quick. When she tried to stand, pain radiated up and down her left leg and she immediately flopped back down. With great effort she hauled herself from the ditch hand over hand, and tried to get her bearings. She saw that the Highland host was much closer now, and that Sorley was moving his people off the ridge and down the hillside, out of sight of the enemy. The men

began to form ranks, their muskets at the ready. As Highlanders came up behind them, they too fell into place and
raised their firearms.

"They've set a trap for those English foxes," she muttered to herself. "Now if only the foxes are obliging enough
to rush into it."

A strange quiet settled over the field, broken only by the
noise of the storm and the incessant thunder of Hawley's
horsemen. In that quiet, Flora began to pray. "Hail Mary,
full of grace, the Lord is with thee. . . ." Her teeth chat-
tered. She wished she had her rosary.

Flora felt a tap on her shoulder, then another on her
face, and another. White blobs fell before her eyes. She
wondered if she had injured her brain, until she realized
that hail was falling all around her. Soon it was hammering
her so hard that she had to cover her head with her arms.
When the barrage let up a little, she peered around at a
misty, half-hidden world peopled with the martial shapes
of Highland soldiers. The ridge was visible in the distance,
a dark gray shelf against a pale gray sky.

Then she saw the first dragoons. Pelted by hail, their
vision dimmed, they burst over the summit and down the
hillside in a roar of hoofbeats and exultant shouts. A thousand or more riders galloped after them, directly into the
line of fire of the Highland army. Too late a few saw the
danger and swerved their steeds abruptly to one side. The
horses directly behind slammed into them. Mounts stumbled and fell. Riders sailed from their saddles down the
slope or vanished beneath their panicked animals.

Suddenly the field erupted in yellow sparks from thousands of flintlocks. The valley shook with an explosion so
loud that Flora winced and once again hid her head in
her arms. When she braved another look, gunsmoke and
the stink of sulfur filled the air. The ridge was littered with

the bodies of man and beast. Riderless horses galloped madly up and down the hillside. Several hundred horsemen advanced to the front lines of the Highlanders only to be hacked down by a silver forest of claymores. Flora recoiled at the slaughter but she could not take her eyes from it. It was horrible, yet it stirred her in a way she could not name.

A line of dragoons cresting the ridge halted, pivoted back, and fled. They had expected a battle but had inadvertently stumbled into hell itself. It was a heartening sight to the Gaels. The air rang with their battle slogans as the clans charged up the hill in a variegated river of tartan, dodging a grisly barrier of carcasses, foundering horses, and dead riders.

"Sons of the hound, come and get flesh!"

"A Gordon! A Gordon!"

" *'S rioghal mo dhream!*"

In what seemed like a matter of moments, two-thirds of the army disappeared over the rise to a fate that Flora dared not think of. She was about to try standing up again when she heard the clank of metal on metal and the creak of leather. Three red-coated riders cantered toward her. She slithered back in the ditch and lay as still as she could, her heart hammering against the wet earth. These men must have punched through the Highland lines, only to find they had nowhere to go but back from whence they came. A few strides from Flora's hiding place they reined up their steaming mounts and began tossing commands at each other. Officers of like ranks, she thought.

When Flora gathered the courage to glance up at the horsemen, she had to stifle a cry. One of them was Henry Stelton, a captain no longer, but dressed in the flowing wig and braided tricorn of a major. His haughty voice and the patrician angles of his face were unmistakable. *Reveal yourself to him,* screamed a devilishly logical voice deep within her. *He may yet save you from this madness. He's not a monster. Marry him and live. Stay here with your Highlanders and perish.*

To hell with you, she thought. She would rather die than become that Englishman's indentured servant.

Moments passed like hours while Flora shivered in the icy water. At last the riders urged their mounts forward and jumped the ditch. She hoped that, if any of them thought to glance to his left, he would see nothing save a dead boy lying in the mud. Relieved, she listened to the sound of the horses galloping back toward the English lines.

Once more Flora crawled from the water, half convinced that she was dead indeed. Her head ached and her leg felt as though it were on fire. At least she had avoided Stelton. Where were Ewan and the *Damainte*? Where was Sorley? Had he tried to kill her? Or had he been trying to preserve her? She couldn't decide. Her head whirled from exhaustion and hunger. What could have possessed her to think that she might have been of any use in battle?

Then she heard it, the scream of the pipes, ringing and echoing across the plain. The shrill music wasn't an incitement to combat or a lament or a march. It was a dance, a victory dance, alive with a sort of controlled frenzy that seemed to shout, *Long live Prince Charles Edward Stuart, rightful king of England and Scotland!*

Flora felt her somber mood dissolve. The clans had won the day! She gave a feeble huzzah and wondered: who still lived?

Chapter Twelve

"After that, you didn't see him again, did you?"

"Nay, Miss Flora," Gair answered, his teeth clenched shut against the pain of a saber cut to his forearm. The blade had bitten deeply, revealing a pearl-white gleam of bone. "But I was in the thick of the Camerons the entire time and didn't hear of his death, so odds are he's still living."

Flora sighed. If Sorley were alive, where was he? She thought she might be able to live without him if she could account for his whereabouts, but he was forever disappearing, then reappearing, like the shadow that he was. Or like a ghost. It was an unfortunate comparison, and she wished she hadn't made it. She would have to keep all her wits about her if she were to be of help to Gair and the others.

The *Damainte* had taken over a miserable hovel at the edge of the town of Falkirk. Its owner was a wizened crone with a hunched back who looked as if she belonged in their company. The air was so thick with peat smoke that Flora could hardly see, and the light that filtered in through the one small window by the fire was hardly adequate for surgery.

She prepared Gair for his ordeal by pouring a good portion of whiskey down his throat, then sliding a leather scabbard into his mouth, lest he bite himself. Then, with a silver sewing needle and an ordinary bit of linen thread, she began stitching up the ugly gash. She had stitched up many wounds among the servants when she was younger, the only sort of stitchery she ever excelled in, but the wound was jagged and wide, and she knew she must have caused Gair considerable pain. He screwed his eyes shut and clamped his teeth on the scabbard but never once cried out.

What an admirable man, Flora thought as she finished her task. And what a pity he had been shunned for so long as a demoniac. If he had had the patience to feign the inability to speak, perhaps life would have been easier for him. But Gair loved to talk, and she suspected that there was a great deal of feeling inside him that craved expression.

While she worked, the rest of the *Damainte* sat around her, celebrating the rout of Hawley's army with hushed conversations and the occasional dram. Flora was only too well aware of the reason for their lack of enthusiasm. Both Seumas and Creag had paid for the victory with their lives.

Flora had wept when she'd heard the grim news about her dear friends, but she was too levelheaded to become burdened by it. While there was nothing she could do for the dead, the living still needed her help. She had finished stitching Gair's wound and was wrapping it in strips of clean linen when she heard a soft voice behind her. "How is Seumas feeling?"

"Ye poor thing!" cried Flora. She stood up carefully, mindful of her twisted leg, and enfolded Rosmairi in her arms. "Remember what we told ye? Seumas is dead. He and Creag and two hundred other clansmen are buried together in a pit on Falkirk Field. Ye saw him laid in the earth and grieved over his grave. Surely ye recall—"

"Dead? He can't be, mistress. Isn't that him lying there?" Rosmairi pointed to the pile of heather and plaids where Gair lay, half-unconscious, murmuring the names of birds. She peered at him with intense curiosity. "Look at this! His face is all of one color now! Are you certain that this is my Seumas?"

Flora began to explain that Gair and Seumas were two different men, one living and one dead, as she had mentioned before, when Ewan interrupted her. "Leave her be," he said. "What harm will it do if she thinks Gair is Seumas?"

Flora couldn't believe she'd heard him right. "What harm? Seumas and Rosmairi were married; Gair and Rosmairi are not," she said, fuming. She reddened a little, remembering her illicit trysts with Sorley, and quickly veered off on another angle. "It would be neither fair nor moral to fool Rosmairi into thinking Gair is someone he's not. Besides, you told me the *Damainte* had sworn not to wed."

As Ewan puffed on his long clay pipe, a wreath of smoke rose above his head like a halo. A decidedly misleading symbol, Flora thought. "Under the circumstances," Ewan continued, "perhaps it's better that Rosmairi have some sort of husband, even if it's not the one she prefers."

"What circumstances are these?" Flora peered warily at

Rosmairi, who was stroking Gair's unblemished face in rapt fascination.

Whoreson blurted out the answer before Ewan said two words. "She's having a wean," he cried. "I'm going tae be an uncle!"

"God in heaven!" Flora studied Rosmairi carefully. The woman looked as slim as ever, but given the bulky nature of her clothing, it was impossible to confirm or deny her condition. "Did she tell you this?"

Ewan shook his head. For a while he seemed too busy himself counting some coins he had looted from the corpses of English soldiers, but finally he continued. "Nay, Seumas did. If you're worried about seemliness, I'll arrange a wedding right this very moment. A distraction will do us all good, I'm thinking."

"But wait. Ye canna . . . that is, it's . . . we don't . . ." stammered Flora. Her vexation knew no bounds. A marriage wasn't something dashed together for the sake of convenience, despite what her father and Henry Stelton believed. She had run like a coney from just such a contrived union. "Rosmairi and Gair may not even care for each other."

"Gair reminds Rosmairi of Seumas," Ewan replied. "As for Gair, he'll do as he's told and be happy about it. Ye must think about Rosmairi's future. She may not have us to look after her forever, and a woman with a wean and no husband oft gives men a bad impression."

Flora collapsed on a nearby chair. Ewan made an excellent point. Rosmairi could survive, even thrive if married to Gair. But debauchery would destroy her. "Be that as it may, I'd like to know what the participants in this arrangement have to say about it."

"Easy enough," Ewan said, blowing a smoke ring. "Rosmairi, will ye marry Gair here?"

The woman stared at him. "But I'm married already."

"Aye, to Seumas, but he's dead."

"This isn't Seumas here, with his face healed?"

"No, that's Gair. Will you have him as a husband?"

Flora saw at once that Rosmairi was too overwhelmed to think straight, if indeed she ever did. "Gair is not Seumas, Rosmairi," Flora reminded her. "You'll be taking a second husband, which may be prudent, seeing as you're with child."

"With child?" echoed Rosmairi. Her eyes grew as round as two guineas. "Is it true? Then I maun be married, for I'll have no bastard."

"Good enough," said Ewan, not giving Flora the chance to explain that Rosmairi's child would not be illegitimate, whatever she decided. "Now we'll see about the groom." Ewan shuffled over to his groaning soldier and shook his arm. "Gair, man! Gair! We've decided that you must take Rosmairi as your wife, seeing as Seumas has passed over. That's fine with you, is it no'?"

The little scoundrel, Flora thought darkly. He could speak to Gair whenever he wished, but only when he wished.

"Lapwing, chaffinch, wagtail . . . I've sworn not to wed," murmured Gair, obviously lingering at the frontiers of consciousness.

"I'm relieving you of your oath," Ewan informed him. "With Rosmairi about to become a mother and Seumas not here to help her, it's the honorable thing to do, is it no'?"

"I'll abide by your decision," Gair whispered. "I'll do it for Seumas. Only give me some whiskey, for the sake of God and good friendship!"

Ewan was quick to oblige, and plied Gair with enough Highland malt to render him all but inert. "Now that the groom is prepared for anything, we'd best proceed with the wedding straightaway."

Flora looked about the cramped room. "But there's no priest," she objected.

The ancient mistress of the house, who had been taking in the proceedings with awestricken silence, cast in her penny's worth of advice. "We had a priest, but he was trampled to pieces by cattle a year back."

She began to say more, but Ewan cut short her fascinating news with a wave of his hand. "We need no priest," he said, pride swelling in his voice. "A pledge before witnesses is all that's necessary. There's the five of us, counting the Widow MacDonald. Cu, find me two fine Camerons, not too drunk, and bring them back here as quick as you may." Cu was out the door before Ewan finished his command.

"You've included Losgann among us," Flora countered, hoping she could yet find some alternative to the drastic nuptials. "And he's but a boy."

"Man enough for our purposes," countered Ewan.

Cu soon returned with two jolly Cameron soldiers who knew almost no English and were too deep in their cups to say much of anything in any language. The ceremony consisted of Ewan coaxing the dazed couple to repeat some simple vows, though Flora feared that Rosmairi and her groom were as mystified as she was. "You're man and wife now," the dwarf concluded. "Gair, be good to her or I'll rip off your twig and eat it, d'ye ken? Rosmairi, if you remember nothing else, remember that it's Gair you're wed to now, not Seumas. His bride is Falkirk Field."

With that, the wedding was over. The *Damainte* resumed their self-absorbed wake, which doubled as a victory celebration, and consumed large amounts of whiskey provided by the Camerons. Flora tended Dughal, who had cracked several ribs during the battle and required ample bandaging, but her thoughts were with Rosmairi. When she finally was free to congratulate the bridal pair, she saw that Gair had fallen into a deep sleep, as blissful a bridegroom as she could imagine. His new bride was curled up beside him, her eyes shut tight, as though she were trying to blot out her present circumstances.

Flora dozed, but fierce dreams savaged her sleep. She saw herself awaken in a bridal bed resplendent with white satin. Beside her lay Sorley, his naked skin as pale and glistening as the bedclothes. Was he asleep or dead? She couldn't tell. No matter how loudly she shouted into his ear or how frantically she pulled at his arm, she could not awaken him. When she leaped from the bed to summon help, a familiar, terrifying visage leered back at her and a white silk handkerchief dangled before her eyes.

She shuddered awake in the quiet cottage. Long minutes trickled past before she was certain that the terror—so vivid, so threatening—was merely an illusion, even less substantial than Rosmairi's hasty wedding. But could the phantasm have some bearing on the waking world, she wondered? Was Sorley lying in a mass grave, perhaps side by side with kind Seumas and brave Creag? The deaths of her friends had shown her all too clearly how dear ones could be torn from her embrace forever. She might never know Sorley's fate for certain.

And if she didn't? What did it matter? Flora had asked herself the question often before, but this time she knew the answer. She could not suffer the thought of never seeing him again, no matter what sins he had committed. He had been right; their destinies were intertwined, and she had been a fool to rail against so obvious a match. There was but one way she and Sorley might finish out eternity together, and that was in a union of the most intimate kind. But how could she bring herself to accept such a fate, now that she knew the truth about him?

A vague sense of dread overtook her. She had no notion how either her campaign or the prince's would conclude, but she knew she must not surrender to doubt. She had three children to care for—five if one counted Gair and Rosmairi. She sighed and slipped her hand around Sorley's compass. It drummed against her chest, driven by the wild beating of her heart.

The town of Sterling fell to the Jacobites like a ripe bramble berry tumbling into a child's hand. The ancient castle on a windswept hill just outside the city was another matter altogether. Its garrison of seasoned Royalist troops defied the Highland host and refused to be coaxed, driven, ordered, or frightened from their post. In spite of Ewan's speculation that the Sassenach hadn't the wits to leave when they were defeated, Flora admired the brave Englishmen. She reasoned that they were still a goodly distance from defeat, and, with a store of water and provisions at their disposal, might hold out until spring.

To her dismay, Prince Charles perceived the capture of the castle as an absolute necessity. With the city in his possession, the heart of Scotland was in the prince's hands; the castle was but a symbol of control, a tantalizing but sterile fruit that offered no practical benefit. But, as Flora reminded herself wistfully, the prince could never be accused of such a homely virtue as practicality. She watched helplessly as soldiers were recruited to lay siege to the castle.

One of these men, Gair informed her after considerable effort, was Sorley. This was fortunate, she tried to persuade herself. First and foremost, it meant that the shadow-man was alive and well. Second, he was less likely to come to harm during a long siege. It also meant, however, that she and he were almost certain to be parted yet again.

A buzzing restlessness fell over the Jacobite forces, and Flora knew they would not abide in Sterling much longer. After their great success at Falkirk, they were so eager for a fight that brawls broke out between the clans. Even the *Damainte* were not immune from these outbreaks. Gair received a slash on his hand while trying to part two combatants. One day at dusk Cu came limping into the camp of the *Damainte* to report more distressing news to Ewan and Flora: Highlanders were deserting ranks in great numbers—twenty, thirty, forty to a group.

Ewan began sputtering unsavory remarks at Cu as well as the deserters, and Flora wondered whether he had noticed what she had noticed, that Cu had a black eye and a bloody knee. "Have you been trying to stop them by yourself?" she asked the unfortunate man, reaching out to examine his face. Cu whined and twisted away from her, rose-colored in embarrassment. "What can have compelled them to desert now, in the midst of victory?"

"Well, that's the worst of it, Miss Flora," Cu replied. "Cumberland has taken Edinburgh. He's there just now, dining on roast beef and warming his lardy bum in Holyrood House while His Majesty eats cold porridge and shivers in a tent."

"Whaaaat?" Ewan gasped. Suddenly the little man was on Cu's chest, toppling the much bigger fellow onto his back in the dirt. "Who dares speak such shite? The fat duke in Dunedin? It can't be true! If it is, then when do we leave to retake the city, man? When?"

Poor Cu, overcome by his master's barrage, fell into a fit of barking that didn't stop until Gair pried Ewan from him. Flora helped the bedraggled dog-man to his feet.

"Go on, Cu," she urged him, all the while remembering her father's death and imagining what harm might come to her if she returned to the city. If Cu spoke the truth, then the two armies were less than a hundred miles away. One day's desperate march could bring them within striking distance of each other. "From whom did you learn all this?"

"From Alasdair Ard," Cu said, cringing. "As for the deserters, ye may see them for yersel' if ye bide a while at the far edge of town. The prince is said to be ill, but not so ill that he canna put five bottles of single malt and six of claret under his belt in a single day or wrap his doxy, Clementina."

"His Highness well knows how to hold his liquor," Ewan said, ripping himself from Gair's grasp. "As to the other, he will answer to God for it. Only tell me this: when are we to march, man? If we lose Edinburgh, we'll be sore-pressed to stop Cumberland from sweeping in under us and taking the entire Lowlands."

But Cu sat back on his haunches, shaking his head and growling. "He knows nothing more," Flora chided Ewan, who had begun hopping about like a crow on a griddle. "In the name of all that's holy, leave him be." She tore a strip of linen from her sleeve and began stanching the gash on Cu's knee. "If we're to march from Sterling, we'll soon learn our orders."

"Soon may not be soon enough," Ewan muttered, but he left her alone to finish tending to Cu's wounds.

Long after sunset, as Flora was wrapping herself in her plaid before lying down for the night with the Smalls, Crann began to bark a loud alarm. Two men had entered the camp, a runner with a blazing torch and a tall figure

Flora could hardly discern from the night's sable shadows. Ewan accosted the men and all three conversed in clipped, quiet Gaelic as their crystallized breath swirled over their heads. The flame cast wavering yellow streaks on the dwarf's face, but Flora could decipher no emotion in his frozen features. She couldn't begin to understand the men's subdued discussion, but she guessed the tidings were not good. When the shorter man trotted off at last, his torch streaming red behind him in the darkness, Flora could see nothing more. The sounds of conversation ceased and were replaced by the crunch of footsteps on the icy ground. Then there was nothing. It was as if Ewan and the stranger had sunk into the earth.

Hours later a rough voice woke her. She glanced around her, expecting to see the sun, but the sky still looked like a huge black inkblot. A puny campfire gave off just enough light for Flora to notice Ewan crouched beside her. "Awaken, Miss Flora. Get the lads up. We're marching. Now."

"Now? In the night?" Flora sat up, confused by her friend's terse commands. Her head throbbed and her eyes ached. She wiped her face with the edge of her plaid, then looked more closely at Ewan. What she saw made her take a sharp breath. The little man appeared to have been wrestling with a pack of wild dogs. His face was black with dirt where it was not red with blood, a handful of hair was missing from his beard, and one sleeve had been ripped from his shirt, creating streamers of linen that fluttered from his shoulder. "Ewan! My God! What has befallen ye?" She would never forgive herself if she had missed another battle like Falkirk.

" 'Tis nothing," Ewan mumbled. He dragged his stunted arm across his face, redistributing the grime. "A minor disagreement with a clansman. However, I persuaded him to see the worth of my opinions right enough. Now hurry.''

"Hurry where?" Flora persisted. "Are we off to Edinburgh to engage the Royalists?"

Ewan let out a long sigh that seemed to have his soul attached to the other end of it. "Nay, north, into the Highlands, where the Sassenach will be loath to follow. There we'll be able to see ourselves through the winter and drive out Cumberland in the spring. At least, that's what the chiefs and His Majesty's generals have determined."

Flora sat back, stunned. The duke was only a hundred miles away, and the prince was backing off yet again? It was not in the Young Chevalier's nature, and such a plan must have broken his valiant heart. "Another retreat?"

Ewan hung his head. "I'm no' made for tucking my tail and running from a fight," he said, "but a soldier follows orders, and we have no choice in the matter."

"And the prince?" Flora continued. "Did he have nothing to say when faced with such a dictum?"

Ewan popped upright and began to walk away. He hadn't heard her, thought Flora, or else she had offended him. But when he had gone only a few steps he turned and faced her, his eyes glistening. " 'Have I lived to see this?' were his words, so I am told." As if he were appalled to have revealed this much, the dwarf stumped off on his stunted legs as fast as he could go. Though Flora was still halfway between waking and sleeping, she sensed that a dream lay shattered on the ground all about her.

We are already defeated, and without ever losing a single battle, she lamented to herself, then bit her tongue for even conceiving such a disheartening thought.

* * *

Flora's feeling of foreboding grew ever stronger as the army struggled northward through chilling rains and snow showers. Morale among the clans was so low that the soldiers abandoned their English prisoners and even their own wounded by the side of the road to care for themselves. Flora's heart ached to help these lost souls, and as she passed them she did what she could, offering them a mouthful of water or whiskey or at the very least a few gentle words. "What sort of army cannot provide for its sick and wounded?" she stormed at Ewan during a rare daytime rest.

The bristly little martinet was less than sympathetic. "Faith, it's an army worried with feeding its able-bodied men," he replied. And with that he summoned Dughal and instructed him to remove his shirt, which he quickly did. Flora was aghast. Dughal's ribs protruded from his great torso like rafters on a ceiling. "But I and the boys and Rosmairi don't go hungry."

Ewan nodded. "Aye, but some of us do." When she began to object to this inequity, he held out his hand to silence her. "Let this be an end to your moaning, now. I'm your chief, and 'tis my decision as to who gets what. Highland men can fight the Sassenach whether we are lean or fat."

"Thank you," she murmured, "for the lads' sake."

Ewan tapped her slender shoulder. "In truth, I don't see much flesh on your bones either, mistress."

"As I said, I don't go hungry." While she appreciated Ewan's kindness, Flora regretted that she had to lie to him. The truth was that she was usually hungry, since she often gave what she had to the Smalls, who fed some of it to

Crann when they thought she wasn't watching. Though none of the *Damainte* complained, all were famished. Flora's only consolation was that Sorley, who languished with the siege back in Sterling, would have plenty to eat and a warm place to sleep. As she would likely never see him again, it gave her some comfort to imagine him in pleasant surroundings.

The Highland host crossed the Forth at the Fords of Frew, with Rattie and Bugger clinging to Dughal's arms as he plowed through the icy water. Flora had never known such cold before and shivered for hours afterward.

The prince billeted himself at Drummond Castle near the town of Crief, and there, on a field sparkling with hoarfrost, he reviewed his troops. Flora grimaced when Ewan told her the results: a thousand men had deserted since the retreat from Derby. "But the prince has coaxed the Old Fox, Simon Fraser of Lovat, to send almost that many warriors, so we are still a force to be reckoned with." Ewan stretched himself up as he said this, but Flora could see that even the irrepressible dwarf scarcely believed what he'd told her.

"And Sterling?" Flora pondered aloud. "The siege?"

"It continues," Ewan snapped. Flora opened her mouth and said one word when the little man interrupted her. "Aye, aye, your precious Sorley is safe enough. Now perhaps you can clear your mind of him and concentrate on . . . your duties to the campaign." He had hesitated just long enough for Flora to grasp that he had meant to say something different, though she knew not what.

"I have never once been remiss in my duties to the prince," she reminded Ewan firmly. "Nor shall I begin now, no matter what Sorley's fate. Too many require my services."

"Forget it not," said Ewan, turning on his heel.

Desertions continued, but other troops from Clan Grant and Clan MacIntosh joined the cause. Thus the Highland host, alternately diminishing and increasing, worked its way through the Highlands to the outskirts of Inverness, the city on the River Ness near the eastern coast. The Jacobites lay siege to the town and its English garrison, led by one Colonel Loudon. It was February, and the weather remained viciously cold. It was all Flora could do to keep the Three Smalls from freezing and starving. She scavenged the camps of the clans to glean just enough "parritch" to keep them and herself alive. Gair, an excellent shot with his bow, contributed coneys, blackcocks, and other small game to the pot, and somehow the *Damainte* avoided starvation.

As much as she hated the snow and the bitterly cold wind, Flora had to admit that they had their benefits, even as she sat shivering before a tiny fire, digging her hands under her armpits to keep her fingers from freezing. As Cu told her, one glory of the Highland winter was that it kept the Hanoverians at bay in the midland cities of Perth, Dunblane, and Crief, too timid to press their advantage through three-foot-tall snowbanks and acres of ice. Sterling, thanks be to God, was still held by the Jacobites, most of them Camerons like Sorley. The other blessing of winter was that it proved too much for Colonel Loudon and his grenadiers. After defending the city for less than two weeks, they abandoned it to the Jacobites.

The Highlanders converged on Inverness in desperation rather than triumph.

"There's no victory here," Ewan fretted to Flora. " 'Tis cold weather that has defeated those Sassenach fops, not this ragtag excuse for an army."

Flora knew he was right. She pitied the people of Inverness, who could ill afford to give away supplies, but she immediately joined the thousands of Jacobites swarming the town like locusts in a field. She combed house after house in search of oatmeal, bannock, and milk for the boys. In one cottage, an ancient corpse of a man offered her a trade. "Take whatever ye can carry in yer arms," he said. "Only gie me yer lodestone. It's a bonny bit a' work."

Flora looked down at her hand. There lay Sorley's compass, flashing in the light of the fireplace. What in heaven's name was it doing in her palm? She considered the ancient's offer. "Thank you, but no," she said finally. What if the campaign went badly and she ended up on the moors with Rosmairi and the Smalls? She'd need the compass to guide them to safety. Her decision was pure logic and had nothing to do with her feelings for Sorley. Nothing.

With her head bowed she trudged from the decrepit cottage.

At last the ice began to melt and winter began to wane. Flora delighted in the signs of spring. She eagerly pointed them out to the Three Smalls: a tumbling white stream, unfettered by ice; a spike of yellow and green Scotch broom boldly thrusting through the snow, and the gray-and-white checkered beauty of an osprey gliding low over the river. She trembled inside with silent joy to learn that Sterling Castle had at long last fallen to the Jacobites, and she waited ardently for word of Sorley. But she cursed the spring, too. No matter how lovely it might seem, it was a traitor. With the snows gone, Royalists on the trail of the prince would have an easy passage north.

Charles Edward had established a billet in Culloden House on Drummossie Moor, only a few miles from Inverness, and the clans set up camp nearby. Flora glimpsed her genteel young commander on several occasions, and each time her hopes plummeted. A serious ague had overtaken him, rattling his slim frame with violent fits of coughing. His face twitched in pain when he spoke, and when he walked he tottered along like a small child. It saddened and baffled Flora to think that this dispirited wreck of a man was responsible for so many lives.

Once, to her utter astonishment, the prince sent Jean-Paul, the young French gallant, to bring her to Culloden House for a royal audience. Charles Edward met with her in a small drawing room. His speech was slurred and his eyes dull, and he sprawled in his chair as if he cared not one whit if anyone mistook him for a common tippler. She had no idea why the prince wished to see her, and she hoped she would not have to endure his presence for very long. His face had a look of doom etched upon it.

"Your opinions have always served me well in the past," said the prince. "What do you think, mam'zelle? Shall I stay and fight, or disband my brave Highland army and regroup later?"

Flora thought for a moment. In the past, the prince had always done the opposite of whatever she suggested. This time she would lie in order to keep a foot in front of him. "I believe you should stay and face the English, Your Highness," she said. "It will crush the spirit of the clans if they are not soon allowed to do what they do best, which is to fight."

Charles Edward turned away from her, his chin resting on his knuckles. He fingered the lace at his throat in a dismissive manner that caused Flora to wonder if her audience had been concluded. She remained before him, however, and at last he addressed her. "I believe you're quite right, Miss Buchanan. That's precisely my position, too, and I shall not stop defending it until my generals see the wisdom of it. Thank you once again for your frank opinion. Jean-Paul will deliver you back to your people.''

The rogue! He cozened me! Flora thought. She immediately tried to refute her earlier statement, but the prince had diverted all his attention to his brandy glass. Jean-Paul swept her from the room, past two frowning Highland chieftains, a tipsy French officer, and a delicate young woman whom Flora recognized as Charles's mistress.

Her meeting with Prince Charles left Flora feeling defeated and disillusioned. To dispel her bitter frustration, she sought to dedicate herself to useful activities. If there was cleaning, cooking, or mending to be done, she took on the task without complaint. She was preparing griddle cakes one evening when she noticed Crann's ears cock straight forward, his attention fastened on something in the mist beyond her. Suddenly a shadow sprinted up to her at an awkward gallop, knocked the griddle into the fire, and began bellowing commands.

She recognized him by his zeal as much as his size. ''Ewan! You've destroyed our supper!'' she shouted as she picked half-cooked oatcakes from the heather.

''Sassenach!'' he cried. ''The duke and his dirty minions are but twenty miles away. We're to leave at once and join the clans for an attack tonight. Ha! We'll slaughter those gaffers in breeks as they snore in their beds, just as we did at Prestonpans.'' Ewan's voice vibrated with confidence. Apparently he had forgotten for the moment that the *Damainte* had been absent during that early victory. ''Cu! Gair! Dughal! Come with me. Miss Flora, you and Losgann stay and secure the camp.''

''Secure the camp,'' Flora repeated. His announcement all but stupefied her. If the king's forces were so close, they surely intended their own surprise attack. By the time she thought to mention this to Ewan, he and his men were gone, evaporating in the swirling mist as if they had never existed.

Flora longed to go with them, but she refused to abandon Rosmairi and the Smalls. Losgann, however, had no such restrictions. He galloped off after Ewan and the others, only to return a short time later in sullen silence. Although her mind churned with fear and excitement, Flora tried to stay calm for the sake of her second family. After supper, she dosed them all with brandy that Losgann had stolen in town. As she had hoped, they all fell asleep soon afterward, and she settled down next to the dwindling fire. She must keep watch, she told herself. For just what she didn't know.

A sudden chill pricked her spine and she wakened in darkness. Crann darted past her into the mist, growling like a wolf, but sprinted back a moment later, his tail between his legs and his eyes tight shut.

"Who goes there?" called Flora, grasping the scabbard of her dirk. Her heart slammed against her rib cage. Perhaps she was right. Perhaps the Sassenach were attacking. She crept forward and, as the mist cleared and revealed nothing alarming, she walked forward with more assurance. Perhaps a fox or wildcat had frightened Crann, she thought, squinting into the charcoal gray darkness. Or had someone thrown sand or salt in his face? She heard nothing but the cheerful song of an early lark, could see nothing—

Something caught her by the ankle and pulled her down. She tried to scream but a handful of tartan stopped her mouth. Someone crouched beside her, bolting her to the earth with a grip like steel. A face emerged from the mist.

"Now, Miss Flora, promise me you'll hold your whisht." The calm tone of Sorley's voice and the desperation in his face confounded Flora. When he removed his hand, she found it impossible to speak louder than a whisper.

"You," she managed at last. "Why have you come here?" Equally split between love and fear, she waited.

"I swear I'll no' harm you, if you'll only hear me out. I've never told a soul what I wish to tell you."

Flora sat up. For the first time she saw that Sorley's clothes were wringing wet and his face was scarlet. The remnants of a large bruise purpled his forehead. As she gazed at him, the fear in her heart began to melt into concern. "First, tell me what happened to you."

Sorley's fairy eyes were clouded with weariness. "We were returning from Sterling when we came upon the clans creeping toward the Royalist lines in the mist. We joined them, but devil take it! The night was dark, we lost our way, and the path we followed ended in a peat bog. So we returned. The others are at my back, and if you think I look a fright, you should see them."

"And the clout on your head?"

Sorley touched it and winced. "Ah, don't you recognize the work of your chieftain? I tried to approach you when the *Damainte* were still in Sterling, but that halfpenny and his cronies drove me off. And you may be sure it took some driving to keep me away from you."

Ewan! Crann growling at visitors in the mist . . . a hushed discussion . . . footsteps and silence. It had been puzzling. Now it was infuriating. "That jealous wee fiend!"

"He was only doing as he saw fit," Sorley said.

"What! That's the second time he's used ye ill. He might have slain ye! I'll flog him sore with my tongue when next I see him."

Sorley gave a harsh laugh. "Nay, you should keep quiet and let the man get some sleep. God knows the duke won't. Already the English are closing in on Drummossie Moor and drawing up their battle lines. The prince has been spoiling for a fight, and alas! He's about to receive one. You and I have so little time together—"

He stopped, breathed a soul-shuddering sigh, then leaned forward. His lips grazed hers. She could not resist him. He gathered her into his arms, and even fractured memories of her mother's death could not tear her from his sweet, devouring embrace. She had been forced to deceive many people during the past few months, she thought, but she would only be deceiving herself if she drove Sorley from her again.

"Aimil was dying," he whispered into her ear. "I did all I could for her, but it was never enough. I sent for a woman skilled in the art of healing, but she could do nothing. I promise you, I did not betray my wife with the healer or any other woman."

He paused and looked deeply into her face. "I believe you," she said, convinced by the savage flame of truth burning in his eyes.

"Aimil suffered greatly in her sickness. There was scarce an hour that she wasn't in pain. One beautiful summer's evening, when the air was sweet with the scent of heather, she could bear her lot no more. 'Help me, *a' ghraidth,*' she begged me. 'Release me from my suffering.' "

"Oh, my dearest! Such a cruel request to make of a husband!"

"Aye," Sorley said, his voice shaking. "Cruel, but crueler still to deny it. And I could not deny her. I suffocated her, as she wished, and when I drew the pillow from her face . . ." He stopped. The depth of his silence was the saddest sound Flora had ever heard. "A smile lay on her lips. Still, it's no wonder Ewan thought the worst and still does. I only hope that the Almighty will not damn me, and that you will forgive me."

The man she had loved so much in spite of herself

sobbed once and crumpled to the ground. All the scorn and suspicion that had weighted Flora's heart for so long rushed from her like frightened birds. "Forgive you, my love?" She cupped his glowing face in her hands. "For an act of courage and compassion? Nay, forgive me for ever doubting you. Long ago ... Ah! Even now it's hard to frame the words! My own father slew my mother. I was only a child, but I saw her death with my own eyes. And that was no act of mercy, but a stupid, blundering act of fear and anger."

"Ach!" Sorley's face twisted in pain and disbelief. "My poor beauty! What a life of misfortunes you've had. I promise you, if I should be alive on Drummossie Moor tomorrow evening, I'll find you and never stir foot away from you again."

Sorley pulled Flora down atop his chest, gripping her so tightly she wondered if he thought she might try to flee as she had before. She lay nestled in his grasp while the mist floated serenely over them, sealing them off from the dictates of princes and dukes alike. Lying in the damp heather with Sorley was a dream, not of pain and terror, but of love and security, and Flora wished she might never leave it. She breathed in the odor of his steaming skin and ran her hand over his sword belt so she might never forget the scent or texture of their love.

Again his lips lightly touched hers. "My darling Flora!" He sighed. "*Arrah!* but I dread the thought of laying down my life in battle without first having lain with you."

"You will not die," she told him firmly, but in her heart she feared for his safety. If only her desire could protect him! "But if you should perish, I'll not live without you."

"What, love? You'd leave those motherless wee weans to fend for themselves? Nay, I know you won't desert them." Sorley smiled and pulled gently on one of her golden curls.

"See how long it's become. You need another barbering, I'm thinking. Lovely Flora. With me or without me, you must go on. Swear it, my heart. Say that you'll save yourself if I should fall."

Flora gulped. Only days ago she had resigned herself to a life without Sorley. Now that she had him, she could not face losing him. "I . . ." She could not say the words! Instead she lunged at him, meaning to embrace him, hoping to somehow enchant him so that he might never leave her. But he caught her and kissed her full on the lips. Tears were in his eyes; she could taste them. Or were they her own? She couldn't tell. One by one he undid the buttons on her blouse and breeches. She fancied that her clothes slid from her body as if ordered to do so. Sorley's chest, pressed hard against her naked bosom, was warm and bare. She felt the thudding of his great heart. He was magnificently alive and he was with her.

Sorley's hands slid over her breasts. Softly he caressed her skin, then tongued her nipples. Her body rippled with pleasure. She ran her hand down his belly until she felt the firmness of Himself. The Highlander needed no more encouragement. With one ardent thrust he was inside her.

Tenderly they made love, long and slow. Thrice Sorley brought Flora to the very edge of ecstasy, only to ease her back from it each time. She was furious with love and longing. When ecstasy did take her, it sprang upon her unaware. It pushed her head back, ripped the breath from her, and threatened to blast her into a thousand fragments. "I swear it!" she cried, when the power to speak returned to her. She fought to hold back her tears when she recalled the gloomy meaning of her promise.

Sorley gazed down at her and grinned. His face was drenched in sweat, giving him the look of a man who had enjoyed the flames of hell. "Miss Flora, you have a way about you; there's no denying it. Come the morrow, in the thick of combat, I'll recall your face the way it looks at this moment, and I'll know what I'm fighting for."

Flora's curiosity got the better of her. "And how does my face look?" she said, raising a hand to her cheek. It was embarrassingly hot.

"Why, as red as a neep and as wet as an otter. In short, thoroughly degenerate."

"Not as degenerate as you, I hope."

Sorley laughed. He caressed her ears, then her chin. Flora shivered. In a few short hours, the beautiful hands that touched her so lovingly would be wielding a claymore with deadly results. "An unmarried woman traveling in the company of outcast men and keeping midnight trysts with widowed rogues? Mistress, you are right enough depraved!" Flora returned his laughter, despite the fear that had begun to envelop her. They kissed deeply. Finally Sorley drew back. "The only way to put a stop to your wanton ways is to wed you."

"Should we survive," she whispered.

Sorley made an exasperated clicking sound with his tongue. "Our conversation has come full circle, love. 'Tis time for me to leave you."

"No!" Flora gripped his naked shoulders. "Never leave me!"

But the shadow-man was already scrambling to his feet and flinging himself into his clothes. His handsome face was as hard as granite. "Don't seek me. I'll come to you after the battle. Do exactly as Ewan tells you. Watch the weans, and for the love of God, don't venture onto the field, no matter if the earth opens up and swallows us. D'ye mark me, woman?"

"A-aye." Where had her darling gone? A warrior had taken his place, all in a matter of moments. She knew it had to be so, had even anticipated the change, but was shaken all the same. "Pray give no orders to me," she said quietly. " 'Tis not needed. I won't desert the lads. Go, for you must go. I'll not interfere."

Sorley stood, his hand to his chin, as if weighing the truth of her words. Then he extended his arms and helped her rise. In a burst of motion he seized her hand and kissed it with such passion that for an instant she thought he had bitten her. "You have my compass?"

"Always."

He gave her a little nod, satisfied. "Then farewell." Suddenly he spun away from her and strode off into the mist. His image grew dimmer and grayer with each step, until she wasn't sure she saw him. Then she knew that she didn't. He had vanished. She felt numb, panicked, and enraptured, all at the same time. A terrifying possibility engulfed her: the same Providence that had acquitted the love of her life might very well destroy him.

Chapter Thirteen

Flora readily admitted to herself that she was not much schooled in military strategy. But as she, Ewan, and Cu surveyed Drummossie Moor at dawn, she was struck by what a truly wretched place it was for the prince to take a stand against thirty thousand Sassenach troops.

"The ground is as soft as a bog," said Ewan, who stood at her elbow, pulling at his beard in exasperation. "If the clans charge, they'll sink up to their knees."

"Or up to the ears, in your case," Cu added.

"And what of these walls?" Flora interjected, hoping Ewan would ignore Cu's friendly insult. She nodded at the extensive earthworks that traversed the field like six-foot-high molehills.

"Dikes," said Ewan. "They divide one crop from another. Good husbandry, perhaps, but if the clans charge, they'll have to scale those things before they get at the

Sassenach. If we hadn't marched our guts out last night for nothing, we could bound over those walls like rabbits."

"You could burrow under them like a rabbit," Cu suggested.

"To hell with you," muttered Ewan.

"If you please!" Flora cried. "Fight the Sassenach, not each other." The men looked at her in astonishment, and Flora wished she'd said nothing. She knew her companions were half-dead from exhaustion, like the Jacobites on the field who swayed on their feet as they tried to stand at attention under the prince's banner.

With a sense of doom, Flora took in the opposite end of the moor. Her throat tightened. She felt sick to her stomach. A huge expanse of red uniforms outnumbered the Highland host three to one or more. Horses whinnied, frightened and excited. The barrels of brass cannons gleamed golden in the light of daybreak. And what could the Jacobites muster against such a force? she thought. Not heavy armaments, certainly, and only two hundred horse. Their only advantage was raw courage, which they had in abundance.

"Can we defeat them?" she asked, knowing Ewan's answer before he gave it.

"Aye," he said curtly. He tossed his head like an impatient lion. "We've never had a loss, Miss Flora, remember that. The Sassenach have scattered whenever we've charged them. We may be outmanned, but that only means that more of them will be running from us."

Flora wasn't convinced. She knew that Sorley expected to die on the field; why else would he have said farewell to her? She said nothing as Ewan summoned what was left of his fighting force and prepared to set out for the Cameron lines. To her surprise, he took her by the hand and guided her away from the others. "Please, dear Flora," he said, "listen carefully." Flora felt her mouth drop open. She had never heard Ewan beseech anyone, least of all her, and she didn't know what to make of this remarkable event. "Stay with Rosmairi and the Smalls," he continued. "Keep them off the field, and stay off it yourself. If the day goes badly for us and I don't return, search out Gair or Cu. They'll take you to a hiding place where none will find you."

For so many months Flora had had tender thoughts toward no one but Sorley, Rosmairi, and the Smalls. Now she realized with a shock how much the overweening little Cameron meant to her. If he died, she would feel as if she had lost a brother. Her throat felt tight and she choked back tears. "Ewan, what would I do without you? What would the Smalls do? Forgive me for never thinking of your safety before this moment."

He stared up at her a few moments, his bright eyes brimming with a hidden emotion that Flora could not quite decipher. Then he raised her hand to his lips, just as Sorley had done hours earlier, with nearly as much passion. "I care for you deeply, mistress, though I may not always appear to. If I knew you'd come to harm, I would be dead inside. I promise you I'll do all I can to keep living, so that I may return to you."

Ewan loves me, Flora thought, as Sorley loves me. She had suspected as much before. Now she knew for certain, even though he was too conscious of his appearance to state his affections as boldly as her beloved. She felt flattered and uneasy. Quickly organizing her scattered wits, she stammered something that she hoped was noncommittal. They stood in silence, her hand still in Ewan's. At last he unsnapped a pistol from his belt and shoved it toward her. "There's a ball in her, so take care how you handle her. Mind the kick should you have to fire her." Flora took the gun but said nothing. There was no need to speak. She knew she was in danger. They were all in danger.

It wasn't until Ewan turned to go that Flora recovered her tongue. "Sorely killed his wife only to end her suffering," she called out to Ewan. "He's not the monster you make him out to be."

The dwarf smiled. He didn't look angry, just resigned. "You're free to believe whatever he tells you," he replied. "Mayhap he's right. But to me, he'll always be a murderer."

He walked off slowly, proudly. *Just like the Jacobites and the Royalists,* Flora thought, Sorely and Ewan would forever be at odds with each other.

"I want to fight with the *Damainte!*"

"Listen! Thunder!"

"That's the Sassenach cannon, ye wheybrain."

"Let me fight, Miss Flora."

"Maybe it's our cannon, cutpurse."

"Dinna call me that! Our cannon canna fire! I'm no' a thief!"

"I can fight fine. I'll use a dirk, like Ewan."

The Smalls' thin voices crackled in the cold of the tiny hut. "Whisht!" Flora cuffed their shaggy heads. "Stop your bickering. You're to be quiet, remember? And Son, no, ye canna join the fight. The prince isn't so desperate that he's sending lads of nine into the fray."

"I want to join the battle," Whoreson whined. "I'm old enough to fight."

Flora ignored the boy's blather and tried to take stock of their situation. The battle had been raging for perhaps half an hour. She thought they were all fairly safe in the hidey-hole Ewan had found them, a turf-wall shieling on the edge of the woods surrounding the field. Then again, the field was so thick with gunsmoke that, whenever she peered through the doorway, she could not tell which way the battle was going.

Crann began barking. Flora turned around to silence the dog, but snapped her mouth shut, speechless. Crann had been lying in the corner next to Rosmairi. Now he lay by himself. "Where's Rosmairi?" wailed Flora. "How did she leave without me seeing her?" She glanced around the cottage, although she knew there was no place to hide.

"The snow door, Miss Flora," Bugger shouted over a barrage of cannon fire. He pointed to the corner where Crann was still sitting. Flora rushed up to the dog, and sure enough, behind him was a wicker door that stood ajar, the opening so low that Ewan could not have walked upright through it. "If snow blocks the other door, ye can always get out."

"Stay here!" Fighting down panic, Flora dashed out the front door. The air reeked of sulfur and rang with the screams of men and the rattle of weapons. In the distance, Flora could see scattered figures milling in a blanket of smoke. "Rosmairi!"

"Miss Flora?"

The woman stood with her back pressed against the wall of the cottage. Tears glistened in her eyes. "I canna remember where I am!"

Flora enfolded her in her arms and gently guided her back toward the main doorway. She was heartened to see that Rosmairi at least remembered Miss Flora. "You're near Culloden House on Drummossie Moor," she explained. "There's a terrible battle. Ye can hear it and smell it, if not see it. We must go inside." Perhaps under the circumstances, Rosmairi was lucky, she thought. If only they all could forget Drummossie Moor.

Back in the cottage, Flora immediately sensed something

was amiss. "Where's Son?" she asked the younger Smalls. The boys stared at their toes. They didn't need to speak. Flora knew. "Stay here, for God's sake!" she shouted. Then she was out the door and wading into the bank of noxious smoke.

Whoreson's trail through the crushed bracken led straight through the woods toward the churning battle-field. Ewan's and Sorley's warnings to stay off the field came back to Flora, and she quickly dismissed them. She had to find the boy! At the edge of the tree line, she stopped. Ahead of her, all was chaos, and somewhere in that chaos was Whoreson. She knew she had come upon the flank of Clan MacDonald when she saw their banner, a mailed fist gripping a cross. The Highlanders stood in ragged lines, their ranks decimated by Hanoverian marks-men. As she watched, five men fell, one after the other. Why don't they charge? Flora thought, though she knew the answer: they'd been given no order to charge.

Musket balls whizzed past her, inches from her ears. Gunsmoke swirled about her, stinging her eyes and making it hard to breathe. Despite all this, death seemed oddly distant, even unimportant. After she found Whoreson was time enough to relax and allow herself the luxury of being horrified.

Flora crouched low and hurried on, searching for Clan Cameron and their red-and-yellow banner. Wouldn't Whoreson have run off in that direction, trying to find Ewan? He couldn't have run very far. She tried not to think about the dead and dying at her feet and avoided looking into their faces. What if she discovered Sorley among them?

Pain! A hot red stripe burned her forearm. She'd been shot! The shock of the wound made her lose her footing. She stumbled and fell to her knees. I'll not go down until

I find Son, she promised herself, and lurched back to a standing position.

What had happened? It was as if the Highland host had fallen into the mouth of hell. From where she stood, she could see that parts of the army surged forward through the smoke, while others milled about in confusion. She saw a brief flash of Charles Edward on his gray barb, desperately galloping down his lines, entreating the clans to hold their ground. All around her men were shouting in Gaelic or screaming in agony. One Highlander in front of her collapsed, his face shredded to a bleeding pulp by grapeshot. Red rivulets turned the ground beneath her into a grotesque tartan of blood and earth.

Flora forced herself to concentrate on Whoreson. If she gave in to panic she'd never find him. Even if she kept her wits there was no guarantee she'd find him.

It was then that she saw him.

The urchin sat next to a corpse not twenty feet from her. He wailed like a babe but appeared to be unharmed. Flora let out a whoop of victory. She half ran, half crawled over to the terrified boy. "Son!"

His sobs turned into hiccoughs that shook his scrawny frame. "Miss Flora! Cu's dead."

At first she didn't understand him. The desperate clamor of the battle blazing around and above her made it hard for her to breathe, let alone think. Then she recognized the blue-and gray tartan of the corpse beside Son.

"Oh, dear Christ! Let it not be true." Flora rolled the body over, and as she did so a loud growl rumbled from it. "Cu! You're alive!"

"Nay, I'm dead," he whispered. A musket ball had penetrated one eye. Blood gushed from the corner of his mouth. Flora knew all chance of saving him was gone. "Yer shadowman is alive. I saw him pass by a moment ago."

Her heart stirred, not only to think that her beloved was alive, but that Cu had thought to tell her. Dearest Cu! "What shall I do now, good friend?" She patted his hand and he clasped it with surprising strength.

"Leave," he said, coughing. "Take the boy. Now!"

As if to underscore his words, a musket ball sizzled through the wild mass of curls on the crown of her head. Flora jumped. Her father had once said that the margin between life and death was only a hairsbreadth; she wondered if he had ever known how correct he was. She leaned forward and kissed the dying man's forehead. "I won't forget you," she said. She stood up, then flung her arms around Whoreson and dragged the shivering child up beside her.

From the corner of her eye she saw someone streaking toward her. She froze. An English fusilier was bearing down on her, his bayonet dripping with black gore and aimed at her throat. She clasped Whoreson so tightly that he squealed in protest. *I don't mind dying, heavenly Father,* she prayed to herself, *but please! Spare the lad!*

Like a rabbit enthralled by the stare of a fox, she waited for the stab of the hideous blade. The soldier was so close she could see every detail of his face. *By the blessed Virgin!* she thought. *He's barely older than Losgann!*

The pistol! Flora reached for it, but it wasn't at her side. She had left it in the herder's hut. She shut her eyes and committed her soul to God's care.

A whipping sound as sharp as the north wind whistled above her. She opened her eyes in time to see the flash of a claymore. Suddenly the young fusilier buckled sideways. His head toppled from his neck in a fountain of blood. Flora opened her mouth to scream, but the sound stayed within her.

"Go! Run! Save yourself and the wean!"

The hoarse rasp of Sorley's voice brought Flora back to life. She looked behind her, but her champion had already vanished in a raging ocean of redcoats, Highlanders, and horses, swept along by the Furies of war. Again she owed her life to him! How ironic that she had once thought he meant to take it from her.

The tide of bodies washed over her and Whoreson. Worried that so many men might knock her down and trample her, Flora dropped to the ground and began crawling on all fours. Whoreson crept along underneath her, protected by her body. She watched countless times as horses' hooves danced within a few inches of her face and scattered dirt in her hair. A ludicrous thought occurred to her: perhaps her old beau Captain Stelton—now Major Stelton—was careening over her aboard his charger, as unaware of her now as he had been on the Plain of Falkirk.

Inch by inch over the bloody battleground Flora and Whoreson toiled over broken bodies and dying soldiers. She saw Gair, still alive and whole, she noticed thankfully, and a few other men she knew, both the living and the dead. Several times Flora thought she would be ill and almost stopped, but the knowledge that Whoreson would never survive without her drove her on. After an eternity of crawling she could see the end of the field where the line of rowan trees began, the trees that shielded her loved ones from the suffering around them. "Very nearly there, Son," she murmured. "Soon we'll be safe."

She didn't see the riderless horse until it was nearly on top of her. She lurched to one side, expecting it to gallop past. But as it charged by, a hoof struck her head a glancing blow. The pain took away her breath. She crashed to the ground, nearly crushing Whoreson beneath her. "Miss Flora! Miss Flora!" he whispered intently into her ear, but she was already slipping into senselessness. Oh, Sorley! she thought. He had saved her only to lose her.

She was running, running, running, Son in her arms, screeching. Behind her thundered a white horse. She had to avoid it. Suddenly Sorley was at her side, running with her over a field of horribly mangled, bleeding bodies. She wanted to stop to weep for them but couldn't. The horse was right behind her. She could feel its moist breath on her neck. "Stop and face it," Sorley called to her. "It's not a horseman, only a horse."

She was terrified, but she trusted Sorley above all else. Clutching Son, who had become an infant, she stopped and faced the horse. It swerved, slid to a stop beside her, and gave a laugh. A very human laugh. "I bought ye something for yer birthday, pretty Flora," the monster said.

Flora woke screaming in the herder's hut. Rosmairi and Gair peered down at her with deep concern. "It's all right, Miss Flora," Rosmairi said gently. "The battle's over."

"Son! Where's Son?" Flora sat up. She looked around in vain for the fiendish horse. Her head ached, and when she put her hand to her ear she discovered an egg-size lump just above it. She saw also that someone had lovingly bandaged her injured arm.

"Is that the lad ye were with?" Rosmairi asked, nodding toward all three Smalls, asleep in a corner. Who would have guessed that Rosmairi had been with the boys for almost a year? thought Flora. "This kind man found ye both on the moor and brought ye back here."

"That kind man is your husband," Flora mumbled, still in a daze. "Thank you, Gair. I'm indebted to you. You've saved my life, and the child's, too."

"Rivers run blood in the spring," Gair answered, and Flora decided she must force herself to communicate with him. What had Ewan said? If he didn't come to her, she should go to Cu or Gair. Sadly, Cu was gone, and Ewan's fate was a mystery. That left only the wise madman.

"Gair, you saved me, didn't you?"

"Aye, mistress, carried you all the way here. It's good the lad could walk, for I couldn't carry him too."

"Miss Flora," Rosmairi blurted. "All is lost. The clans are defeated." She clutched Flora's arm like a drowning child, and Flora couldn't tell if she meant to give comfort or take it. "The Sassenach are killing the wounded on the field and taking no one prisoner. We're not safe here. If we stay, they'll find us for certain. That's so, Gair, isn't it?"

As the man ran his fingers through his beard, Flora saw that his hair looked as if it had been sprinkled with gray ash. Clearly he had suffered a shock as frightening as his own madness. "Aye, but it's dark now. We can yet escape if luck is with us."

"Escape to where?" Flora asked, then berated herself silently and tried again. "You'll lead us to Ewan's trysting spot, won't you?"

"I'll lead you to the spot," Gair replied in a grim tone, "but I cannot promise a tryst."

Rosmairi woke the boys. All six crept into the cold, calm night, with Crann at Gair's side. Flora's gorge rose at the stench in the air, the sickening stink of a slaughterhouse. She was still so light-headed from her injuries that she could not walk on her own, but held on to Gair's arm for support. Where were they going? She couldn't tell. Finally she remembered Sorley's compass, but although she found it right away she couldn't read it in the dark. Gair seemed to know the way, however. He never slowed, never hesitated, but marched with long, soldierly strides into the darkness.

Once, climbing a small ridge, Flora stopped to catch

her breath. While she rested, the moon sailed out from behind a cloud and spilled its silver light on the battlefield. What she saw made her cry out and reel backward in alarm. Drummossie Moor was littered with the corpses of the bold Highlanders, their naked legs plainly visible in the stark moonlight. Royalist soldiers waded through the mountains of bodies, bayoneting those who showed signs of life. As she listened in horror to the shrieks of the dying, Flora felt rage and repulsion, but little by little another feeling trickled into her consciousness: fear. Fear for Sorley. She had worried for him at Falkirk, where so few Jacobites had fallen. Now it seemed unlikely that he or anyone else could have lived through such massive devastation.

Someone pulled her to the ground. She was about to protest when she heard the thump of hooves. The moonlight revealed a horseman who swayed slightly in the saddle as he sang a bawdy song under his breath. She shivered when his shadow passed over her. He was so close she could smell the brandy he had been drinking. Flora guessed he hadn't seen her or the others, but his horse did. It stared at her as it passed and flicked one ear backward, blowing steam from its nostrils. She gave thanks to God that the man was not as alert as his beast.

After the rider passed, Gair set off like a hound on a scent, making it all but impossible for the others to keep pace. Flora kept one hand on Rattie and the other on Rosmairi, driving the boys before her over the moor and hoping they would not lose sight of Gair. At one point they stopped to rest, and Flora fell asleep. She awoke just as dawn was breaking, obliterating the protective darkness. Her arm throbbed a little, but her head pains and dizziness were gone.

Flora was waking Rosmairi and the boys when she heard Gair give a shout and receive one in return. Her heart brightened. Ewan's voice was unmistakable. Thank the Lord, Ewan had survived the slaughter somehow!

Flora gazed around her, searching for her friends, but could make out nothing save rolling green moorland, an occasional stunted pine, and hundreds of gray granite boulders. Crann, responding to nothing Flora could hear or see, galloped into the wilderness. Flora waited, but when Gair did not reappear, she grew anxious.

"That man . . . my husband's gone underground with the fairies," Rosmairi mumbled, and Flora could not say whether she spoke in jest or not. A few more months and her friend might very well be giving birth amid these bleak surroundings. It was a somber thought. Briefly she wondered if she might be carrying Sorley's child.

A stone moved, then headed toward her.

Flora blinked. It was the dwarf. But he wasn't the dwarf she remembered. His head hung low and he limped slightly, giving his odd gait a halting, lopsided twist. She had never seen him walk so slowly, as if an invisible demon were dragging him across the moor against his will. When he was a double arm's length from Flora's bedraggled crew, he stopped. "Miss Flora, Rosmairi, lads," he said, as if to reassure himself of their identity.

"Oh, Ewan! You're alive!" she cried.

"Only in a manner of speaking," he retorted. "In the past two days I've seen what no man should ever have to see. But it does my heart good to see that the five of you have outsmarted Stinking Willie."

"And you as well. I'd be nowhere without you." She wished she could show Ewan how deeply she appreciated him, but when she tried to take his hand he stepped backward, eluding her. She drew back, hurt to the quick, then realized that she had no reason to feel rebuffed. Who knew what the little man had been through in the past few hours?

She wished she could distract him from the horrors that ate at his soul, but he was deep in grief; she could see that. "You're wounded. You can't walk properly."

Ewan shrugged. "Mistress, I couldn't walk properly before, so there's no harm done now." A fiery trace of the old Ewan returned to his eyes, then died down. "Follow me," he said abruptly.

"Where?" Flora puzzled aloud. "There's naught here."

Ewan mustered a smile. "Oh, but there is! Come, I'll show the lot of you."

Flora trusted Ewan with her life. She knew he would never place Rosmairi or the Smalls in danger. Even so, it took every grain of conviction within her to gather up the children and herd them toward the dwarf's retreating back. She grabbed Rosmairi by the elbow. "There's nothing here but rocks!" she complained to the patient woman.

"Oh, Miss Flora!" Rosmairi smiled in the dazed, happy way she had about her. "Highlanders live among the rocks. You'd be surprised at the secrets a rock can hide."

Flora was used to strange conversations, but this, she thought, must surely be one of the most inane. She followed Ewan and the boys up to a heap of stone slabs that had a vaguely architectural look about them. "A cave? There's no entrance."

Ewan turned around and gave her a ferocious, not altogether friendly grin. "Mistress, there is an entrance, but there's no cave. This is a dolmen, the work of the ancient ones who lived here long before us Gaels. No one knows why they built these places, perhaps to house their dead or conduct their heathenish rituals. One thing's sure: this one is a haven for us." The boys helped him move some brush and branches at the foot of one massive stone to reveal an excavation about four feet deep. "Come down here, as I'm doing," Ewan said, lowering himself into the ditch.

The boys followed eagerly, despite their utter exhaustion. Rosmairi climbed down next. Flora hung back, afraid of descending below the earth. She felt as if her friends were entering a grave. Ewan looked up at her and reached his stubby arm toward her. "Have no fear, Miss Flora. I'll assist you. As you'll soon see, you have all the reason in the world to come down here."

Flora frowned. She didn't understand Ewan's cryptic comment, but now was scarcely the time to solve riddles. At the edge of the pit she hesitated, then stepped onto a small stone that seemed to serve as a step. Immediately it gave way and her leg plunged downward, followed by the rest of her. She screamed, imagining the impact of earth and stone on her head. Instead she fell on something soft and pliant. Ewan. The little man had leaped forward to break her fall. "God save you!" She gasped. "What a fool I am!"

"Not at all, Miss Flora. A fine bold entry, if a little lacking in dignity." Ewan picked himself up with the agility of an otter, then replaced a few of the branches that covered the pit. "Now all of you, stoop down and duck under the stone."

The stone Ewan referred to was one of the great rectangular slabs that composed the dolmen. It was oriented in a horizontal fashion, like a wall, but with an opening some three feet high beneath it. The Smalls scurried underneath it like badgers. Rosmairi dropped on all fours and wriggled after them.

"You do as well," Ewan ordered Flora.

Flora felt her heart hammer in her chest. "I'm no' fond of tight places," she said. In her mind's eye she saw a little girl wedged in a corner against a railing, too shocked to weep.

"It can't be helped," Ewan countered. By dint of much gentle prodding and cajoling, he succeeded in coaxing Flora down on her hands and knees. Under Ewan's constant encouragement, she began to crawl under the stone, as she had seen Rosmairi do moments earlier. She heard Crann barking and crept toward the sound. But the ancient granite block was lower than she had thought, and she scraped her back against its dirk-sharp edge. The dank scent of earth overpowered her senses, stifling her breath. Panic seeped into her heart. She was entombed. She couldn't breathe!

Flora began to scrabble backward out from under the stone, but a swat on her bottom made her squeal in surprise and sent her lunging forward.

"No dawdling now, mistress," said Ewan. He'd been right behind her all the time. "Breathe deeply. You can smell our campfire and see its light."

Flora took a hesitant sniff. The fragrance of burning peat filled her nose, almost as pleasant as incense. She saw the fire's red glow and heard the sound of hushed voices. Then, all of a sudden, she found herself in a cavelike chamber. A small fire in its center cast fantastic shadows all around the dolmen's interior. Besides Rosmairi, Gair, and the children, she spotted Losgann and Dughal, now both so gaunt they might have passed for skeletons recently added to the huge burial vault. The lad and the giant stared at her, awestruck, as if they were looking at a ghost. They took me for dead, she realized, and smiled at them.

Ewan edged out from beneath the stone, brushing dirt from his plaid. "Not a palace, to be sure," he said, his laughter not quite hiding his bitterness. "Still, it's as safe a place as we're likely to find."

As Flora's vision adjusted to the smoky dimness, she saw that the dolmen was in fact a hollow, artificial mountain. What had appeared to be a jumble of granite chunks from the outside changed, on examination of the interior, into a parquet of giant stones cemented by an amalgam of peat, small rocks, branches, and thatch. The chamber itself was neatly stocked with crockery, kindling, peat, and a cache of oatmeal and other foodstuffs. It was beautiful and orderly, a cruel counterpoint to the Jacobite cause and her own chaotic life. "His Highness would be fortunate to have this as his palace." She sighed, imagining the prince hiding in the heather with hordes of red soldiers in frenzied pursuit.

"Floraidh!"

The guttural cry ripped her thoughts into fragments. At once Flora saw what she had been too dazed to see earlier: a bed made of heather branches and bits of clothing, and on it a man so tall that his legs protruded well beyond the limits of the makeshift cot. Not just any man.

Flora was at his side before she knew she had taken a single step. She reached out to touch him, then stopped, her hand an inch from his sweat-stained face. What she beheld made her soul scream in outrage. What had they done to him? She stared hopelessly at his face, and the words she had meant to say froze in her throat.

"I thought you'd wish to see him," Ewan drawled, shuffling up beside her, "though faith! King Geordie's troops didn't leave much of him behind."

Flora tried to ignore Ewan's cruel words but found them uncomfortably true. Sorley Fior's body had been slashed, punctured, crushed, and beaten to within the far reaches of his endurance and then some. His shout of recognition had cost him dearly, and he now lay panting on the bed, trying to keep his eyes open so that he might look at her. Flora stroked his wrist, but stopped when she saw him

wince. "Oh, my poor Sorley! He's burning with fever!"
She found a damp rag and laid it on his forehead.

"Aye, and the wrist's broken," Ewan explained, with a
casual wave of his hand. "As are some ribs, I think. But
that's the least of it. He took a thrust from a bayonet, and
that's drained him almost dry of blood. If Dughal hadn't
carried the devil away in his arms, Sorley Fior would be
but one more corpse on Culloden Field. It seems as if I
have merely changed his grave site."

Flora tore her gaze from Sorley and glowered down at
the impertinent dwarf. "Even now you can't speak well of
him," she said quietly. "In the name of God, why did you
pluck him from death's grip and bring him here?" Ewan
looked around the dolmen as if seeking help, but the other
Damainte were occupied in feeding the fire and heating
some broth. Though the Smalls' bright laughter struck
Flora as being very much at odds with their solemn surroundings, it was a relief to think that someone could still
laugh. "Why?"

Ewan reached up and laid his crooked fingers on her
face. "Miss Flora," he murmured, with all the tenderness
of a lover, "I wish to do right by you. I engaged you in
this pretty mess and I would like to save you from it. If
that means saving my rival, who is unfortunately the man
you love, so be it, though in truth I doubt he'll tarry much
longer in the land of the living."

Ewan's bold words, seemingly so careless and unfeeling,
seared Flora's brain and made her eyes sting with tears.
She dug her fingers into the dwarf's plaid and thrust her
face into his. "A surgeon!" she cried. "The English officers
travel with their personal surgeons. My father told me so
years ago, but surely it's still true. Ye must find a doctor
and bring him here. Ye must, or I shall! Else Sorley will
die."

Ewan broke free with difficulty, and only then did Flora realize how ferociously she had been holding him. She felt the gazes of the other *Damainte* on her back and tried to ignore them. Then the terrier of a man who had so often consigned Sorley to the flames of hell said the one thing Flora had never thought to hear from his lips: "Very well. I'll do all I can for the wretch." The dwarf barked a brief command to poor Gair, who had just sat down to a bowl of broth, and both men scurried out of the dolmen into certain danger.

What had she done? Flora pressed her hand to her head to quell a sudden, stabbing pain. She had sent her friends on a nigh impossible errand, straight into the maw of an enemy devoted to their destruction. But what else could she do?

She stole a glance at Sorley, who lay with his eyes closed, the plaid over his chest barely stirring as he breathed. Suddenly his fingers gripped her own, then relaxed. What would she do without him? There was no question: she had to save him. No matter what the cost. She had not survived thus far to give him up without a struggle. And a struggle, she knew, was the best that awaited them both.

Chapter Fourteen

How long had Ewan been gone?

In the constant night of the dolmen, Flora had lost track of time. It might have been dawn, it might have been midnight—she didn't know, and the uncertainty added to her apprehension. With each passing minute she feared that Sorley slipped farther and farther away from her. At one point he fell into a deep, black sleep that hideously mimicked the last sleep. She stitched his wounds and washed his body to keep him cool, but she could not wake him.

"Is he dead yet?" Rattie craned his neck over Flora's shoulder for a peek at the sick man.

"No, and he shall not die," Flora replied, trying to keep her voice steady. The boy meant no harm, she reminded herself. For most of his five years, death had probably been as commonplace as life, and neither had really mattered to him. "I shall not let him die."

Rosmairi wandered up to Flora, sat at her feet, and laid her head in Flora's lap. It was a sweet gesture, as innocent as a child's, and Flora loved her all the more for it. "Who's this man here?" Rosmairi asked.

"Sorley Fior," Flora replied. She had been awake for more than a day, and her exhaustion was beginning to erode her patience. "You've seen him month after month. Is his face not at all familiar to you?"

"I remember Sorley Fior," the woman answered quietly, squinting down into Sorley's face. "This is not Sorley Fior. This man is white faced and sickly and cannot hold up his head, and Sorley Fior is fine and strong, as pink as a salmon and as proud as a stag. They can't be the same man, mistress."

That her addled friend remembered Sorley yet could not recognize him shook Flora to the quick and made her wonder if her beloved had changed in some vital and intrinsic way that she had failed to notice. She was brooding on this forbidding prospect when Crann barked, the boys gave a collective shout, and she heard a great deal of grumbling and shuffling about behind the stone wall. Ewan scrambled under first, followed by a portly gentleman dressed in a flowing coat and begrimed white breeches. His peruke was missing, and his hair stood up straight on his head, as if trying to match his expression of unfettered terror. Because of his twisted features and the darkness of the vault, Flora did not recognize him right away, but when she did, she leaped up and rushed straight toward him.

"Dr. Barclay! Why aren't you attending the prince?" she said.

Barclay tried to speak, but Ewan gave him such a clout on the back that the pudgy physician stumbled forward and nearly fell on his face. When he regained his footing, Ewan answered her. "Mistress, this lump of walking shite is a turncoat, the lowest of the low. When things began to go badly for us, he switched his allegiances, just as a rat runs from a burning building. I found him at a public house in Inverness, feeding that great gut of his.''

The doctor laid a protective hand on his substantial midriff, which quaked like a pudding. Flora felt his desperation and touched his sleeve with a gentle hand. ''You're in no danger,'' she reassured him. ''We need your skill to help save a dear friend.''

Barclay stopped shaking and seemed to gain some control over his terror. He squinted at her long and hard. ''Miss Buchanan, by my soul! What in the name of all that's decent has brought you to this condition?''

Ewan buffeted the doctor yet again. ''Enough of that,'' he muttered. ''Your business here is to tend the sick, not ply the lady with questions. Here.'' On Ewan's command, Gair, who had stolen up behind the doctor, grabbed him by the shoulder and pushed him to Sorley's bedside. A black leather bag materialized from Gair's plaid, and he threw it on the floor at Barclay's feet.

The doctor was a professional despite his shortcomings. He gave Sorley a brief examination, then let out a long, shuddering sigh. ''This man's exceedingly ill,'' he said. ''I'm not at all certain I can do him any good.''

''Oh, ye must!'' On a wild impulse born of hopelessness and fatigue, Flora snatched Barclay's dirt-splotched hand and pressed it to her lips. ''This is a great man, a heroic man, and he must live. Without him I'd lose my senses.''

Ewan frowned and sidled in between Flora and the doctor. ''The lady is tired and knows not what she's saying,'' he said in a rumbling voice. ''Nevertheless, you sniveling Sassenach sawbones, do what you can for your patient. If you succeed in saving him, you'll live and be rewarded. If not . . .'' Ewan casually ran his hand over his dirk. ''Well, we won't consider that just now, and mark me—you wouldn't want to consider it.''

Flora was relieved to see that the doctor required no further inspiration but set about his business without delay. He put her to work grinding medicines with a mortar and pestle while he studied Sorley's wounds and bathed them with a foul-smelling concoction. Flora fought to stay alert, but sometimes she dozed off, only to wake with a start, afraid that Sorley needed her. He was still unconscious, however, no better than before, but no worse either.

Adam Barclay was a curious man. He scrubbed his hands often in cool water that Gair fetched from a spring near the dolmen. "Why do you wash your hands with such devotion?" Flora asked him, after one especially long ablution. "Can't you abide the smell of the wounds?"

The doctor smiled. "Believe me, Miss Buchanan, I have smelled worse. Nay, it is a habit I acquired in Africa, where I served as ship's doctor aboard a merchant vessel. The Moorish doctors clean their hands often, claiming it benefits their patients, and, as they saved more afflicted than they lost, I began to emulate them."

During her long vigils with the doctor, Flora learned much about the man. He was in the joint service of a major and a colonel, who treated him with all the respect due someone who had the skills to bring them back from the edge of the grave, if needed. "If only the good officers were as generous with their purse as they are with their compliments," the doctor complained. "I have alas grown accustomed to life's little luxuries during my travels and in my practice at Edinburgh, and it's a hardship indeed to be without good tobacco and a keg of dry sack."

Flora had no idea just how Ewan intended to reward the doctor, as he had promised—assuming, of course, that Sorley recovered. It was difficult to tell if his condition was improving or declining, as his fever broke occasionally, only to roar back again with renewed vigor. Day and night became one enormous well of darkness, brightened only by the peat fire and whatever sunlight filtered in through chinks in the great stones. She relied on Ewan and Gair to keep her informed of the passing days, for only they were permitted outside the safety of the dolmen for more than a few minutes at a time. If luck was with her, she was allowed to fetch water from the spring, and occasionally she went with Ewan on his rounds.

One evening at sunset, she accompanied Ewan on his watch, sitting outside the stone fortress in the half-light of sunset, hoping the Sassenach kept their distance. "You must try to get some rest," he told her. "You'll fall ill yourself, and what good will that do?"

"I'm well, thank you," she said. "It's good to be out in the air, away from the smoke." She looked out toward the west, at the red ribbons shed by the setting sun, and found her heart inexplicably flooding with sadness. She had been through so much with Ewan, yet she had never thanked him for all he had done for her. He had even rescued Sorely, all for her sake.

Flora reached out and took the dwarf's crabbed hand in hers. He was a prideful man, an unpredictable man, and she was unsure how he would react to what she had to say. "I'm so grateful to you, Ewan Fada," she began. "Even if all goes amiss and Sorley doesn't recover, I'll still hold you in highest esteem. Few men indeed would be"— she paused only an instant—"big enough to succor the man they hated for the sake of a . . . well, a foundling, I suppose. I fear I've been more hindrance than help to you these past months."

The little man for once had nothing to say. He merely gazed at her, his brown beard gilded by the dying light, his eyes blazing with some private secret. Minutes passed, and at last he spoke. "Come with me, Miss Flora. I'll show you something fine."

Intrigued, Flora rose and followed Ewan to the side of the dolmen. A dozen small rocks the size of a person's head lay heaped next to a much larger stone. As she watched, Ewan lifted the stones to reveal a small depression in the earth. In it lay a leather bag. "Do y'see this?" he said, dragging the satchel from the dirt.

Flora recognized it at once as one of the saddlebags that Dughal had lugged on his shoulders ever since she had fallen in with the *Damainte*. They carried extra weapons, and what else she could not guess. "Pistols?" she said. "Powder?"

Ewan shook his head, and a faint smile lit up his boyish face. He pulled the bag from the earth and opened it as tenderly as he might have undressed his own child. A dazzling glint of light caught Flora's eye. She stared at the contents of the bag, wondering if she had gone mad and had begun to see illusions. "Gold!"

"Aye, and silver." Ewan fished some items from the saddlebag and spread them out with loving care on the ground before Flora. Guineas, silver coins, rings, snuff-boxes, chains, buttons, buckles, clasps, spurs, even a knife and fork.

"Is it yours?"

"Aye, mine and Cu's, but as he's dead, it's mine alone now."

Flora picked up a beautiful golden ring set with sapphires. A love token perhaps? She gingerly placed it back among the other baubles. "Wherever did you get it?"

Ewan smiled and waggled his finger at her. "Why, Miss Flora, you mean to say you have never seen me after a battle, searching among the fallen, pocketing this and tucking away that? The dead have no need of their silver, so I'm more than happy to relieve them of it."

Flora hated the idea of looting, but life on the moor had taught her that it was better to be practical than judgmental. The *Damainte* had no other way to support themselves, she reasoned, and if the money could be used to help the afflicted, why, then it was a sort of charity, and therefore legitimate. "What's the worth of all this, do you reckon?"

The dwarf shrugged, far less impressed by his wealth than she. "Six hundred pounds, I'd say. Maybe eight."

"Ah! A fortune! Surely you can purchase your freedom." Flora remembered how Sorley had bribed Dr. Barclay without a second thought. "Judges and jailers can be bought and crimes excused, if one's purse is great enough."

"Ha! If the cursed Hanoverians knew of my cache, they'd confiscate it outright and not wait for me to buy their cooperation. No, I'd hoped to put this treasure to another use."

Flora leaned toward him, drawn by her curiosity. When she was so close she could feel the little man's breath on her face, she drew back in sudden embarrassment. "Pray what use is that? Would you try to buy passage on a ship away from here?"

Ewan looked at her intently, and it seemed to Flora that he was struggling to say something. "I would, but not alone." He reached for her hand and held it captive in both of his, and even though she tried to free herself she could not. "Oh, mistress! List to me a moment! I'm weak with words, so I'll speak plainly." He paused. An uneasy feeling settled in Flora's stomach as she sensed what Ewan was about to say. "I know your love for Sorley, but the man is deathly ill. He might pass on, and where would that leave you, orphaned and unwed and alone?"

"Ewan, I beg you not to continue," Flora whispered, not wanting to hear what she knew he was about to say.

"I must, Miss Flora. Here is my proposition, straight and simple: if Sorley dies, wed me."

"What?"

"Aye, you heard me correctly," Ewan went on, his face alternating between a smile and a frown as he spoke. "I swear I'll protect you, though it would cost me my life. As to children, I have the means to provide for them all, even if they're as stunted as their da. We'll take the Smalls with us, and Rosmairi and Gair. God knows they need protecting."

Again Flora tried to object, but Ewan interrupted her with so many kind, earnest words that she found herself agreeing to let him finish. "I know I'm not handsome, tall, and straight like Sorley, but I'm a decent sort and God-fearing. Scandal's never been connected with my name. Most important of all, I love you, my heart. There. It's said. They're not easy words for a man like me." The dwarf's face flushed scarlet and he was obliged to draw several deep breaths before he could continue. "That you don't love me in return is understandable. However, mistress, in time love will grow. I'm sure of it." He kissed his forefinger, then gently applied it to her lips. "If you but allow it."

Flora could think of nothing to say. She was struck dumb by Ewan's love and generosity, although she wanted no part of either. If only she could be certain that Sorley would recover from his wounds, but doubts had attacked her before. Should the unspeakable happen, then Ewan's plan might be all that was left to her. Flora closed her eyes. How could she contemplate such a betrayal? Sorley would not die; he must not die! If he did, he'd take with him all her joy in living. She must dissuade her diminutive benefactor without making light of his disastrous proposal. "Ewan, you'll always be in my heart, if not as my husband, then as my dearest friend. Your offer's taken me by surprise, to say the least. In several days we should know how Sorley stands. Let's wait till then to discuss this further."

Keen disappointment darkened the dwarf's face. "Well, now, I could hardly expect you to be wrapping yourself around my neck," he murmured. "I suppose this will do."

Flora felt as if she had been in a trance. She looked up and saw that the crimson and violet clouds of sunset had melted away, leaving the sky a luminous black. "I must return to the weans. I'm sure they're hungry," she said, standing up. As she hurried away, tears of anger burned her eyes. She had no wish to hurt Ewan, but Sorley alone was the star in her sky, the commander of her desire. There was no other for her, and never would be.

As for Ewan, he was her friend. But now that he had become her unwelcome suitor, she could not quite think of him only as her friend. She had seen his affection for her growing, yet like a frightened child she had done nothing to stop it. Now it was too late. Damn her for being so timid! Damn him for falling in love with her!

For days it seemed to Flora as if Ewan's plans might go forward according to his wishes. Sorley hung poised on the lip of the grave, and even Dr. Barclay could not understand how the Gael managed to go on living. But Flora knew.

She sat beside him during the dark nights and equally dark days, sleeping very little and worrying a great deal. Whatever she could do for Sorley she did—changed his dressings, bathed his aching body, rubbed oil into his skin to keep it from becoming sore and inflamed. Whenever he awoke for a few moments from his unnatural sleep, she stroked his matted hair and assured him that he was still alive, that she loved him. Sometimes the confusion would clear from his eyes and he would speak to her just like the old Sorley who always had a battle plan: "Find that man, Skeleton, and give yourself up to him for safekeeping," he told her once. She could only gawk at him in wonderment. How could he possibly have remembered Stelton? And another time: "If I pass on to the other side, take Ewan as your husband. He'll love you like no other, save myself, and you'll never want for anything."

"Save you," she answered, but he had already fallen into a faint.

Five tense days passed in the dolmen. Flora discovered that it was far from a perfect hiding place: almost every time she chanced outside she saw red jackets in the distance or heard a horse's whinny or the terrible hammering of regimental drums. She felt like a rabbit in a warren patrolled by foxes. Certainly, she thought, the *Damainte* fared no better. Ewan and the other men were sullen and quiet, while Rosmairi wept each day, deep in despair, though she often forgot why. The Three Smalls whined and begged to go outside so often that Ewan threatened to whip them, and the poor doctor fretted aloud over whether he would ever survive his horrid ordeal. Crann, meanwhile, gamboled about like a pup, delighting in the close contact of so many people.

Then, the afternoon of the sixth day, sunlight returned to Flora's world. As she was trying to spoon some water down Sorley's throat, the man sputtered, sat bolt upright, and wrenched the spoon from her hand. "For God's sake, have you no whiskey?" he said. Then, his energy spent, he sank back onto his bed. Flora felt his cheek: it was cool. The fever will come back, she worried, but when hours passed and Sorley's temperature remained normal, Dr. Barclay annouced that the Highlander's fever had broken.

"Oh, Sorley! Thank God and all the saints!" cried Flora. She leaned forward and kissed Sorley's still-muscular neck.

"A miracle," Barclay muttered. "I daresay there's some hope for him now, mistress. With exhaustive care, I've no doubt but in time he'll make a full recovery."

Flora beamed, but as the doctor continued, detailing all the work she had ahead of her, she caught sight of Ewan's face. For the briefest of moments his eyes flared open wide, and he looked as stricken if he had just been told he had but three days to live. Then his face returned to its customary mask of bored vigilance. Flora pitied him, but she knew that nothing she might say or do could help Ewan through his misery. She had already tried and failed. He would have to suffer on his own, as he always did, until she summoned the wits to try to explain her love for Sorley and his innocence yet again.

Several days passed without event, other than Sorley's continued return to health. He was far from hale and as weak as a newborn lamb, but vitality gleamed in his beautiful mismatched eyes for the first time since Culloden, and Flora basked in the certainty that she would not lose him this time either.

Her serenity was broken one morning when she woke from a deep sleep to the whimpering of the children, the barking of the dog, and a general deafening chaos. Gentle Jesus, let there be no troops about this time of day, she prayed, crossing herself hastily. She looked for Ewan, but the dwarf was gone, as well as Gair and Losgann. "What has happened?" she asked Whoreson, who appeared to be less distraught than the others.

"The doctor's gone," the lad explained.

Two shots punctuated the boy's words. Flora shuddered,

Megan Gray

remembering the disaster on Drummossie Moor. Her fear lasted only an instant, replaced by a driving need to make certain that her impetuous chieftain had not gotten himself killed.

Flora bolted under the stone and crouched in the grave-like opening. The sky arched bright blue over her head, and she realized with sudden fear that the protective branches were missing. She listened intently but heard nothing. Climbing out of the pit, she scouted the immediate area, but all was peaceful. "Ewan!" she called.

"Miss Buchanan?"

Flora sprang straight into the air like a skylark. Directly behind her stood a very sheepish-looking Dr. Barclay, and beside him a warlike figure in a flowing wig, imposing red-and-gold uniform, and black boots up to his thigh. "H-H-Henry?" she croaked, unable and unwilling to believe she had recognized Maj. Henry Stelton.

"My God! What are you doing here?" he blurted. "Are you all right?"

Flora said nothing. There was nothing to say.

"I don't wonder I appear strange to you," said Stelton, in a gentle voice at odds with his martial dress. "We've been separated too long. But you're safe now. Have these savages injured you?"

He thinks I've been abducted, she thought, and decided not to disabuse him of the idea just yet. "I've been treated very well," she said cautiously. "But what of the shots? Where . . . ?"

Flora couldn't bear to state her fears aloud. Stelton seemed to sense this, for he immediately led her to the rear of the dolmen. What she saw made her cry out and falter backward. Six scarlet-coated fusiliers stood over the inert bodies of her friends. Losgann and Dughal lay crumpled up in pools of blood in the green heather, while Ewan sprawled flat on his back, his tiny, immobile limbs giving him the look of a broken doll tossed aside by some giant child. Gair alone was still standing, his wrists bound together in front of him, mumbling incoherently in Gaelic.

Flora's heart felt like lead in her chest. "Are they dead?"

The major tossed his handsome head like a spirited horse. "Not the dwarf, not yet, anyway," he admitted. "He had an altercation with the butt of a Brown Bess, and Bess won. But don't fret. He shan't frighten you anymore. I'll have him shot down like the dog that he is, and his mangy companion as well."

"No!" Fear gnawed at the back of Flora's neck. "Henry, spare them both!" She ran to the major and clasped his gloved hands. "They're good men, and Gair is a family man. I beg you, have mercy. Is there nothing you can do?"

Stelton's demeanor changed and he broke into a charming smile. "For you, my pet, I shall be as merciful as I'm allowed to be and then some. We'll take the cripple and his crony into Sterling and have them dance a jig on the gibbet. That's as merciful as the law allows."

Flora struggled to speak but no words came. She choked back tears at the sight of Losgann's and Dughal's twisted bodies. Sorley . . . Ewan . . . Gair and Rosmairi . . . even the Smalls were in danger of being strung up and hanged like dogs, and all because she had insisted on having a surgeon for Sorley. She eyed Barclay with murderous ferocity, and the physician cowered at the menace in her gaze. Flora felt she might fall down in a swoon at any moment. Nevertheless, she forced herself to talk. Sorley, Ewan, and her second family were in mortal danger. "The others . . . inside the dolmen. There's an expectant woman and three small children. Surely you don't intend to take them to Sterling as well?"

"Others?" Stelton looked at her with great interest, and

at once she realized her mistake. Dr. Barclay hadn't revealed the hiding place; she had! "Is it true, Barclay?"

The good doctor, his ample body jiggling in distress, gave an agitated nod. Stelton ordered his men into the dolmen and in a short time they returned with Rosmairi, the Smalls, and Crann, all of whom huddled together in fear and confusion. She had unwittingly betrayed her own people, Flora thought angrily. Again she tried to plead their case. "Henry, if I ever meant anything to you, you must free Rosmairi and the weans."

Stelton sighed as he adjusted his black gloves. "You're overwrought, my dear," he said. The cold spring wind played with the long curls of his wig. "That's to be expected, of course. But pray, try to understand my position. All rebels must face the grim consequences of their treason. Why, I'm breaking a number of regulations simply by taking them into custody instead of executing them outright. When we get to Sterling, I'll seek to arrange a pardon for the woman and her children."

He thinks the Smalls are Rosmairi's sons, Flora thought. A fortunate mistake. It might be easier to free a mother and her children than a pregnant woman and three unrelated orphans, who didn't even have the consolation of kinship with each other. Still certain that Stelton was being obstinate, Flora began an angry reply to his offer when reason overrode her fury and stopped her. She *was* obliged to the major. Anyone else less besotted with her would have ignored her pleas, or, more in keeping with regulations, blown her head to pieces with a Brown Bess. For she was a rebel herself, or at the very least a woman of questionable repute consorting with rebels. "Thank you," she whispered. "I'm beholden to you."

The major bowed graciously. "Nay, mistress, it's I who am beholden to *you!* I trust my compassion will have a

positive effect on your decision regarding my earlier proposal," he said in formal tones that would have been more
at home in a town house parlor than on a barren moor.
"Keep in mind that it might be rather difficult for you to
obtain a husband if word were to spread about your . . .
hmmm, adventures."

The bastard! Flora thought. *He's blackmailing me!*

She drew her head away from him, but Stelton leaned
forward and flicked the collar of her disreputable blouse.
"I shall do what I can to obtain some suitable clothing
for you," he said with a sniff. "In the meantime, a clean
blouse and breeches may have to suffice. I think it best
that you—"

A fast-flowing river of Gaelic interrupted Stelton's
smooth words. Flora recognized Sorley's resonant voice.
She turned just in time to see the injured Highlander
emerge from the dolmen on a litter borne by two fusiliers.
Too weak to resist but painfully conscious of what was
happening, Sorley could do nothing but curse his tormen-
tors in his native tongue, then translate the obscenities for
their benefit. Flora was glad to see he had that much
strength. She knew he would need it if he were to live
beyond a fortnight.

"What a pity," said Dr. Barclay, "to have expended so
much skill and effort in saving a man, only to see him get
his neck pulled on the scaffold."

The cruel comment stung Flora's heart, and she vowed
she would keep the words from becoming prophetic. The
doctor wasn't a wicked man. In truth, he had saved Sorley's
life. It was a pity he couldn't be convinced to help the
courageous Gael now. Then, seemingly from nowhere,
Flora remembered something Sorley had told her during
the start of their improbable history: *Physicians are easily*

bought. Flora wondered if the scent of guineas might lure the turncoat doctor back to the Jacobite camp.

"Henry," she said, touching the major's sleeve in her best drawing-room manner. "Will you help me? I've hidden a few things in a satchel under some stones. Shoes, letters, a necklace—naught but trinkets, really, but I should like to have them."

"Then you shall," Stelton said. He summoned a fusilier with one swift movement of his hand. Flora hadn't anticipated an escort, but when the soldier began following her to the pile of rocks beside the dolmen, she knew she had no choice in the matter. She chewed her thumb like a worried child, contemplating how she would explain why she possessed hundreds of guineas to the trooper, much less to the major. But when she cleared away the rocks and examined the hole underneath, she was both relieved and dismayed to discover that she needed no excuse. The hiding place was empty.

"Someone has taken my belongings," she cried, looking among the stones in utter vexation. Perhaps Ewan had removed the money or a soldier had stolen it.

"A shame, miss," said the guard, bored yet sympathetic. "Shall we join the others?"

The small troop with its ragged prisoners was waiting to depart when Flora returned. Poor Ewan was trussed up like a Christmas goose. Although he was awake and walking, his dazed look told her he had not yet recovered from his injury. The two soldiers continued to carry Sorley, who had exhausted himself so thoroughly he was forced to resume his blasphemous tirade in a whisper. Stelton, mounted on a lean gray hunter, trotted up to her. "Come, Miss Buchanan," he called. "You may ride with me for now."

"But we cannot leave yet," she insisted. "We must bury

Losgann and Dughal in the fashion of their countrymen, with a cairn of stones atop each grave.''

"Oh, yes," Stelton replied, reaching his hand down to her. "And each should have a fine funeral, with an oaken casket and garlands of roses. What nonsense! Really, Miss Buchanan, you must not waste your sensibilities on these barbarians. You're fortunate I could effect your rescue.''

A wave of sorrow washed over Flora as she resigned herself to the painful fact that she could do nothing more for her dead friends. Stelton leaned down, caught her around the waist, and swept her benumbed body up before him on the saddle. She hated the feel of his arms around her. Sorley's embrace had always felt protective; the major, however, clearly had domination on his mind. Flora fumbled at the strong arms around her waist, but the major's grip was like a shackle.

She considered attacking her self-styled rescuer. Her rigorous life had made her stronger than most women, and she knew she could unhorse him if she took him by surprise. But even if she did, what would she accomplish? Sorley, Ewan, and Gair would be killed on the spot, and the others endangered. No, she couldn't take the risk. Nor could she bring herself to hurt the major, who was her only ally in the ranks of the Hanoverians and as kind a soldier as could be found under such harsh circumstances.

Instead of resisting, Flora lay back against Stelton's powerful chest as the horse jolted forward. Thunder rolled above her. The dark sky had grown darker. Bolts of lightning sizzled through the black clouds. Even the heavens are against me, she thought. The first drops of rain had begun to fall when Flora at last gave vent to the sobs that she had restrained for so long.

"You have no reason to weep now," murmured the major. "You're perfectly safe.''

I have everything to weep for, she thought. For Sorley and the *Damainte,* for the prince's ruined dream. And for her own dark future.

She heard a cry of surprise and saw a soldier fall on his bottom as if his feet had been yanked out from under him. What was happening? Stelton shouted. Someone was running toward her. A very short person—one of the weans?

No, it was Ewan. Somehow he had freed himself from his bonds and was coming to her rescue, though she needed none. He had mistaken her sobs as a sign of abuse, Flora thought. She had to stop him. "Ewan! Wait! Go back," she screamed. "Go back! I'm in no peril."

Thunder boomed and lightning cracked.

Ewan seemed to hear her, for he slowed, then stopped. He opened his mouth as if to call her name. Blood spurted from his lips. Flora called out his name in horror. He staggered, then pitched forward, struggled onto his knees, and finally tumbled facedown in the dirt. His stubby legs thrashed the ground and churned the earth into a blood-red morass. Finally he lay still.

"No! My God, no!" Flora shrieked. What had just happened did not happen, she thought. It could not have happened. She had heard lightning, not a shot. Ewan might be injured. But he could not be dead.

With strength born of panic, Flora tugged herself free from Stelton and slid down the horse's shoulder. She ran toward Ewan's body and had almost reached it when someone grabbed her and wrenched her back. Flora fought the soldier with all the fury of a lioness whose cub has been ripped away from her. "Ewan!" she shouted. "Ewan, rise up, for the love of God!"

Two other soldiers joined the first and struggled to subdue her. She clawed and kicked at them, knowing all the while that she battled to no avail. Dr. Barclay joined the melee and clamped a foul-smelling cloth over her mouth and nose. The more she resisted, the weaker she became, until she felt herself finally sink backward into the doctor's arms. Over the thunder and the clanking of weapons, she heard Sorley's heart-stopping wail of lamentation. "Ewan! Alas! Not Ewan! *Mo dhia!*"

Before the drug overwhelmed her, Flora heard another voice, much weaker, like that of a small child falling asleep. "Remember me, Flora. I . . . I love you." The voice dropped into silence as Flora fell into darkness.

Chapter Fifteen

"Look at the fine ship, Miss Flora. Is that one ours?"

Rattie, whom Flora had renamed Robbie, had clambered onto a stool taller than he was and stood balancing on it to look out the window at the harbor. Flora left her embroidery on a chair and walked over to stand beside him. It felt strange to feel long skirts rustling against her legs after so many months in breeks. Then again, her whole world was foreign to her now—the cozy apartment the major had rented for her and Rosmairi and the boys, the scent of lavender, the little town of Greenock, the lively sounds of people, horses, and wagons passing beneath her windows. It seemed like a dream, all of it. It was only when she looked at Sorley's compass or saw a short man in the streets that the past crushed down upon her and she struggled to breathe.

Sorley! Oh, why had she thought of him? Her memories of him ate at her heart like acid. He had remained behind in Šterling when she and her second family had gone on to Greenock, but that was a month ago. By now he could be dead, hanged on the gibbet or ravaged by disease in a prison barge on the Thames, for all she knew. Thank God she still had the children!

Flora laid a steadying hand on Robbie's back. "Mind you don't fall." She peered through the open window. "The tall black one? I don't know. Major Stelton said our ship was called the *Bonhomme*, but I can't see the name of this one."

"Let me look! Move aside, simpleton."

"Devil take you! I want to look, too."

Whoreson and Bugger, who had been playing draughts on the floor, dashed to the window with Crann right behind them. No longer ragged urchins but miniature gentlemen in waistkits and white hose, the boys reminded Flora of the merchants' children she used to play with in Edinburgh, in her other life so long ago. "Horton! Roger! Such coarse language!" she admonished them. "I can't think Ewan Fada would have approved of young men speaking this way."

Flora had found that the boys would do nigh anything in Ewan's memory. At first it had hurt to mention his name. Sometimes she blamed herself for his death, thinking she could have prevented it if only she had been quicker or cleverer, louder or more perceptive. By and by the pain diminished a little, and speaking his name often had become a pleasure. In a way, it was as if Ewan were still with her.

The lads apologized, then stared out the window at the ship, discussing its appearance and possible destinations. "It's damned big," Horton said. "Very big, I mean to say. Bound for Africa, probably."

"No, the Indies."

"It's Africa we're going to, isn't it, Miss Flora?" Robbie asked.

Flora laughed. She had been through so much hardship lately that even the sound of her own laughter seemed exotic to her. "Nay, not Africa. America. Boston, the city is called. I hear it's a grand place."

"Are you coming too?"

"Aye, for certain, Robbie. Such a thing to be asking," she said, tousling his shiny hair. "You know I'd never leave you and your foster brothers."

The boy clasped her around the legs and laid his head against her skirts. "I thought you were going to wed the major."

"For a time it seemed I might have to," she replied, "but no, I shan't be marrying him after all."

"That's fine." The lad sighed. "I dinna like the Sassenach *bodach.*"

Robbie skipped back to the window, leaving Flora steeped in memories. God knows, Stelton had tried, she thought. He had proposed on three separate occasions, the last time threatening to send her to trial to Sterling. But she had called his bluff and refused him, and won the hand. That was when the major had offered to send her, Rosmairi, and the boys to Boston. "You'll be safe there," he'd told her. "My cousin lives just outside the city, and she'll see you established. At least I'll have the satisfaction of watching that Jacobite seducer dance on the gallows." It was a wicked remark by a scorned man, and it had pierced Flora's heart with sorrow. Yet she'd said nothing, only thanked Major Stelton for his kindness as she ushered him out the door.

Flora shook herself from her painful reverie and was returning to her embroidery when Crann barked once. Rosmairi entered the room, followed by Gair. Flora smiled to see them, especially Gair. She considered it a great victory that she had duped Stelton into thinking that Gair was an idiot. Coaxing the major into releasing Gair into her custody had taken much more effort, but she had succeeded there, too. The only man among the *Damainte* to survive Culloden, Gair was her steadfast friend, a resourceful ally, and the sun in Rosmairi's universe.

"Back so soon?" Flora asked. "Was the market not too crowded?"

"We didn't get as far as that, Miss Flora," Rosmairi said shyly. "We met a man who wishes to see ye, and so hurried straight home." In her discreet blue gown and neat mob-cap, Rosmairi looked like any other goodwife in Greenock on a market Saturday. How odd to think that she had been living in the heather with a band of rebels for more than a year!

"Why, who is this mysterious fellow?"

Rosmairi gave Flora such a look of distress that Flora regretted she had asked at all. "I canna remember his name, miss, but he's a plump auld toad." She paused, then patted Gair's hand. "Isn't he, husband?"

"Aye. It's the leech," Gair answered. "Barclay."

Flora stiffened, remembering the doctor's betrayal. Then again, he had not told Stelton about the children hidden in the dolmen. "You'll bring him up, won't you, Gair?"

"I cannot," he said. "He's waiting in the street for you. Doesn't care to come up."

"How unusual," Flora said as she reached for a shawl. It was a bright May morning, but the winds from the sea were brisk and cool. "I must see what he wants. I can't imagine why he wishes to see me. Mayhap he knows what became of . . . of Sorley Fior."

"Who is that, now?" Rosmairi took the shawl from Flora's hands and helped her arrange it around her shoulders.

Flora sighed. Sorley had already fallen out of Rosmairi's frail memory. "A dear friend of mine from the campaign. Taken prisoner, alas." She would have gone on but her voice had begun to quaver like a harp string as she contemplated Sorley's most probable fate. She slipped her feet into iron pattens to protect them from the mud of the streets. Then, fearing the worst and steeling herself to accept it, she darted from the apartment and down the stairs into the street.

Flora breathed in the smells of the town—fresh-baked bread, sweat, sea salt, and manure. It was a rich mixture that she had grown quite fond of and had missed out on the moors. She saw Barclay at once, standing across the street from her, dressed in a suit of the finest nut-brown brocade trimmed in silver, with a beautiful lace jabot at his throat. He had been stout before but now he was considerably stouter, his belly bulging as much as Rosmairi's. When he saw Flora, she dropped him a curtsy. "Good day, Doctor. I see you have prospered greatly since you left the employ of Major Stelton."

"Thank you, mistress, I do well enough," said Barclay, with an abbreviated bow, made difficult because of his girth. "But it's Colonel Stelton now. He's quite the hero ever since he captured the cousin of a leader of the rebellion. Forgive my haste, but we mustn't tarry. Will you walk with me, please?"

Without waiting for an answer, Barclay swooped upon her, took her by the elbow, and began marching down the lane like a grenadier. Startled at this indignity, Flora accompanied him as best she could, but she kept slipping on the dirt and tripping on the cobblestones. "Really, sir, the mire . . . these pattens. Wherever we're going, can we not go there a little slower?''

The doctor obliged happily, since he was by now quite out of breath.

"Would it be presumptuous of me to ask where you're taking me?"

Barclay squinted at her, as if estimating the depth of her character, then led her to the side of the lane in front of a sailmaker's shop. "I'm only just arrived from Sterling last evening, and I don't mind saying it's been a harrowing business, a harrowing business indeed. Once I thought we were undone, but fortunately I was mistaken. That's not to underestimate the potential for dangers ahead. I have the papers, but it will take more than that. I assume you'll want to help, and indeed you'll have to, if this plan is to work."

Flora tried to make sense of the doctor's ramblings. Clearly he was involved in an intrigue of one sort or the other, but why had he come to her? "You're in need of my help?" she asked. "For what purpose, pray? Something to do with the 'harrowing business,' I suppose."

The doctor's face glistened with sweat. He swept the street up and down with his glance, then drew a silk kerchief from his pocket and mopped his dripping jowls. "We mustn't speak here, Miss Buchanan, not out in the open. Come with me and all will be clear, I promise you."

"If this concerns money," Flora said pointedly, "be aware that I have none."

The doctor shook his head, and his several chins shook as well. "Thanks to your friend, Ewan Cameron, I want for nothing. But come!"

Before Flora could question him about his dealings with Ewan, Barclay pressed his palm against her back and propelled her down a narrow lane. The chase is on again, she thought, but where or why she still did not know. At length they came to a small, neat house and were admitted by a maid. The moment Flora entered the hallway, a hideous shriek of mortal agony vibrated throughout the timbers of the building.

Flora felt the blood drain from her face as memories of Culloden leaped out at her with fangs and claws. When she thought she had recovered, she glanced at the floor, only to find it covered with scarlet streaks. "What manner of torture chamber is this?" Flora demanded as she grabbed Barclay by his plush brown sleeve. "Or is it a slaughterhouse? Why did you bring me here?"

"Wrong on both accounts, mistress," replied the doctor with a tight smile. "This is the local surgery. I've brought you here to show you something interesting." Barclay began to waddle down a long, dark hall and beckoned Flora to follow him. As he walked, he dropped explanations behind him like bread crumbs. "The town surgeon and I are longtime acquaintances. He has graciously allowed me to stay with him and, seeing as I value my privacy, this is the perfect retreat. It's not the sort of place Colonel Stelton would choose to stick his nose into, eh?"

"Nor I mine," Flora said, listening to another cry, weaker than the first. "However, I can't see what business it is of yours whether he does or no'."

"Oh, I assure you, I wish to have no business with him whatsoever," the doctor said. "In truth, the less seen of him the better." Barclay stopped by a door, opened it, and stepped aside to allow her to enter first. "Now you'll discover why."

Flora had had enough of the pompous doctor's enigmatic ways. While she knew he was really a harmless sort and inspired no fear in her whatsoever, she did not altogether trust him. She entered the chamber warily.

To her relief, it was light and airy, devoid of the fetid smell Flora associated with inns, hospitals, and all chance gatherings of strangers. The furnishings were sparse, but the room did have a cozy fireplace and a hearth bedecked with blue and white Dutch tiles. A man deeply engaged in reading a book sat facing a small fire. He had close-cropped dark hair and wondrous long legs, and was dressed rather plainly in breeches, blouse, and jerkin. Even though only half of him was visible, he had a noble air about him that Flora found curiously familiar. "Sir?" she said. Surely it couldn't be . . .

The man turned toward her.

"Sorley!" Flora's legs turned to jelly and she dropped to her knees on the floor. Fortunately the good doctor caught her under the arms and prevented her from falling outright. "You're alive!"

The shadow-man rose. He was as lean as a greyhound but otherwise bore little likeness to the invalid who only weeks before had languished near death in the dolmen. "My God, woman!" He gasped. "It's like being in paradise to see you again!" Then his fairy eyes glittered and his face glowed with his beautiful smile. " 'Tis a pity all the ladies don't swoon when they meet me."

"You scoundrel!" Flora cried, laughing in relief. Barclay helped her to her feet, then discreetly retired to another room on the pretext of finding her a suitable chair. Before she could take a step toward him, Sorley was at her side, wrapping his long arms around her. She succumbed to his embrace like a butterfly unfolding its wings in the sunlight. And to think she'd never expected to see him alive again! She stretched up as high as she could to kiss his searching lips, and he drank her love down like brandy.

"Oh, my darling!" she murmured, longing for privacy and knowing she'd have none. "How came you to be here . . . ?'' She stopped just short of adding the word *alive*.

"You must thank Barclay for that, my heart," Sorley answered, brushing his lips across the crown of her head. "He plucked me out of prison and brought me to Greenock."

How could he have arranged such a miracle? Flora thought as the doctor entered the room with an embroidered chair for her.

"Here you are, Miss Buchanan," Barclay said cheerfully as he placed the chair behind her, apparently oblivious of the passion that simmered between her and the Highlander. "I heard your comment, so I hope you will allow me the liberty of explaining this extraordinary situation."

"Pray continue." Reluctantly Flora lowered herself into the chair. To her joy, Sorley sat down on the floor beside her and laid his head in her lap. She thought the doctor might be embarrassed by such an open display of affection, but either he was a man of the world or simply too full of himself to care.

"Earlier you inquired about my financial state," he said, pacing up and down the length of the parlor. "Forgive me for being evasive then, but I can be more direct now. I owe my newfound wealth to Ewan Fada, as I said before. Only a day before Colonel Stelton's arrival, Ewan showed me a hidden cache of guineas and other valuables, and bade me take them. However, I had to swear to him that I'd use a portion to try to secure the release of you and Sorley, should you fall prisoner to the king's forces. Well, as you see, fate has provided me a chance to keep my word."

Flora gave a tiny cry of remorse. "Oh, poor, dear Ewan!" He had taken great pains to save the man he hated, for her sake. He had even given his life to protect her. She knew she would never have another friend as staunch as he. "How I wish he were with us now! But tell me—how could you bring Sorley here without Stelton knowing?"

Sorley gave her knee a loving squeeze. "He's a wise old fox, that one, love," he said. "He has more wiles than all of the duke's officers put together."

Barclay beamed in self-satisfaction, then seemed to realize that humility would make him appear more gallant. "Nay, Mr. Cameron, you flatter me. My dear, my greatest asset in the work was Ewan's fortune. Silver is the grease that makes short work of burdens, so they say. By the blessing of Providence, I was able to locate another prisoner who had the look of Sorley about him, as well as a turnkey and several other scamps greedy enough to say any words I put in their mouths, for a price, of course. That man swung on the gallows, and when he died, he died as Sorley Fior Cameron, even though the poor creature was of Clan Donald all along."

"He participated in the ruse?" Flora asked.

Barclay shook his head.

"He could not, even if he wished to," Sorley interjected. "He knew no English, and his judges no Gaelic. The accusation, the conviction, the sentence—all was only so much empty prattle to him. He was never given an opportunity to defend himself. Fortunately Stelton was not there to identify him."

"But you are not to fret for him, Miss Buchanan," said the doctor hastily. "He would have been executed for treason no matter what his name. At least this way his death has done some good."

Flora sighed, trying not to think of the wife and family the unknown man had surely left behind. "I marvel that you've come this far unscathed, but what next? The boys and I are scheduled to sail for Boston in three days, and I assure you I'll go nowhere without Sorley."

"Nor I without you," Sorley said. He stood up, went to a nearby cabinet, and returned with three cups of brandy carefully balanced in his hands. "Barclay has obtained forged papers for me."

"Aye," said the doctor, "but I'm worried we'll be discovered." He removed a cup of brandy from Sorley's hands with surgical exactness. "I had no notion Stelton was here in Greenock. He'll recognize Sorley the moment he sets eyes on him, even with his head shaved like a sheep and breeches on his posterior instead of a belted plaid. Then our amusing game will come to a sorry end, and all three of us will be swinging from the devil's axletree."

Flora frowned as she sipped her brandy. Barclay was right. Sorley's proud carriage and long limbs were every bit as distinctive as his mismatched eyes. He required a clever disguise. But what?

Without a moment's thought Flora crossed her legs like a man in trousers, a habit she had acquired during her ten months in boy's clothing. But the fabric of her long skirts pulled on her legs, and when she became fully aware of what she was doing, she chastised herself for behaving so improperly.

With the speed of an osprey plummeting into a mountain loch the solution came to her. Sorley would wear skirts again, but not the manly skirts of the Gael. "I have a suggestion," she said, with the calm assurance that comes of solving a dilemma. "I'm not certain you'll like the sound of it, however."

Sorley laughed nervously. "As long as emasculation isn't involved, I'll consider it."

Flora chucked Sorley under the chin. It wasn't like her to be playful, she thought, but she was glad to see that both she and her beloved still had a bit of spirit left in them. "Well, emasculation is involved, symbolically speaking, but it's no' painful and it's no' permanent."

Sorley's jaws dropped open and his eyes rolled like a stag's. *"Dia!* What do you mean to do to me, woman?"

Flora chuckled at his fright, part comic and part real. In truth, there was little humor in the situation at all, and she knew that the plan she was about to present was at best highly dangerous and brimming with risk. "I propose that you dress as a woman to evade Stelton's notice."

"Interesting," muttered Barclay. "Highly deceptive. Just like a woman to think of it. After a night of merrymaking, the colonel won't be very perceptive come morning."

Sorley shook his head in woeful acceptance. "I suppose it's worth a try. Still, if given my choice, I'd prefer to be emasculated."

"And I," said Flora, "prefer that you not."

The weather had turned chill and dreary, and the smells of salt and dead fish hung thick in the harbor air. As the timbers of the masts creaked their strange music overhead, Flora walked down the slick dock with as much dignity as she could muster, trying to avoid seagull droppings and the gaze of lecherous sailors. Beggars in various stages of hardship and deprivation dragged themselves up and down the harbor, but Flora paid them no heed. Even the most pitiful ones with missing limbs and eyes failed to rouse much of her sympathy. She had to concentrate on the welfare of her second family.

Robbie danced along at her side, his mind on the sea voyage before him, perhaps, and not on the perils of the next few minutes. Flora dared not look behind her for fear of drawing attention to the others, but she could hear them thumping along on the wooden planks of the dock and she could imagine them perfectly. Rosmairi and Gair each held a boy firmly in hand, and Crann paced by Gair's side. Dr. Barclay pushed a small cart bearing two monstrous travel bags, each almost as round as he. The good doctor had begged Flora to take him with her, since, as he'd explained, his life would be "as safe as a fox at the inn on meet day" once word of Sorley's escape became public.

Flora could easily picture the tall, stately woman who walked beside the doctor. She wore a midnight blue gown that Flora herself had sewn, and a chestnut red wig, surmounted by a mobcap. The lady appeared to have the ague, for her eyes were red and swollen and all but closed, the result of lime juice applied liberally to the eyelids. A skillful layer of cosmetics concealed the remains of a beard and softened her masculine features. And if the lady stumbled now and then and tugged at her long skirts, it was only to be expected, since "she" had never before worn such cumbersome garments.

They made a peculiar troop, Flora thought, but in such motley company Sorley didn't appear quite so out of place. They had begun to draw near the *Bonhomme*—the black-hulled ship that had so intrigued Robbie—when Stelton and four well-armed soldiers marched up and clanked to a stop in front of Flora. Several beggars too close by for their own comfort scurried back into the shadows like rats. The colonel, elegant in his crimson coat with gleaming golden braid, made a leg. Flora dropped a curtsy. "Miss Buchanan, the thought of never seeing you again distresses me no end," he said.

"I'm sorry for that, Henry," Flora said, and she meant what she said. Even now, after so much suffering and bloodshed, she held no ill will against the colonel. He was risking his commission and possibly his life by letting her leave

the country. No, it wasn't him she hated; it was his commander's brutality that enraged her. "But I do believe it's
best for us all if I leave."

The colonel clasped his hands before him, clenching
and unclenching his black-gloved fingers. "Are you certain
you won't reconsider my proposal, Flora? You'd live like
a queen instead of a renegade. I can find good homes for
the children."

"They have a good home, thank you."

The colonel gave her a humorless smile. All at once he
became another man, efficient and detached. If he were
suffering distress from the effects of overindulgence, as
Barclay had prophesied, he concealed it well. "Your
papers," he demanded.

Flora could not help herself; her hand shook as she held
out the documents Stelton himself had procured for her.
"Not yours, mistress," he said with a dismissive wave.
"Those I'm already acquainted with. Barclay?"

The doctor appeared unperturbed as he handed over
his documents. The colonel examined them carefully.
"Leaving for the New World? We have need of physicians
in this one."

"My mother and brother have emigrated and require
my assistance, as my mother is quite ill," Barclay replied.
What an accomplished liar, Flora thought. The old fox
had told her he had no living kin at all.

"Your credentials are in order," Stelton said. Next he
studied the boys' papers, then Gair's. Nothing seemed
to be amiss. Flora held her breath. "And the children's
mother?" He nodded at Rosmairi.

"Here are her papers of passage, all in order," Flora
said, eagerly pulling the documents from the velvet bag

she carried for just that purpose. God bless Barclay for
conjuring up proper-looking papers! Again her hands
trembled. The colonel made some remark about the chill
weather and perused Rosmairi's traveling papers. "Rosemary Cameron?" Stelton stared into Rosmairi's face as he
spoke, making Flora want to seize the front of his uniform
and thrust him out of the poor woman's presence.

"That is she," Flora said.

Stelton ignored her. "Rosemary Cameron?" he repeated.

Rosmairi collected her wits at last. "I am Rosmairi . . .
Rosemary if you will, sir," she said in a trembling voice
scarcely louder than a whisper.

"A lady's maid," Stelton continued, reading from the
papers. Then he raised his eyes. "But what is this?" He
glared boldly at Sorley. "I don't remember seeing this
woman before. Is she part of your party, Miss Buchanan?"

"She is, sir," Flora said, with more force than she
intended to use. "She's Effie Cameron, Rosmairi's sister.
As you can see, Rosmairi is expectant, and she needs her
sister's care." Again Flora handed Stelton a set of wrinkled
documents. This time she drew a deep breath and held it.

The colonel looked over the papers, then eyed Sorley
up and down. He took two steps to the right and surveyed
him again. "I don't believe I've ever seen a woman this
tall before. What's wrong with your eyes, mistress?"

"A touch of the grippe, sir," Sorley said, in a soft alto.
His Perthshire accent was almost the twin of Rosmairi's.
"It always settles in my eyes."

"I cannot make out the handwriting here, Rosemary,"
said Stelton, still gazing into Sorley's well-shaven face.
"Pray repeat your sister's name."

Rosmairi was quick with an answer. "Flora, sir," she said.

"Flora?" Stelton frowned as he reexamined the traveling papers. "There is a discrepancy here. On closer inspection, the papers clearly state 'Effie.' "

Rosmairi thinks of me as her sister, Flora thought with a mixture of pride and terror. *Oh, we are undone!* She was desperately patching together some sort of explanation for the puzzled colonel when Sorley intervened.

"Flora Cameron is my given name, sir," he murmured, "but Effie is my pet name, the name I answer to. 'Tis common in my part of the country."

Stelton walked a complete circuit around Sorley, regarding him with either distrust or disbelief. Flora couldn't say which for certain, but she had a sickening feeling that Stelton suspected a ruse. "Tallest woman I've ever seen," he muttered to himself. "And why do you seek to travel to the colonies, Miss Cameron? It's a tiring, dangerous journey. Surely you have kin here."

"Nay, sir. And if I did, none would be so dear to me as my beloved sister." Sorley grabbed Rosmairi's hand. "What would she do wi'out me, puir lamb, and her so close to her time?"

Sorley's voice and manner were the image of femininity. He completely charmed Rosmairi, who smiled at Sorley as if he were indeed her sister. Flora hoped that Stelton was equally duped. But the colonel still stared at Sorley's face with such hawklike intensity that Flora thought he might identify him despite the painstaking disguise. "What happened to your cheek, mistress?" Stelton finally inquired. "You're bleeding."

Flora saw it was true. A tiny nick from Barclay's razor had bled through the layer of talcum she had applied to Sorley's face.

The Highlander raised a finger to his cheek but he maintained his composure. "Ach, sir! It's naught but a scratch from the innkeep's cat. I should hae kept my distance from it."

Did the colonel believe Sorley? Or had he already seen through the Gael's deception? Flora couldn't tell. She held her breath, waiting for Stelton's response.

"Your documentation is somewhat misleading, mistress," the colonel said in a measured tone that masked his emotions. "It doesn't include your given name. By regulations I should detain you."

Flora began to object, but her protests were hidden behind a sudden stream of wailing. Sorley was weeping! Flora noticed he had the presence of mind to bring his shawl up to his face, lest his tears wash away all her cosmetic handiwork. "Oh, sir! Dinna do that! Ye wouldn't tear apart two sisters, would ye?"

Gair, Rosmairi, Barclay, and the boys stared at Sorley in fascination, as if they believed he actually had been enchanted into a woman. The colonel snorted. He fidgeted with his gloves. *He's perplexed,* Flora thought. *The poor man doesn't know what to conclude.* Perhaps he'd decided that "she" was a "he," then changed his mind. Seizing the moment of confusion, Flora sprang to "Effie's" defense. "If there's a fine or a fee to be paid, we'll pay it," she said coldly. "But I implore ye, don't make us abandon poor Effie. She has her heart and hopes set on accompanying her sister."

Stelton hesitated. He had the better of her, Flora realized with a jolt. If he wished, he could make "Effie's" release contingent on Flora's acceptance of his marriage proposal. A bitter taste rose in her mouth. How might she best argue in Sorley's defense? Stelton was a soldier. Tears might move him, but he would not admire them. What he admired was steel. "Come, come, Henry. Her husband fell at Culloden; her country has been ravished by your merciless duke. Has battle hardened your heart so deeply that her plight means nothing to you? You can either save her or destroy her."

An exasperated look flashed over Stelton's face. Adding to his distress was the small crowd that had gathered around Flora's party, tossing insults at the colonel for bullying a group of women. "Very well!" Stelton waved his hand in a manner as elegant as it was impotent. "Both sisters may proceed. Only cease this incessant blubbering!" Sorley's sobs at once subsided. "Miss Buchanan, consider this concession my personal favor to you," Stelton continued in a much softer voice. "I've never intended to force you into marriage, and my only desire is to see you happy. But for the last time . . . will you reconsider? Are you quite sure you cannot be happy with me?"

Flora shook her head, afraid to speak for fear of saying something that might raise Stelton's suspicions. Her silence was loud, however, and Stelton understood it. He went up to Sorley and murmured something to him sotto voce, then dispatched one of his grenadiers, who soon returned with a quill and inkpot. Snatching the papers from Flora's hands, Stelton scrawled the word *Flora* next to Effie's name and handed the pages back.

"I suppose you'll want the dog as well," he said.

"Aye," Flora replied. "He's the lads' dog."

"Fortunately he needs no papers. You're free to board."

Flora felt so relieved she thought she might collapse on the spot. Instead she thanked the colonel and praised his compassionate nature. While she spoke, she exulted to herself. They had gulled him!

After Stelton dispersed the gawking crowd, he and his

troops began to escort Flora and her party toward the *Bonhomme*. But as they neared the gangplank, one of the tattered beggars who had slunk away only minutes earlier shambled out from behind a stack of crates and made straight for Flora. She glimpsed him from the corner of her eye, a miserable cripple who looked as if someone had crumpled him up and later tried to straighten him out. Flora drew back, then cringed as she felt his yellow clawlike hand grasp her wrist. "Something for a poor old man, miss," he whined in a voice like steel on glass.

Flora found herself looking into the face of her nightmares. Somewhere deep inside her soul she screamed silently, but she neither turned away nor stepped back. Life with the *Damainte* had taught her to stand firm and hold her ground against transgression. Now, staring into the face of her childhood defiler, she expected to encounter a devil but saw only a wretch who had suffered greatly for his sin. She tried to hate him but couldn't. All she felt was an overwhelming wave of pity. Instinctively her hand flew to her bosom. The neck of her frock had loosened a little, revealing the very top of her mark of shame. "Macinally, you're alive after all," she said in quiet surprise.

The old man's eyes grew round and white. His face lost all color. "My God! It's you!" he cried. "You did this to me!"

By the time Stelton came to Flora's aid the poor devil was already scrabbling away from her as fast as his crippled legs could carry him. "Filth!" the colonel shouted after him as he scuttled down the wharf, and Crann began barking.

Stelton laid a steadying hand on Flora's shoulder. "You look quite pale, Miss Buchanan," he said. "That knave didn't hurt you, did he?"

"Nay, he didn't," Flora answered. And as she continued

on her way toward the ship she added to herself, *not any longer.*

Flora stood near the stern of the ship, watching and listening as her husband clung to the rail, roaring a wild Gaelic song into the waves. How strange, how wonderful to think of him as her husband, but he was, now and forever, as he often told her. The French captain had married them their first day on board. As he knew no English, Flora had worried that he might make an error she could not detect and thereby void the ceremony. Sorley had some knowledge of the language, however, and assured her that the captain had the situation well in hand. She laughed at herself now to think how foolish she had been.

Sorley stopped singing when the wind became so brisk he could no longer shout it down.

Flora came up to him and wrapped her arms around his middle. "Oh, my love! You must miss Scotland so terribly!"

Sorley gave a curt nod and folded her in his arms. Flora thrilled to the steady drumbeat of his heart and thought how close she had come to losing him so many different times. His hair had grown back a little in the two weeks they had been aboard ship, and now it fluttered in the breeze like a frayed black banner. His garments felt rough against her skin. She still wasn't used to him in breeches and waistkit, but he would likely never wear a plaid again. According to Barclay, tartan, plaids, bagpipes, and Gaelic had all been banned by the Crown.

"Thousands dead," Sorley said. "Thousands of my people, gone forever. And for what? The dream of a rash young man who drank five bottles of wine a day."

"You must not be bitter, love," Flora murmured as she stroked his rock-hard back. "It's over now, and we're away

from it. The lads, Rosmairi, Gair, you and I have all survived. A fine new future lies before us." She paused, then
added, "And I promise that you won't have to wear wom-
en's skirts ever again."

Sorley smiled and kissed the top of her head. "Thank
you for that, my beautiful bride. I can't imagine anyone will
ever attempt such a ridiculous rescue ever again, either."

The memory of Sorley in skirts made Flora recall something she had tried to forget. "Love, what was it Stelton
said to you, just before Macinally ran up to me?"

The Highlander burst out laughing. "Oh! I fear he
wasn't as witless as you and I thought, my heart. He said,
'You play the part well, but you have an Adam's apple,'
and then, 'Take good care of her, you rebel bastard.' "

"Ach!" Strange, a fortnight ago the idea of Stelton dis-
covering their ruse had terrified her. Now she found it
amusing. "He was really most perceptive, wasn't he? And
kindhearted, as well." That was a lesson the *Damainte* had
taught her: the dearest friends surfaced in the oddest ways,
and always when least expected.

"Have you my compass?"

The question took Flora off guard. Of course she had
Sorley's compass. She was never without it, though she
rarely looked at it since boarding the ship. Reaching into
her bodice, she plucked the tiny instrument from between
her breasts and laid it in Sorley's palm. The Highlander
examined it a moment, gave it a kiss, then flung it into
the foamy waves that dashed themselves to pieces against
the hull of the ship.

"Sorley!" Flora leaned over the rail, but the compass
was gone, part of the sea now and not part of her life. She
didn't feel sad or angry, only perplexed. "Why would you
do such a thing?"

Sorley kissed the back of her neck. *"A' ghraidh,* we need

it no longer. It led you and me on a twisted path, to be sure, but now we're where we ought to be. Together. In each other's arms. From this moment on, you are my compass, my lodestone, the fixed point in my life. I need no other guide."

He was right. She needed no love tokens when she had something a thousand times more valuable. Again they kissed, long, deep, and hard, but as they did so, a sea swell lifted the ship. Flora and Sorley were hard put to retain their balance on the pitching deck.

"Let's retire to our cabin, my calf," Sorley said, snatching the rail just in time to prevent a fall. "If I'm going to roll and bounce about anyway, let it be on you."

"Ha! Always the rogue!" Flora tapped him playfully on the shoulder. "But wait. There's something I must ask you."

"Ask it in haste," he said.

"Do you like the name Aimil for a lass, and do you agree that Ewan is a good name for a lad?"

Sorley stared at her a moment, then threw back his head. Laughter rang from him like music. "You saucy creature! You've become so used to deceit that you can't tell anything plain. Is it true? Are you with child?"

"I am." Flora chuckled to see her beloved so happy. She knew he would never forget Culloden or his friends who perished there, just as she would never forget them. But they would not be the only contents of his heart or hers. "And I intend to start knitting some garments for the tyke straight away, so it won't be a naked Highlander, as its father has been for most of his life."

Sorley drew himself up as straight as the swaying deck would allow. "Mistress, there's important business to attend to first down below. And indeed, it's business best done naked."

Flora feigned a cry of alarm as Sorley picked her up in his arms and made his way toward the hatch. "I'm undone!" she said, laughing.

"Not you, my love," Sorley countered. "Only your clothing."

Put a Little Romance in Your Life With
Fern Michaels

__Dear Emily	0-8217-5676-1	$6.99US/$8.50CAN
__Sara's Song	0-8217-5856-X	$6.99US/$8.50CAN
__Wish List	0-8217-5228-6	$6.99US/$7.99CAN
__Vegas Rich	0-8217-5594-3	$6.99US/$8.50CAN
__Vegas Heat	0-8217-5758-X	$6.99US/$8.50CAN
__Vegas Sunrise	1-55817-5983-3	$6.99US/$8.50CAN
__Whitefire	0-8217-5638-9	$6.99US/$8.50CAN

Put a Little Romance in Your Life With
Rosanne Bittner

__Caress	0-8217-3791-0	$5.99US/$6.99CAN
__Full Circle	0-8217-4711-8	$5.99US/$6.99CAN
__Shameless	0-8217-4056-3	$5.99US/$6.99CAN
__Unforgettable	0-8217-5830-6	$5.99US/$7.50CAN
__Texas Embrace	0-8217-5625-7	$5.99US/$7.50CAN
__Texas Passions	0-8217-6166-8	$5.99US/$7.50CAN
__Until Tomorrow	0-8217-5064-X	$5.99US/$6.99CAN
__Love Me Tomorrow	0-8217-5818-7	$5.99US/$7.50CAN

Put a Little Romance in Your Life With
Hannah Howell

___**My Valiant Knight** $5.50US/$7.00CAN
    0-8217-5186-7

___**Only For You** $5.99US/$7.50CAN
    0-8217-5943-4

___**Unconquered** $5.99US/$7.50CAN
    0-8217-5417-3

___**Wild Roses** $5.99US/$7.50CAN
    0-8217-5677-X

___**Highland Destiny** $5.99US/$7.50CAN
    0-8217-5921-3

___**Highland Honor** $5.99US/$7.50CAN
    0-8217-6095-5

___**A Taste of Fire** $5.99US/$7.50CAN
    0-8217-5804-7
